Jon Evans
BLOOD PRICE

HarperCollins*Publishers*

To my parents

Blood Price
© 2004 by Jon Evans.
All rights reserved.

Published by
HarperCollins Publishers Ltd

No part of this book may be used
or reproduced in any manner whatsoever without the prior written
permission of the publisher, except
in the case of brief quotations
embodied in reviews.

First trade paperback edition by
HarperCollins Publishers Ltd: 2005
This mass market paperback
edition: 2006

HarperCollins books may be purchased for educational, business, or
sales promotional use through our
Special Markets Department.

HarperCollins Publishers Ltd
2 Bloor Street East, 20th Floor
Toronto, Ontario, Canada
M4W 1A8

www.harpercollins.ca

Library and Archives Canada
Cataloguing in Publication
information is available.

Evans, Jon, 1973–

Blood price / Jon Evans.

ISBN: 978-1-55468-213-3

OPM 9 8 7 6 5 4 3 2 1

Printed and bound in
the United States

Set in Sabon

Acknowledgements

My thanks must begin with my rock-star agent, Vivienne Schuster at Curtis Brown UK. Thanks also to her across-the-pond counterpart, Deborah Schneider of Gelfman Schneider, and my publishers: at Hodder and Stoughton, Carolyn Mays and especially Alex Bonham, about whom enough good things cannot be said; at HarperCollins Canada, Iris Tupholme and Siobhan Blessing; and at HarperCollins USA, Michael Shohl.

Thank you, Maria Alexander, for the Magic Castle and other L.A. expeditions. Nate Basiliko, for your helpful advice and spare bed. Pablo Bawdekar and Judith Cox. David Brown, for driving me across the Sinai despite my woeful condition. Michael Carlin, for making your now-customary appearance. Chong Chan and Andrea Schnebel. Maggie Cino. Amanda Garnham. Martina Hatlak, for showing me Zagreb. Chris Hemming. E. Anne Killpack, especially for those Belize contacts. Sarah Langan. Allegra Lundyworf, for being you, for Burning Man, and for being there while I wrote. Rachael Nicholson and Benjamin Brown. Chris Nielsen, for making an appearance. Bill Hanage and the Paddington Discussion Group. Max Pentreath and Kelle Link. Isaac Pinnock. Tom Redekopp, because you asked for it. Michael and Laura Smit, for dinner, dammit. Sasha Smith and Paul Hendrich. Zorana Spasojevic, for showing me around Belgrade, and general Balkans fact-checking—those errors that remain are entirely mine. And Peter Stanton, for providing the venue. And, as ever, forever, my family.

The following books aided me greatly; *My War Gone By, I Miss it So* by Anthony Lloyd; *Love Thy Neighbour: A Story of War* by Peter Maas; *Endgame: The Betrayal and Fall of Srebrenica, Europe's Worst Massacre Since World War II* by David Rohde; *Safe Area Gorazde: The War in Eastern Bosnia 1992–1995* by Joe Sacco; *A Bed for the Night: Humanitarianism in Crisis* by David Rieff; *Crossing Over: A Mexican Family on the Migrant Trail* by Ruben Martinez; *Coyotes: A Journey through the Secret World of America's Illegal Aliens* by Ted Conover; and *Killing Pablo: The Hunt for the World's Greatest Outlaw* by Mark Bowden.

1 Bosnia, April 2003

1 The Child

The taxi arrived at exactly the wrong time. Ten seconds earlier and I wouldn't have seen the child at all. Ten seconds later and it would have been too late to help him. I would have moved on, uninvolved, and I cannot even imagine how different the rest of my life might have been.

When I encountered the little boy it was two in the morning and I was somewhere in the back streets of Sarajevo, completely lost, muttering incoherent fury at my absent girlfriend. My soon-to-be-ex-girlfriend. I was just drunk enough to admit that to myself for the first time. We were finished, Talena and me; our two-year relationship had frayed beyond repair. This vacation, our last desperate throw of the dice, had come up snake eyes. She would dump me as soon as we got back to California, and I couldn't blame her. I would have dumped me a long time ago.

We had been at a party, a reunion hosted by friends Talena had not seen in eight years, held in a lushly decorated apartment, elegant furniture and tasteful paintings and acid jazz on the turntables, American cigarettes and French wine, lean and beautiful people, everyone but Talena and me decked out in designer clothes. Only the groaning plumbing and low cracked ceiling hinted that we were in a dazed and shambling nation still trying to recover from the most vicious civil war in all the bloody history of Europe. Talena's friends were very good at keeping up the façade of urbane cosmopolitan high life. For some of them I think it was all they had.

Everyone but me was Bosnian, though many spoke good English, and I knew no one but Talena, who was absorbed with her long-distant friends. I felt excluded. I drank too much slivovitz, Bosnia's lethal plum brandy. I told Talena I was leaving. She accused me of avoiding her friends. It had escalated into a bitter fight, as our disagreements so often did these days, and I had turned and stormed into the night, fuelled by slivovitz and wounded rage.

Losing myself on the steep slopes of southern Sarajevo shouldn't have been possible. All I needed to do was to go downhill until I reached the Miljacka River and then follow it upstream. But in my drunken emotional haze I found myself climbing as often as I descended; somehow the winding streets never went in quite the right direction, and every time I caught a glimpse of the few dim lights of downtown they seemed no nearer than before. I was beginning to wonder if I should try to go back when I turned yet another a corner, saw the family in the pick-up, and stopped dead with surprise.

The street was typical suburban Sarajevo. A pair of street lamps shed barely enough light to navigate by, but bright light from an open doorway illuminated the street. A pitted and crumbling road, no sidewalk, barely wide enough for two cars, its edges slowly eaten away by a thousand ravenous generations of grass. Little houses of five or six rooms were arrayed on either side, their walls, like the street itself, still pockmarked with bullet scars from the eight-years-ended war. The plots of land between houses contained lawns and vegetable gardens, but no trees; the war had swallowed almost all the trees within a mile of Sarajevo, cut down and burned for warmth. There was a pervasive air of neglect and decay—peeling paint, a plank fallen from a wooden fence, a cracked window, gardens that were mostly weed, little clumps of debris—that the few new or brightly painted houses could not dispel.

A beat-up white Mitsubishi pick-up was parked in front of the lit doorway. In the bed of the pick-up a dark-skinned family sat atop a ragged collection of bags and bundles. They were so out of place they startled me out of my self-righteous reverie and nearly into sobriety. Other than a few NATO troops they were the only non-white people I had seen in Bosnia. Two adults and four children ranging in age from high single digits to mid-teens. I guessed they were South Asian, probably Tamil, judging by their features and the darkness of their skin.

Three young white men emerged from the house, all sporting the Menacing Gangsta look: black clothes, shaved heads, tattoos, alpha-male attitude. They approached the pick-up, obviously intending to get in and drive away, and the dark-skinned parents, alarmed, started objecting loudly in a strange and sonorous language. The white men hesitated and looked at one another. The driver replied in annoyed Serbo-Croatian. After a brief, confused pause, both groups started speaking at once. It quickly became apparent that neither side understood a word the other was saying.

I didn't know either language, but I understood that the white men insisted on driving off, while the Tamils passionately wanted to stay. The dispute was serious, and exacerbated by the mutual miscommunication, and as I watched the volume and emotion escalated rapidly until both sides were shouting. Everyone was much too engrossed in their argument to notice me.

It took only a minute for matters to come to a boil. One of the white men withdrew keys from his pocket and started towards the driver's seat. The adult Tamils leaped to their feet, howling with anger and dismay, obviously about to step down from the pick-up and take their children with them.

Then another white man, short and thickly muscled, drew a gun, a big all-metal handgun that gleamed dully in the light, and the cacophony of angry voices went quiet like somebody had pulled a plug.

The third white man, skinny and tall, followed his companion's lead and drew another, smaller, gun. I thought from his body language that he was only reluctantly following along. The hulking eager gunslinger aimed his weapon at the Tamil father and barked an order, pointing to the bed of the pick-up with his free hand. The father looked at his wife and children. A moment passed where I wasn't sure which way things would go. Then, slowly, unwillingly, the father sank back down to a seated position, and his wife did the same.

The two armed men got into the back of the pick-up as well, their guns still out, and motioned and shouted at the Tamils until the family was lined up against the front of the pick-up, their backs to the cab, while the two white men sat in the back corners. The engine wheezed and groaned and started. The father started shaking uncontrollably. The mother began to speak breathlessly to the white men, pleading with them desperately, waving her hands weakly, tears leaking out of her eyes, her voice so drained of strength that

I could not hear it. Their children stared dully at me. I think the eldest, a teenage girl, may have registered my presence.

The woman's pleas met with no response. The light in the house went out. After a moment the door shut, and a fourth figure left the house and entered the passenger side of the cab. In the newly dim light I couldn't tell if this new arrival was a man or a woman, black or white. The side door closed and the pick-up started forward. I could hear the father weeping over the engine's growl as they moved away.

Now that the house light was out I saw that the street went straight downhill, towards the Miljacka. I shook my head and slowly started to walk, beginning to actually think about what I had seen. Until then I had reacted like it was entertainment, unscheduled street theatre. I had felt no fear when the guns came out. I suppose too much slivovitz had something to do with that, but even sober I think I would have stayed calm. I was so much and so obviously not a part of whatever happened on and around that Mitsubishi pick-up that I couldn't imagine actually being threatened. The setting and the people involved were too foreign, too apart from my life, to impinge on my existence in any way.

I developed a vague idea of what had happened. I knew that Bosnia, still a basically wild and lawless country beneath the rigid order imposed by NATO's peacekeepers, was a nexus for people smuggling. That had to be why that family was here; there was no other conceivable reason. They were trying to get themselves into Europe, make a better life for themselves than what they had had in Sri Lanka or wherever. This house was a transfer station on the way. And for some reason the Tamil family really, really hadn't wanted to leave it yet. As I walked I vaguely wished them the best, hoped

5

they weren't being taken someplace unspeakably awful, and idly wondered why they had so desperately wanted to stay. I was already categorizing the incident as a minor anecdote, something to recount to Talena tomorrow, nothing that had anything to do with me, when I saw the little boy.

He was maybe five years old, wearing ragged blue shorts and little sneakers with holes in them and, oddly, a torn and too-big Tupac Shakur T-shirt. His hair was dirty and unruly, his skin so dark he looked almost African or Aboriginal. He looked around, up and down the street, and then at me, very confused, his mouth open.

I put it all together. The family's other child. He had wandered off or gotten lost or decided to play hide-and-seek just as the Bosnian refugee-smuggling gangsters had come to take them somewhere else. And now the family, unable to make their loss understood, had been dragged off at gunpoint, to who knows where, without their youngest son.

The lights and sound of the pick-up dwindled in the distance.

The little boy and I stared at each other.

My instinctive, overpowering, primal reaction was this: *don't get involved*.

It wasn't like this was the first time I had witnessed something awful, or potentially awful. I had spent a good portion of my twenties travelling to and through various exotic Third World destinations. I had seen countless hordes of men, women and children whose lives were measured in suffering: AIDS babies in Zimbabwe, mutilated beggar children in China, whole villages with malnutrition-distended bellies in Mali. I had seen scores of skin-and-bones families, their bodies pockmarked with scars and boils, somehow surviving on the streets of Calcutta, staring at wealthy passers-by with eyes too dulled by pain and hunger even to be greedy any more, and I had walked casually past without sparing them a rupee or even a thought. This planet is full of terrible things, and if you want to travel and see its wonders, you have to inure yourself to its anguish.

I rationalized that the world's awful suffering was not my responsibility and as long as I didn't actually do anything to increase it I was on solid moral ground. I told myself that I did a little good each time I travelled, bringing in much-needed hard currency, spending money on hostels and taxis and street vendors who in turn spent it on their families and neighbours, my own personal trickle-down effect. That was good enough for me. I was a traveller, not a missionary, and I wasn't willing to turn into Mother Teresa. I gave a little money each year to Amnesty International and Doctors Without Borders, and that gave me a licence, I thought, some kind of licence to watch terrible things without ever getting involved.

Easy enough to tell yourself. Hard to tell a little boy staring at you quietly with big betrayed eyes as his family disappears into the darkness behind him.

Whatever happened, I reminded myself, it wouldn't be my fault. The boy was not my responsibility. I couldn't take him under my wing. The hassle and confusion would become incredibly oppressive, and most of all I would violate the Prime Directive: don't get involved.

I half expected him to start crying but he somehow maintained a kind of solemn dignity. For a moment I wondered what his name was. Then I got hold of myself, looked away from him, and began to invent a reason to walk away from

7

this abandoned child. Surely his family would eventually talk someone into bringing them back to find him. If I took him with me I might actually destroy their only chance of reunion. So the best thing to do was to leave the boy here. QED. A solution so plausible that if I tried very hard I would eventually be able to convince myself of its truth. Though maybe not tomorrow. And maybe I wouldn't tell Talena about this. It might be hard to explain to somebody else, anybody else, even her.

The boy's face started to grow brighter, and I turned around to see the lights of a car behind us. Two headlights beneath a trapezoidal call light. A taxi. Almost as out of place as a Tamil family in this distant neighbourhood. I still don't know what it was doing roving Sarajevo's late-night back streets instead of looking for passengers downtown.

I looked back down the street. The lights of the pick-up were still visible.

If I had stopped to think about it, I probably wouldn't have done anything. But there was no time to think. I waved violently and the taxi stopped and I grabbed the little boy around his waist—he was heavier and much warmer than I expected him to be—and then we were in the taxi and I pointed desperately at the vanishing tail-lights of the pick-up and ordered, 'Follow them! Follow that car, now!'

2 Involved

The driver may not have understood me, but he didn't need to, my desperation was infectious. Tyres squealed as he launched us down the street and after the pick-up. The boy squirmed in my arms and I let him go sit in the corner of the back seat, arms around his knees, staring at me. He was so soundless I began to wonder if he might be mute.

The pick-up crossed a bridge over the Miljacka to Zmaja od Bosne, a street once bitterly nicknamed Sniper's Alley, and turned right. We followed it through the ancient, elegant and often devastated buildings of downtown Sarajevo. To our left, mortar-scarred mosques and cathedrals, a synagogue abandoned since the Nazis slaughtered most of the city's Jews, and the boarded-up, burned-out hulk of the National Library, across from which Gavrilo Princip had fired the shot that killed Archduke Ferdinand and began the First World War. On our right, across the river, a concrete stadium built to host the 1984 Winter Olympics, upon which the five Olympic rings had once been inscribed. It took some imagination now to reconstruct those rings from the keloid pattern left by bullets and shellfire. For a moment I tried to imagine how much worse the city had looked in 1995, given that it was still so battle-scarred eight years later.

The boy said something in a soft musical language. So much for the mute theory. I realized that the taxi driver had not started his meter. Pretty typical in Bosnia or any non-First World country. Normally I made sure to negotiate the fare before I got in, and since I had neglected to do so, the driver would now try to charge me an outrageous price when we finally got wherever we were going.

The pick-up climbed up the hills east of Sarajevo. The lights of the city began to diminish behind us as we picked up speed on the wide, smooth, NATO-rebuilt road. I began to wonder how far they were going. For all I knew they could be en route to the Croatian border. The taxi driver wasn't likely to take me that far. Even if he did, I couldn't afford it. I wondered if I could convince the driver to cut them off and force them to stop. My guess was no. I would have to wait for the Mitsubishi to come to a stop.

The boy, still huddled in his quasi-foetal position, began loudly and insistently to repeat some incomprehensible phrase, his voice quavering.

I looked at him and shook my head. 'Sorry, kid. It's all Greek to me.'

He didn't seem to find the sound of my voice comforting and kept chanting his mantra. Around us the street lights grew further apart and the road wound its way past overgrown bushes and weeds. We were now the only two vehicles on the road, and I hoped that maybe the pick-up would stop to see who was following them, but they didn't.

The taxi driver turned to me and said something I didn't understand, and just then the boy finally began to cry, to bawl really; the floodgates opened and he sobbed and shrieked with a voice incredibly loud for someone so small.

'Where we go?' the taxi driver shouted over the howling child.

I looked at him. Then I took a mental step back and looked at myself. Ten minutes ago I had been walking back to our hostel. Now I was in a taxi I couldn't afford, accompanied by a shrieking five-year-old boy I had just met, following armed criminals and a family of refugees to God only knew where.

'Beats the hell outta me,' I assured the driver.

'I no—sorry,' the driver said carefully, 'I *don't* understand. Where do you want to go today?'

Great, I thought. *Here I am adopting children and chasing gangsters and my driver is quoting Microsoft ads.* I was saved from having to answer by the Mitsubishi's squealing brakes. The pick-up made a sudden left turn on to a gravel road it almost overshot, changing course so suddenly that my taxi flew right past before I could tell the driver to stop.

'There!' I said excitedly. 'There! Turn around!' I mimed a U-turn.

The driver looked dubious. I saw his point. The winding road had narrowed to typical Bosnian size, much too skinny for a U-turn, with a ditch on one side and a steep hill on the other. If a car piloted by your typical Bosnian driver came from either direction while we were in the middle of the eleven-point turn probably required to reverse our course, we would all become footnotes in tomorrow's Sarajevo obituaries.

'Wait,' the driver decided.

We drove for another minute until he found another offshoot road and used that to turn around. The boy's howling tantrum had begun to dissipate and by the time we turned on to the gravel road it had diminished to coughing and soft, pitiful sobs. I ignored him. Under other circumstances I might have tried being fatherly and sympathetic, but I had begun unfairly to blame the kid for getting me into this mess in the first place.

The gravel road went downhill, through shoulder-high bushes and across disturbingly jittery bridges that spanned little streams, presumably tributaries of the Miljacka. Out here there were no street lights and the darkness on either side of the taxi was so thick it seemed solid. The driver glanced back at me nervously. I didn't feel too confident either. The situation seemed to be deteriorating with every passing minute.

I looked at the child and wondered what would have happened to him if I hadn't grabbed him and hailed the taxi. Maybe nothing. Maybe the family would find a translator at the pick-up's destination, and after a quick explanation the Mitsubishi would have returned and retrieved the boy. Possible. But it didn't seem likely.

Maybe a neighbour would have discovered him in a yard and adopted him. Bosnians, like all the denizens of the Balkans, were famous for their hospitality. Maybe he would have grown up here, learned the language, only vaguely remembered his early childhood, and one day ten years from now one of his elder sisters, by now a doctor in London, would have tracked him down for a tearful and joyous reunion.

Or maybe he would have been abandoned, ignored, turned over to the rough shelters and violent tutors one finds on the streets of Sarajevo. That seemed a lot more likely. Bosnians were also famous for their racism.

I could have taken him back to our hostel and tomorrow turned him over to the police. I still could. What would happen next was hard to imagine: the Bosnian government was as minimal as possible and I doubted they had procedures in place for alien children who showed up out of nowhere. But surely some well-meaning NGO would take him in and try to find his family, or put him in an orphanage here, wouldn't they? Though I couldn't imagine who. Maybe the government would deport him back to Sri

Lanka, a callous move but the world is a callous place, and few countries more so than Bosnia. It was easy to imagine the boy returned to his homeland, spending his youth in some Dickensian orphanage, a place worse than jail.

The taxi's headlights uncovered a bumpy dirt and rocks trail that veered away from the gravel to the right. The driver slowed us to a crawl and enquired, 'Go here?'

'Excellent question,' I said. 'Brief, to the point, well put. I have no fucking idea.'

The driver stopped the taxi. 'I don't understand.'

'Me neither.' I looked at the dirt road. Were those fresh tyre tracks? They might be. I was an out-of-work computer programmer, not Aragorn the Ranger, but those tracks did look distinctly darker than the soil around them. I looked down the dirt track and in the distance I saw a tiny flicker of light.

'Yes,' I said. 'Turn here.'

The driver advanced into the dirt road, then stopped so abruptly that the child next to me, who had thankfully fallen silent again, slid forward and nearly off the seat. There was a gate in front of us, part of a rusting metal chain-link fence that intersected the dirt trail about twenty feet up from the gravel road. The gate was locked with a thick chain and padlock.

For a moment I felt defeated. We could go no further. I would have to take the boy back to the city and go to the police. Then the driver said something and pointed at the gate, and I noticed what should have been obvious. The vehicular gate included a pedestrian doorway, like a house door might include a cat-flap, and that doorway was latched but unlocked.

'Right,' I said. 'Okay. Godfuckingdamnit.' It was either walk or turn back, and I wasn't ready to turn back. 'Okay, stop here, and wait for me. Wait for me until I come back.'

I tried to think of a reason for the taxi driver to wait. My mind replayed a helpful scene from *Eyes Wide Shut*, and I withdrew my Eagle Creek travel wallet from beneath my slacks, dug out a pink fifty-euro note, tore it in two and handed half to the driver. Just then I remembered all the warnings that US dollars in Bosnia had to be in pristine condition for anyone, including banks, to accept them. Fortunately this stricture didn't seem to apply to euros. My driver looked at it, nodded slowly, and said, 'I wait.'

'Good,' I said. I probably wasn't even overpaying him that much. Sarajevo was an expensive place to travel and fifty euros or a hundred KM—'konvertible marks,' the local currency—seemed almost right for a cab ride to and from the outermost boonies.

I reached out and gently took the boy by the arm. He looked at me, his face soaked with tears, shuddered, and began to cry again, quietly this time.

'Dogs and small children are supposed to naturally trust me,' I muttered. 'I guess you didn't get the memo.'

I picked up the boy, who sobbed but didn't resist, exited the taxi, passed through the gate, and began to trek down the dirt road towards that faint spark of light. As always while travelling, I had my keychain with me, a small Swiss army knife connected to a mini-Maglite flashlight, and once again it came in handy. After some awkward juggling I wound up with the shaking, weeping boy in the crook of my right arm and the flashlight in my left hand.

I thought uneasily of all the land-mine signs and warnings

in every guidebook. There were still a million live land-mines in this country, and we were close enough to Sarajevo that the field surrounding this dirt track probably contained its share. As long as we stayed on the road we should be all right, but if the boy decided to wriggle away and run off . . . I tightened my hold on him and picked up my pace, trying to walk without thinking about where I was, or what I was doing, or why. No good would come of that.

We walked maybe half a mile. There were no sounds but the child's soft sobs and my Doc Martens against the dirt ruts and tyre tracks. The weeds on either side of the road had not been touched for years. The spark of light grew and resolved into a single bare fluorescent bar, the only illumination outside a big concrete and metal building, some three hundred feet long and a hundred feet wide, surrounded by a flat gravel field. Once upon a time it had been some kind of factory, but it looked long deserted, almost all the doors and windows boarded up. The light glowed above a set of concrete stairs that led up a few feet to a loading dock. The door next to the light was an eight-foot-square sheet of horizontally corrugated metal that slid up and down. There were two vehicles parked near the light. A gleaming new Land Rover, the vehicle of choice for Bosnia's warlords, criminals, thugs and venal officials, and a familiar empty white Mitsubishi pick-up.

I stood before the steel door for a long moment. The boy had given up on crying and buried his face in my shoulder instead. I could feel his quick panting breaths and his warm damp face and his thudding heartbeat. He felt very heavy now but I didn't want to put him down. It wasn't just fear of him running away. Some kind of paternal instinct had

15

arisen during our walk down that dark dirt road. I felt jealously protective of him and afraid for us both. I didn't know exactly what lay behind that steel door, but I was pretty confident that the answer included violent armed criminals. Maybe my refugee-smuggling theory was wrong. Maybe for some reason the family had been brought here to be executed and the child was lucky to have been left behind.

I considered my options. The smart thing to do was obvious. Turn around, go back, take the taxi back to the city, confer with Talena, and turn the kid over to the police in the morning. Hell, the Bosnian police were so corrupt they probably knew these smugglers by their first name, they could deliver the boy to them during their first doughnut break.

But I wanted to return this child to his family. I knew that his family were just behind that door. I did not really think they had been brought here to their deaths. And, yes, it was kind of insane that I was standing here at all, but now that I had come this far it was too late to chicken out and turn around.

That last was really the deciding factor. A stupid motivation, granted, but enough. I banged on the door with my left fist, using my Swiss army knife to generate a pleasingly loud metal-on-metal sound. The boy started to cry again.

Loud but muffled voices behind the door expressed surprise in the guttural warlike sounds of Serbo-Croatian. I heard the tromp of heavy boots, followed by a few questions aimed in my direction. I banged on the door again. There was a moment of silence. Then the grating rattle of metal on metal as the door rose up, revealing three men and one woman, all of them carrying guns, all of them aiming at me. I had planned to say 'Avon calling' or something equally amusing, but staring down four gun barrels really saps one's desire to be flip and entertaining. I barely forced an unconvincing smile.

The woman, a tall slender black-clad redhead who would have been intimidating even unarmed, unleashed a jackhammer sequence of harsh syllables which I was sure translated to something like, 'Who the fucking fuck are you?'

'Sorry, I don't understand,' I said, trying to make my voice as soothing as a hypnotist. 'Does anyone here speak English?'

They stared at me, dumbfounded. The guns stayed aimed at my head and body as if magnetically attracted. It took a lot of effort to keep the smile on my face. It had been a long time since I had faced a situation anything like this. My slivovitz courage had evaporated in the face of all those guns, and my whole body trembled with adrenaline and fear.

I looked past the guns, hoping to find a willing interpreter. The door opened on to a large room, a loading bay I supposed, concrete floor beneath a wooden ceiling supported by concrete pillars. The room stank of sweat and urine and cigarettes and sawdust; there was a thin layer of sawdust everywhere. At the back and sides of the room a few dark door-sized openings led deeper into the building, and there was a big open space from which a conveyor belt protruded into the loading bay. The part of my mind not frozen by fear decided this place had once been a furniture factory or sawmill or something like that.

About thirty people were clustered in the back right-hand corner, sitting in little groups, all of them near or atop one or two bags. At first glance it looked almost like

17

a typical backpacker scene: single travellers, smoking cigarettes and playing cards, waiting for a bus or for something to happen. But these travellers were dressed in rags, layered in filth, gaunt and desperate, equipped with polyester duffel bags rather than Eagle Creek backpacks. Most of them were some flavour of Indian or Middle Eastern. Almost all were men, a few of them accompanied by a woman.

In the other back corner of the room were a dozen white women, mostly young and slender but already visibly victims of hard living, almost all of them blonde. They were dressed slightly better than the other group, mostly in tight jeans, navel-baring T-shirts and cheap flashy jewellery, although a few of them wore dumpy misshapen dresses and no jewels. They sat and stood in a tight group in the absolute corner of the room, mostly with their backs to the walls, smoking up a stormcloud. Like the men in the other corner they had paused in their conversation to stare at my dramatic entrance.

About halfway along the wall to my right sat the family I had seen in the Mitsubishi, all six of them huddled together in a heap of grief, heedless of the possessions that lay haphazardly piled beside them. They did not even look up to see the return of their lost son. But he saw them. He shouted so loudly that I winced, and he began to wriggle in my grip like a rabid cat. I managed to lower him most of the way to the ground before he broke free and scrambled past the nonplussed gunmen to rejoin his family.

His parents and siblings stared at him open-mouthed as he approached. Then his mother, disbelieving, held her arms out wide, and he ran into them, and the rest of his family mobbed him like a football team that had just scored a game-winning touchdown, weeping and laughing with relief.

That broke some of the tension. The gangsters held a brief uncouth conversation, after which the men developed a little less hostility in their eyes and stances. The woman approached me.

'I speak English. That is their son?' She pointed at the rejoicing family.

'Yes.'

'Where do you get him? How do you find us?'

I almost reflexively corrected her tense but decided it wasn't a good time. Instead I explained my recent history. She looked sceptical. I couldn't blame her. It was a bizarre and unconvincing story. By the time I finished telling it, one of the men had shut the door behind me, which was bad, but the guns had all been put away, which was very good.

'Papers,' the woman said. 'Identification.'

'My passport's back where I'm staying,' I said. 'But I have a copy . . .'

I opened up my travel wallet and dug out the sheet of paper I carried at all times, a photocopy of my passport's ID page and my California driver's licence. I also had a credit card, two hundred euros, and a hundred US dollars, in cash. I expected to lose all that when the gangsters saw it, but they paid no notice. Maybe it was small change to them. I tried to remember what I had read about people smuggling. Something like five thousand dollars per person to go from India to Europe, if I recalled correctly. Even if these particular gangsters only got a tenth of that for this leg of the trip, that meant the desperate men and women in this room represented nearly thirty thousand dollars. I wondered why they looked so poor if they could muster five grand, a fortune in India, to travel. Maybe these were the ones who went on credit and had to pay it off by working illegally once they arrived. I suspected the women in the corner would all spend their first year in the West turning tricks on the street, whether they knew it yet or not.

The male gangsters all sported the same designer-dangerous look; leather jackets, black jeans, black army boots, thick steel necklaces over the identical tattooed flames that encircled their necks and disappeared below their black T-shirts. I imagined them modelling a new clothing line, Menace by Armani. The short hypermuscled one wore no shirt beneath his open jacket, revealing mountainous pectorals and the remainder of what I assumed was their gang-membership tattoo: a flaming sword, its hilt at the collarbone and its point at the navel, with Oriental dragons dancing in the flames that covered the rest of the torso.

The woman, who was definitely in charge, was about my age, harshly beautiful, marathon-fit. She had no leather jacket, steel necklace or tattoo, but something about her demeanour, her flat detached expression, made her the scariest person in the room. I was dead certain she wouldn't hesitate a microsecond to use the gun she carried.

'America or Canada?' she demanded.

'I'm Canadian. But I live in California. America.'

She frowned at the ambiguity. 'You NATO? NGO? Journalist?'

'I'm a tourist.'

She, and all the others—I supposed the word was the same in their language—stared at me in disbelief. This was arguably the least plausible part of my story. Nobody came to Bosnia for pleasure; the war was too distant for ghouls and too recent for everybody else.

'No, really,' I said. 'A tourist. My girlfriend . . . ' I paused and then decided not to explain, it was too complicated and they probably didn't really care.

'A tourist,' she repeated. She sounded baffled, rather than angry or disbelieving, which was good. 'What is your work, in America?'

'Computer programmer.' That wasn't strictly speaking accurate, but it sounded a lot better than 'Unemployed loser who can't find a job and supports himself by sponging off his parents and girlfriend.'

She spoke to her minions and then turned to me. 'Stay here,' she said, quite unnecessarily seeing as how two of her thugs stood between me and the door, and she walked away. I watched her disappear down one of the shadowy corridors that led deeper into the building.

'You live California?' one of the thugs asked.

'Yes,' I said, surprised that anyone else spoke English. I looked at him. Tall and thin, a big hook nose and features that did not aesthetically agree with his shaved head, early twenties. At twenty-nine I was probably the oldest person in the room except for the parents who had just regained their child.

'Los Angeles?'

'San Francisco.' He seemed disappointed, so I added, 'But I go to Los Angeles sometimes, I have friends there.'

'I always want to go Los Angeles,' he said. 'Make movies there.'

'It's the place to go,' I said banally. The English-speaker, I realized, was the one who had seemed reluctant to pull his gun and order the family around at gunpoint back in the city. I decided to think of him as the sensitive reasonable gangster.

'Pretty girls there?' He grinned.

I put on my lecherous heterosexual-man leer. 'You have no idea. It's like all the pretty girls in America, they all go to Los Angeles. And the weather is beautiful, and everybody has a car, and you can swim at the beach every day.' Actually I hated LA with a passion but I didn't think it was a good time to rain on his delusions.

'Los Angeles.' He shook his head reverently. 'I go there some day.'

I smiled and nodded.

The miniature Hulk lookalike said something to Sensitive Reasonable Gangster, who nodded and said to me, 'He want to know if you like the tattoo.'

I looked at the enormous flaming sword on Mini-Hulk's chest. 'It's great,' I said, and then, it just sort of popped out, 'Very phallic.'

Sensitive Reasonable Gangster looked at me, perplexed. 'Phallic?'

'California slang,' I assured him. 'It means really cool. Very good.'

'Phallic,' he said, nodding and smiling. 'Very phallic.' He turned and said something to the other gangsters, presumably expanding their California-cool vocabulary. By turns they each said 'phallic,' trying out the word. I managed to maintain a straight face, but only just. It wasn't just the word that was funny, it was the way the whole conversation's power dynamic had changed. Sure, this was their country, and I was a suspicious unwanted intruder, and they were the violent criminals who did whatever they wanted; but I lived in America, in California no less, and thanks to the almighty global power of Hollywood that made me infinitely cooler than these backwater Bosnian thugs; next to them I was the Fonz, and they knew it.

The woman returned, and two men followed behind her. I was no longer the oldest person in the room; she was near my age, and both of the men looked mid-thirties. One of them, tall and impressively craggy, hung back in the shadows, but I kept a wary eye on him all the same. He had the same dull expression that the woman did, lifeless, like a snake. He and she were far scarier than the other gangsters. Those boys were too young to have fought in the war, but I was sure the woman and the man in the shadows were veterans of casual and terrible violence.

The other man was my height, slender, wearing rimless eyeglasses, dressed in a charcoal-grey suit and black tie that even I could tell were designer and expensive, his long blond hair tied back in a ponytail. Except for the ponytail he could have been a Wall Street CEO. This man was clearly the boss. Even the body language of the woman and the shadowed über-thug indicated deference.

The businessman walked straight up to me and offered his hand. 'Good evening,' he said. 'Mr Wood, I presume?' A smooth, confident voice, accented but cultured.

'That's me,' I said. We exchanged firm handshakes.

'My name is Sinisa. I understand you claim to be a tourist who happened to find this boy and followed my people to return him, correct? A tourist and a computer progammer?'

His English was nearly fluent. His accent was like no other I had ever heard, not quite Eastern European, not quite anything else.

'That's correct. I know it's weird, but it's true.'

'You will be happy to know I am inclined to believe you,' he said. 'I do not think anyone would invent such a ridiculous story. But I would like to verify some things. Where are you staying in Sarajevo?'

'This, crap, I forget the name exactly. Pansione Karnak or something, not that exactly but something like that. It's a really cheap little backpacker place, thirty KM a night, downtown, next to a parking lot. Right on the streetcar line, near the old synagogue, you know? Shit. I forget the name right now.'

'I know the place,' Sinisa said, sounding amused. 'One moment. I will put an engineer on the telephone to ask you about computers. Try to convince him you are a real programmer.'

He withdrew an expensive cellphone from his suit pocket and selected a number to call. I was surprised he got any reception out here. He explained the situation to whoever answered, in English, and passed the phone to me. I took it gingerly, as if it might explode, and put it to my ear.

A gruff voice with yet another unidentifiable accent asked me, 'What languages do you code in?'

'Uh, Java, mostly,' I said faintly. 'I can find my way around in C and Smalltalk and a bunch of—'

'Java. Fine. Why would you use the synchronized keyword in Java?'

I had not thought that the evening could get any more surreal. And what kind of gangster overlord had a computer expert on staff at this hour? 'Well . . . basically it's a way to indicate that while a thread is running a given block of code no other threads may concurrently access that object.'

'Yeah,' my interrogator said. 'Good description. Give me back to Sinisa.'

I returned the phone. I was beginning to feel much better about my predicament. For one thing, I was beginning to understand my situation. I had stumbled into a gathering of refugees who had been staying in various different safe houses. They had probably all been brought here to move on to the next stage of their journey, probably tonight. Sinisa and his people were no doubt unhappy that I was here but they had already concluded that killing or kidnapping a Canadian tourist, and I was sure they now believed I was a tourist, was going to bring far more grief upon their heads than letting me go. I figured they would probably keep me here overnight, until the refugees had been taken away, and then release me. I hoped they would give me a drive back to Sarajevo. My cab driver wasn't going to wait all night.

Sinisa listened, said, 'Good,' hung up, and said to me, 'You are free to go.'

'I . . . what? Right now?'

'Yes. Now.'

This I hadn't expected. 'I can just walk away right now?'

'Yes,' he said impatiently. 'Go.'

He motioned to the door. Mini-Hulk scurried over and pulled it open, one-handed.

'Right,' I said. 'Okay. I'll go.'

I stared at Sinisa for a moment, waiting for the punchline, but none came.

'Well, see you guys, thanks for everything,' I said, automatic Canadian courtesy, and I walked out into the night.

25

For a moment I was afraid they had just lured me outside so they could shoot me with less mess, but the door rattled back down into place behind me.

I was so surprised I nearly pitched off the edge of the loading dock instead of going down the steps. I didn't understand. I show up out of nowhere, I find out exactly where they are and what they are doing, and they let me go? What kind of criminals were these?

The answer came to me halfway back to the taxi. Very confident ones. Certain that there was nothing I could do to harm them. Go to the police? The police got a percentage. Sinisa and his people-smuggling ring had to be abetted, if not outright aided, by the Bosnian authorities. Why wouldn't they let me go? They had nothing to hide. They had no one to hide from.

The taxi took me back to Sarajevo.

I never saw the child or his family again. I hope they made it.

3 Fraying

My adventure had taken up much of the night and I expected Talena to be up waiting for me, worried and angry. When I walked through the Pansione Konack's battered wooden door, the little brass bells crudely rigged above it rang loudly. But when I climbed up the uneven wooden stairs into the common room, there was no one there but the old troll-like woman who worked there and seemed to have given up sleep years ago. She sat in one of the much repaired chairs, squinting at an ancient magazine, paying no attention to me.

I went into our room and turned on the light. A dingy room that contained a sagging too-small bed, a bedside table, a chair, and nothing else. The walls and ceiling were pitted and cracked. Our backpacks barely fitted into the available floor space. The light was a single dim bulb dangling from bare wire. We could have stayed with any of several of Talena's old friends, but neither of us had felt comfortable with that idea, given that it had been eight long years since she had seen them. I wished we had taken up one of those offers. I suspected Talena wished the same thing, but I didn't want to ask. It was one of an increasingly long list of subjects I was reluctant to bring up for fear they might trigger another icy communication breakdown. We had had more than enough of those in the last six months.

Talena was curled up in bed, asleep. Not so worried about me after all. Without pausing to wonder whether it was a good idea, I sat next to her and shook her shoulder. I wanted to tell her all about my adventure while it was fresh in my mind. I was proud that I had done something bold and reckless and gotten away with it, that I had had an adventure. Maybe it was stupid macho bullshit, but it was the only stupid macho bullshit I had had for a long time, and I wanted to share it with her.

'Huh?' she mumbled, eyes flickering open. 'Wha? The— what is it? What time is it?'

'You're not going to believe what just happened,' I said.

'What the fuck *time* is it?' She squinted at her watch. 'It—Jesus Christ, it's four in the fucking morning!'

'Seriously. Listen. It was unbelievable. I was walking down this random street, I turned the corner, and I saw this Tamil family—'

'Paul, *what the fuck?* I'm trying to sleep! Jesus fucking Christ! Do lives depend on you telling me this shit right now? Do they?'

I hesitated. 'No.'

'Then shut the fuck up and let me sleep.' She rolled over, turning her back to me. 'And turn the fucking light out.'

After a moment I rose, deflated, and turned out the light.

I stood in the darkness for a moment. Then I went back out into the common room. I knew I should try to get some sleep, we had an early bus ride to Mostar tomorrow, but I was still wide awake. I sat down in an uneven wooden chair and looked around like I had just noticed where I was. Which was how I felt. A strange and disturbing feeling. Like some kind of film had been peeled off my eyeballs and I was really seeing the things around me, in full vivid colour, for the first time in ages.

Like the rest of the pansione the common room was grey, low-ceilinged, undecorated, poorly lit, too small, encrusted with grease and dust, and smelled old and sour. Everything, walls and lights and furniture and bedding and plumbing, was old and faded and rickety and barely worked. I wished we had more money. I was twenty-nine years old now, Talena twenty-eight, and I didn't associate squalid accommodation with desirable backpacker chic any more. I would have been happy to sacrifice gritty authenticity for comfort, but we couldn't afford comfort. We couldn't even afford the air fare that had brought us here. This holiday was entirely financed by MasterCard.

I sat in one of the uneven wooden chairs. The troll woman continued pretending that I didn't exist. I felt itchy, physically dissatisfied. After a moment I realized to my surprise that I wanted a cigarette. I had never been a regular smoker, and I hadn't had a cigarette in two years, not since starting to date Talena.

What the hell. She would be angry if she found out, but that hardly mattered; these days she would find reasons to be angry with me if I morphed into the Angel Gabriel and started healing cancer patients. I got up, went downstairs, exited the pansione, and headed for the twenty-four-hour convenience store a few blocks west.

It was dark out, only a few street lights, and the street was utterly deserted, as if the city had been evacuated while my back was turned. A warm breeze drifted eastward. The street-car rails in the middle of the street gleamed in the moonlight. As I walked I wondered how many people had died on this stretch of road during Sarajevo's three-year siege. It was easy to imagine it, now that the streets were as empty as a deserted movie set, easy to superimpose bloodsoaked scenes of anguish, terror and war. I didn't have to imagine bullet marks, or bear-claw-shaped mortar scars, or apartment towers blasted into gargantuan Swiss cheese. The signs of war were still easy to find in this city overflowing with angry ghosts.

The convenience store was a reassuring island of bright lights, modern technology and Western brand names. I bought a pack of Marlboro Lights and a box of matches. I walked back to the pansione, unwrapped the pack, and lit my first cigarette in two years. I choked a little on the first few puffs, but old habits kicked in and I was soon smoking like I had never stopped.

I still wasn't tired. Far from it. I was electrically awake. I hadn't experienced tonight's kind of adrenaline rush, or anything even close to it, for a long, long time. I felt like I had woken up from a long, deep sleep. From a coma.

I thought of the last time I had faced down a loaded gun. The smell and taste of smoke reminded me of how I and my friends had smoked our way through a pack of cheap Moroccan cigarettes on our way back to our hotel, that day more than two years ago. I hadn't thought about that night in ages. I hadn't thought about anything outside the bleak rut of my day-to-day life in ages. It had hurt too much, remembering how good my life had been.

Once upon a time I was a man who had adventures, who travelled several months a year, crossed oceans and continents on a whim, who had friends around the globe who would risk their lives for me and I for them, who had a beautiful girlfriend whom I loved and who loved me, who was happy. Once upon a time I had money. Once upon a time my skills were in demand and I was able to get a well-paid job whenever I wanted one. Those two things hadn't seemed so important. How wrong I had been.

I still had Talena, but, I told myself, finally able to artic-ulate it because it had moved from fear to certainty, not for much longer. I still had those friends, but most were oceans away, and I wasn't likely to have enough money to cross oceans again any time soon. I didn't have much else. Two years ago, I had everything. Now I was running out of things to lose.

At the party that night, I had watched Talena laughing with one of her old rediscovered friends, a tall, easy-going, model-handsome man with chiselled muscles and designer clothes, trading jokes in a language I did not understand, and for the first time I had thought: *She doesn't belong with me. I wish she did, how I wish she did, but she doesn't. She belongs with someone better.*

The troll woman said something. I started out of my reverie and looked at her. She reached for the Marlboros with bony claw fingers and looked at me for approval. I nodded. She coaxed a cigarette from the pack, lit it, and sucked at it like it was the source of life. I wondered how old she was. She looked about seventy, but Bosnians, like all residents of recent war zones, usually looked older than they were. Maybe sixty. I wondered where I would be when I was sixty, if I might be alone in a room like this, bumming cigarettes from strangers. Just then it seemed like a terrifyingly plausible future.

I lit up another cigarette and contemplated myself and my prospects. I hadn't done so for a long time. Eighteen months of poverty and boredom and rejection, of living off handouts from my parents and Talena, of being an unemployed bum with fuck-all to do, had shrunk my life to a barren rut from which I dared not lift my head. For a long time now the mental subjects of *me* and *the future* had been too repellent to dwell on. But tonight, being in Sarajevo, carrying that little boy back to his family, staring down the smugglers' guns, tonight seemed to have jolted me out of my lethargy and depression, for a little while at least. Tonight I could look at myself without cringing.

I stayed up all night, smoking and thinking, sometimes sitting in that common room, sometimes wandering the deserted streets, until my throat was raw and my mind was numb and the sky above Sarajevo had turned pale with incipient dawn. Then I went into our room, sat on the chair, and watched Talena sleep, peaceful and beautiful, her slender body curled up like she was cold, her face half obscured by her long dark hair. I loved her. I wondered if she still loved me. I knew she had at one point, very much, but I also knew that she could not love someone she did not respect, not for very long.

I knew it was too late to save what we had. Much too late. Unless something extraordinary happened.

4 Mostar Tigers

'Paul? Are you okay?'

I opened my eyes. Talena was sitting on the bed, looking at me, concerned. I had fallen asleep sitting on the chair.

'Sure,' I said slowly, still slightly dazed.

'What . . . why did you sleep on the chair?' Her voice half incredulous, half accusatory.

'I didn't sleep much. I was up most of the night.'

'Why? What happened?'

'I'll tell you over breakfast,' I said.

We dressed and had bread and sliced meat and yoghurt and Turkish coffee in one of the many cafés in the nearby Bascarsija district, a cobblestoned warren straight out of the Ottoman Empire. I told her about my encounter with the little boy and the smugglers. I tried to make the story into a light-hearted anecdote, but her expression as she listened was grim. She let me finish but I could tell she wanted to interrupt and chastise me on several occasions.

'You make them sound charming,' she said when I was finished. 'You and your friendly neighbourhood gangsters. Jesus, Paul, how could you have been so stupid? They're monsters. You understand that? They're rapists and murderers and . . . and . . . and I can't believe you're sitting here cheerfully talking about it like you had a fun little adventure and you saved a child and you're all proud of it now. Those people are practically going to be slaves, you know. Those women will all be raped. Every one of them. And you, you should never have gotten involved. You should have just kept walking. You don't know how lucky you are you walked away. If they weren't in a good mood, if you weren't a foreigner, they would have beaten you to a pulp just to teach you to keep your nose out of their business. You might never have walked again, that's the way this country works, you understand? And then you went and told this Sinisa where you were staying, told him the truth. Maybe your little adventure isn't even over yet, maybe they'll change their minds and come find you, find *us,* wouldn't that be fun? I can't—I just can't believe you. I would never have imagined that you would do something so reckless and stupid and then act like this. Like you're so fucking proud of it.'

'I'm sorry,' I mumbled, wilting in the face of her righteous wrath, looking down at the table, away from her icy blue eyes. 'I'm sorry.'

But that was a lie. Lack of sleep had caught up with me despite the jet-fuel Turkish coffee, and I was too tired to argue, but I wasn't sorry for what I had done. I was sorry that I had upset Talena, I appreciated that what I had done was foolish and reckless, but she was right when she said I was proud.

33

After the silent remainder of our breakfast we gathered our packs and took a streetcar to the bus station. The Croat/Muslim station. Post-war Sarajevo had two bus stations, at opposite ends of the city, one for the Serb-controlled part of the country—the Republika Srpska, a name which always reminded me of the satirical *Onion* article 'Clinton Deploys Vowels To Bosnia'—and one for everywhere else. A typically crazy consequence of the ethnic fault lines that had cracked Bosnia open like an egg.

'Ethnic' isn't really the right word. Serbs, Croats and Muslims are physically indistinguishable and their spoken language differs only in accent if at all. Religion was the theoretical dividing line, Orthodox vs Catholic vs Islam, but pre-war Bosnia had been one of the more secular places on earth, and it still seemed a whole lot less religious than the good old USA. It didn't matter. Despite all their similarities, each side had found plenty of reasons to hate and slaughter the other two.

Post-war Bosnia was a stable place only because stability had been forced upon it by thousands of NATO troops. Without them it would have fragmented in weeks. People paid lip-service to Bosnia being a single indivisible nation, but it was effectively partitioned into the Republika Srpska and the Bosnia-Herzegovina Federation, which in turn seemed to be subdivided into the largely Muslim Bosnian Federation and Croat-dominated Herzegovina. Sarajevo itself seemed a quasi-independent entity. My Lonely Planet guide claimed that the presidency rotated between the three ethnicities every six months, and the ruling cabinet was equally divided among them, which meant that it never reached any decisions at all because each side vetoed all propositions brought by either of the other two, which was fine because in practice NATO completely ignored the cabinet and made all the country's important decisions and would for the foreseeable future. Like everything else in Bosnia, half tragedy and half farce.

At least the bus station was halfway civilized: snack shops selling various configurations of meat and starch, kiosks of junk food and newspapers, computer-printed bus tickets. We boarded the 8.40 bus to Mostar, off to visit Saskia, Talena's half-sister.

Lonely Planet: Eastern Europe reported that Mostar, a town of about eighty thousand, was a town divided by a river between the Muslims on one side and the Croats on the other, still recovering from being on the front line of war, each side mistrusting the other. It did not sound like a fun place to spend a weekend and I was already looking forward to leaving. After Mostar we would return to Sarajevo for a couple more days, then take the bus to Croatia and fly from there back to California.

The bus to Mostar was more comfortable than I expected. I dozed through most of the three-hour ride. During my periods of waking I saw to my surprise that Bosnia was an achingly pretty country. The road followed a rushing river, its water a deep pure blue, along breathtaking gorges and canyons, up and down high rocky hills covered with thick wild forest, past lazy scenic postcard vistas where the river grew fat and slow for a few miles before narrowing into whitewater cataracts. The hills were as craggy and rugged as any I had ever seen. Geography alone explained why Bosnia had been the poorest, most backward, least developed part of Yugoslavia. This simple two-lane road must have been a beggar to build, over endless steep hills and through the occasional tunnel. Sarajevo had been a thoroughly modern and cosmopolitan city. It still was, albeit a crippled one. But most of the rest of Bosnia was rough and wild. A natural haven for mystics, misfits, outlaws and smugglers.

Or, as the nineties had shown, a haven for slavering hatred, concentration camps, mass rape, mass murder, torture, slaughter and genocide. A natural home for war and for warlords.

'I'm nervous,' Talena said, when we were about half an hour away.

'About what?'

'Seeing Saskia again. I know it's stupid. But I'm nervous.'

'That she'll be different? Or that you've become different?'

'Of course we'll be different,' she said impatiently. 'We've had eight very different years since I last saw her. I think we'll still get along fine. I'm nervous that she's miserable.'

'What does she say in her emails?'

'She always says things are fine . . . but the way she says it . . . It always follows a list of things that are definitely not fine. And she hardly ever writes about her husband, and when she does it's just a really quick thing about how he's really a good man after all, always winds up sounding like she's trying to convince herself. But, you know, email, no context, no nuance, maybe I'm reading too much into it.'

'Is she jealous that you went to America?'

She nodded. 'Sure. Everyone was jealous. Most of my friends applied for that scholarship, and I was the only one who got it. Saskia was the only one who had enough space left over after being jealous to be happy for me too. I tried to bring her over, you know. In nineteen ninety-seven. Two years after I came to America. She wasn't married yet, and she had this temporary break-up with Dragan. I tried to sponsor her as an immigrant. It's supposed to be easier for family members, but Immigration and Naturalization seems to think half-sisters don't count as much as sisters, and they dug up this bullshit criminal record she had, so no go. And she went back to Dragan and got married and lived who-the-fuck-knows ever after.'

After a pause I asked, 'What if she is miserable?'

'I don't know,' Talena said. 'I don't know. I'd do whatever I could to help her out. But right now whatever I can basically do amounts to nothing. I have no money and I live ten time zones away.' She sighed. 'I guess that's what I'm worried about. That she'll be miserable, and here I come home at last from the great American dream she was so jealous of, here I am her glamorous half-sister who lives in California and works for the big famous publishing company, and I can't do fuck-all to help her or anyone else.'

I couldn't think of anything to say.

'We were best friends,' Talena said. 'We used to tell people we were identical twins who happened to come from different mothers. I mean, we looked different, but . . . sometimes when we went out we'd call each other by our own names; it was a little game. So when I see her, that'll be like seeing what would have happened to me, you know? There but for the grace of God and all that shit. And . . . *damn* it. And her husband better fucking deserve her, that's all. He better at least be trying to make her happy. But I

37

don't know. She doesn't say. But it doesn't sound like it.'

'Half an hour till we find out,' I said.

She nodded. 'Half an hour.'

We rode on in silence.

'Paul?' she said after a minute.

'Yeah?'

'It was still really stupid of you. But I'm glad you helped that little boy.'

'Thanks,' I said. 'Me too.'

'There she is,' Talena said as the bus pulled into its slot, clutching my arm so tightly that I later found fingernail bruises. I followed her gaze to a small, dark-haired, porcelain-skinned woman, pretty in a waifish-pixie way, dressed sexy and skimpy like most Bosnian women, black leather skirt and tight grey shirt and boots with two-inch heels. Her long hair was arranged in such a way that a canopy of it almost covered the left side of her face. A man, presumably her husband Dragan, stood beside her. Dragan had the Wild-Man-of-Borneo look, ragged shoulder-length hair, thick beard, brooding eyes. He was much taller than Saskia, in torn jeans and, despite the heat, a black leather jacket with a red CCCP emblem.

Saskia was so tense with anticipation that she was almost vibrating. Dragan's arms were folded and he scowled uncomfortably. We disembarked and Talena immediately dropped her pack and rushed to embrace Saskia. Both of them were in tears. I had almost never seen Talena cry before.

Dragan and I nodded to each other. He was clearly not the touchy-feely type. Up close he was downright scary, six foot four at least, with a wide build and a big belly. His hands were covered with pale jagged patches of scar tissue. From shrapnel, I later learned, during the war. Another scar ran down his left cheek and disappeared beneath his beard.

Maybe he's a big sentimental softie underneath, I told myself, but unconvincingly. Dragan seemed a lot more Hell's Angel than Brother Bear. He held himself like he wanted to smash something.

After a while Talena disengaged and waved me over to greet Saskia. I shook Saskia's trembling hand, and turned to Dragan, but before I could offer my hand he took a step back and said something. In Croatian, presumably, given that both he and Saskia were Croats. His voice was unnecessarily loud and whatever he said made others nearby stop and look at us with distaste. Saskia winced.

Talena looked at him for a long, silent second and then turned to me. 'Dragan would like to go now,' she said, her voice neutral and her face rigidly expressionless, 'because this is the Muslim side of the river. He says he doesn't like staying here longer than he has to because Muslims are all criminals and thieves.'

'No kidding,' I said. 'Jeez. I guess we better go before they take all our stuff, huh?'

Dragan, insensate to my sarcasm, took Saskia's arm and led her towards the small parking lot. Talena frowned after them. I picked up our packs, already wishing we were back in the bus's air conditioning. The crippling, unseasonal heatwave that hung over the Balkans showed no signs of going away; the temperature had to be near forty degrees already.

Their car was an ancient diesel Mercedes, not a luxury vehicle despite the brand, though in Bosnia owning any car at all was luxury. A huge zigzag crack spanned the windshield, and the back windows didn't work. It felt like a mobile sauna. Dragan was silent at first, but when we crossed the Neretva River, only two blocks west, he sighed as if an enormous weight had been lifted from his shoulders, turned to face the back seat with a huge grin spread across his face, and all but bellowed, '*Dobrodasao u Mostar!*' which even I knew meant 'Welcome to Mostar!'

'*Hvala,*' thank you, Talena said faintly, as surprised as I was.

Dragan looked back to the road just in time to avoid a fatal collision with an all-but-rusted-out Peugeot. He pounded the horn with his fist, released a toxic stream of Croatian at the offending vehicle, turned back to us with a smile and said something good-natured.

'A party,' Talena translated. 'They're having a party for us. Not just him and Saskia, his . . . it's hard to translate. His clan, maybe.'

'A party,' I said absently. 'That's nice.'

I was a little distracted by what I could see out the window. We were moving too fast to focus on any details, but outside its entirely rebuilt city centre, pleasant three- and four-storey office buildings buzzing with bureaucrats, Mostar was clearly in much worse shape than anywhere in Sarajevo. We passed a bombed-out trapezoidal building eight storeys high, its walls charred black, every single window shattered. On the other side of the road was a long concrete wall, half papered over by ads for cellphone companies, the remainder cracked and cratered by some kind of weapon more serious than small arms.

Dragan and Saskia lived on a long and tree-lined street on Mostar's outskirts that at first looked prosperous, if overgrown. Leafy trees and thick bushes and tall grass were ubiquitous west of the Neretva. The east side, I later learned, had no trees at all. That was the Muslim side, and like Sarajevo it had been besieged during the war, forcing its inhabitants to cut down and burn all their trees in order to survive. But parts of the Croatian side were nearly jungle, streets that seemed to be under attack from Mother Nature herself, seeking to turn Mostar back into forest, erase all traces of mankind. After spending a couple of days there it didn't seem like such a bad idea.

In Dragan and Saskia's neighbourhood the riot of weeds and bushes made their street look green and peaceful and briefly concealed the fact that half of its houses had been razed to the ground. Dozens more had been half destroyed but were now patched up enough with wood and concrete and corrugated aluminium that families actually lived in the two or three remaining usable rooms. Maybe one in four had been mostly spared by the war, just a few bullet holes here and there, a roof that leaked in the rain where a shell had struck but failed to explode, shrapnel marks on the wall. Like much of the rest of Mostar their street looked and felt like the war had ended only eight weeks ago rather than eight years.

The party had already begun. Men barbecued two pigs on spits over a pit in one of the larger vacant lots, drank beer and passed bottles of slivovitz around although it wasn't even noon. Women sat beneath a temporary tented canopy, arranging food on big folding tables, sitting on plastic chairs, talking and smoking, watching over the children and the dozen teenagers playing football in the street who paused the game to let us pass. About sixty people

41

in all. There were hardly any old people, and noticeably more adult women than men, and while there were teenagers and small children, there were very few children of any in-between age, which said a lot about the demographics of the war's victims. Everyone waved and peered curiously into the car as we passed. The attention made me uncomfortable. I wasn't a party person at the best of times, and Honoured and Somewhat Resented Rich Foreign Guest was not a role I liked to play.

We parked outside Dragan and Saskia's house. There were many cars parked on the street. That at least made the neighbourhood seem vibrant. Theirs was one of the good houses, small but in a plot of land big enough to boast a vegetable garden. Their property was clean and well cared for, inside and out, with garden implements hanging neatly from a rack outside, comfortable couches and fresh flowers and small landscape prints indoors, threadbare but comfortable sheets and pillowcases. Upstairs there were two tiny bedrooms; downstairs held the living room, a kitchen and a bathroom. There was no attic and no basement.

Saskia led us up to the guest room, where we deposited our packs, and then out to the party, whose participants surrounded us and welcomed us with a boisterous cheer. They were flashier and prettier people than I had anticipated. I had half expected country bumpkins with banjos and patched clothes and half their teeth missing, a Bosnian *Deliverance*. Admittedly there was a minority who fitted that profile, men like Dragan with tangled hair and beards who didn't seem to have bathed lately, women who wore rough simple dresses that had had all the colour washed out of them, but most of them, especially the younger ones, wore designer jeans and shiny skirts and leather boots and football shirts made of space-age materials adorned with the names zidane or rivaldo or mihajlovic, and the music thumping out of the CD player beneath the table full of bread and cheese was not banjo but Eminem.

After greeting us with a cheer, the men returned to the roasting pigs, the children returned to their games, and the women milled about and talked and laughed and asked us questions. Talena smiled at a few of the things they said and answered the questions politely. I didn't understand a word and she didn't have time to translate. After a moment Dragan clapped his hand on my shoulder, hard enough that I almost stumbled, and half led, half dragged me to the cooler next to the barbecue pit. He dug through the cooler's ice and unearthed a cold bottle of Niksicki Gold for me, improving my opinion of him immensely. Technically it was too early to start drinking, but I figured, when in Bosnia . . .

I stood next to Dragan and the other men in a semicircle around the pigs, sipping beer and watching as a lanky old man carefully basted and rotated the glistening flesh. The smell made my mouth water. I looked around and smiled, partly to seem polite and friendly, partly because I was amused by the universal human nature of the scene: the women gossip with the newcomers, the children play games, the men stand around the roasting meat.

Dragan said something to one of the other men, in his forties with grey hair and a beard, both a few inches long but neatly clipped. They exchanged a few words and then the older man turned to me and said in careful but good English, 'Hello. My name is Josip. They call me the Professor, but I am not really. I studied in London for two

43

years, once, that is all.' He smiled. 'Many years ago, when I was young.'

'Paul,' I said. We shook hands.

'Your girlfriend is very beautiful,' Josip said, looking at Talena. 'You are a lucky man.'

'She certainly is,' I agreed.

We smiled at each other stiffly.

'Do you all live on this street?' I asked, waving my hand at the assembled masses.

'Yes,' Josip said. 'But there are also other people on this street who do not live here. Those of us here, we are not just neighbours. All the men you see here around you, we fought together in the war. We were the Mostar Tigers.' He said the name proudly. 'First we fought the Chetniks. Then we fought the Turks. We fought for three years.'

'The Turks?' I asked, bewildered. I knew from Sarajevo that 'Chetnik' referred to the Serbs, but the second reference confused me. I was no historian but I was pretty sure Turkey had never gotten involved in the Bosnian war.

'The Muslims,' Josip said, spitting out the word. 'The people across the river.'

'Oh, right, them,' I said. 'I take it you're still not friends.'

'You must be careful while you are here,' he warned me. 'Especially near the river. Don't believe anything they say. They smile and smile, but they're all fundamentalists, fanatics; they want to make all of Europe an Islamic state, they want every woman in a chador, every man in a mosque; they won't rest until either they win or they're all dead. If we aren't careful, your people and mine, if we aren't careful they will win. This is still the front line, here, the battle for

Europe is still going on; never mind this peace, it's still jihad to them, it's just a different kind of war now, now they're terrorists. They were always terrorists. They're no different from the people who destroyed your World Trade Center, no different at all. There are high-level connections to Osama bin Laden; he sends money and weapons and Arabs and blacks here to fight for the Muslims. It's well documented, ask anyone, ask a Muslim; they are proud of it.'

'I see,' I said, nodding expressionlessly, hiding my shock. I hadn't encountered anything like this virulent bigotry in Sarajevo. The people there, at least those friends of Talena I had talked to, were disgusted by their country's past, eager to turn their backs on nationalism and embrace the West, considered themselves European rather than Bosnian.

'You must be careful. At night they come across the river, they break windows, they cut electricity, they cut car tyres, they steal anything they can, they try to burn our churches, and if they find one of our women . . . Animals. No better than animals. There are still Muslim war criminals walking around on the other side of the river, dozens of them, in broad daylight. And your people, NATO, they do nothing to stop them. Nothing.'

I smiled politely and took a long swig of my beer. When the slivovitz came around, I took a big swallow of that. I could see why Bosnians drank so much. Sometimes it was the only way to deal with the place.

Dragan conferred briefly with Josip, who then turned to me and said, 'But enough about the Muslims. Enough about the war. God willing the war is only history now. Even so we shouldn't talk about history here. We have too much history. Surely you have seen that already. We have too much history and it has too many teeth. Let us focus on the future. To peace and hopes for the future.'

I clinked my bottles against his and Dragan's, who bestowed a toothy smile upon me.

'My good friend Dragan here,' Josip continued, 'tomorrow he and I would like to show you something. We have a business proposition for you that you may find interesting. A very promising business proposition for which we need an outside investor like you. An investor who I truly believe will become very rich.'

My stomach sank. I considered explaining to Josip that I was unemployed and already in debt to MasterCard to the tune of eight thousand dollars, but I knew he wouldn't believe me. Everyone in places like this knew beyond any doubt that all Americans were impossibly rich, and any attempt to deny this would seem a rude and transparent lie. I smiled and nodded.

'Good,' Josip said. 'Tomorrow. But we shall speak no more of this today. Tomorrow is for business, and today is for living!'

We clinked our beers together again. I looked over at Talena; she and Saskia stood next to one another, ignoring the rest of the world, talking fast and laughing, making up for so much lost time. Josip introduced me to the rest of the fifteen Mostar Tigers, whose names never made it past my short-term memory. They were as scary as Dragan. Three of them were missing limbs, and two others walked with pronounced limps. Even the ones who didn't have visible scars, even the several who were of the lean, fine chiselled features almost effeminate type that seemed to be grown *en masse* in a pretty-boy factory somewhere in the Balkans, all of them had the flat, arrogant demeanour of men who are casually comfortable inflicting and receiving violence.

Woody Allen once said that every time he met a woman, on some level he was thinking about having sex with her. Whenever two men meet, on some level they are both thinking, *Could I take him? If it comes down to him or me, in a fight, who wins?* Usually there is some element of doubt in the answer. Here there was none. Against any one of them I would lose. The Mostar Tigers were friendly, and at that point they were still mostly quiet and reserved, but like Sinisa's lieutenants last night, the woman and the über-thug, they had the feral aura of wild animals. Carnivores.

I noticed that several of them looked towards Talena more often than necessary, and let their gazes linger. I was used to Talena attracting attention; she was tall and slender and startlingly pretty, even in khaki cargo pants and black T-shirt. But for the first time I felt irrationally threatened by it, as if she might decide on the spur of the moment to replace me with one of the pretty-boy Tigers, or one of them might challenge me to a duel for her.

The group dynamics of the Tigers made it clear that Dragan was their leader. The others came to talk to him. They asked questions and he answered. On the rare occasions when he initiated conversation, those around him immediately fell silent and listened intently.

Well, I thought, *at least Saskia got the alpha thug.*

The party went on all day and into the night. I didn't enjoy it. I was tired and hot, and I wasn't accustomed to drinking as early or as much as the Bosnians, and by mid-afternoon I was wobbly and exhausted. I'm not a people person to begin with, I'm uncomfortable in big groups, quickly bored by small talk, uncertain of the appropriate conversational protocols, although in Mostar that wasn't a big deal as the only people I could communicate with were Josip and Talena. I was actually glad that the language barrier walled me off from everyone else. I wasn't used to being at parties without Talena by my side. Here, she and Saskia were inseparable and didn't want company, and I couldn't blame them, but it made me feel like I was an awkward teenager again, lounging around a party looking for someone to talk to, pretending I wasn't bored and embarrassed by my solitude. I passed my time by drinking more beer, which didn't help. And in addition to my usual party insecurity I had to swallow the angry contempt with which I responded to the all-too-common manifestations of the endlessly deep vein of blood-curdling hatred and bigotry that lay beneath Bosnia's unconvincing veneer of civilization.

And, I didn't want to think about this and walled it off, but the more I drank the more my awful understanding began to seep in through the cracks and around the edges that I had to start dealing with the conscious knowledge that Talena and I were through. She was the only good thing in my life, and I was about to lose her for ever. I tried to tell myself that maybe this would be the best thing for me. Maybe, like the US economy, like Bosnia itself, I had to hit the rock bottom of my pit before I could start clawing my way up towards the light again. But no matter how much I drank I couldn't even begin to convince myself.

Some time near dusk I looked around from my intoxicated self-pitying haze and realized that Talena and Saskia were nowhere to be seen and that I badly wanted the party to end. I was very tired, my clothes were thickly crusted with my own dried sweat, and I wanted to curl up and sleep. But Josip wasn't around either, so I couldn't even tell this to anyone, and I didn't remember which house was Dragan and Saskia's. I got another plate of roast pork and bread and cheese, all of it dry by now, but I had the vague idea that it would sober me up a little and make me stronger. I washed it down with another beer. The soccer ball came my way and on a whim I tried to play with the teenagers.

Like all Europeans they were frighteningly good and like all North Americans I was laughably bad. After clumsily stepping on the ball and tumbling on to the street, scraping my hand and cueing a stinging chorus of mocking laughter, I retreated back to the vacant lot next to the food tables, found a rotting concrete block in the weeds, and sat atop it for a while. Nobody paid me any attention. By this time everyone was too drunk to feign interest in their Honoured Canadian Guest. That suited me fine.

I vaguely noticed that the party had escalated into loud ragged laughter, short emotional bursts of song, men grabbing women and kissing them roughly, brief impassioned arguments. I watched as one of the Tigers, the one with a prosthetic leg, drunkenly tried to make the teenagers march like they were soldiers and shouted at them, spittle flying from his mouth, when they refused. Instead of laughing at him they backed quietly away. A woman hesitantly approached the one-legged man and gently tried to convince him to leave the kids alone. He rewarded her with a shove that sent her sprawling to the street. Nobody seemed to notice or care as she scrambled to her feet and retreated to her plastic chair with a newly skinned elbow, tears staining her face. I wondered if they were married.

'Paul,' Talena said.

I jerked with surprise and looked up at her. She and Saskia had returned from somewhere. I had a dim notion that they had been gone for hours. Saskia's eyes were red with tears and she clutched Talena's arm as if she would collapse without its support. She looked like a child next to Talena, who was eight or nine inches taller. Talena was pale and tense, and I could tell she had been crying too.

'What happened?' I asked.

She shook her head. 'You're drunk.'

'No,' I said, shaking my head. 'Shit. Yeah, a little, I guess.'

'That's great,' she said. 'That's just fucking great. You go get drunk.'

'What happened?'

'You fucking—I can't rely on you, you know that? I used to think I could rely on you.'

I was drunkenly confident that her anger was unjustified. So I'd had one beer too many, it was a Bosnian party that started at noon, what the hell did she expect in this nation of alcoholics? I nearly said that, nearly picked a fight with her. Only the sight of Saskia, drained and despairing, prevented me.

'We're going to bed,' Talena said. 'Don't wake me up when you come in. If you come in. You can sleep out here for all I give a shit.'

'Okay,' I said, and watched her depart. I wanted to follow and find out what terrible thing had happened. It occurred to me that maybe she wouldn't tell me, not even tomorrow when I was sober and we were alone together. We had grown far enough apart that that was possible.

Darkness fell. Women and children began to drift back to their homes, or to the half-ruined buildings that passed for them, but the Tigers remained, standing in a cluster in the middle of the street, circulating their umpteenth bottle of slivovitz, talking and laughing, probably reminiscing about the good old days of killing and maiming. I looked over at them. Then I sat bolt upright, alarmed, as I saw Dragan walking down the street holding a Kalashnikov. Before I could figure out how to react, he aimed the weapon at the sky, howled like a wounded animal, and fired a whole magazine straight up at the stars. I hadn't heard the loud, curiously hollow sound of gunfire for a long time.

I told myself I should go home. I was getting maudlin and weepy again, but more to the point, drink and guns and ex-soldiers were a bad combination. If 'soldiers' was the right word. I suspected that the Mostar Tigers had been one of the Bosnian war's many highly irregular warlord paramilitary units, not part of any formal army. Which made them even more volatile and dangerous. And even if they fired only at the moon, bullets that go up must eventually come down. I remembered reading somewhere that if they tumbled they would only hit hard enough to bruise, but if they came straight back down they could kill you; 'space bullets' the article had called them.

I knew I should go home. But I felt about as mobile as the concrete block on which I sat. The beer and slivovitz seemed to have hardened into glue in my joints. I just watched and stared as all fifteen of them linked arms and hoarsely began to sing. Some of them began to weep. They were midway through what I had begun to recognize as the chorus when NATO arrived.

5 Broken Bridges

They came from both ends of the street at once, two Jeeps with four blue-helmeted soldiers in each, and both of them pulled up on the side of the street opposite me, stopping at an angle to one another, headlights crossing right where the group of Tigers stood. The Tigers split off into two groups, one facing each Jeep. It was dark but the headlights and bright rear-mounted searchlights of the Jeeps illuminated the scene clearly and kept the British hidden. The block on which I sat was just far enough away that I remained in darkness.

'Put down your weapon *immediately*,' a crisp British voice demanded. His voice was quickly followed by the Croatian translation.

Dragan bellowed something. I didn't hear what the NATO translator said, but it certainly didn't defuse the situation. The doors of the Jeeps opened and the soldiers took up armed positions behind them.

'Go fuck yourself,' Josip said loudly, his English slurred and accented but unfortunately very understandable. 'This is our city. Our city. We fought for it, we bled for it, we fucking died for it. Fuck you. Fuck NATO, fuck you. This is our home. Our home. Not your home. Ours. So we, we'—he staggered with the force of his inebriated emotion and just prevented himself from falling—'*we* will do what we want here. So fuck you, fuck every one of you, fuck your mothers, fuck your sisters, fuck your daughters, fuck yourselves, fuck yourselves up the ass, fuck each other, fuck you, fuck off, eat shit and fucking die.'

I thought it was an impressive display of profanity considering that English was at best his second language. The British leader didn't seem to share my admiration. 'You have ten seconds to put down that Kalashnikov,' he said coolly, 'or you will be arrested.'

Josip and the NATO translator raced to convey their versions of that. The threat of their leader's arrest galvanized the other armed Tigers—half a dozen, it turned out, carried small pistols on their persons—into drawing their weapons. No guns had yet been aimed at the NATO troops, but it seemed like just a matter of time.

The British leader agreed with my estimation: I heard him speak, probably into a radio, and calmly report, 'This is second squad. Our situation has escalated. Request back-up.'

The searchlight of one of the Jeeps described a slow arc around the street and latched on to me. I shielded my face with my arms against the blinding light.

'You!' a young and nervous voice shouted, not the leader's. 'Get up here with your mates!' When I didn't respond immediately the same voice barked, presumably to their translator, 'Tell him to get his bloody arse up here. Last thing we need here is more of them skulking around.'

'All right!' I said angrily, loudly enough that the Brits could hear me over the dark muttering of the Tigers. 'Christ. Stop pointing that fucking thing at me already, will you? Jesus.' I stood up, still shielding my eyes, and walked over to the space between the Jeeps, moving fairly steadily; the sight of guns and the incipient stand-off had half sobered me in a hurry.

'Who the fuck are you?' the young voice asked, astonished. 'What's a fucking Yank doing here?'

'I'm Canadian, asshole,' I said. And then, inspiration striking: 'And these are my friends, and if this is anyone's fault, it's mine, so why don't you cool the fuck down and stop pointing your guns at my friends here? And for Christ's sake get that goddamn light out of my face!'

My stew of poisonous emotions had found an unexpected outlet: the British army.

My appearance and irritable complaints were so out of place that they alone half defanged the situation. The Bosnians, coming from a land where you never trusted armed authorities, who could not even imagine treating soldiers as if you had rights that they dared not violate, were bewildered and to some extent impressed by my grumpy demands and almost total lack of fear that Brits might shoot me or arrest me, and my strange behaviour crowded the worst of their macho persecution complex from their minds. The British, on the other hand, nonplussed at finding an annoyed Canadian amidst this gang of thugs, were suddenly no longer certain what they should do.

'Redirect the light,' the leader ordered, and I could see again. 'And we are not pointing guns at your friends. Not yet. Now who are you and how precisely are you responsible for this?'

'My name is Balthazar Wood,' I said. I hardly ever used my full name but I had learned that in confrontations its lengthy ring was psychologically advantageous. I indicated Dragan. 'Dragan here is a friend of mine. He was telling me how they used to shoot guns into the air at parties, and I asked him if he could show me. So he did. As a favour to me, that's all. And who exactly are you?' The best defence, it's a good offence.

After a pause he answered me. 'Lieutenant Simon Taylor, Second Paratroop Division, British army.'

'Yeah. I had the British part figured out. Paratroopers, huh? Old friend of mine used to be in your outfit. Hallam Chevalier, ever heard of him? . . . Okay, never mind. Look, I'm sorry. I asked for a little too much authentic Bosnian culture. I'm just a stupid tourist.' An old traveller's trick: *stupid tourist,* an amazingly effective and almost universally applicable ploy that had gotten me out of countless scrapes in the past. Everyone knows that tourists are such incredible idiots that they're effectively mentally damaged and can't really be held responsible for their actions. 'I've been drinking,' I continued, 'we've all been drinking, I guess you can see that. I'm very sorry it came to this. But it's over now, and nobody really wants any trouble. Can't we all just go home and sleep it off?'

I hoped for a 'yes.' I expected a long, stern lecture, followed by a grudging 'yes.' I feared that Dragan or one of his men, who so far had been perplexed into letting me do the talking, would ruin everything by doing or saying something stupid during the lecture.

I did not expect what I heard next, from a third British voice, this one rough and middle-aged and surprised: 'Chevalier? Sergeant Hallam Chevalier? You're a mate of his? The South African?'

'I—well, yes,' I said. 'Zimbabwe, not South Africa. Yes, he's a good friend of mine.'

'I've heard that name before,' the leader said thoughtfully.

'He was a fucking legend, sir,' the old voice said. 'I met him a few times, my first tour here, ten years ago. I heard

55

he was nominated for the VC. Just bloody politics he didn't get it.'

'Hallam was nominated for the Victoria Cross?' I said, amazed. 'For what?'

'We don't have time for this,' the leader said sharply before the older soldier could answer. 'Klein, this is not a gossip shop, and you will not waste our time exchanging war stories with one of our suspects.'

'Yes, sir,' the older voice said, chastened.

'And you, Mr Wood, tell me, how does one descend from being friends with a widely respected member of the finest military unit in the world to fraternizing with your current set of associates?'

I looked over at the Mostar Tigers, looked back towards the NATO Jeeps, rolled my eyes, shrugged, and said in a regretful you-know-how-it-is voice, 'My girlfriend.'

There were a couple of quickly smothered chuckles on the other side of the headlights.

'And where is she?'

'Asleep.'

The leader sighed, loudly. Then he said, 'I'll tell you what, Mr Wood. If you talk your friends here into following her example this very minute, then I shall arrest no one and confiscate nothing. This is your last and only chance.'

I turned to Josip, who was already translating. Dragan thought about it for a minute. I wondered just how big an idiot he was. Then he said something back, and Josip announced: 'Dragan says two things. First thing, we are already tired, so the party is over and we will go to sleep, fine. Second thing he says, he says fuck you, NATO. Fuck you all.'

Pretty big, I decided. A solid 7 on an idiot scale of 1

to 10. And there were more engines approaching. NATO's reinforcements. If they decided to take offence, then Dragan, and possibly I, would probably spend at least the night in jail.

Fortunately, Lieutenant Taylor actually sounded amused. 'Tell your friend that the feeling is more than mutual,' he said drily. 'Now put your guns away and go home. By the look of the lot of you, you need all the beauty sleep you can get.'

I followed Dragan back into his house. I was very tired, eager to sleep, but as I began to climb the stairs to the guest bedroom, he put a meaty hand on my shoulder and dragged me back to the front door. I tried to protest politely but the language barrier made the attempt futile. We waited, the door open a crack, until NATO's headlights vanished. Then Dragan advanced into the night again, half pulling me behind him. In the dim glow of the two functioning street lights I saw shadows emerging from other houses. The party was not over. The Mostar Tigers were reconvening.

I followed Dragan and the others across uneven grassy fields, led by several darting flashlights. I thought uneasily of unexploded land-mines. I wanted to turn back to the warm bed I had almost reached, but doing so would clearly be very rude, and offending Dragan and the Tigers seemed like a bad idea.

A building loomed out of the night, a big ruined house, its stone walls scarred and chipped, every window shattered. I followed the flashlights up old stone steps, through a doorway with no door, and into a big draughty room. Something scurried as we entered. I soon realized that the room was draughty because an irregular hole the size of a Volkswagen had been blasted into one wall. Shattered limbs of lacquered wood that had once been fine furniture were piled in a corner. A big and vaguely Persian rug remained, torn and covered with dust. Someone, presumably the Tigers, had redecorated the room with big logs and concrete bricks, and improvised a firepit out of the rubble beneath the hole in the wall.

The Tigers, who had been absolutely silent on the walk over, began to chatter brightly to one another. I sat on one of the logs, between Josip and Dragan, as a fire was lit. A new bottle of slivovitz was opened and plastic cupfuls passed around. I tried to demur but a roar of disapproval forced me to accept a cup.

Dragan lifted his cup. 'Paul Wood!' he said. With his other hand he clapped me on the back so hard I nearly spilled my slivovitz.

'Paul Wood!' the Tigers chorused, and they raised their glasses to me, then drained them. I was so surprised I forgot to drink.

'It is friends like you we need, Paul,' Josip said. 'Friends who can stand up to NATO and make them listen. Friends who can support our business.'

'I'm happy I could help,' I said cautiously. The appreciation was flattering. I had to admit I got a bit of a buzz from all those battle-hardened warriors smiling approvingly at me. But I wasn't sure I really wanted to be an honorary member of the Mostar Tigers. A subject change seemed like a good idea. 'What is this place?'

'One of the rich Turks lived here,' Josip said. 'It was our headquarters during the war. We did great things here.

Great things. And now, now we come here to drink. Look at us. Hiding here like children escaping their parents. It is a humiliation. Look at these men around you. Every one of us has killed men in battle. We saved one another's lives times beyond counting. Our enemies trembled at our name. And now, now the war is over, all we do is drink and curse NATO and talk about how bold we once were. But look, Paul, look, I tell you, these are some of the bravest and most dangerous men in the world. We are not useless. But this peace'—he spat the word out—'this NATO peace, it comes with nothing, no opportunity. If we were given an opportunity, I tell you what we would do with it. We would make a miracle. We would make an empire.'

It was a stirring speech. I wished I was a rich Western investor, wished there was some way I could help Dragan and Josip and the Tigers. But they were aiming their speeches at the wrong man. I couldn't even help myself.

'You are tired,' Josip said. 'I understand. We will speak of this further tomorrow. But do not forget what I tell you. You are with men capable of great things.'

I woke early. Partly because ten time zones' worth of jet lag was still making my metabolic clock spin like a compass in a magnet factory. Partly because I always wake up early when I'm badly hung over, as if my body wants me to suffer through as many hours of my self-inflicted agony as possible, some kind of moral lesson. It was barely dawn. Talena slept beside me. I didn't remember coming into the house and going to sleep. I hoped I hadn't woken her up.

The bathroom, I remembered, was downstairs. Standing up was a terrible mistake. A sledgehammer began to pound at my skull from the inside. I felt so weak that I tottered rather than walked. I descended the stairs slowly and clumsily. There was no rail, so I pressed my hands against the wood-panelled wall next to the stairs for support. The steps creaked beneath me. Eventually I reached the bathroom door and pushed it open.

The toilet lid was down, and Saskia sat atop it, her face in her hands, tears leaking from her closed eyes. She was crying without making a single noise, absolutely silent even though her whole body shook violently. She wore sweat pants and a black bra, and her long dark hair was tied back in a ponytail. Her stomach and upper arms were mottled with bruises the size of apples, vividly purple and yellow against her otherwise porcelain skin.

I stood there, stunned, my mind wrapped in my hangover's thick blinding cloth, barely able to parse what I was seeing. No wonder Talena was so upset, was my first coherent thought. You'd be upset too if you met your half-sister and once-best-friend after eight years and found that she was a battered wife. I wondered if I should turn around and go upstairs and pretend this encounter had never taken place. It seemed horribly rude to intrude on Saskia's misery like this. But she would hear my retreat. She must have heard me coming downstairs.

'Sorry,' Saskia managed to whisper through her silent sobs. 'Sorry. Wait. Please wait.' Her eyes had at least flickered open, so she knew who stood before her.

I waited, amazed at her noiseless weeping, at the discipline it takes to control an involuntary physical reaction like that. Easy, and terrible, to imagine how it had happened. Dragan liked beating her, but he didn't like the way she sounded when she cried afterwards, so he punished her even more severely when she cried until she learned how to be silent. A kind of self-control that didn't come easy. Hindu fakirs practised for half their lives to have so much control. Years upon years of patient, methodical, endless abuse must have been inflicted on the woman before me until she had learned to cry silently. I shivered at the thought.

'Sorry,' she whispered again, getting control of herself. 'I am sorry, Paul, I am sorry.'

'It's okay,' I whispered back. 'Saskia. It's okay.'

'I am think you are Talena,' she said. She frowned, trying to find the right words in her broken English. 'But it is okay it is you. You are good man, Paul. Talena tell me. You are good man. She tell me. I tell her to stay with you. It is okay you see me.' She spread her arms wide to display her bruises, almost proudly. 'But no tell Dragan. No tell. Please. No tell. You tell, is bad, is most bad for me, okay?'

'Okay,' I said. 'I understand.'

'I am sorry. I not, I do not know English. Not good. In German I am good. In English I am so stupid. Please know, please know, I am not stupid. I am . . . what is word? Good, not stupid.'

'Smart,' I said.

'Yes. Smart. I am smart like Talena, I am, please know. But in English I am not say the words I want. It make me . . . ' She shrugged with a frustration that required no translation. 'I am not stupid. I have diploma, good school. In Croatian or German I am smart. Big smart. In my school I was most smart, girl or boy, I was most smart. I know you must think, stay with Dragan, must be stupid. But please, I am not.'

'I don't think that,' I said. 'I don't think you're stupid.' And I didn't. I had some idea how hard it was to flounder in a language you had only a bare and broken understanding of, and she was doing wonders to convey what she needed to with her hundred-word vocabulary, on the fly, without hesitation. I would never have done near as well in French.

'Talena want me to go with you now. To Sarajevo. To go and stay.' She shook her head. 'I no go. No now. Is not smart. I want to say what is not smart. I want to say big many things to you, Paul, but I not have words, I am sorry. You go back to Sarajevo. I stay here. I want to go to Sarajevo with you. I want it big, most big. If I go, then Dragan go. I go before. I know I have baby, so I go. Dragan want baby. Dragan want baby most big. I no want Dragan baby father, so I go. Dragan go. Dragan . . . ' She hesitated, lost for words, then she formed a fist and mimed punching herself in the belly. 'Many times. So no baby. Dragan want baby most big, but he want me know Dragan most big more.'

I stared at her, speechless.

'Talena want me to go with you. But if I go, Dragan go. Dragan go, Dragan kill me.' She shrugged. 'I think, I kill Dragan. But is others. I kill Dragan, I go, they go, they kill me. I go Sarajevo, Banja Luka, I go Bosnia, they go, they kill me. So I no go with you. If I go America, I go with you. But Talena say, I no go America.'

Which was true. It would take months to get a visa.

'You and Talena, you go America now. I wait. You go do things so I go America, you go Bosnia, I go America. I stay America. Is good. Is most good. Is smart? Is good?'

'Is good,' I assured her. I wanted to cry. 'Is smart.'

'Good,' Saskia said. 'You good man, Paul. You good man.'

We looked at each other. It was clear that the conversation was over.

'Do you go to . . . ' She couldn't think of the word, and mimed using her hands as a pillow.

'Sleep,' I said.

'Sleep. Yes. Do you go to sleep now?'

'Yes,' I said. 'Except I need to use the bathroom first.'

She looked at me, confused, and I pointed to the toilet.

'Oh, yes,' she said, and smiled, amused and slightly embarrassed. I hadn't seen her smile before. It was a smile that seemed to belong to an entirely different woman, confident and beautiful and insouciant, rather than the frightened, huddled, desperate person who had conducted the rest of this conversation. She got up and padded silently past me. On impulse I reached out and took her shoulder. I was going to hug her, but she pulled away, fast, her smile fading to fright.

'Sorry,' I said, kicking myself for being an idiot, for not realizing that she associated any male touch with terror and pain. 'Sorry. I just . . . sorry.'

'Oh,' she said. 'Okay. Sorry. Is no good. Sorry.'

'Goodnight,' I whispered, although it was now day.

'Goodnight.'

I woke the second time to a pounding headache and an angry girlfriend.

'Sure hope you had a good time yesterday,' Talena said, when I made the mistake of opening my eyes. She sat on the edge of the bed, fully dressed, reading my Lonely Planet

63

guide. 'Hope you had a wonderful time with all your new friends. Why don't you ask them to take you hunting later on? Maybe they can explain the fine points of how you set land-mines so that they'll kill small children.'

'Nguh,' I protested. It was hard to talk. I cleared my throat. 'Land-mines . . . what?'

'But that's all old news. What they're really expert at now-adays is beating their wives. Ask them all about it. I'm sure they can teach you all the details. Where you hit them so that they piss blood for a week but it isn't visible in public. How you hit them on the soles of the feet so they can't walk if you don't want them to leave the house. You know what? I just realized. I bet actually they learned all this from torturing people during the war, and now that the war's over, they're just keeping in practice with their wives. That's how Saskia got that black eye. Dragan's just practising for the next war.'

'Black eye?'

'There's a reason she dragged all her hair over one side of her face and put make-up on like she was about to go on TV.' She paused and in a slightly less angry tone said, 'I didn't notice it either at first. He stopped hitting her in the face a couple of weeks ago, because we were coming to visit. He told her that if she told either of us he would cut her tongue out. You hear that? Cut her tongue out. And it's not some empty hyperbolic threat, he actually means he would take a steak knife and hold her mouth open and saw her fucking tongue off. That's your new buddy Dragan for you. She was crying all day yesterday. It took her all day to start talking about it. He wouldn't give a shit whether we knew or not, not Dragan, except he wants to make a good impression because he's hoping you'll give him money.'

'Yeah,' I said. 'He mentioned.'

'He did? He talked to you? In English?'

'His friend. Josip. Speaks English.'

'Josip. Right. The Professor. Well, Saskia says Dragan doesn't, so we can speak freely as long as Josip isn't around. But if you so much as hint that we know about him beating her . . . ' She tried to come up with some kind of consequence equal to the enormity of that action, and failed. 'Don't. Just, don't. Please, Paul, for God's sake, wake the fuck up. This is bad. This is really fucking bad. All those men last night, all your new best friends? They're monsters. Don't think of them as people. Think of them as demons in human form. I'm not exaggerating, not one fucking bit; if you heard the stories she told me . . . God. Crucifixions, old men and boys crucified alive, live impalings, locking children into houses and setting them on fire, shooting pregnant women in the belly, stopping buses and picking out girls to drag outside and rape in front of their families, war or no war, and it wasn't a war; it's fucking unspeakable what they did, and I don't care that half the rest of the country was doing the same kind of thing, they're still monsters. It's like Saskia was kidnapped by orcs eight years ago and they kept making her send letters saying she was okay. Except they didn't make her. She just didn't want to trouble me. If she'd only told me, if she'd just called or written and told me . . . Fuck. It makes me want to scream. I guess she didn't get email until a few years ago anyway and by then he'd already kicked all the good sense out of her.'

'You don't need to worry about me,' I said defensively. 'They were already definitely not my new best friends.'

'That's not what Josip said you told the NATO troops.'

'I was trying to mediate. That's all. Defusing the situation. Come on, Talena, you know me, do you really think I was male bonding with those animals? I was just trying to be polite and friendly so that you wouldn't be pissed off at me for ruining your reunion. If it wasn't for you I wouldn't have stayed at that party more than ten minutes.'

'That's why you told them that you were one of their blood brothers? That's why you told NATO to go fuck themselves and dared them to arrest you? To be polite?'

'Blood brothers?' I asked, incredulous. 'I told NATO what?'

'Well . . . that's the story he told me this morning,' Talena said, seeing from my reaction that the tale had grown considerably in the telling. 'That you're the new local hero who told NATO to piss off, and because it was you, for once they actually did. Usually three or four of them wind up spending a night or two in jail.'

'Usually? There's a usually?' That made the whole encounter retrospectively even weirder. 'Jesus Christ, this town is fucked up.'

'Tell me about it.'

'There any water left in your bottle?'

Talena dug out her half-full litre bottle and passed it to me. I emptied it.

'Dragan wants to drive you out somewhere as soon as you're up,' she said. 'His big business opportunity. He's very excited, he was almost going to tell me all about it but then he remembered that he was talking to a woman. After that he probably wanted to break my nose just to keep in practice. That fucker.'

'What are you going to do?' I asked.

'I'm going to cut *his* tongue out, and break all his fucking fingers one at a time,' Talena said fiercely, and for a moment I feared she meant it. But then she sighed, and said in a slightly more sane tone, 'I'm going to get her out of here.'

'How?'

'I don't know,' she admitted. 'I want her to come back to Sarajevo with us. That'll be a start.'

'She won't come,' I said. 'She's afraid they'll kill her. She won't come unless we can get her an American visa. These days that could take months. If we could do it at all.'

Talena stared at me, amazed.

'What?' I asked.

'How do you know?'

I realized that Talena had not spoken to Saskia this morning, at least not in private, and did not know about my conversation earlier this morning. 'I talked to her. This morning.'

'You . . . how? When?'

I explained. Talena listened intently.

'I didn't see her bruises,' she said quietly when I finished, no longer angry at me. She brought her knees up and put her arms around them, unconsciously curling her athletic body into a foetal position. 'I wanted to see them. I don't know why. But I didn't want to ask.'

'They're bad,' I said.

'The feet, he's done that. With a coat hanger. The wire from a coat hanger. She wasn't able to walk for six weeks. That was after she ran to Sarajevo and he found her and kicked her baby into a miscarriage. He came back and he actually flayed most of the skin off the soles of her feet.

67

She showed me that.' Her face wrinkled like she had bitten something rotten and needed to spit it out of her mouth.

'Jesus,' I said.

'We have to get her out of here. I don't care what she says. I don't care if Dragan and all fucking Mostar comes after us.'

'They would, you know. These jokers, they probably would.'

'I know.' Talena sighed. 'I'll talk to her again when you and Dragan are gone. There has to be something we can do. I don't know. But we can't leave her here. We have to get her out of here. Out of the country, now. We're going to get her out of here and I don't care how.'

'It is very simple,' Josip said. 'So simple it is perfect. We have friends who can supply us with automotive parts, very easily, very high quality, very inexpensive. We have other friends who are expert mechanics, can repair anything, but right now like everyone else they are unemployed, no one can afford them or even the equipment that would allow them to work. This would be our repair shop.'

I looked at the squat unfinished concrete shell of a building, a hundred feet square and two storeys high. It was post-war, I could tell by the absence of bullet marks. There was nothing here but the foundation, the four walls, the ceiling, a few dozen slender internal columns, a skirt of gravel around the building, and a gravel trail connecting to the road. Vacant doorways and window spaces created gaps like missing teeth in the walls.

'Our investor, I will call him you for the purposes of our discussion'—he grinned as if it were a very fine joke—'will serve two purposes; one, allow us to purchase this land and construct our repair shop here, not very expensive I assure you, everything is cheap in Bosnia; and two, arrange for the vehicles. Worthless, damaged, ruined vehicles come in; they have perhaps been in accidents, or are too old for the owners to bother repairing them, automobiles that would otherwise go to the scrap heap. We repair and replace as we need to, we have endless cheap parts and expert cheap labour, and then what do we have? Cars good as new that we can sell anywhere for an enormous profit. We get work. You get rich. Bosnia gets a new industry. Is it not perfect?'

The pathetic thing was, he was right. It was perfect. It sounded like a completely viable business model, taking advantage of Bosnia's only competitive advantages: lax law enforcement and cheap labour. Take smuggled auto parts from thieves and chop shops in Western Europe, add the work of desperate long-unemployed mechanics, and *voilà*, instant profits. In its own sleazy way it was an inspired idea, but they were reduced to pitching it to a random Western visitor because nobody in their right mind would invest in Mostar and the Mostar Tigers.

I sipped from my bottle and nodded as if I were interested.

'How much money are we talking about here?' I asked.

Josip and Dragan conferred briefly. There was some kind of disagreement. Dragan won. Josip turned back to me and said, 'We estimate one hundred thousand euros.'

I raised my eyebrows. 'I don't have anything like that kind of money,' I said.

Josip's expression condensed to a mixture of disbelief and betrayal.

'I have some friends, though, in London and New York and other places'—I paused a moment before diverging from the truth—'who I think might be interested in this. At the very least I can go home and put together a business plan for you. If I can get five or six of my corporate friends interested . . . well, then there are some very real possibilities.'

Josip's eyes widened at my use of the word 'corporate,' and he hurried to translate to Dragan, who grinned broadly and nodded.

'There are a lot of things I need to know,' I said. I dug into my backpack and came up with a pencil and paper. I figured that, as in most social situations, asking a lot of specific questions would convince them that I took them seriously. But for a moment I couldn't fight my way through the painful mental shroud of my hangover, couldn't think of any questions to ask. They waited for me as I stared dumbly. I pretended to be thinking, muttered to myself inaudibly and incoherently for a little while, and then my brain kicked into gear and I began to rattle off questions about ownership percentages and mortgages and supply reliability and wages. Most of the questions were completely bogus, I didn't really know anything about running a company in any field other than software consulting, but they knew even less.

Sometimes they looked at each other and talked in low voices and then admitted they didn't know. Sometimes my questions made them fervently excited and Josip would explain vividly imagined details of how their international body shop would operate. I almost felt bad about inflating their expectations. Heartless killers and wife-beaters, sure, but when it came to business and to the myth of the end-lessly wealthy West they were very much like children. I kept reminding myself of the image of Saskia weeping silently, her stomach carpeted with bruises, and of what Talena had said about them. Setting children on fire, shooting pregnant women in the belly, raping teenage girls in front of their families. It was hard to believe, hard even to imagine, watching rumpled Josip and suddenly jolly Dragan grin eagerly at one another, their eyes lit with long-suppressed hope.

It was noon when we finally departed the shabby concrete shell that contained Dragan and Josip's dreams of wealth. The heatwave had if anything intensified. I had them drop me off at an Internet café so I could send emails to my investors. I did send an email, but it didn't mention their business plan. I emailed Hallam in London, my friend the ex-paratrooper, asking him if he still had any friends in Bosnia, because I had gotten into a bad situation here, and I was probably going to need help.

Before plunging into the colourless pit of poverty and unemployment I had led a strange and much travelled life, and I had many unusual friends scattered about the globe. Most importantly I had my close friends, my tribe, the people with whom I had travelled across Africa five years ago. Hallam was one of that tribe. Two and a half years ago he and I, and his wife Nicole, and our friends Steve and Lawrence, had avenged the murder of one of our members. I knew they would do whatever they could to help me, the same way I would help them, or Talena would help Saskia. I couldn't imagine how Steve or Lawrence could be of assist-ance but I cc'd them on the email just in case.

After spending half an hour on the Net for the princely sum of four euros, twice the going Sarajevo rate, I decided to walk around Mostar a little, get the lay of the land, see the sights if any, go over to the Muslim side and see how different it was. My Lonely Planet map indicated where the front line had been during the war, just west of the Neretva River that divided the town, a five-minute walk from the Internet café. I decided to go stroll along the front line and then cross the river to the Muslim old city.

Most of Mostar was in considerably better shape than the distant neighbourhood in which Dragan and Saskia lived. Parts of it seemed hardly affected by the war. En route to the river I passed a few bombed-out, bullet-cratered, war-scarred buildings, but only a few, standing out like rotting teeth amid new or rebuilt houses and offices and apartment complexes. Most of the freshly built or freshly painted buildings had plaques indicating that they were part of the vast EU-funded reconstruction effort. The streets were buzzing with cars and well-dressed pedestrians, every intersection had a couple of cafés crowded with men drinking coffee, and I began to realize that the Tigers lived in Mostar's equivalent of the ghetto.

The front line, Santiceva Street, was staggering. It was lined by rows of half-collapsed heaps of grey concrete and brick, torn open by ragged misshapen gaps and holes like Godzilla had taken bites out of them, punched full of bullet holes, many of them roofless, covered with dust, full of rubble. Chimneys and jagged concrete spurs that had somehow survived the tank and shellfire jutted out like broken bones. Bushes grew within the gaping shells that had once been buildings. It went on like this for a dozen blocks. A few randomly located houses had been rebuilt, and EU plaques proudly pronounced the reconstruction effort in five languages, but in that setting the words seemed like a sick joke. I understood for the first time the difference between Sarajevo and Mostar. Sarajevo had been scarred and crippled by the war. Mostar had been gutted.

I walked silently along Santiceva Street, keeping close to cover as if a sniper might shoot at me, holding my breath as I had done as a child when driving past a cemetery, afraid that one of the spirits of the dead might enter my body when I breathed in. At the north end I crossed the bridge. The bridge at the south end, a centuries-old World Heritage Site, had been destroyed during the war. There was talk of rebuilding it, scaffolding hung over the river there, but there was so little traffic on the existing bridges between the severed halves of the city that building another seemed ridiculous. I wondered whether it might be best to dynamite all the remaining bridges instead, leave the Neretva River as an uncrossable barrier between Mostar's two seething hatreds.

The river was gorgeous, deep blue water racing through a steep twenty-foot-deep ravine of huge boulders and thick bushes. A few people frolicked in the water, escaping the heat. The Muslim old city was a few square blocks of cobblestones and old cafés, quaint but smaller and nowhere near as picturesque as Sarajevo's Bascarsija district. I sat among the men, old and young, who sipped coffee and talked. On this side of the river they dressed more simply. I gratefully drank a cold Coke and looked down on the river. The usual madman's connect-the-dots of bullet and mortar scars dotted the walls all around, but I barely even noticed them. By now they were just standard Bosnian wallpaper, and, besides, I had too much to think and worry about.

This time yesterday my biggest concern had been whether Talena was about to leave me. Now I was riding the horns of a terrible moral and practical dilemma. The only way to help Saskia was to get her away from Dragan, away from Mostar, and if we did that, he and his fellow thugs might very well come after her and us. They had done so before. If we tried to help Saskia, Talena and I would be putting ourselves in serious danger.

But we couldn't abandon her, not now that we knew what had happened to her. We had to help Saskia. I felt that almost as strongly as Talena, even though I hardly knew her. Her whispered baby-talk tales of horror had moved me to overwhelming pity. And I had been primed by helping the Tamil boy; my don't-get-involved reflex had been disabled. I was unable to watch Saskia through my usual detached, dehumanizing lens. We had to help. But how?

We could get her to Sarajevo, if she would go. But the Tigers, Dragan's band of blood brothers, veterans of the most savage civil war Europe had ever seen, would track us down anywhere we went in Bosnia. And despite NATO's presence Bosnia was still a morass of crime and corruption, a place where competent murderers stood a good chance of getting away free.

We could not get her to America. We could buy her a plane ticket to the UK or the USA, have her claim refugee status, but in this new world, the world that had changed in the time it took the twin towers of the World Trade Center to collapse, she stood no chance. A refugee from Bosnia? The

Bosnian war was over, and Bosnia was a smuggler's haven, a forty per cent Muslim one to boot. She would be on the next plane back. And Dragan would be waiting for her.

We could follow her plan, work to get her an American or Canadian or British visa, but that would take months. Even then, would Dragan really let her get a passport, get a visa, get away to Sarajevo and on to an airplane? Could she do all that by herself, when she spent her whole life surrounded by the Tigers and their wives and children, watching her, willing to go to Dragan if they saw anything suspicious? Not likely.

She could only get away if we were here to help. I had no idea when Talena and I would be able to come back to Bosnia. Given our bank balances and my job prospects, the answer was likely measured in years. We had to do something now. But what? There seemed to be no way to help. We could not get her out of Bosnia.

I let myself fill with rage at the bureaucrats and politicians and immigration officers who erected and manned the borders and barriers that stood between Saskia and safety. All we needed to do was get her out of the country, a simple thing; but we couldn't, it was unthinkable, impossible, just because she didn't have the right kind of paperwork. It probably happened all the time. There were probably thousands of people like us, with relatives and friends caged in terrible situations like Saskia's. And there was nothing they or we could do. Never mind what was right, what was humane. Saskia had been born on the wrong patch of the planet, she had the wrong citizenship, so the immense ignorant power of Western governments stood against her, condemned her to her cage. We were powerless to help.

6 Cynosure

I checked email on my way back; no answer from Hallam or my other friends. I forked out over twenty KM to call him, but got only the voice of his wife Nicole, asking me to leave a message. I asked them to read their email as soon as was humanly possible. I wanted to go to the Brits and ask them for help, but without Hallam's intervention that would do me no good. NATO was here to keep the lid on Bosnia's seething cauldron of hate, a tough enough job already. Helping battered women was way outside their duties.

By the time I returned to Dragan and Saskia's street another party was in progress. Maybe they wanted to show that they hadn't been intimidated by NATO. Maybe this was all they did, all day, every day. The only difference from yesterday's party was that instead of pigs they were cutting and roasting steaks from half a butchered calf. The calf lay on the ground, wrapped in brown paper, it and the pool of its blood covered with flies. The Tigers stood around it, drinking and watching the flames, just like yesterday. Maybe I had walked into some kind of sick black-comedy Bosnian version of *Groundhog Day*. I wondered if Dragan beat Saskia out of nothing more than boredom.

Dragan smiled at me but his eyes were wary. I all but ignored him. I got a beer from Josip, who wanted to talk about their business some more. He did not share Dragan's wariness. His instincts were not as sharp. I suggested we leave business until tomorrow, walked back to the same concrete block I had sat on the night before, perched on it again, and began to drink. Talena looked at me, confused and hurt and a little angry. I knew she wanted me to join them, distract Dragan away from her and Saskia.

But what was the point? We couldn't help her. That was the hard unbearable truth. There was nothing we could do. We would have to leave tomorrow, leave Saskia here to struggle through the rest of her life alone, though uncountable years of abuse and suffering until Dragan lost his temper one day and beat her to death.

I returned to the barbecue pit for a slab of beef and another beer. Josip, worried and solicitous, asked me if I was all right. I said I was fine, just tired, hung over, a little sick. He laughed and clapped me on the back and told me to have some slivovitz. I had a swallow and returned to my concrete block and my despairing reverie. I couldn't help Saskia. I couldn't help anyone. Even that little boy—for all the pride and righteousness I felt for having gotten involved with him, for saving him, I had sure gotten uninvolved in a big hurry. I had left him and his family in the care of animal thugs, less dangerous than the Mostar Tigers maybe, but probably no less vicious. What if I had *really* gotten involved? What if I had taken a little fucking responsibility? What if I had done all I could to care for him, make sure that he got to the West, to civilization, to a bright future? Just once, what if I had picked someone out of the suffering throngs and done what I could, really done *everything* that I could, to help?

Talena reluctantly left Saskia with Dragan and approached me.

'What are you doing?' she asked, both worried and angry. 'What's wrong?'

'Will she come with us?'

'No,' she said. 'We have to talk her into it. We can sneak her out tonight. He'll be drunk, like last night. You have to help me. She says she won't do it. I don't know how to convince her. I have to talk to her in English around him; it's like pulling teeth, and he gets angry and tells her to stop, he even told *me* to stop last time. You have to get him away from us so I can convince her. I told her we could get her to America, but she didn't believe me.'

'Because you were lying.'

'We can. Somehow. I don't know how.'

'We're flying home in three days. You're going to get her a visa by then?'

'We don't have to go home,' Talena said. 'We can stay and help her.'

'Oh, good, so then you lose your job, too, and when we're completely out of money, which will be all of what, a week later, then we have to fly back anyway. How does that help her again?'

'I'm not leaving her here, Paul. I told you that before. I meant it.'

'I don't want to leave her any more than you do,' I said. 'Believe me. I want to help her. But how? Are you going to move back to Bosnia to protect her? From these crazy fuckers? How?'

'I don't know! I don't fucking know. I don't have any logical answers, I know that, so shut your fucking logic up already. I know I'm not being logical. All I know is that she's my sister and I can't leave her here like this. I'm sorry for not having a rational plan. And if you don't want to go along, I understand. I do. I'm not even angry at you for it. Not at all. She's my sister, not yours. You go back. But I'm getting her out of this hell-hole and then I'm getting her out of the country. I'll carry her over the border myself if I have to. If that means staying here, then it means staying here. I'm not asking you to stay with me. But while you're here, please help me. Please.'

I started to shake my head at her ruefully.

Then my head stopped in mid-shake and my eyes widened. My mind began to fit jigsaw pieces together, pieces I had not previously realized were part of the same puzzle.

Carry her over the border myself.

Hallam.

The little boy.

'Paul,' Talena said. 'Paul?'

'Sit,' I said. I motioned at another nearby block. 'Sit there. Don't look at Dragan and Saskia. Look depressed. Like you've given up.'

After a moment she did just that.

'Where's your passport?' I asked. 'And your money and credit card?'

'Right here,' she said. 'In my travel pouch.'

'Good.' I patted my own travel wallet to reassure myself that I had passport and money and MasterCard and airplane tickets. 'I guess he probably has all Saskia's ID anyway. Doesn't matter. She won't need it. We've got everything we need.'

'Need for what?'

What I was about to propose was certifiably insane. It was also insanely exciting. It felt like the moment before a bungee jump, standing on the brink of an abyss, about to jump into it for no good reason.

'We can't sneak out tonight,' I said. 'Dragan's suspicious.

79

He's watching us. Don't look. We want him to think we've given up, but even if he does, he won't get drunk tonight, just in case. He's not dumb, not about things like this. He's a cunning motherfucker. We have to go right now. During the party. No packs, no preparation, nothing. Clothes on our backs.'

'She won't come,' Talena said.

'She will when you convince her that we're going to take her to America.'

'I tried that already, remember? She didn't believe me.'

'That's because you were lying,' I said. 'This time you'll be telling the truth.'

'How?'

I actually smiled. 'The hard way,' I said. 'How else?'

7 Shelterless

Saskia shivered with terror and excitement. Certainly not with cold; the air conditioning was broken, and even though it was well past sunset the Mostar–Sarajevo bus was a mobile sauna. Every seat was occupied: old ladies wearing babushkas and faded dresses, young couples in tight jeans and glittery shirts bedecked with logos, bearded middle-aged men in cheap suits who walked with limps. I supposed buses to Sarajevo, Bosnia's alpha metropolis, were always busy.

The three of us had disappeared individually into the darkness, met at the end of the street, and raced to catch this 8:40 bus. There was another at 10, but waiting that long might have been disastrous. In the end we got to the station on time by hailing a passing car and offering the driver twenty KM to drive us. *Instant Taxi,* another veteran traveller's ploy. We had feared that someone at the bus station might recognize Saskia and carry news back to Dragan, but Mostar was big enough that one could be anonymous, and the bus station was after all on the Muslim side, little travelled by the Tigers and their ilk.

I sat behind Talena and Saskia, next to a remarkably ugly teenage girl with bottle-blonde hair who read some Croatian equivalent of *Seventeen* while listening to angry hip-hop on her Walkman. I was nervous too. They had to be beginning to suspect that we weren't coming back. Maybe Dragan was already in hot pursuit in his Mercedes. This bus was the only way to Sarajevo, but it was also a death trap, impossible to escape. Maybe they would cut us off on this dark and lonely road, force the driver to stop, drag us out and shoot us. It wasn't likely. But it wasn't completely impossible either.

I realized that we were going to live in a haze of constant fear until we got Saskia out of the country. We would spend every moment knowing that the Mostar Tigers might suddenly appear and attack. It sounded like we were being pursued by some kind of demented football team, but I found myself entirely unable to smile at the idea.

In front of me, Talena put her arm around Saskia, who quietly began to cry on Talena's shoulder. I wished she would make noise when she wept, like a normal human being. Her silence was unnerving. I put my hand on Talena's other shoulder and squeezed. She put her hand on mine. We rode like that for a long time.

Eventually I broke the silence. 'Do you think we should go back to the pansione?'

'Would anywhere else be better?' she asked.

'No,' I said. Dragan didn't know where we had stayed in Sarajevo. The pansione was cheap and unobtrusive. If—when—they came after us, they would probably start their search at Sarajevo's famous Holiday Inn and other expensive hotels, what with their certainty that we were rich Americans. The pansione was also located next to a parking lot, which was useful, since I planned to rent a car tomorrow. A car is a very practical investment when you're running for your life.

The journey to Sarajevo seemed to take several anxious days, but eventually the lights of civilization began to glimmer around us. I was worried that Dragan might have us followed from the bus station, so I had Talena convince the driver to let us out a few blocks away.

It was a relief to be back in Sarajevo's busy streets, out of Mostar, with Saskia, all of us still in one piece. But I knew that this initial escape had been the easy part. Getting Saskia out of the country would be harder. But with Hallam's help, we just might pull it off; maybe even, if we were very lucky, in the next three days, before our non-refundable flights from Zagreb expired.

Our problem was not that Saskia couldn't leave Bosnia. Our problem was that no other country would allow her to enter. The obvious solution, once I rid myself of my instinctive desire to follow the law, was to bring her in illegally. And we could hardly be in a better place for that. If refugee smuggling was an Olympic event, Balkan countries would be regular medallists. Bosnia's human traffic went to Western Europe, not the USA, but that was fine. If we could pay smugglers to get Saskia into Germany, where she spoke the language, or England, where my friends lived, she would be safe. It wasn't exactly an airtight plan, granted, more like a vague notion, but it sure beat no plan at all.

Talena led Saskia to the pansione while I checked email at the Internet café around the corner on Dalmatinska Street. There were three responses, from Hallam, Lawrence and Steve.

```
From:    niclam@freeserve.co.uk
To:      balthazarwood@yahoo.com
Subject: Re: Urgent request for help—not a
joke
Date:    5 Apr 2003 14:03 GMT
```

Paul mate,

I have a number of contacts still on duty in Bosnia. The most useful to you will be Major William Botham. You'll find him at NATO headquarters in Sarajevo. I've already called him and told him to expect you. He will be willing to bend the rules for you. The rest are enlisted men. I'm not sure how to get in contact with them immediately but I've started tracking them down. Let me know right away if you need their help. You have our mobile number. Call us any time, day or night, reverse charges. Take care of yourself and for God's sake

don't do anything stupid unless you absolutely have to. I suppose Bosnia is better
than it was when I served there—it could
hardly be any worse—but I expect it's still
a very bad place to be in any kind of trouble.

Hallam

From: lcarlin@rbs.co.uk
To: balthazarwood@yahoo.com
Subject: Your poor decisionmaking skills
Date: 5 Apr 2003 16:48 GMT

So you're kidnapping Bosnian women now. Are
you sure that's wise? I know a harem sounds
like a good idea on paper, but just imagine
what happens when they all get simultaneous
PMS. They might start acting like Bosnian
men.

The many-tentacled corporate-banking monstrosity that signs my pay cheques does
business in Sarajevo, and has an office
there. If you need money sent there quickly,
let me know. I'll divert it from Steve's
account, he'll never notice.

If you need any other kind of help, needless
to say I'll do whatever I can. As you know
I normally charge five hundred pounds a day

```
for acts of derring-do. Please note that my
Balkans rate is twice that.
How's the beer there?
```

```
Lawrence
```

```
From:    greasysteve@hotmail.com
To:      balthazarwood@yahoo.com
Subject: Re: Urgent request for help—not a
joke
Date:    5 Apr 2003 17:33 GMT
```

```
Gday mate. Sounds like a spot of trouble.
Want me to come help sort it out? Cheers.
```

Just opening up my inbox and seeing the three unread emails, Lawrence's with his usual snarky subject line, cheered me up. Talena and I were not in this alone. Hallam's email, in particular, was good news. I'd thought he might still have friends in the military here, but I hadn't dared hope for anyone as high-ranking as a major.

I sent a quick update back to the three of them and went back to the pansione. I walked on the shadowy side of the street, looked for people who might be looking for me. Nobody obvious. En route I stopped in at the same convenience store where I had bought cigarettes. We had abandoned our packs in Mostar, we had nothing at all. I bought soap, toothpaste and Snickers bars. That would have to do for tonight. Tomorrow, Talena and Saskia could go shopping while I tried to arrange for Saskia's escape. A vaguely sexist division of labour, but Talena had the credit card that was not on the verge of disintegration. Though in Bosnia, even in Sarajevo, point-of-sale credit-card authorization machines were not common; a foreigner like me could probably go a long way with a maxed-out card and a confident smile.

Unfortunately, that wouldn't work at a bank, and last I checked refugee smugglers did not take MasterCard. It would be cash only once we found a gang willing to spirit Saskia out of the country. If we found such a gang. But it couldn't be that hard. I had already stumbled on to one by accident.

'This is crazy,' Talena said, lying next to me in bed, finishing off her Snickers bar.

'You don't say.'

'I keep sort of forgetting what we're doing. I was going to take a shower when I remembered we have no towels and even if we did I have no clothes to change into. And then I was like, oh, that's right, we all but kidnapped Saskia and we're running for our lives and tomorrow we're going to try to find some criminals to help us get her out of the country. It doesn't seem real.'

'I know.' I shook my head. 'I'm worried about the shopping. Maybe I should do that too. You two should stay here. The more we're outside, the more chance they'll have of seeing one of us.'

Talena paused and then levered herself up on one elbow, facing me sternly, blue eyes flashing. 'Are you seriously suggesting that Saskia and I stay in here like we're in jail while you go out and have all the fun?'

'Fun?'

'I'm trying to think of it as an adventure,' she said.

'Adventure. Noun. Long periods of tedium interspersed with brief moments of terror.'

'No, that's being besieged by the Serbian army for three years. In an adventure you're the one going out and doing something. Makes a colossal difference, believe me.'

I forgot sometimes that Talena was a war veteran too.

'I've made my mental shopping list for tomorrow,' she said. 'Top of the list: towels, underwear, guns.'

'Guns?'

'Guns.'

She was serious. 'Uh . . . Talena . . . I don't know if that's such a good idea.'

'I don't seem to remember asking you.'

Which sounded bitchy but was said good-naturedly. Now that we had embarked on this insane venture, the frost between us had thawed a little. For one thing we were both scared. The couple that prays to be spared together, stays together. For another thing, she was right, this was an adventure. Now that we lived in constant danger the world was enormously more vivid. Every breath was an event, every moment pungently intense. It was scary and painfully stressful, yes, but it was also exciting, and it made our last year of unhappiness and drudgery and petty sniping seem small and tawdry and irrelevant.

I wondered if Saskia, across the hall in a room even smaller than ours, was at all excited. I didn't think so. I thought she was probably nothing but frightened, and would be until we got her out of Bosnia. Saskia knew what happened when this kind of adventure turned sour. You were beaten with fists and boots and an iron bar until you

87

heard your own bones breaking, your face was so thick with blood that you couldn't see, and finally your baby died inside you and you were reduced to a huddled, broken heap, whimpering for mercy.

For a moment I involuntarily imagined Talena, captured by Dragan and the Tigers, helpless and alone with them in a cold concrete cell. I imagined what might happen to her. It made my stomach clench violently with fear. The part of me that enjoyed this adventure was suddenly nowhere to be found.

'I don't think you should go outside,' I said again, my voice a little hoarse. 'Especially not alone.'

Talena opened her mouth to say something intemperate, then studied my face for a second. 'You're worried about me, huh?'

I nodded.

'That's nice of you. But you should really be worried about yourself. You're not from here. You don't know the streets. You don't know the language. People notice you. If they find us, they'll definitely find you first.'

'Oh.' I hadn't thought of it like that.

'Maybe you should stay hidden in here while I take care of things.'

'There's no fucking way I'm—' I began, then stopped halfway to outrage. 'Okay. Fine. Point made.'

'We're in this together, understand?' she asked. 'Partners in crime. Got it?'

'Got it.'

'Good. Now turn the light out and come here.'

They say power is the ultimate aphrodisiac but, believe me, it's got nothing on danger.

The next morning I rented a diesel-fuelled stick-shift Citroën. I hadn't driven a stick for years and it quickly became apparent that the most terrifyingly dangerous parts of my adventure might take place behind the wheel. I nearly died three times on the road out of Sarajevo.

It took me an hour to locate the right gravel road. I knew that the expedition would be fruitless when I found that the pedestrian gate on the dirt-road offshoot was locked, but I had to see for myself. I tore my jeans climbing over the fence.

The abandoned factory where I had returned the Tamil boy to his family was utterly deserted. There were no cars and the loading-dock door was locked. I got in through a broken window, dug out my Maglite and found my way through rusted machinery and along a conveyor belt to the room where the refugees had huddled. There was nothing and nobody there. Aside from scuffed sawdust the room might have been empty for a decade.

So much for my plan to track down Sinisa the refugee smuggler. I wondered uneasily if finding someone willing to take Saskia out of the country would turn out to be a very difficult process. Criminals don't exactly advertise in the Yellow Pages, and none of Talena's friends seemed the type to hang out in shady bars with suspicious characters. If Major Botham couldn't help us, we would be in trouble.

HQ SFOR—milspeak for the headquarters of NATO's Stabilization Force—was a compound called Camp Butmir, near the airport, smack on the border between the Republika Srpska and the Federation of Bosnia-Herzegovina. There's symbolism for you: NATO standing between the combatants like a boxing referee. The main gate stood amid a forest of rippling flags, one for each of NATO's members.

Major Botham was a short, wiry man in his mid-forties with so much restless energy that his office felt a little like a cage. He greeted me with a short handshake and invited me to sit. I did. He remained standing.

Through the window behind him I could see Sarajevo's airport. During the siege, the UN had controlled the airport proper, the Serbs had controlled either end of the runway, and the Bosnians had controlled either side. The east side of the runway was besieged Sarajevo, and the west was relatively free Bosnian territory. The usual bewildering Bosnian war insanity which was hard to believe even now. There had been a tunnel under that runway, the one route other than the ongoing UN airlift through which people and goods could move in and out of the city in relative safety. That was just what I needed now: a tunnel to the West.

'Hallam informed me that you needed some extracurricular assistance,' he said. His accent was South African.

'That's one way of putting it,' I said. I paused. I didn't know how to phrase what I wanted to say. Now that I was here, actually talking to a NATO major, my plan seemed like the stupidest, most ridiculous notion ever conceived. Was I really going to open my mouth and ask him to help me break the law?

Apparently, yes. 'Look,' I said. 'I'm not going to try to sugarcoat this. I need help to get a woman out of Bosnia. I don't think I can do it legally, but I have to do it as soon as I can, and I have to do it before her psycho husband and his psycho friends catch up with us. It's not like it sounds, I'm not involved with her. She's my girlfriend's sister.'

Major Botham looked at me for a long moment. Then he said, 'Details, please.'

I told him the whole story. When I was finished the major stood with his arms folded, staring into space, for some time. Eventually he nodded.

'Yours is a difficult situation, Mr Wood,' Major Botham said. 'And it will be difficult for me to assist you in any meaningful way.'

'I know.'

'Hallam said you saved his wife's life once.'

I blinked. 'Not really. I just kind of stalled things long enough for him to show up.'

'He saved my life twice, during the war. I asked him to come back when I was posted back here, but he wasn't interested. Can't say I blame him. This place is a snakepit.'

I nodded vigorously.

'I can't help you get her out legally. I expect you knew that already.'

'I did.'

'I'm afraid I can hardly do anything for you at all. What I can do is provide you with some phone numbers. My mobile number, for one. If her husband shows up and seems to be a tangible threat, give me a call, and I can get a patrol to you within ten minutes. We're a lot more reliable than the Sarajevo police, I assure you. Do you have a mobile phone here?'

I shook my head.

'I have a spare,' he said, digging into his desk and unearthing an antique Nokia and a charger cable adorned with a two-circular-prong Balkans adapter. 'It still works. Take it. Try not to make too many trunk calls to Tokyo. NATO pays the bill.'

'Thanks,' I said inadequately. A phone with which I could call my very own military back-up. That was one heck of a start.

'And I can make some enquiries, try to find an organization which, shall we say, provides the relevant assistance to people like your friend Saskia. I should be able to get some answers by, say, ten hundred tomorrow.'

'Wow. Thanks.'

'Don't look so surprised. This is the least I can do for a friend of Hallam's.'

'You . . . Not to be blunt, but I'm surprised you're helping me break the law.'

'Am I?' he asked. 'Whose law?'

'Well . . . ' I stopped and thought about it. What I planned was illegal, wasn't it?

'It remains legal to try to leave the country,' Major Botham said. 'Legal and, if you ask me, in Bosnia generally a good idea. It may become illegal when she actually reaches the border, but even then she will be violating the laws of the receiving country, not this one. If you call this a country at all. It's possible that Bosnia's so-called government may have signed laws that attempt to prevent human trafficking. But even if they have, it doesn't concern me. We may occasionally turn unstable elements over to the local police, as you nearly witnessed in Mostar, but SFOR is a military presence, not a police force. Our mission does call for us to respect local law, but we are also explicitly outside the jurisdiction of that law, and respecting it is very much secondary to maintaining a safe and secure environment.'

'Oh,' I said.

'In short, we run this godforsaken hell-hole, and we can do whatever we want here.'

'I'm glad to hear that,' I said sincerely.

'I'll call you on that phone by ten hundred hours with any information I can garner.'

Our conversation was obviously over. 'Thank you, Major. Thank you very much.'

'You're welcome. Where are you staying?'

'The Pansione Konack.'

'I know it. Centrally located, that's good, but there's only one entrance. If you need to escape you'll have to go out of a window.'

'Oh. I hadn't thought of that.'

'Keep that phone charged,' he said as he walked me to the door. 'And be careful. I can get men to you in ten minutes, but that's plenty of time to die in.'

That was apparently his version of goodbye. He closed the door behind me. I looked at the phone in my hand. I felt better. I was confident that with Major William Botham on our side, one way or another, shit was going to happen.

I got back at mid-afternoon. Talena and Saskia had bought three polyester Adidas shoulder bags, one black, one blue, one red, and filled them with new clothes. They looked disturbingly like the bags that the Middle Eastern refugees in the abandoned furniture factory had carried.

'Here,' Talena said after I had told her my story. 'Keep this with you.'

She dug into the black bag and offered me a small snub-nosed revolver. I took two steps back, eyed the gun like I might a live rattlesnake, and made no move to take it.

'I bought three,' she said impatiently. 'It's not loaded yet. Take it.'

'Where did you get it?'

'A guy I used to know.'

I wanted to know more but didn't want to push our new-found camaraderie too far. 'Where . . . where do I put it?'

'Put this shiny new windbreaker on and tuck it into your belt. You've fired a gun, right?'

'Once.' At a firing range in Australia, years ago. I took it from her like it was made of nitroglycerine. It was lighter than I expected. 'I don't . . . I don't know how to load it, or . . . Jesus, Talena. What the fuck?'

'How very Canadian of you,' she said fondly. 'But listen, Toto, we're not in Moose Jaw any more. Time for Firearms 101.'

She taught me how to load it and how to arm and disarm the safety. Saskia didn't pay attention. I supposed she had learned during the war.

'How much were they?' I asked.

'A hundred US dollars each.'

'You spent three hundred dollars on guns? Jesus. Sounds like a waste of money.'

'You'll sing in a very different key if we ever have to use one.'

'Yeah? And what if we don't?'

'Then you'll be so grateful that we were so incredibly lucky that you won't give a shit about a measly three hundred dollars.'

She had a point.

'I bought an English textbook for Saskia,' Talena said. 'She's going to start studying again. Her English used to be pretty good, ten years ago. I bet it'll come back in a hurry.'

Saskia caught enough of that to understand and smiled hopefully at me.

'Good,' I said, and smiled back at Saskia. It was weird to be risking my life for and spending so much time around this person with whom I could only communicate in baby talk. I wondered how she felt. She seemed pale but determined, and a little colour had returned to her doll-like features. Spending the day with Talena had probably been good for her.

A phone rang. It took a couple of rings, and perplexed stares from Saskia and Talena, before I remembered the cellphone in my pocket. I dug it out and answered.

'Hello?'

'With whom am I speaking?' Major Botham's clipped South African accent.

'Major Botham, hello. This is Paul.'

'Good.'

'Did you find anyone who could help us?'

'Not yet. I'm ringing because I have important information for you. I had some troops keep an eye on the bus station today. Dragan, a man who fits your description of his friend Josip, and four associates arrived in Sarajevo approximately thirty minutes ago.'

A cold chill gathered at the base of my spine and slowly began to work its way upward. I wasn't surprised. Stealing Dragan's wife was an unforgivable insult, and the Balkan cultural mindset has a penchant for melodramatic revenge. I imagined some of the Tigers were actually grateful for this juicy little blood vendetta; this hunt was probably the most excitement, the closest thing to the war they had so loved, in ages. I hadn't doubted they would come for us. But knowing and *knowing* are two different things.

'I recommend you maintain high awareness of your surroundings,' Major Botham said.

'I understand,' I said faintly. 'I'll do that.'

'You have my number. I'll keep at least one patrol near the Pansione Konack all night.'

'Thank you.'

'And I'll call you by ten hundred. If nothing happens before then.'

'Great,' I said, but he had already hung up.

'Who was that?' Talena asked.

'The bearer of bad news.'

'What kind of bad news?'

'Dragan arrived at the bus station today,' I said.

A hush fell.

Then Talena snorted, a black-comedy chuckle, and said, 'Tell me again how upset you are that I bought you a gun.'

We spent the rest of the afternoon inside the Pansione Konack, teaching Saskia how to play Shithead and Hearts. She was a natural. After nightfall Talena and I went out to pick up some *cevapcici*, a Bosnian snack that like all Balkan food was about eighty per cent meat, and pizza and Coke. It was a nervous expedition. We were glad to get back into the relative safety of the pansione.

I wondered if Talena was going to jump me again when we returned to our room, but after we got into bed she turned her back to me. I lay and watched her for a little while. I could tell she was wide awake, thinking. I wondered how she would react if I reached over, took her shoulder, told her I loved her, told her I wanted a second chance.

Not yet, I decided. I leaned over, kissed her cheek, and murmured, 'Sweet dreams.'

Her answering smile, like all her smiles, made my heart skip a beat.

'Back atcha,' she whispered.

8 Pursuits

'Mr Wood,' Major Botham said. 'I have two phone numbers for you. Either one of them should be able to provide you with the services you require. Feel free to mention my name during negotiations, but understand that I cannot provide you with any tangible assistance.'

'I understand.'

'The first number is for a man named Mladen.' I wrote it down. 'The second is for a man named Sinisa. The number is—'

'Wait,' I said. 'Sinisa?'

'Correct.'

'Does he, does he have a weird accent?'

There was a brief pause. 'Yes, he does,' Major Botham said curiously. 'Half Dutch, half Serbian. I understand he was raised in Holland. Did Hallam mention him?'

I hadn't told the major about my expedition with the Tamil child. I didn't want to get into the story now, for one thing because I didn't want him questioning my judgement and general sanity. 'We've made some other enquiries as well,' I said lamely.

97

'Yes, I see. Sinisa is supposed to be more reliable but also more expensive. Do you want his number?'

'Yes, please.' Better the gangsta you know than the gangsta you don't. Sinisa had at least been polite.

I explained the situation to Talena, who in turn explained it to Saskia.

'So are you going to call him?' Talena asked me.

I didn't want to. My stomach was rumbling with hunger and I wanted to go get breakfast. I didn't feel ready to have a conversation with a dangerous criminal overlord. But that was only part of it. I was reluctant to make this connection, to open this particular door. I wasn't exactly sure what lay behind it but I suspected the path was long and dark.

But on the other hand Dragan was already in town looking for us and immediate peril does tend to trump existential angst. I dialled the number. It rang five times and I figured I would get voice-mail. I couldn't even begin to imagine what message to leave and decided to call back instead.

'Da?' A human voice, not a machine.

I almost passed the phone over to Talena, but decided that would be ducking responsibility. 'Does anybody there speak English?'

'Yes. Who is this?' Sinisa's unmistakable accent.

'My name is Paul Wood. I'm the Canadian guy who barged into your factory outside the city'—I did the math and the brevity of the period since came as a shock, it felt like weeks had passed—'four days ago with the little boy.'

After a pause Sinisa asked, an edge in his voice, 'And how did you get this number?'

'From Major William Botham of SFOR. He suggested

you as a person who could possibly help me out with a problem I'm having.'

'You are Canadian and you need to employ my services?'

'Not me. My friend who is not Canadian.'

'Mr Wood, I am a very busy man, and I do not appreciate intrusions on my private line. Give my regards to Major Botham and remind him I am not a help service for troubled Canadian tourists.'

'No,' I said desperately. 'Wait. Don't hang up. This is serious. This is life and death.'

'Perhaps. But not my life. Not my death. Why should I care?'

I didn't know what to say to that.

'Goodbye, Mr Wood. And if you ever call this number again, I assure you—'

Then he paused.

'Wait,' he said. 'You are the computer programmer, yes?'

'That's right.'

'You are Canadian, but you live in America.'

'Yes.'

After a moment he said, 'I can meet you on Thursday at noon.'

It was Tuesday. Our flight would leave Wednesday night. 'If it's at all possible to make it earlier—' I began.

'Thursday at noon or not at all.'

I swallowed and looked at Saskia. Well, it was only money, and compared to what Sinisa would charge for Saskia's escape, an airfare wasn't much. I could declare bankruptcy when I went home and spend the next year

99

saving up enough to pay back what I would soon owe to Lawrence. If I could find a job. But compared to worrying about Dragan breaking into the pansione and riddling us all with bullets, a job hunt would be a day at the circus. One thing about a life of constant physical danger is that it puts everything else into its proper minuscule perspective.

'Thursday at noon,' I said. 'Where?'

'I will call you at eleven a.m. Thursday and tell you.'

He hung up without saying goodbye. I suppose terrible phone manners are a common side effect of near-absolute power.

'We have an appointment,' I reported.

'Good,' Talena said. 'Well done.'

'Should we call the other guy too?' I asked. 'We might save money.' Comparison shopping for criminals. On the other hand it would complicate matters even further, and Mladen was the devil we didn't know, and while Miss Manners might not approve of Sinisa's conversational skills, he certainly sounded professional.

'How much money?'

'He didn't say. I'm expecting about five thousand dollars.'

Talena shook her head. 'Never mind the money. The important thing is that Saskia gets out safe. Major Botham said Sinisa was the reliable expensive one, right? And he's the one you met? Well, if what you saw in that factory was the Nieman Marcus version of smuggling, there's no way in hell I'm sending her to Wal-Mart.'

'Fair enough. So we've got two days to kill.'

Talena sighed. 'You have to work on your word choice.'

They found us on Wednesday.

It was near sunset. Talena and I were lined up at a pizza stand in the pedestrian thoroughfare near Sarajevo's ravaged cathedral. We had grown almost complacent. We only had to get through this expedition and the next day's breakfast before meeting with Sinisa. The streets were churning with people, mostly teenage and twenty-something men and women preening and flirting. I was sure we were veiled by the crowd.

'Paul,' Talena murmured hoarsely, and when I heard her tone, my false sense of security popped like a soap bubble. 'That guy on the church stairs. Was he with them?'

I looked up. A man who looked very familiar, a pretty-boy type in his mid-twenties, stood on the cathedral steps, looking our way. He reached into his pocket without taking his eyes off us. For a moment I was afraid he might pull a gun and shoot through the crowd at us, but his hand emerged holding a cellphone.

He caught my eye and smiled. It was the smile that made me remember. I had seen him playing soccer in Mostar. He had smiled like that, wide and childlike, after scoring a goal. He was one of Dragan's Tigers. The pit of my stomach dropped nauseatingly away.

'Yes,' I said. 'Shit. Yes.'

'He's calling the others, shit, shit, come on.'

We abandoned the pizza line and walked away as fast as we dared, westward, away from the pansione. I felt sick and clumsy with fear. The crowd was too thick to break into a run. I looked over my shoulder and saw him following us while punching numbers into his phone, shouldering people out of his way to keep up. I didn't think we could lose him in the crowd, he was too close. I pulled out my own Nokia and dialled Major Botham with shaking fingers. Up to ten minutes before NATO could arrive. If we didn't run, if we just stayed in this public place, would the Tigers try anything? They just might. Where could we go? Out of the pedestrian area and into a taxi, maybe. If one arrived in time. We didn't dare wait for one. The pretty boy behind us was sure to have a gun.

'Left, turn left, down here.' Talena's voice vibrated with tension.

Major Botham's phone began to ring.

'Where are we going?' I asked, as we turned into a narrow, pedestrian-filled alley.

'Across the river. The Yugoslav embassy. Tell him.'

I couldn't imagine why but I didn't have any better ideas.

'Major William Botham,' the major said.

'Major. This is Paul Wood. We're in trouble. One of Dragan's men has seen us and he's chasing us. He's called the others. We're near the big church and we're going to the Yugoslav embassy.'

'The embassy. Good. I'll despatch immediately.' He hung up.

I looked over our shoulder. The pretty boy was still about fifty feet behind us. He didn't seen to be in any hurry to catch up, which was good, but he had transferred the phone to his left hand, and his right was hidden in the pocket of his denim jacket, which was bad.

I had a gun too, tucked uncomfortably into the back of my jeans. So did Talena. But I had absolutely no desire to draw my weapon. Shooting it out with the Tigers was the craziest idea of all; there was no way we would get out in one piece if we got into a firefight.

'Why the embassy?' I asked.

'They have guards.'

Of course. The Yugoslav embassy, being the official representation of the widely hated Serbian government in Belgrade, had to be heavily guarded at all times. Hopefully its guards would not allow an armed confrontation to take place there. The Tigers couldn't just shoot us down from a distance, they needed us to find Saskia. Hopefully we could stall until NATO showed up.

But if not . . . the embassy was next to the river, on the other side, and only a thin pedestrian walkway ran between its gate and the bank of the Miljacka. There would be nowhere to hide there, and no escape.

'We should split up,' I said.

'No.'

'Yes. That way if it goes bad one of us can go back and get Saskia out.'

She didn't have an answer for that.

'Not yet,' I said. 'When we cross the river. Who do you think he'll follow?'

After a moment she said, 'You. He'll follow you.'

Near the edge of the pedestrian zone the crowds thinned out, and Talena broke into a run. I followed, even though irrationally I didn't want to. Our previous brisk walk had maintained the illusion that the situation was under control, but running was an admission of panic.

A horn blared and we only just avoided being pancaked by a van as we dashed across the street. I could see the river a block ahead. We accelerated towards it. People scampered out of our way. The gun protruded painfully into the small of my back and I was afraid it might fall out. I wondered if our pursuer was running too. We dodged in and out of the pedestrian traffic. I knocked over a little girl and barely overcame a crazy impulse to stop and apologize.

We finally emerged on to Obala Kulina, the main road that paralleled the north side of the Miljacka. Traffic was too thick to cross and there were no available taxis so we turned right and sprinted for the next crossing, where there was a bridge. By the time we arrived there was a gap in the flow of cars, and we danced through the traffic, across the road and on to the bridge. I looked back, hoping that we had lost him. No joy. Our pursuer looked relaxed, like he was out on his regular afternoon jog. I told myself this couldn't really be happening, this was just a dream, we weren't actually being pursued by an armed gunman, it wasn't the kind of thing that really happened.

I was already covered with thick sweat, and panted like a dog with adrenaline and exhaustion. We had run for only a couple of minutes, but fear had caused all my muscles to tense up so strongly they actually quavered, and my strength had begun to ebb. Midway across the bridge I looked down at the Miljacka's dark steady flow and for a moment thought crazily about jumping in, escaping by river like Butch and Sundance. But that would never work. I forced myself to relax a little, to try to think.

'You go straight,' I said, trying to keep my voice steady. 'I'll go to the embassy.'

I was afraid Talena would insist on accompanying me, but she kept going as I turned right and sprinted along the pedestrian walkway that paralleled the river. I ran straight through a couple walking hand in hand, severing their connection. Occasional walkways led south, away from the river, but I ignored them.

I glanced over my shoulder. Talena had been right, our pretty-boy pursuer had followed me; that was a relief. At least they wouldn't get her. He was only a hundred feet away, talking into his phone as he jogged, doubtless reporting my movements. I knew the chase wouldn't last much longer. My lungs were thick with exhaustion and he didn't look like he had even broken a sweat. Somewhere in a deep detached corner of my mind I told myself I should really get in shape if I got out of this mess.

The Yugoslav embassy was just ahead of me. Razor-wire fence to my left, Miljacka to my right, nowhere to escape to but the river itself. There was a security cubicle next to the gate, a box of bullet-proof glass.

The security cubicle was empty.

I halted. For a moment my mind went blank with sheer panic.

Then a cool, precise voice, one I did not entirely recognize as my own, cut through the fog of fear in my head. *Two choices, Paul,* it said. *Always two choices. Fight or flight.*

The Miljacka, where it coursed through downtown Sarajevo, was walled on both sides by concrete, and looked more like a giant sewer than a river. The drop into it was sheer but modest, maybe ten feet. I had no idea how deep the water was or what the surface beneath consisted of. A jump could easily result in shattered legs if the river before us was just a few feet of water over uneven stones. But better that than falling into the hands of the Tigers.

On the other hand, the voice reminded me, *you do have a gun.*

'Good point,' I gasped. I turned around and fumbled for the revolver in my waistband. My throat was so dry it chafed painfully with every panting breath. My hand shook as if I were suffering from an epileptic seizure.

The pretty boy slowed down when he saw the gun, but when he saw how it shook he smiled widely and accelerated towards me, past one of the walkways that led away from the river. I crouched down and tried to aim, ready to launch myself into the river if I missed. I remembered I needed to switch off the safety and attempted to do so with a trembling thumb. I wondered if I was really about to shoot a man.

Then Talena thundered out of the intersecting walkway and slammed into the pretty boy like an NFL linebacker. He flew off the riverside path and hung in the air like Michael Jordan, pure surprise etched on his face, before tumbling into the Miljacka with a violent splash.

I stared disbelievingly at Talena.

'Come on,' she said, breathing as hard as I was, '*hurry!*'

I stuck the gun in my windbreaker pocket and ran towards her, giddy with relief. We pelted side by side down the walkway from which she had emerged, then sprinted down random Sarajevo streets for several minutes, newly energized by our narrow escape, until we finally came to a stop in a parking lot and collapsed against each other. We were utterly drained. But when we got our breath back we looked at each other and started to giggle uncontrollably, like children.

'Did you see the look on his face?' she gasped. 'Oh, my

God, it was so funny, it was like holy *fuck* where did that truck come from? I hope he can't swim—'

'—are you kidding,' I said, 'pollution in this country, he probably dissolved, or now he's Blinky the Three-Eyed Gangster—'

'—I can't believe you actually pulled a gun, I thought you were Canadian—'

'—I can't believe I was actually going to shoot it—'

'—Jesus, if I knew you might actually use it, I would never have given you bullets!'

Both of us burst into slightly hysterical laughter that went on for over a minute. Then we grabbed each other and kissed for a long time, heedless of passers-by, before we were interrupted by my warbling phone. Major Botham, whose men had arrived too late, wanted to know if we were still alive. I told him we were. He didn't seem surprised by my giddy voice. I guess he'd heard its like many times before.

'God,' Talena whispered. 'Maybe it's worth it being so scared.'

In the middle of the night we had both woken from bad dreams and all but attacked one another. The most frenzied sex we'd had for years, maybe ever. We lay drained in each other's sweat-slippery arms, a tangled curtain of her dark hair draped across my chest.

'It was like this during the siege, sometimes,' she said. 'After Zlatan got shot sometimes it was with a total stranger. You'd meet at some party or, I don't know, on the street, and we'd find some filthy blanket in some corner and try to just fuck our way into amnesia. I don't mean, it's not like it happened all the time. But some days I just needed it.'

She paused, but I didn't say anything. Talena almost never talked about the siege. I didn't want to interrupt.

'The week after my parents' funeral, I did it twice in one day with men whose names I didn't know. Without a condom with one of them. Condoms were like gold. With Zlatan we washed them out and reused them, but with strangers, I don't know, it seemed like too much to ask. Is this shocking you?'

'A little,' I admitted.

'Don't think about it too much. I'm not that girl any more. She was so scared, and so fucked up, and so not willing to admit it. Coming back here, and being scared again . . . it's weird. It's like, I don't know, it's like she's following me around, whispering in my ear.' She grinned, lightening the mood considerably. 'Maybe I'm just going crazy. I sure hope so. That'll probably make things a lot easier to deal with.'

'Maybe you were always crazy,' I teased.

'I'm with you, aren't I?'

'Very funny.'

'If it wasn't for her I would never have made it,' Talena said, nodding towards Saskia's room. 'She was the strong one. And she was friends with all the gangsters and the black marketeers. They were like heroes, you know. If it wasn't for the criminals, Caco and Juka and the others, there would have been no siege, they would have rolled right over Sarajevo in the first month, probably sent half of us to concentration camps. Saskia was in tight with them. She fought on the front line a few times, can you believe that? With a sniper rifle. She killed two Serbs. She was a lot braver than me. I never went near the front line unless I had to. She kept me going. Whenever I or my friends were really in trouble, out of food or something, or the one time I had this crazy boyfriend for like one week who decided both of us should kill ourselves in some highly photogenic way to get world attention, or, shit, whenever I just couldn't take it any more and I felt like I was just minutes away from going completely crazy forever, whatever it was, I went to her and she took care of me. She could always make me laugh. You know how amazing that was? We were living in what was like the deepest pit of hell, always hungry and cold and tired and scared and angry and desperate and just sick of being alive, and she could always make me laugh. After Mom and Dad died, when the building I was in got taken over by all these refugees, they pushed me out, and I stayed with her for the rest of the war. My big sister. Half-sister, whatever. I fucking hero-worshipped her.'

I didn't know what to say. It didn't seem possible that Talena could be describing the same woman who was now the fragile timid creature in the room across the hall.

'I bought the map,' Talena said.

'What map?'

'The survival map. At the bookstore. I want to show you.'

She climbed halfway over me to turn on the light and dig something out from under the bed. A poster tube. She opened it, dug out a poster, and unrolled it.

'I don't know why I hid it under the bed,' she said sheepishly. 'I just didn't want you asking about it until . . . I don't know. Here. This was where I grew up.'

The Sarajevo Survival Map was the visual equivalent of a kick in the gut. A hand-drawn aerial perspective of downtown Sarajevo during the siege. A thick red line depicted the front line that surrounded the city, a tight red noose around and often through the city which ran right down to the Miljacka in places. Thick spiky rows of menacing tanks and artillery pieces were arrayed just outside the line. The overall visual effect was like looking at a picture of a boot about to stomp on a woman's face.

Talena had lived here for three years, from age eighteen to twenty-one, with Serb artillery and snipers firing into the city from all directions, at any time. Her parents had been killed. Her boyfriend had been killed. Many of her other friends had been wounded. She had lost more than most, which was part of why she had been selected for the American scholarship. But everyone in the city had lost someone. Ten per cent of the population had been killed or wounded.

'We lived in Ilidza, over there,' she said, pointing on the map. 'But it wasn't safe and we had to move. So we moved here, by the cemetery. There's the hospital, Kosova hospital. There's the market where my parents were killed. They went out to buy bread. Zlatan's apartment was here. He died here, running across this square. These pink dots, they show sniper areas. He was trying to pick up a little girl who had been shot and carry her to the hospital and the sniper got him too. I was screaming at him not to try it. Screaming. This is where I was interviewed by the BBC once. I was hung over and I guess I looked enough like hell that they thought I was pitiful. And because I could speak English because of my mother.' Her mother had taught English at the university. 'And here we are, right here, the pansione. This area was pretty safe because the buildings were tall, so the snipers couldn't see the streets.'

'God,' I said, inadequately.

'You know something?' Talena said. 'California's never really felt like my home. I've been there seven years, and I love it, but . . . you know? It just never felt like my place. I was afraid that maybe Sarajevo would feel like home, even after all this time. But it doesn't. Not at all. It feels like . . . ' She shook her head. 'It feels like visiting a cemetery.'

9 Negotiations

Sinisa called at 11 a.m. sharp.

'I will send a car for you,' he said. 'How many are you?'

'Three.'

'The car will arrive in fifteen minutes. The three of you will turn over any weapons you are carrying to my men. They will escort you to our meeting place.'

I opened my mouth to acquiesce but he had already hung up. Obviously his cellphone provider charged by the second.

The car was a familiar white Mitsubishi pick-up driven by two familiar men I had not expected ever to see again: Sensitive Reasonable Gangster and Mini-Hulk from that abandoned furniture factory to which I had tracked the Tamil family.

'Hey, California man,' SRG greeted me. 'How you going? Everything phallic?'

'Very,' I said.

'You have no guns, yes?' he asked, looking past me at Talena and Saskia as they unloaded their bags in the bed of the pick-up.

'Actually, we do,' Talena said. She passed our three revolvers over to Mini-Hulk. SRG widened his eyes and raised his hands in mock fear. Talena said something curt to him, and he shrugged and returned to a normal stance.

'Let's go,' he said to me. 'Sinisa no like if we are late.'

We sat in the back of the pick-up atop the Adidas bags that contained all our possessions. The Mitsubishi's suspension was creaky and we bounced and swayed as the pick-up rattled along Sarajevo's often rough streets. I thought of the Tamil family who had sat here in this same vehicle. Now, less than a week later, I sat in their place.

I expected to return to that factory or some equally far-flung location, but we only travelled about half a mile, through Bascarsija, across the river, and up winding house-lined streets, until we came unexpectedly into a huge grave-yard that occupied a steep promontory above the Miljacka.

The pick-up found a dirt trail leading into the heart of the cemetery. It was a Muslim cemetery, I could tell by the tall and narrow obelisks used instead of Western-style grave-stones, and by the names, Nasir, Ahmet, Camila. Some of the gravestones were made of carved marble, some of them monuments sculpted with beautiful patterns, but many were marked only by whitewashed wooden panels, now cracked and peeling. Those were the ones dated between 1992 and 1995, during the siege, when even that wood had been precious.

A Land Rover stood parked on an empty plot near the summit of the cemetery ridge. Sinisa stood next to it, dressed in a dark suit, wearing mirrored sunglasses. He was accompanied, I noted uneasily, by the red-haired woman and craggy über-thug man who had been in the factory. Their electric presence, the air of potentially imminent violence, was undimmed by daylight. Also present was a short man who resembled some kind of overgrown rodent, with long greasy hair and a ski-jump nose, carrying a laptop case.

'Mr Wood,' Sinisa said. 'We meet again.' Sinisa and I shook hands.

'This is Talena, my girlfriend, she's American,' I said. Sinisa kissed her cheek twice as if he were French. 'And this is Saskia, who needs to emigrate.'

'You have met Zoltan,' he said, indicating the über-thug, 'and Zorana,' the redhead.

I smiled at them. They did not smile back. Both of them were even scarier in daylight. Zoltan was all craggy muscle, with a zigzag, much broken nose, and despite his bulldog build he moved with athletic grace. Zorana was stunningly alpha-female beautiful, long, lean, muscled body, perfect features, fiery red hair. Both of them openly carried guns on their belts.

A slightly awkward silence ensued. I realized Sinisa was waiting for me to talk. Maybe the criminal conversational protocol was that the customer spoke first.

'Should we talk about money now?' I asked hesitantly. 'Or work out the details first?'

I had no idea what the details were. Were we actually willing to turn Saskia over to Sinisa? What would happen to her? How could we be sure she would be safe? How much would we have to pay, and when?

'I do not want money from you,' Sinisa said.

'Excuse me?' I didn't know much, but I knew smugglers didn't work *pro bono*.

'I want to employ your skills. If they are relevant.'

I was too surprised to speak.

Talena stepped in. 'You *what?*'

'I need a skilled computer programmer, and quickly,' he said. 'You need this woman taken to safety, and quickly. I propose an exchange.'

'I . . . ' I traded an astounded glance with Talena. 'I think we'd rather just pay you. We just need you to get her to Germany or England. How much will that cost?'

'That is not on offer. I am not interested in your money.'

'This is crazy,' Talena said. 'If you want to hire someone, put up an ad on HotJobs. We're here to do business with you.'

'No. You are here because you have had the good fortune to approach me at a time when I require the services of a computer programmer. Otherwise I would never have agreed to this meeting.'

I shook my head, bemused. 'A programmer for what?'

'Arwin.'

For a moment I thought it was a code name, or some Tolkien reference, neither would have surprised me much at that stage. Then the little weaselly man with the laptop came forward and I realized that it was his name.

'We talked on the phone,' he said to me. His voice was shrill and nasal in person, and his accent was not from the Balkans. 'Synchronized, remember?'

'Right.'

'We need a guy with strong Java, Web, and database

skills. Also someone familiar with security and cryptology and who can read C.'

'Well . . . I'm your guy, but . . . ' My voice trailed off.

'You got a CV?'

'What?'

'A CV. A résumé. You don't have one?'

'Not on me. Um, I have one online.'

'Come show me.' He turned and walked towards the Land Rover.

I looked back at Talena and Saskia.

'The interview will not take long,' Sinisa said.

My interview. This was a job interview. Possibly the strangest job interview in the history of computer science. I followed Arwin to the Land Rover, head spinning. He already had the laptop out of its case and a Web browser open. I supposed it had a cellular modem.

'What is the address?' he asked, fingers poised over the keys.

'I'll drive,' I said.

He reluctantly stepped aside. 'Do you recognize the browser and the environment?'

'Sure. Mozilla. KDE. Linux.'

He nodded, satisfied, and watched as I pointed the browser towards the computer in San Francisco that contained, among other things, a copy of my résumé. My usual job-interview nervousness and sense of unworthiness flooded into me despite the surreal context. I was glad that I had kept my résumé semi-fraudulently updated by listing open-source projects I had dabbled with over the last eighteen months as if they were ongoing activities. It covered up my lengthy period of unemployment, and if Arwin was ignorant of these projects, which was quite possible, he might interpret them as jobs.

'Java work, database work, lots of websites,' he summarized after a quick pass through my résumé. 'You sound perfect.'

I shrugged. 'Maybe I am.'

He fired off a half-dozen more Java questions at me, all of them easy. Then he asked me questions about design patterns and recursive algorithms and object modelling and database denormalization, all of them integral to my long-dormant professional life, basic enough that the answers came easily despite my year and a half away. It only took five minutes. It rarely takes more than that for a true techie to identify another, and both Arwin and I, despite my rust and Arwin's many later-discovered flaws, were hardcore coders.

'He'll do,' Arwin announced as we returned to the others.

Talena looked worried.

'Excellent,' Sinisa said, awarding me a proprietary smile. 'Then it is time to discuss the logistical details.'

'We haven't agreed to anything yet,' I said. I didn't like his certainty. 'You're not the only game in town.'

'No. But I am the only game that will take your friend all the way to America.'

'America?' Talena asked.

'America.'

'How?'

'You do not really expect me to reveal my trade secrets. But I assure you, if you agree to our arrangement, and if Paul performs the tasks I require, Saskia will be in California six weeks from today.'

'How do we know she'll be safe?' I asked.

'Because you will be with her.'

'I—what?'

'You do not expect me to let you work from home, do you? I know America has its New Economy, but here we still live in the old world. You two, and you as well if you like,'—to Talena—'will come with me to my operational headquarters. You will work for me there, with Arwin.'

I exchanged a dazed look with Talena.

'You are very fortunate that I need someone like you,' Sinisa said. 'Otherwise I would not take your friend to America regardless of how much you offered. This is the deal of a lifetime, Mr Wood.'

'Yeah? How long a lifetime?'

He chuckled. 'I am glad to see you have a sense of humour, but I assure you, if you hold up your end of the agreement, you have nothing to fear from me.'

'Nothing to fear except you making sure I don't walk out with your trade secrets.'

'An understandable concern. But if you have done your research with your NATO friends, you know that I am not a man who does such things. I have never reneged on an agreement, Mr Wood. But obviously it is impossible to prove a negative. It is up to you. My offer is on the table. You have ten minutes to decide.'

'Wait. One question. Why me? There's plenty of coders around here, aren't there?'

'You'd be surprised,' Arwin piped up. 'Anyone with real skill'—the last consonant was stressed, hacker-speak rather than an accent—'got the hell out of this country a long time ago. He brought me in from Russia.'

'You speak pretty good English for a Russian,' Talena pointed out.

'Lived in Brooklyn for three years. Illegally. Fuckin' INS deported me. Sinisa's my ticket back too. Just like he can be for your little friend.'

'Nine minutes,' Sinisa said.

'I can tell you're not going to be one of my favourite bosses ever if I do accept,' I said sarcastically. 'We're going to talk it over for a bit.'

Talena, Saskia, and I retreated back into a huddle.

'This is so messed up,' I said.

'Do you think he's serious?' Talena asked.

'That or he's got one sick sense of humour. But Arwin's the real deal, I'm sure of that.'

Saskia said something.

'She says she wants to go to America,' Talena said, 'but not if it puts you in danger.'

'Yeah? Tell her it's a little fucking late.'

'We could always go to the other guy.'

'Yeah,' I said. 'But maybe Sinisa's right. Maybe this is good luck.'

Talena shook her head. 'I don't like it. I'd rather just pay him. We just happen to show up at his door when he needs a programmer? No way. There's something else going on.'

'Maybe so. But this way I'll be able to keep an eye on her, make sure she's safe.'

'What if he doesn't want to let you go?'

'He knows I've got friends in NATO,' I said. 'That helps. And he let me go before, remember? That's something.'

'I don't trust him. He's too smooth. And he's a Serb. I know that sounds crazy but it makes a difference around here, it really does, he's a Serb and Saskia and I are Croats, it makes a difference. I don't trust him.'

'Me neither. But I trust the alternatives even less.'

We looked at each other for a moment.

'Besides,' I said, 'you know, I need a job.'

She quirked a smile but her expression turned serious in a hurry. 'He's a criminal, Paul.'

'You remember some of the dot-coms I worked for? This dude can't be any worse.'

'I'm serious. Never mind how slick and charming and Western he is, never mind his nice suit. He's a monster too. Probably no better than Dragan.'

'Yes. I agree. He's probably a monster. And I'd be helping him. And I'd have to trust him to let me go after. But if he's telling the truth I'd also be getting Saskia not just out of here but into America. And I think he is telling the truth.'

'There's a whole lot he's not telling. Why would he need someone like you so badly?'

'Kind of curious about that myself,' I admitted. 'But he's not exactly in the world's most transparent business. He's given us a pretty good offer. Maybe we're dealing with the devil, but, you know, why the fuck did we let him give us a ride out here in the first place, right? So he's a monster. Maybe he can be *our* monster for a little while.'

'You want to accept.'

'Yes.'

'All right,' Talena said, nodding. She passed the decision on to Saskia, who closed her eyes and smiled with relief, and turned back to me. 'Then we're all staying here.'

'Absolutely not,' I said quickly. 'You'd lose your job. You have to go back.'

'Never mind my *job*, Paul, this guy is dangerous, you could lose your fucking *life*.'

'An even better reason for you not to come with me. So you can orchestrate help from outside if we need it. If he does fuck us over then you won't be able to do much good if you're sitting helpless in his clutches too.'

'Paul, there is no way I'm going to fly back to California and leave you and Saskia all alone with this Serb smuggler with nothing but his word protecting you. End of discussion.'

'What if he does turn on us?' I asked. 'What good will you be here?'

She didn't have any answer to that.

'One of us has to stay away from him,' I said. 'It can't be me, it can't be Saskia, so it has to be you. I'm sorry. I know you want to stay here. But if you do, you endanger both of us.'

Try as she might, and she tried, she couldn't think of a counter-argument to that.

'Don't worry,' I said. 'It probably sounds more scary than it is. I bet it'll just be another boring programming job. I'll be craving danger after three days but all I'll get is bug hunts.'

She didn't seem convinced.

'So it's settled,' I said, barrelling on before she could think of some other reason to protest. 'We accept the offer.' I paused as a brainwave hit. 'Well, sort of, and then Saskia and I stay here, I work on a job that will never ever make it on to my résumé, you go home, and we meet up in six weeks. Piece of cake.'

'What do you mean, sort of?'

'Come on. I'll show you.'

I led Saskia and Talena back to Sinisa.

'One condition,' I said.

His expression darkened. 'I do not like conditions.'

'Twenty thousand US dollars deposited into my American bank account. Half today, half when the job is done.'

He looked at me, appalled and insulted, though I suspected both were negotiating ploys. 'Absolutely not. I am already being far too generous with you, Mr Wood. Do you know how much passage to America would cost if I were to allow you simply to buy it? Fifty thousand dollars!'

'How interesting. Do you know how much expert coders cost per hour in California?'

He sighed. 'Ten thousand dollars.'

'Fifteen.'

'Fine.'

We shook hands. To him it was obviously petty cash.

'Will Talena be staying here with you?' he asked.

'Talena will be flying back to California tonight,' I said.

Talena looked like she very much wanted to object, but she stayed quiet.

'All right,' Sinisa said. 'Arwin. Take his bank details and arrange the transfer for my authorization.'

Talena and I followed Arwin back to the pick-up and watched him unfold and launch the laptop. I was in a bit of a daze. I had just agreed to join a criminal conspiracy of Bosnian thugs. Talena would be leaving me tonight. The future had become a grey and unknowable void.

'Tell me everything you know about the bank,' Arwin said. 'I should be able to find the SWIFT code online, if they're—'

Arwin was interrupted by Zoltan, who stood on the cab of the Mitsubishi pick-up, keeping watch. He barked something which made the previously unflappable Sinisa pause for a moment, then turn, vault atop the Land Rover, and look where Zoltan pointed.

'There are cars stopped at the cemetery entrance,' Talena said to me quietly. 'Men are getting out of them.'

After a moment she and I followed Sinisa up to the hood of the Land Rover and looked around. There were nine men climbing towards us. They had divided into three groups, coming from three different directions. One of the stopped cars was a battered diesel Mercedes with a visible zigzag crack across the windshield.

'That's Dragan's car,' Talena said, just as I was thinking it. Saskia emitted a tiny, barely audible whimper of terror.

The three groups approached from west and north and east. They carried shotguns and Kalashnikovs, and they moved fast, with military discipline. They would reach us in a few minutes. As they passed, a half-dozen kids playing soccer on a green patch near the entrance picked up their ball and scurried off. Startled mourners backed away and fled out of the graveyard. Trouble was brewing, anyone could tell.

'Friends of you?' Zoltan, the über-thug atop the Mitsubishi, asked me with a thick accent.

I considered lying. I doubted Sinisa would be willing to get into a firefight for our sake, especially when he was outnumbered. But it wouldn't take long to figure out why they were here. Might as well go down telling the truth.

'They're after her,' I said, nodding to Saskia, who stood with fists tightly clenched, looking from me to Talena and back, her eyes blank with terror.

Talena said, 'Paul. We should run. Now.'

Behind us, to the south, the ground sloped downwards for a few hundred yards, then, just past the graveyard's perimeter fence, it rose abruptly into a steep rocky slope. A thin ribbon of dirt path wound its way up that slope.

'That is what they want,' Sinisa said to her.

'What? How do you know?'

'Basic tactics. They would not come like this unless they wanted to drive you that way. There are more of them waiting on top of that path, I assure you.'

If he was right then we were surrounded. I reached for my phone.

'Who do you call?' Zorana, the red-headed woman who had greeted me in the factory, asked sharply.

'NATO.'

'You have interesting contacts,' Sinisa said. 'We must discuss them some day.'

'Yeah, sure,' I said. 'If this isn't my last day on earth that is.'

'Hang up,' he said.

'What?'

'Do not call them. I would prefer not to owe Major Botham any perceived favours.'

'Well, I would prefer not to be dead.'

'You will be fine,' he said. 'Everything is under control. Trust me.'

He looked at me and waited, calmly and patiently, as if nine armed and extremely dangerous men were not within a minute or two of arrival. I paused. My finger hovered over the dial button. We were surrounded and outnumbered. Sinisa was a professional criminal and therefore completely untrustworthy. Maybe he was the one who had called Dragan here, and was deliberately betraying us. It was entirely possible.

But if that was the case we were dead anyway; it didn't matter whether I called or not. If Sinisa didn't help us we would be dead well before NATO ever showed up. Mistrusting him was no longer an option. I pushed cancel.

'Good,' Sinisa said. He switched to Serbian and started barking orders. Zoltan, Zorana, Mini-Hulk and SRG took positions behind the vehicles and the bigger marble tombstones. Arwin folded the laptop, replaced it in its case, and got into the Mitsubishi. Sinisa vaulted nimbly to the ground.

'Get inside,' he said, patting the Land Rover fondly. 'Fully bullet-proof, solid rubber tyres. But do not get too comfortable. They may have grenades. Tell me, who are these men?'

Talena and Saskia and I climbed on to the Land Rover's leather seats. Talena had to help Saskia, who was numb and shivering.

'They're called the Mostar Tigers,' I said.

Sinisa stiffened with surprise. My stomach clenched with fear. He had heard of them, and not in a good way. Now, I was suddenly and terribly certain, he would decide to abandon us to our fate rather than fight the Tigers.

Instead he rolled his eyes, drew his cellphone, and said, 'Good God almighty, why can nothing ever happen the easy way?'

The nine men had fanned out into a semicircle, like pack animals on the hunt, moving with coordinated precision from tombstone to tombstone, using them as cover. Dragan and the Tigers, with more waiting atop that path. Maybe all fifteen of them were in Sarajevo; he must have called in reinforcements from Mostar.

Sinisa joined us in the Land Rover, in the driver's seat, still holding his cellphone to his ear. He opened the window a finger's width, and we waited.

Sinisa's eyes were alive with excitement, and muscles jutted from his neck, but he seemed otherwise calm. Saskia's eyes were closed and every breath was a soft groan. Talena and I were somewhere in between: my right leg twitched nervously, she wound a loop of hair around a finger and pulled hard enough that it had to hurt, both of us as taut as guitar strings but still in control. I was intensely aware of all my senses, the rich smell of leather, the sound of Saskia's breathing, the soft textures of Talena's hand as I took it in mine.

They stopped about fifty feet away from us, sheltered behind gravestones.

Sinisa had a quick muttered conversation with his phone.

Then Dragan's bellowing voice sounded. Talena muttered a translation into my ear.

'We want the Canadian and the two women!' he shouted. 'Give them to us and we will all leave this graveyard alive! If not, that Land Rover will be your mausoleum! We are the Mostar Tigers! I am Dragan Kovacevic! The woman, Saskia, she is *mine!* She is my *wife!* I will not rest, not a single day, not an hour, until I have my woman back, until I have my revenge and the streets run red with the blood of my enemies!'

That last sounded much too poetic for Dragan, but Talena assured me that it was fairly basic hyperbole around these parts, sort of the Bosnian equivalent of 'Yo' momma.' Sinisa lowered the window a little further and called out a reply.

'The Mostar Tigers,' Talena translated. 'I know of you. Perhaps you know of me. My name is Sinisa Obradovic.'

There was a pause.

'I know who you are,' Dragan said, his voice less strident.

'These people are under my protection. Leave while you still can.'

'If you know of the Mostar Tigers, you know we never run from a fight.'

'This is no fight. This is suicide.'

Dragan laughed. 'Bold words from a man surrounded and outnumbered.'

Sinisa muttered something else into his phone. I looked at Talena, who shrugged, she hadn't caught it. Sinisa then closed his window, interlaced his hands behind his head, and leaned back in the leather seat, a slight, confident smile on his face. I began to wonder if we had turned ourselves over to a deranged megalomaniac.

There was a loud crack, not gunfire, more like a big log snapping in two. Then another, and another, and I caught some kind of puffing motion out of the corner of my eye. I looked out at the graveyard. Something flickered in the distance. I blinked. One of those marble obelisks, over by the Tigers—had one of those just vanished?

Another loud crack, and this time I saw the top half of one of those marble spires disappear into a puff of dust and gravel. Then another. And another. Somebody in the distance, one of the Tigers, yelled with rage and fear.

Sinisa spoke into his phone, and the pace of destruction

accelerated. All around where the Tigers huddled, grave markers snapped and burst and fell to the ground. It was like watching loggers clear-cut a forest. I covered my ears against the piercing cracks, feeling slightly guilty about the desecration, but only slightly. Better to destroy others' tombstones than to qualify for our own.

Finally Sinisa spoke a single word into his phone and the onslaught stopped. My ears rang like I had spent the day front row centre at Lollapalooza. A stunned silence hung over the cemetery.

Sinisa lowered the window and shouted.

'You have one minute to leave,' Talena translated, 'before my snipers stop shooting at stones and start shooting at you.'

There was no immediate response. I wondered where the snipers were. There were many houses on the slopes to the south, and several tall buildings across the Miljacka, with a clear view of the graveyard.

Sinisa glanced at his watch. 'Forty-five seconds!' he called out.

'That woman is my wife!' Dragan shouted. 'My wife!'

'Forty seconds.'

'I make a bad enemy, Sinisa Obradovic. If you do this thing then you too will have taken my wife from me. I make a bad enemy!'

'Then perhaps I should just kill you now,' Sinisa suggested.

'Perhaps you should!'

'Christ,' I muttered. It wasn't bravado. Dragan really was nuts.

'If you stay here for only thirty more seconds,' Sinisa said, 'I will.'

I held my breath. I wanted them to stay. I wanted Sinisa to wipe them out. But just before Sinisa's deadline the Tigers began to retreat downhill, towards their vehicles.

Sinisa looked back at us, grinning smugly.

'They'll be back,' I warned him.

'I doubt that.'

'Paul's right,' Talena said. 'Those guys are crazy. And crazy dangerous. You know that, right? If they find out where you are . . .'

'If they find out where we are they will be very frustrated. If Dragan Kovacevic tries to leave the country, believe me, I will know.'

'Leave the country?' I asked, perplexed.

'I am no longer based in Bosnia,' Sinisa explained. 'You will come with me to my new headquarters.'

'I what? Where? What country? When?' Everything was happening too fast.

'Albania. Today.'

'*Albania?*'

'No worries, Mr Wood,' he said. 'I think you will like it.'

Sinisa was in a hurry. We didn't have time to drive Talena to the airport. Instead we dropped her off downtown where she could catch a taxi. I exited the car with her, and she turned to me, and we hugged each other so hard that after a moment I relaxed my grip for fear I might crack one of her ribs.

'You take care of yourself,' she whispered. 'Take care of Saskia too. But take care of yourself. Most of all. Don't you dare do anything stupid and get yourself hurt. Don't you dare. Promise me you'll come back safe.'

'I promise,' I said.

'I shouldn't go,' she said. She let me go and shook her head angrily. 'This is crazy. What am I doing? I'm not going. No. I'm staying here with you.'

'No,' I said. 'You can't. I wish you could, believe me, but no. You have to go back to work, and you have to be the one to help us if we get in trouble.'

'I can't. Fuck the job, Paul, I can't go, this is *wrong*. It feels so fucking wrong to turn around and walk out on you. Fuck. Fucking fucking *fuck*. You better not just be telling me to leave so I'll be safe.'

'I'm not. Talena, I don't want you to go any more than you do. But we'll be safer if you leave.'

'How am I supposed to help you if you get in trouble in Albania?' she asked.

'Call my friends. Hallam and Steve and Lawrence. They'll come if I'm in trouble.'

'Goddamnit. I better hear from you every fucking chance you get. Every single day. No exceptions.'

'Every chance I get,' I promised.

'You better. I . . . ' She sighed. 'This is so fucked up. We shouldn't be doing this like this, not here, not now, but . . . Paul, listen, I know this is all crazy, this whole, everything that's been happening. And I know we haven't talked, I can't even remember the last time we really talked. I know things haven't been good between us for a while. But these last few days, I've been thinking . . . maybe, when you get back, maybe we could try one last time. Things will have to be different. Very different. But maybe we could try.'

'I would like that,' I said quietly. 'Very much.'

'Okay. Good. Okay.' She took a deep breath. 'You know, I almost, I almost forgot how much I like you. I forgot how good you are. How did that happen? How did we let that happen?'

'It was my fault,' I said.

'Never mind. Dammit. Of all the fucking times, you know? Right now I want to sit you down and just talk for six straight days. Make up for our whole lost last year.' She closed her eyes. 'But we can't. So let's, okay, shit. You better'—her lip started to quaver—'you better just go now. Just, please, turn around, go, tell Saskia goodbye for me, tell her I'm sorry, tell her I couldn't tell her goodbye myself or I'd just start bawling in the middle of the street, and, Paul, please, please be okay. Please come back okay. Please don't get hurt. Don't get her hurt but most of all don't you get hurt.'

'I love you,' I said, and kissed her softly. She didn't answer. I turned my back on her and got into the Land Rover, and I sat stiffly with my heart pounding and a lump as big as a grapefruit in my throat as Sinisa drove me away from the woman I loved.

At least she would be safe. I was sure of that. That was something.

2 Albania

10 Human Traffic

'Paul,' Saskia whispered, touching my shoulder so tentatively I barely felt it. 'Paul.'

'I'm awake,' I lied, shook my head to clear it, looked around, tried to remember where I was and what I was doing. The back of Sinisa's Land Rover. Driving south, towards Albania. No, wait, we were in Albania, I remembered shivering in the chill mountain wind, waiting outside the Land Rover at three in the morning while Sinisa talked to the guards at the Montenegro border, dispensing cigarettes and envelopes full of money. Seven hours had passed since then, and our convoy of two, the Land Rover leading the white Mitsubishi pick-up, rolled along a smooth two-lane road that wound its way through green rolling hills flecked with red brick buildings, groves of olive trees, herds of sheep and cattle. My expectations of Albania, vague television memories of angry men in filthy grey cities waving AK-47s while dishevelled Western reporters explained how pyramid schemes had looted the whole country's savings, had never included this vision of rural paradise.

'Did you sleep well?' Sinisa asked. He was in the passenger seat; at some point Arwin had taken the wheel.

'Fine,' I said. There was a crick in my neck, and my clothes felt thickly uncomfortable, but I did feel rested, albeit several coffees away from alert.

'There is a café by the side of the road here. A good place. They know me.'

'Everyone knows Sinisa,' Arwin added. 'In case you hadn't figured it out already.'

Sinisa beamed at the tribute.

I looked over to Saskia. 'How are you?' I asked.

'Good,' she said, forcing a smile. I didn't believe her. I guessed it had to be traumatic, fleeing your country, turning yourselves over to refugee smugglers, still pursued by your monstrous husband and his friends. I guessed the road to freedom was always bumpy.

'Your NATO friends helped build this road,' Sinisa said. 'Three, four years ago, this was all pot-holes and cracks. It took all day to go from Tirana to the border. Then Kosovo happened, NATO started bombing the Serbs, a hundred thousand refugees came into Albania, and the aid organizations finally started pouring money into this country. The Kosovo crisis was the best thing that ever happened to Albania. Here we go. The coffee here is splendid. Italian coffee, not Turkish, we left Turkish coffee behind at the border.'

The café was clean, well lit and spacious, the scrambled eggs and ham and Greek salad were excellent if an odd mix, the gleaming new cappuccino machine was put to good use, and our waiter refused a tip. Yesterday's notion of Albania whimpered briefly in my head before disintegrating for good.

Our convoy stopped for a cigarette in the gravel parking lot outside the café before resuming our journey. Zoltan and Zorana smoked unfiltered Camels as they leaned against the Mitsubishi, piled high and riding low with bags and boxes and crates and canisters. I was glad they were on our side. I

felt uneasy around them, like I was in the presence of wild
and possibly rabid animals.

Sinisa and Arwin were Marlboro Light men. I bummed
a cigarette off Sinisa. He offered one to Saskia as well, and
after a moment she took it. I didn't really intend to take
up smoking again, but I figured it would make for good
relations with my new boss to be a smoking buddy. Also
I associated smoking's degenerate decadence with travel.
And this journey felt like travel. I suppose technically it
was more along the lines of desperate survival; I was, after
all, working for a criminal overlord while helping Saskia
escape a murderous group of thugs, but we were a long way
away from Bosnia, and despite their morally dubious business model Sinisa and Arwin seemed like they might be my
kind of people; I was even getting the unexpected chance to
explore this most remote corner of Europe. I felt like I was
back on vacation.

'It is not all like this,' Sinisa assured us, as the nicotine
hit me and I involuntarily shuddered. 'Remember, this is the
poorest country in Europe, the only country where you do
not dare drink the tap water. The countryside is nice, but
the cities are ugly, the factories are filthy, there are chemical
leaks and oil spills, the medical standards are disastrous,
only the main roads like this are any good. And the people,
backward, corrupt, no education. But despite its difficul-
ties, I tell you, this is a land of opportunity. The economy
is booming, the trade barriers are falling, the government
is slowly becoming competent, the people work hard when
they can find work. And we are so close to the West. It
is fifty kilometres to the Italian coast. This will be holiday
country in a few decades. Lake Ohrid, to the east, huge,

beautiful, almost untouched: last year I bought a whole kilometre of waterfront property, not a single building on it, less than a one-bedroom flat in London.'

Arwin snorted. 'Don't kid yourself,' he said to me. 'This place is a shithole.'

Sinisa sighed. 'Arwin, you have no dreams in you.'

'Sure I do. I want to spend a long weekend driving around Manhattan in a stretch Hummer limo with two slutty supermodels. If that isn't the ultimate dream, tell me what is. Lake Ohrid? Fuck that. The girls here, sure, they're pretty, but they're all Muslim, you'd have to pry their legs open with a fucking crowbar.'

'I keep Arwin around for his delicate sensibilities and his valuable cultural insights,' Sinisa said to me.

I chuckled. Zoltan growled something in Serbian.

'English,' Sinisa said. 'Around Paul, both of you speak English, always. It is a valuable opportunity for you two, to be able to practise with a real American English speaker.'

Zoltan looked away and took a long drag on his cigarette before saying, 'Yes, okay.'

'Are you two going to America too?' I asked.

Zoltan and Zorana looked at each other and then at Sinisa. I sensed I was not supposed to know the answer to that question. Which by itself pretty much told me the answer. It was hard to picture the two of them in America; they seemed too raw, too primal, for the modern civilized USA. Like bringing wolves into a city.

'English skills are important everywhere today,' Sinisa said blandly.

I suddenly realized, by how they stood and the way they had looked at one another, that Zoltan and Zorana were a couple. I noted identical plain gold wedding rings. Husband and wife. I repressed a chuckle. Of course. With names like theirs, how could they not be married?

We smoked the rest of our cigarettes in silence and piled back into the Land Rover and Mitsubishi for the five-hour ride to Vlore. A long and interesting drive. Near the city of Elbasan we passed a gargantuan chemical factory, the size of a small town, the land around it blighted to a sooty lunar grey decorated only by stunted bushes and weeds. From Elbasan south at least half the vehicles were mini-vans carrying up to a dozen passengers apiece, here called *furgons* but no different from African *tro-tros* or *matatus*, Indonesian *bemos*, New Guinean *PMVs*, Central American *colectivos*. The poor world's public transit is everywhere the same.

The road veered around the capital of Tirana and headed west for the Adriatic, briefly becoming a proper four-lane highway before it hit the ocean, turned south, and shrank back to two poorly maintained lanes. We paralleled a rail-road track for a long time but I didn't see a single train. The buildings we passed were either red brick houses or cheap grey concrete blocks still sprouting rusting bundles of rebar, sometimes with scarecrows attached. I saw lumberyards, machine shops, bales of hay piled in enormous pyramids, gas stations, but mostly the road went through fields, maybe half of them under active cultivation, the rest abandoned to waist-high weeds and grass. We overtook *furgons*, groaning tractors, ancient Fiats belching dark filth from their tail-pipes, an old man on a rusted Vespa scooter with an eight-foot pitchfork strapped to his back. Occasionally we caught a glimpse of the Adriatic Sea to our right.

The craziest thing was the bunkers. They were everywhere. 'Hoxha's mushrooms,' Arwin called them, pointing them out to me and explaining. Enver Hoxha, Albania's strange and paranoid Cold War dictator, during his forty-year tenure had ordered the construction of some seven hundred and fifty thousand concrete bunkers from which his loyal Albanians could resist the onrushing hordes of invaders that Hoxha feared. Now no Albanian landscape was complete without a couple of dozen of Hoxha's bunkers, squat concrete mushrooms four feet tall and six feet in diameter, clustered along roads and waterfronts and any vaguely strategic location but also sitting in ones and twos in the middle of green farming fields or lurking deep in the forest. Their existence seemed like evidence of Hoxha's complete insanity, but maybe, given what had happened to neighbouring Yugoslavia after his death, he hadn't been so crazy after all.

By the time we finally reached Vlore we had been driving for a full day and I was too tired and punch-drunk to pay close attention to the town. My first impressions were of a sea of squat grey concrete blocks, wheezing old cars, a big open-air market, uneven streets, a huge decrepit pier jutting into the sea like a rotting tooth, a long arc of beach covered with flotsam and filth. We went through the downtown and up a high bluff that overlooked the harbour, a bay of the intensely blue Adriatic ringed by high green hills. The grey sprawl of Vlore proper looked like a fungal infection on the otherwise gorgeous panorama.

We switchbacked up the steep slope, past chains of Hoxha's mushrooms, and emerged on to a surprisingly pleasant little street lined with olive trees. There were a half-dozen small houses on either side and one very large house at the end, on the lip of the bluff. We turned into a gravel driveway midway along the street.

'I figured the one at the end was yours,' I said.

'These are all my houses,' Sinisa said casually. 'This is the one where you will live.'

'Oh.' Sinisa didn't just have a big house; he had his own *neighbourhood.*

Saskia and I got out of the car carrying the Adidas bags that contained all our worldly possessions. It was good to stretch my legs again.

'The door is open,' Sinisa said. 'Come to the house at the end in thirty minutes. Then you will begin your work.'

I opened my mouth to agree but he was already reversing back on to the street and driving towards his mansion. Saskia and I looked at one another.

'Well,' I said. 'I guess this is home. Let's take a look.'

It was like walking into a cave. Our new home was nothing but a barren shell of uneven drywall and pitted concrete floors. Albanian construction standards were obviously lax. It might have been an okay little place if it had come with any furnishings whatsoever. At least it had electricity and running water. The whole house smelled of fresh paint and was uncomfortably hot. Vlore was cooler than Bosnia, thanks to the nearby Adriatic, but the heatwave that had hung over the Balkans for two weeks had not yet abated. I thought longingly of the cool mountain air at the Montenegro border.

We dumped our Adidas bags and went back outside, where the air was cooler and there was no unnerving emptiness.

I was both exhausted and restless from our twenty-four-hour drive. I wanted to go for a walk, get the lay of the land, but there was nowhere to go; Sinisa's private hillside neighbourhood was at least a mile away from any other buildings and a good hour's walk from downtown Vlore. I saw that several of the other houses on the street were adorned with satellite dishes and wished that ours was similarly endowed. A little CNN or better yet Fox Sportsworld was just what the doctor called for. But it seemed I would have to go without.

This was where I would live for a while. A very weird notion.

'Nothing,' Saskia said. She looked even paler than usual. 'Nothing inside.'

'Don't worry,' I said. 'I guess he wasn't expecting us. I'll have him get some stuff out here. Beds and chairs and, I don't know, stuff.'

She smiled hesitantly. I doubted she had understood a word. I was speaking fast and mumbling, tired from the drive. 'It will be okay,' I tried again, speaking as clearly as I could.

'Good,' she said. 'That is good, Paul.' But I wasn't sure she believed me.

The first day of work is always surreal. It is ten times more surreal if you are now working for a criminal enterprise, if you have just parted from your girlfriend for an extended period, if you have just driven from Bosnia into Albania after a cemetery firefight with the gang of thugs pursuing the woman you are trying to rescue, and if it begins with a long speech from Sinisa Obradovic. Take my word for it.

'My parents were from Belgrade,' Sinisa said, leaning back against his desk, as I sat in one of his overdecorated office's overstuffed leather chairs. 'They moved to Amsterdam in the sixties. I speak Serbian because they spoke it at home, but I considered myself Dutch. I joined the army. I was a paratrooper, a lieutenant. Because I spoke the language they transferred me to the Thirteenth Air Mobile Battalion and sent me here as a peacekeeper. To Srebrenica.'

'Oh,' I said softly.

'You know of it. Seven thousand unarmed men, slaughtered. I was there. It was despicable. The UN, my own army, they betrayed those men. An airstrike would have stopped the Serb advance, the massacre would never have happened; that airstrike was cancelled because the man who requested it filled out the wrong UN airstrike form, did you know that? Children were dying, but the UN would not intervene because the paperwork was filled out incorrectly.'

'I didn't know that,' I said, tentatively appalled in case it was true.

'That was where my faith in armies and governments collapsed. I went back to Holland. I left the army and went to school. Let me tell you of my qualifications. I am of course a citizen of the Netherlands, an EU citizen. I was a lieutenant in the Dutch army. I have a diploma in business from a university in Eindhoven. I am a licensed pilot. I speak Serbian, English, Dutch, German, I am learning Spanish, one day I hope to learn Chinese. Here in Vlore I own a cement factory, eight and a half hectares of olive groves, three fishing boats. I have various business interests in Amsterdam and Belgrade and Sarajevo. But, with you I can be blunt, my major business, my *raison d'être* as the

French would say, is illegally smuggling refugees from poor countries into rich ones.

'Illegal. Not immoral. On the contrary, my business is as moral as the work of Médecins sans Frontières, Amnesty International, UNICEF. I take people from danger, hunger, fear, desperation, unbearable poverty, unendurable despair, and I deliver them to the land of opportunity. What is immoral is that my business is illegal. You remember that famous motto on the Statue of Liberty? "Give me your tired, your hungry, your poor, your huddled masses yearning to live free." No more. Not today. Today the tired and hungry are no longer wanted. Now the huddled masses must have visas, money, connections. Now they are guilty until proven innocent, guilty of being Muslim, guilty of being dark-skinned, guilty of being poor, guilty of wanting a better life for themselves.'

He obviously wasn't ad libbing. This was a spiel, some kind of sales pitch. I wondered who else it was used on. Investors, contributors, potential employees, the refugees who were his clients, the officials who looked the other way in return for regular envelopes filled with US dollars? Had Arwin heard this pitch? I didn't think so. Arwin didn't seem like a man who would be moved by any attempt to awaken his inner Gandhi. This speech was saved for people whom Sinisa thought might become True Believers.

While I was a long way from shaving my head and joining his cult, I had to admit he had some good points. That said, for an altruist working to help the world's poor and struggling, he sure had done well for himself. His mansion had two fully equipped Land Rovers out front, an armed guard at the wrought-iron gate, a pool, a Jacuzzi, a clutch of satellite dishes. As he spoke Sinisa leaned on a magnificent mahogany desk adorned with a top-of-the-line Vaio notebook, dressed in Armani finery like some Eurotrash male model, outlined by a bay window which framed a spectacular view of Vlore's harbour. I felt like I was in a *Town and Country* photo shoot.

'Do you know why I hired you?' he asked. 'I suppose you are good at your job, but not only that. I hired you because I can trust you. I know this because of that little boy you saved, because you walked into that place and returned that child to his family. I know you understand that the people I carry across borders, it is our moral duty to help them.'

'What happened to that family?' I asked.

He shrugged. 'My business has grown too large to track all my clients. I will find out and let you know.' But he never did.

'My business,' he continued, stressing the word. 'A business, not a charity. People will give money to help the poor, but not to help bring them to places where they can provide for themselves. I run a profitable business. I see no contradiction. One can both do good and do good business. And this is a good business to be in. People are the ultimate commodity. They supply themselves, transport themselves, hide themselves, they can travel halfway around the world with only minimal assistance and coordination.

'My total business income last year, Mr Wood, was four million United States dollars. You see how open I am being with you. A considerable amount. But around the world, every year, more than ten *billion* dollars are spent on services such as mine. This market is wide open, fragmented, populated largely by incompetent organizations. You might be surprised to learn that modern business management techniques are almost entirely absent in the world in which I work. When they are introduced, I assure you, they are completely applicable and fantastically successful. I am in a market that is ripe for growth, Mr Wood. I intend to grow. I intend to expand around the world. I intend to be number one. Not the Microsoft of people smuggling, Bill Gates is too public and visible, but the Intel. Do you know what the maxim of Intel's CEO has always been?'

I did know. 'Only the paranoid survive.'

He beamed with approval. 'Exactly. And that, Mr Wood, is why you are here. Intel is one good analogy to what I hope to build, but perhaps another, better analogy is Amazon, or eBay. My business, going forward, will be an Internet business. You and I and Arwin are going to move my business into the New Economy.'

I opened my mouth to tell him that in America the New Economy had died eighteen months ago—rumour had it you could find its tombstone somewhere in Silicon Valley's eighty million square feet of newly empty office space—but decided not to argue with Sinisa's increasingly bizarre ideas. No sense talking myself out of my new job before I even found out what it was.

'At present this industry has an unbelievably inefficient organizational structure. Because our business is illegal, we work in small groups, like revolutionary cells, unable to betray one another, never contacting one another directly. Suppose a fixer in Sri Lanka has thirty people he wishes to convey to the Netherlands, he has to get them by boat to a group in Iran, perhaps, and from there to a group in Turkey, and from there by air to my people in Bosnia, then down here to Vlore, and on one of my fishing boats to the Italian coast, where the Mafia picks them up and puts them on a train to Holland. Enormously complicated and difficult, so many things that can go wrong, a fragile chain of unreliable gangs, safe houses that move every week, misplaced mobile phones that are the only contact point for the next stage, money stolen or skimmed off, payoffs by all sides to police and border guards, confusion and suspicion whenever the clients are passed from one group to another: it is a horribly, horribly inefficient business, because of a constant lack of information, but this lack of information has been necessary, because of the security risk.

'At first I saw no alternative. And then I read a book. A work of surpassing genius. It is called *The Moon is a Harsh Mistress*, by Robert Heinlein.'

'I've read it,' I said warily.

'It inspired my new business model. All this model requires is secure communications, and that, Mr Wood, that we have. Does it surprise you when I tell you that today it is easy to encode information in such a way that, without the right password, all the computers and code-breakers in all the world would have to work for ten thousand years to unlock the hidden message? Does it surprise you that this can be done on the simplest of home computers with a program available for free? And that these unbreakable coded messages can then be hidden in sounds or pictures?'

I looked at him. The question did not seem to be rhetorical, so after a moment I shook my head. I was surprised, not by what he said, but by the fact he was even mentioning it. I was an expert Internet programmer and this was old and basic information for anyone who was even remotely a techie. It was like Sinisa had just asked a NASA engineer whether he had heard about this amazing thing the Wright Brothers had done.

'It surprised me,' Sinisa said. 'Incidentally you may wish to be careful of shaking your head in Albania, it means "yes" not "no" here. To continue. It surprised me greatly. I had thought this was a dying industry. I had thought technology would make crime a thing of the past by making privacy, secrecy, a thing of the past. When Arwin told me that instead it made true secrecy possible for the first time in history, I began to think. Unbreakable codes. And the Internet, available everywhere. A business where the major problem is lack of information due to fear of discovery. I realized what I need to take the next step, to become a global player. I will build a perfectly secure, perfectly secret Internet communications system, one that all the people, all the organizations I work with, can use. A central communications hub for everyone I work with.

'There is nothing like what I am doing in this world, believe me. No one else is thinking of this. And with this competitive advantage, simply allowing the fixer in Sri Lanka to talk to everyone up the chain all the way to Italy, to fix schedules and agree on payments and discuss problems and make corrections at any time, instead of having meetings in dark alleys with gunmen on both sides because both sides fear being robbed or arrested, or calling the one number each side has and hoping the message goes up the chain without being lost or intercepted by the police or some competitor with a grudge—it will be revolutionary, Mr Wood, absolutely revolutionary. And we are almost halfway there. Arwin is building me an unbreakable code system. You, Mr Wood, you will build our website. And it will change the world.'

I stared up at Sinisa and tried very hard not to laugh. I succeeded, I kept a straight and serious face, but only barely. At last I understood him. He wasn't really a criminal overlord at all. At heart he was a self-deluded dot-com CEO, three years behind his time. The only difference was that he was talking about the criminal world instead of the business world, but, as he had all but said, sometimes there was a damn fine line.

His proposed system was not even remotely revolutionary. That Heinlein novel had been written in 1968. The implications of strong crypto had been well understood for decades, and I strongly doubted his would be the first criminal organization to make use of it. But maybe not; what did I know about the criminal underworld? Maybe gangsters were even more hidebound and resistant to change than the most sluggish behemoths of the corporate world, maybe Sinisa's MBA tactics really were bleeding edge, at least here in the Balkans.

At any rate if I did build this system it would definitely streamline his business and make it harder for the authorities to catch him. But I didn't feel bad about that. Sinisa seemed a lot more Robin Hood than Scarface. He wasn't near as smart as he thought he was, but his heart was in roughly the right place. I was convinced, utterly convinced, that he believed every verging-on-ludicrous word he had spoken.

After the speech Sinisa took me to the office, an overgrown closet on the second floor. There were two slightly obsolete computers and one network hub. Arwin was working on one computer. The other was mine.

'Arwin will give you all the technical details,' Sinisa explained, and left.

It really wasn't so different from the first day of work at my other jobs. First, listen to the CEO give a speech that was supposed to be stirring and morale-building but instead made me wonder whether he had any idea what planet he lived on; then, get the real scoop from my fellow techies.

'Did he take you up on a high mountain and show you all the countries of the world?' Arwin asked.

'I didn't figure you for a Bible quoter.'

'Only the New Testament. I'm Jewish, it's heretical. I used to read it to piss my mother off.'

'Cute,' I said. 'So what am I supposed to do?'

'Build a website so brain-dead even goat-fucking retards can use it.'

'Uh-huh. Any particular kind of website, or should I use my imagination?'

'Basically,' Arwin said, 'we're talking the world's most paranoid chat room.'

'Doesn't sound like rocket science,' I said.

'Thank fuck for that. We've only got a month.'

It was midnight when I got back to our house, the long-dormant technical side of my mind spinning with details, ideas, plans, questions, fragments of code. Whatever the reason, whoever the employer, it was a real physical relief to be working again. I was eager for morning to come so I could get up and go to work. And check email. My new office had Internet access, which I had been worried about, and I had sent a brief I-am-okay update to Talena, and cc'd Hallam, Nicole, Lawrence and Steve.

Sinisa had outfitted our new house with camp-beds, blankets and a few floor lamps. It was a start. I looked into the bedroom nearest the street. Saskia was already under the sheets, her eyes closed, looking younger than she did when awake, breathing with the soft rhythm of sleep. I was glad of it.

I went into what was now my room, undressed, and got on to the camp-bed. It squeaked and moved alarmingly on its wheels when I first put my weight on it, but was surprisingly comfortable once I lay down. It was hot but not too hot to sleep. I closed my eyes and wondered where Talena was.

11 Stegosaurus

These days total secrecy is both easy and free. All those Hollywood scenes of computers breaking codes and unscrambling secrets? *Sneakers* and *Hackers* and *Swordfish* and so forth? Amusing and utter nonsense. Codes aren't breakable, secrets can't be unscrambled, not any more, not if anybody competent did the scrambling.

Go ahead, do it yourself. Download PGP; stands for Pretty Good Privacy, free software available to anyone with an Internet connection. Pick a password—pass phrase, actually, seven or eight words; it has to be fairly long for the math to work. This is your 'private key.' Keep it very secret. Run it through the PGP software to generate your 'public key,' called that because you give it away to all and sundry, friends, enemies, post it on the Internet, doesn't matter. Then anyone who wants to send you a secret message takes the message, takes your public key, plugs both of them into PGP, and out comes a stream of gibberish that can only be deciphered by you with your private key. No one else can ever break the code.

Let me repeat that. *No one* else can *ever* break the code. The combined forces of the entire United States government could work full-time on it for years, and all the mathematicians and supercomputers and National Security Agency cryptography experts in the world still couldn't put your Humpty Dumpty message together again. There are vague rumblings of quantum computers that might be able to do so, a few decades down the line, but long before that happens we'll have unbreakable quantum encryption. The ancient war between code-makers and code-breakers is over. The code-breakers lost.

It's kind of a cool thought at first, that Big Brother might watch you, but he can't read what you wrote. Then it's a little bit scary, when you start thinking about terrorists, child pornographers, arms dealers, drug smugglers. Or Sinisa Obradovic.

The only problem with unbreakably coded messages is that they still look like coded messages. But that too is an easy problem to solve, thanks to steganography, 'covered writing,' the art of hiding a message. In ancient Greece they tattooed secrets on a messenger's head, let his hair grow out, and sent him on his mission. In the eighteenth century two conspirators might write apparently chatty and meaningless letters to one another, in which one could read the real message by extracting every thirteenth letter. Nowadays, again with free software, you can invisibly hide a message inside a picture, in a snippet of music, even in email that looks like spam.

Our job, Arwin's and mine, was to build a secure communications system for Sinisa's smuggling empire. When I showed up, Arwin was putting the finishing touches to an encryption engine he called Stegosaurus, which first encoded messages, then hid them inside pictures—inevitably some kind of unpleasantly explicit porn shot, Arwin being Arwin—so even if someone intercepted a picture as it was beamed over the Internet, they wouldn't be able to distinguish a hidden message from garden-variety Internet pornography. My job, in turn, was to build a website around his Stegosaurus, a site so user-friendly that barely literate criminals everywhere could use it.

After a couple of days of flailing around for a catchy name I would up calling the website Mycroft. Partly a nod to the Heinlein novel that had inspired Sinisa, partly because the image of Sherlock Holmes's brother riding Arwin's stegosaurus was freakishly amusing. Us techies are nothing if not whimsical.

Pretty basic stuff. Suppose Mustafa in Moscow wants to warn Ivan in Istanbul that next week's shipment will be a day late. He logs into Mycroft, picks Ivan from the list of people he's permitted to send messages to, and types in his message. My Java program does all the rest: encodes the message, folds two copies of the message into one of Arwin's porn pictures, and uploads the new picture to Mycroft, looking just as tawdry as before. Ivan, for his part, logs on to the site, finds a new message waiting for him, types in his private key, and out comes Mustafa's original memo.

Note: *two* copies of the message. Only Ivan can decode what is encoded with Ivan's public key, and Sinisa wanted to be able to look over the virtual shoulder of everyone who used his system. So every message was encoded twice, once for the intended recipient, and once, secretly, for Sinisa himself.

There were a few bells and whistles. Sinisa wanted the system occasionally to generate random empty messages from one user to another; this prevented a hypothetical observer from drawing conclusions from the sheer fact of a message being sent. And of course they needed secure logins and user admin, fallback plans in case their website was taken down by a denial-of-service attack or incompetence on the part of the Albanian network host, a heap of other little things; but it was still basically a simple job. Simple, not small. Writing Mycroft from scratch by myself in one month, then testing it to ensure it worked perfectly, was an awful lot of work.

From: balthazarwood@yahoo.com
To: talenar@lonelyplanet.com
Subject: the albanian times
Date: 9 Apr 2003 17:17 GMT

Well, we're still here, and here still seems safe. Heck, here is starting to feel down-right comfortable.

When we said goodbye, you said you felt like you wanted to sit down and talk for six days. Me too. Maybe we can talk here? I

don't know, maybe it's not the right time or
place or medium, but maybe it is.
I want you to know I'm sorry for the way
I've been for the last year and a half. And
I promise, I swear, I will not screw up a
second chance.

I miss you. I love you.

Paul

From: talenar@lonelyplanet.com
To: balthazarwood@yahoo.com
Subject: Re: the albanian times
Date: 10 Apr 2003 04:16 GMT

Hi.

I miss you too. I spend all day worrying
about you two. It's exhausting. I feel like
I'm a World War II widow-in-waiting, like
my man's on the battlefield and all I can do
is sit around and hope the telegram doesn't
arrive today. I've been biting heads off
people at work. Mmm, tasty heads. Today I
overheard Lisa telling Julian not to take it
personally, she thought I was having 'relationship problems.' Hah. If she only knew.

I mean, it's not like we weren't having
relationship problems, but now this is all

so weird and tense that those seem like they happened a long time ago in a galaxy far far away.

OK, no. I'm going to leave that in, but it's not true. Arg. Arg arg arg arg. This is so fucking confusing. I'm all worried and grateful and proud and amazed by what you're doing, and I wake up every morning wishing you were next to me, and at the same time, Paul, part of me, lots of me, is still angry at you. I'm sorry. I know this is absolutely the wrong time. I know I should just be supportive, but I can't bring myself to lie and pretend like we're all roses and honey.

So, yeah, I'm scared for you and mad at you at the same time. And now it's like you suddenly turned back from Mr Hyde into the guy I fell in love with in the first place, and you're out there being all daring and intrepid and risking your life to save Saskia and I feel horrible about saying anything bad to you at all at a time like this. So I'm angry and confused and guilty and terrified pretty much 24/7 these days. Yep, it's shaping up to be a real good month, how about you?

I don't know what else to say right now.

Wish you were here. A lot.

Talena

'Fuck it,' Arwin said late one night that first week, a night when separate bug hunts were proving fruitless and turning our brains into mush. 'Let's go get a beer.'

I greedily agreed. Finding and fixing hard-to-reproduce errors is the most difficult and frustrating part of programming, and I was eager for a reprieve. We went to Sinisa's lavish kitchen, liberated two bottles of Tirana Pilsner from his fridge, and went out to the deck that overlooked the harbour. Arwin produced a packet of Marlboro Lights, and we smoked, sipped Albania's surprisingly drinkable national beer, and watched the moonlight shimmer on the Adriatic.

My thoughts gravitated from Java code to Talena, and the email she had sent. I didn't know what to write back. She was right to be angry at me. I had been a shit, especially since we had moved in together, six months earlier.

We hadn't decided to live together because everything was wonderful between us and we were eager to take that step, but because I couldn't afford rent any more and it was that or move back to Canada and away from her. So for months on end I had woken up, checked the online job boards to see if there was anything new, sent off résumés to anything even vaguely in my line, and then faced another grim day in Talena's cramped apartment, too poor to leave, too bored to live. Time on my hands and no money to fill it. I sat around all day, reading, watching TV, playing video games, and when she came home we either ignored or snapped at each other, like animals trapped in a cage. I know that there were other options, that plenty of people in similar situations lead full and interesting lives, but I didn't know how. Living with poverty is a skill. I had spent my whole adult life being independent and overpaid, and I was no good at being poor and needy.

The worst, the most unbearable thing, had been living off Talena's pay cheque. I knew it was Neanderthal of me but I couldn't stand being supported by my girlfriend. I couldn't bear asking her for money, it made my stomach twist with rage and self-loathing, but I had to do it every week. And her employers at Lonely Planet had made cutbacks too, like everyone else in the Bay Area when the depression hit. She wasn't laid off but she had to work long hours to make up for the people who were let go, so she came home tired and drained and found me unwashed and unshaven, watching empty TV, too lethargic to muster the energy to get up from the couch to greet her, and if she managed to crack open my thin veneer of sloth all she found was rage and frustration and resentment, directed at myself and at the world and much of it, unfairly, at her. I deserved her anger. I had earned it.

'I can't wait to get the fuck out of this place,' Arwin said, shattering my reverie.

'How long have you been here?' I asked after a moment.

'Jesus fuck. We were supposed to go months ago. That's why he brought you in. The zombies are getting itchy.'

I blinked. 'Zombies?'

'That's what I call all those other Serbian fucks.' He waved a hand in the general direction of the road. 'Your neighbours.'

The other houses on the road were occupied by a group of about two dozen people, mostly men, mostly middle-aged and badly worn down by life's sandpaper. Only two of them stood out; a tall white-haired man with an aristocratic look, and a very short goateed man about my age. Whoever they were, they didn't seem to have any official role in Sinisa's organization. In fact they rarely left their houses, and when they did they passed by me as if I didn't exist. The only time I had encountered them in Sinisa's mansion was on an occasion when I had passed his office, looked in, and witnessed the white-haired man arguing with Sinisa in Serbian as several others looked on.

'Who exactly are those guys?' I asked.

He opened his mouth, closed it again, gave me a look, and shook his head.

'All right. I won't ask.'

'One more month to American pussy,' he said, stretching his short hirsute frame. It struck me that Arwin looked more like a rodent than any other human I had ever met. 'And that fuck-me-dead girlfriend of yours. How did an ugly loser like you get so lucky?'

'I wonder that sometimes myself,' I admitted. 'You know, nobody's told me, how are we getting to the States? I figure it's on a ship, right?'

Arwin sighed and gave me another look.

'Okay. Okay. No more questions.'

'I got a question for you. What's the job situation like in California?'

'Terrible,' I said. 'But you're going back to Brooklyn, right? Oh, sorry, no questions.'

'Nah, you can ask about me, no one gives a shit what I

do. I can't go back to New York, I got fucked over by these Russian mafia assholes; one of them was my fucking cousin, you believe that? Flesh and blood and he fucked me over for five thousand dollars. That little shit. Except now he's a big shit. I show up there again he'll rip my balls off just for the practice. Nah, I'm thinking California. Surfer girls with big tits, right? Like *Baywatch*. And all the dope you can smoke, and it's almost legal.'

'It's not all like *Baywatch*,' I warned him. 'And even in Berkeley pot isn't exactly legal.'

'Whatever. I'm sick of Brooklyn. Too much like Russia. California sounds good. As long as I don't have to help out any more. All these fucking zombies, they make me sick. Think you can help me find a job there? Under the table?'

'I'll try,' I said, truthfully. I liked Arwin. He was incredibly crude but often hilariously so; on my second day of work, his lengthy rant about the professional limitations of Vlore's one and only whorehouse had left me simultaneously squirming with discomfort and shaking with laughter. And he was a hard worker, a reasonably good C programmer who knew his limitations and was making a point to learn what he could about Java and Web and database programming from me. He had the real hacker thirst for knowledge. Sure, he was also venal, criminal, sexist, racist, arrogant and obnoxiously opinionated, but at least he never pretended otherwise. He was fun to be around and to work with, and was even fairly generous and considerate given his other moral limitations. He never once complained about my constant leeching of his cigarettes. If that didn't qualify him for a perverse kind of sainthood, nothing would.

That night, when I left Sinisa's mansion, a half-dozen of the zombies were clustered on the porch of the house two doors over from ours, where their patrician white-haired leader lived. He sat on a wooden chair while the others, the little goateed man and four sour-faced middle-aged men, stood around him, gesticulating and talking loudly in Serbian. They looked like they were petitioning him for something. Then one of them saw me looking at them, and all of them fell silent and stared at me suspiciously as I passed.

I wondered who the zombies were, and why Sinisa had invited them to come from the former Yugoslavia and stay in his private neighbourhood. Try as I might, I couldn't come up with a single plausible theory; they were too numerous, and too apparently useless. Insufficient data, I decided. But I didn't believe Sinisa was housing and feeding them out of sheer altruism. They were surely, in some way, part of his plans.

```
From:     balthazarwood@yahoo.com
To:       talenar@lonelyplanet.com
Subject:  Re: the albanian times
Date:     11 Apr 2003 11:03 GMT
```

I'm sorry. I've treated you badly, I know that now, and I'm so sorry. I know how inadequate that sounds. I don't think sorry ever counts for much, you know that, but I guess it's at least a start. I hope I'm at least beginning to make it up to you.

I don't know what else I can say. I wish I did.

Things are fine over here. The work's actually interesting. It's a tight deadline, I'm working probably 70-80 hours a week, but I'm pretty sure I'll make it, and you don't know how good it is to be building something, doing something tangible again.

I love you.

Paul

I almost didn't write that email. Not because it wasn't heartfelt, but because I had discovered that my computer had a keyboard monitor and packet sniffer running at all times, meaning that anything I typed, and all my Internet traffic, was recorded by virtual eyes perpetually looking over my shoulder, presumably to ensure I wasn't posting Sinisa's trade secrets on the Web. I didn't like the thought of Sinisa or Arwin reading anything so personal. But if I wanted to write freely I would have to walk an hour to downtown Vlore and one of its Internet cafés, and in those early days of Mycroft's development I didn't dare take that kind of time away from work. I feared that if more than a day or two passed Talena would misinterpret my silence, so I resigned myself to Arwin and Sinisa reading every word I wrote.

There was a boxing gym in Sinisa's basement, with a full-sized ring, jump ropes, punching bags suspended from the ceiling, speed bags dangling from head-high wooden discs, gloves hanging on wall hooks, a chin-up bar, a set of dumb-bells, a big wall clock counting out three-minute rounds and thirty-second intervals, and the thick smell of dried sweat. I started going there daily to work out and clear my head when it grew clogged with cobwebs of Java code. At first I just used the dumb-bells, but the temptation to hit things was overwhelming and I soon took to donning gloves and clumsily pummelling the punching bags.

Near the end of the first week, I was interrupted in mid-punch by a voice from the door: 'Do you want lesson?'

Zoltan's voice. Zorana stood next to him, both of them dressed in workout gear. I hadn't seen them since arriving in Vlore.

'Okay,' I said tentatively.

'You must make many changes,' Zoltan said, approaching. 'First your stance. Right now you show your opponent all your body. In real fight, very bad. You must turn, like this, show him only left shoulder, with feet like this. Feet are very important. Most of boxing is feet and hips. Forget fists. When you throw punches they must come from hips. Even jab. Jab, you throw like this . . . '

After demonstrating, he strapped flat little pads with bull's-eyes on to his hands, 'focus pads' he called them, and had me punch them for five rounds. Fifteen minutes doesn't sound like much, but during the last round I was on the verge of collapse and twice fell over throwing wild roundhouse hooks. In those five rounds I learned quite a lot about boxing. Most importantly the fact that you had to be in much, much better shape than me. When the final bell rang I slumped against the wall, gasping for air, so drenched in sweat I might as well have gone swimming. The world reeled around me and I closed my eyes, afraid I was about to faint.

'You are fat and slow,' Zoltan scolded. 'Punching is most easy part of boxing. Being punched, that is hard part. You must do much running, much ropework. You are very weak.'

I was in no condition to argue.

'Do you come here every day?' Zorana asked.

'I guess,' I eventually managed.

'Good,' Zoltan said. 'Every day, very good.'

'Yeah,' I said. 'Sure, yeah, sure. I should, I should go shower, work, lots of work to do, very busy.'

'Tonight, you would like to come for dinner with us?' Zorana asked. 'We would like to talk to you, practise English, ask questions.'

'Uh . . .' I looked from one to the other, slightly unnerved by the invitation. It was like being asked out by Special Forces troops. But I was too dazed to come up with a polite out, and I couldn't refuse and insult them. 'Sure.'

'Excellent. We will come and find you,' she said.

'Great. I should, yeah, shower. See you, uh, tonight.'

When we arrived at one of the vaguely Italian beachfront restaurants, the proprietor scurried out and all but kowtowed to Zoltan and Zorana. He was visibly nervous as he took our order. We decided on pizza.

'We want to know about California,' Zorana said, as three draught beers arrived.

'Like what?'

'Everything. We go to live there, you understand.'

'Really?'

'Yes,' Zorana said. 'There is nothing for us in Serbia any more.'

'Serbia is weak,' Zoltan said bitterly. 'Our people are weak. No strength. No pride. No, how you say?' He barked a word in Serbian.

'Brotherhood,' Zorana said sadly. 'Serbia has forgotten its history and brotherhood. Our people have betrayed their own brothers and sisters. The traitors, the false-hearted, they have taken over. We fought for Serbia, Zoltan and I. We bled for Serbia. Many like us died for Serbia. Now they have driven us away, they have destroyed our country, sold our home, they kneel and lick the boots of England and France for a few euros like beggars on the street.' Her face wrinkled like she wanted to spit something foul on to the table.

'America took Kosovo from us,' Zoltan said. 'Kosovo, home of Serbian heart. Now we must go make home in America.'

They exchanged a long, sorrowful look, as if they were discussing the painful demise of a close family member. I wished I was somewhere else.

'So,' Zorana said. 'California. We have money, but we need to know everything else. Where to live, how to move around, where to go if we need a doctor, how to stop the police from finding us. Remember we will be illegal.'

'Not really.'

They looked at each other. 'That is what Sinisa says,' Zoltan said cautiously.

'Well, technically, yes, but nobody talks about illegal immigrants there. There's too many of them; there's at least a couple of million Mexicans who snuck over the border to work there; the state's whole economy would collapse without them. Calling them illegal is considered, well, insensitive. We call them undocumented. I don't know much about living undocumented, but, you know, two million poor Mexicans do it; a white couple with money like you, I don't think it'll be that hard.'

They nodded, pleased. The pizza arrived. As we ate I began to explain life in California to them. What a Social Security number was and how not having it was going to make their lives difficult. How in order to have a good life anywhere but San Francisco you had to have a car, but the undocumented couldn't get driver's licences. The congested web of American health care that I didn't fully understand myself, but which, contrary to what many Europeans believed, at least guaranteed that if you walked into an emergency room you would be cared for, although they would try to bill you later. How much rent would cost; I suggested that they sublet from someone else for cash. The contempt with which American banks treated retail customers and how hard it would be for them to get an account without a legal identity. They listened raptly and Zorana even made some notes.

'Tell us about the police,' Zoltan said.

'The police?'

'We know some things from television, but . . . is hard to say.'

'We have many questions,' Zorana added. 'When are they allowed to arrest you? When can they come and search your house?'

I answered as best I could, although my knowledge of the American justice system stemmed mostly from watching *Law & Order*. They were weirdly interested in the niceties of warrants and jurisdictions.

'You have not been police trouble, in America?' Zoltan asked.

'No,' I said. 'Remember, I'm not American; if I got convicted they'd send me back to Canada and not let me back into America ever again.'

'You have never been arrested?' Zorana asked.

I shook my head, then, remembering Sinisa's warning, clarified, 'No.'

'We worry about American police,' Zorana said. 'Sinisa says they are not like here, you cannot pay them not to go to jail.'

'That's true,' I said. Maybe not a hundred per cent always true, but I didn't want to drown them in subtle distinctions.

'If we go to America, and there is trouble,' Zorana said, 'you will help us?'

After a moment I said, 'Sure.' I couldn't very well say no. And besides, I kind of meant it. I was still nowhere near comfortable around Zoltan and Zorana, but they appeared to be on my team, at least at the moment. There was obviously a lot being kept from me. I wasn't clear on why they were abandoning their much loved Serbia and jettisoning their lives to move to America. But the fact they were doing so at all made me sympathize with them a little. I knew it was no easy thing, leaving your home, trying to find and make a new one.

'Thank you,' Zoltan said, reaching over and clapping his hand on my shoulder hard enough that my chair rocked back and forth a little.

'Tell us, Paul,' Zorana said. 'If a friend of yours, a good friend, asked you to break an American law for them, for an important reason, would you do it?'

'Well,' I said cautiously, 'it would depend on the friend. And the reason.'

'Suppose there is woman like Saskia,' Zoltan said. 'Suppose she need safe San Francisco home. You help this woman?'

'Or suppose your friend gives you a'—Zorana made a square shape with her hands and frowned a moment before finding the right word—'a box, and asks you to take it to their friend in Los Angeles.'

Subtle, they weren't. I considered my options. I didn't want to endanger our newfound rapport. But I didn't want to promise them they could start using my apartment as a safe house, and me as a courier, if and when I made it back to San Francisco. I already wished I had never made my magnanimous offer.

'It would have to be a very good friend,' I said.

'You are loyal to your friends, yes?' Zorana asked.

'Very,' I said.

'Good,' Zoltan said. 'Is good. Loyal is very important.'

I nodded, hoping they didn't think I was agreeing to anything more than that sentiment, hoping they weren't going to pursue this subject any further.

'Maybe we go now,' Zorana said, to my relief. 'We talk like this again, yes?'

I'd really rather not, I didn't say. 'If you like.'

'You good man, Paul,' Zoltan said, giving me another of his bone-rattling back-claps. I tried not to wince. 'You good man. I think we become good friends.'

From: talenar@lonelyplanet.com
To: balthazarwood@yahoo.com

Subject: Re: the albanian times
Date: 13 Apr 2003 02:11 GMT

Is there anything you need or want over
there? DHL and FedEx deliver to Albania.
It's a bit expensive but they say they can
get stuff there in 72 hours.

Your apology is received and understood. I
think maybe we should postpone the relationship part of this conversation for now, what
do you think? We've both got too much to worry
about in the next month to start brooding
about what might happen after that. My mother always said that if you took care of the
present the future would take care of itself.
Of course look what happened to her.

Shit. I'm just babbling. I'm scared, Paul.
I stay up late every night and wake up every
morning worried that something's happened
to you two.

Maybe I should just start drinking and doing
crack, hold up convenience stores, that sort
of thing, you know, unwind a bit. :)

I miss you. I can't wait to see you. I want
you home. Be safe. Write every day.

Talena

Blood Price

From: balthazarwood@yahoo.com
To: talenar@lonelyplanet.com
Subject: Re: daily update
Date: 12 Apr 2003 17:47 GMT

Brain hurts. Poor brain, so tired, all its crenellations mashed flat by evil Apache Web Server arch-enemy.

Work going well. Saskia a little bored but learning English amazingly fast, and excited to come to SF. I still have no idea how exactly we're going to get there.

Thanks for the offer, but actually we're pretty well supplied with stuff. This place isn't as boonie-remote as all that.

I hear what you're saying about now and the future. Worry about the future when we know there is one, sure, okay, that sounds right. Sorry, I'd be more eloquent, but brain is dead.

Love,

Paul

12 Out on the Tiles

When I was twenty-one years old, on the verge of graduating from university, infected by a feverish wanderlust that eight years later I still hadn't fully recovered from, I made a list of cities where I would like to live for a month. The top ten were Cape Town, Paris, London, Montreal, New York, Rio, Sydney, San Francisco, Tokyo and Vancouver. The thriving metropolis of Vlore, Albania, was nowhere to be found. In fact I am willing to bet that it has never been found on any such list ever.

But I almost liked it. Sure, there were a lot of downsides. It was in Albania, for starters, a country well above the sub-Saharan level of development I had expected but still definitely a Third World nation, and Vlore was a poor and mostly ugly town: Stalinist concrete architecture, old groaning vehicles spewing diesel fumes and dark clouds of smoke, rusting cranes on the single pier that jutted into the Adriatic. Most of the streets were cracked and potholed tarmac, or uneven hard-packed dirt strewn with filth and broken glass. During Albania's several recent periods of violent instability Vlore had been openly ruled by warlord gangs, and it still had a certain Wild West feel. Wandering the side streets after dark set off every street-smarts alarm I had even though I knew I was under Sinisa's protection. Saskia and I eventually got a TV, but no satellite dish, and discovered that Albanian TV tended to have extremely low production values, high levels of visual and audible static, and a schedule that consisted largely of Jean-Claude Van Damme movies dubbed into Albanian.

But once I got used to it Vlore really wasn't so bad. I

liked walking down the main drag at sunset, a wide flat road bustling and thriving with people, small businesses, cafés, *pasticeris* and a half-dozen banks. The *pasticeris*, ice-cream stalls, sold good Italian *gelato* for twenty leke or approximately fifteen cents a cone. The people dressed sharply given that they couldn't afford much, and although it was theoretically a conservative Muslim country all the younger women seemed to have adopted the standard Balkan fashion of skimpy and two sizes too small. Every evening, the town's teenagers and twenty-somethings flooded on to the main street; the men stood around in small packs, sipping beer and smoking cigarettes, and the women paraded up and down the street, occasionally deigning to stop and flirt with the men. This was called the *xhiro,* or 'stroll,' the standard mating dance of the young Albanian. Vlore's youth seemed almost a different species from the middle-aged and old people who watched indulgently; the elders tended to be thick, lumpy, wrinkled and unattractive. I supposed Albania's forty years of hard-core, hardscrabble Communism had been tough on all its inhabitants.

Capitalism had worked its usual tawdry magic. Booze, cigarettes and Internet cafés were all cheap and addictively popular, satellite TV dishes had sprouted like mushrooms from the city's squalid apartment complexes, bright new Coke and Marlboro signs and posters were everywhere, a counterfeit Discman and a sheaf of pirated CDs cost me all of forty euros, and a row of cheap seafood restaurants lined the waterfront, occasionally patronized by gaggles of Italian tourists. The water of the Adriatic was crystal clear and warm enough to swim in. Unfortunately, the beach was filthy with flotsam, broken glass and oil slicks from the rusted hulks that loaded and unloaded at the pier. Still, it was nice to sit on a chair by the waterfront, listen to the sea lapping at the shore, and watch the scenery.

Like the rest of Albania, Vlore would have been a very pretty place if most of its buildings were razed to the ground. It was set in a glorious natural harbour, a horseshoe of steep green hills surrounding a placid salt-water lagoon. The city itself expanded from the docks and rose slowly to the east and north. Just south of the city, high rocky bluffs cascaded down from a hill two thousand feet high, a bed for the pearl of Sinisa's mansion.

I fell into a comfortable routine. Ten to twelve hours of work a day, every day. Not that I kept regular hours. Sometimes I needed a break, and fresh air, so I beat up on the bags in the boxing gym, or walked up and down the hill on which Sinisa's private enclave perched, or hitched a ride down to Vlore and wandered for half an hour, letting my subconscious pick at whatever coding problem was bothering me. Lots of smoke breaks with Arwin, occasional drinks and life-in-America lectures with Zoltan and Zorana, nightly English lessons with Saskia.

I was actually happy. I had escaped the miserable rut that had been my life for a year, and I was, at least to a first approximation, living a strange and exciting adventure. If you squinted at me the right way, I was a professional hacker on the run from lethal enemies, living in a criminal overlord's Albanian compound, helping him with his dastardly plans in exchange for the rescue of an innocent imperilled woman. For the first time in a year I felt good about myself. I felt tough, confident, debonair. I felt like the kind of man Talena might want, and even if she didn't, like the kind of man who might be able to handle that rejection. It became possible to imagine a future without her.

Of course it wasn't *really* an adventure, I told myself, because adventure meant danger, and once I grew accustomed to the routine, my life in Sinisa's compound seemed placid, safe, downright ordinary. It's amazing what you can get used to. For three weeks my Albanian existence felt like little more than a working holiday, a lucrative and entertaining pause before my return to the real world.

One day I came down to the boxing gym and found Zoltan and Sinisa in the ring, wearing gloves and headgear, doing their level best to knock one another out. Zorana watched from the ringside as Zoltan, bigger and much stronger, prowled around the ring, hunting Sinisa, who ducked and blocked and bobbed and weaved around Zoltan's punches, moving with graceful speed, his blond ponytail whipping through the air behind him, managing to avoid dozens of power punches that would surely have felled him had they landed cleanly. He even tagged Zoltan with an occasional counter-punch, not that Zoltan seemed to notice.

The bell rang. Zoltan and Sinisa embraced like brothers, then began to peel off their sparring gear. Both of them glistened with sweat. Sinisa looked over at me and raised his eyebrows. He looked much younger in shorts rather than his usual tailored suits. I realized he was only a few years older than me.

'I did not know you were a boxer,' he said, approaching.

'I'm not,' I said. 'Just started working out here.'

'He comes every day,' Zorana said approvingly.

'Good,' Sinisa said. 'Stay with it. It is the purest sport. It makes you strong. It teaches you who you are.'

I wasn't sure about the latter part, but the former was beyond dispute. Thanks to two weeks of training I could now jump rope for three rounds without gasping like an asthma victim. That wasn't much compared to the Olympic-calibre fitness of the other three people in the room, but it felt like accomplishment to me.

Sinisa looked at me closely as he unrolled his hand wraps. I looked away, slightly uncomfortable in his scrutiny.

'This afternoon, we will go for a walk, you and I,' Sinisa decided. 'I will show you something. I will show you an empire.'

The Roman Empire, to be exact. In the foothills south of the city, about midway between the town proper and Sinisa's mansion, there nestled an ancient Roman amphitheatre with room for several thousand, its terraced seats cracked and worn, two thousand years old but still the most impressive structure in Vlore. It took us about twenty minutes to walk there.

'When I first came here, all this was overgrown,' Sinisa said, leading me to the centre of the amphitheatre, the stage. He was dressed down, for once, in a grey shirt, black slacks and sports jacket, and hiking boots. 'I had it cleared. The Albanians, none of them understood why. They thought it was nothing more than old stones.'

I nodded.

'What do you think?' he asked. 'What does this say to you?'

I looked around at the haunting, silent reminder that

this forgotten backwater nation had once been an integral part of the Roman Empire, civilization's apotheosis. Only a handful of Hoxha's mushrooms indicated that we were still in the twenty-first century. I imagined the stone terraces full of thousands of theatregoers in bright togas, waiting to see a few Christians fed to the lions.

'"Ozymandias,"' I said.

'Yes,' Sinisa said, pleased. 'Every empire crumbles. Every man dies. In the end we are all forgotten. Our lives are like sparks from a fire, gone in a heartbeat. All we can do is burn as brightly as possible. Tell me something, Mr Wood. I am a rich man. I have enough money for all the rest of my life. And the list of those who would like me dead is long. Why do you think I do not retire to Amsterdam, to safety?'

I resigned myself to being the straight man in this Socratic dialogue. 'Because you think what you do is important?'

'That is part of it,' Sinisa said. 'Until the world sees sense and throws open its borders, someone must do what I do, operate the escape valve for those who need it. But more than that, it is because to me a comfortable life is no life at all. Have you ever seen war?'

'Not really,' I said, a little taken aback.

'When I came here from Holland, as a peacekeeper, I was young, troubled, without direction. I drank too much. I took drugs. Do you know when that changed? The first time I was shot at, in Srebrenica. The *intensity* of it. It changed me on the spot. Every breath, every motion, was an event, because I knew it might be my last. Most people in Holland, all the rich Western nations, they go decades without living as intensely as I did in those few seconds.

'After the war, Holland seemed a country of shadows.

Meaningless. Like living without colour. I decided then that I would not live half a life. I would not follow the laws that grey old men write because they are afraid. You have no place in this world, not truly, unless you have fought for it. A home is not a home unless you have conquered it. You have done nothing with your life unless you have built an empire from dust.' He waved at the amphitheatre. 'One day your empire will crumble back to dust. One day it will be forgotten. One day you will die. That is not important. It is the fighting and the building that matter. Your heartbeat spark of life must burn brightly, but not for its own sake, you must forge something with that fire. That is why I do what I do. Do you understand me?'

'Yes,' I said. And it was true. I wasn't a war junkie, I had no intention of building a criminal empire, but I understood in my bones what he was saying. The need to live as intensely as possible—I felt that too, though my version was much more muted than his. I got my kicks from travel rather than war. But travel for its own sake, aimless wandering and spectating, was ultimately unsatisfying. Eventually you had to do something constructive with your life. I had always assumed that it was one or the other, live intensely or be constructive. It had never occurred to me that you might combine the two. Empire-building, he called it. I had to admit the notion sounded tempting.

'Good,' Sinisa said. 'Very few of those who serve me understand me. Zoltan and Zorana, they are my friends, they are loyal until death, but they do not think like you and I do.'

'What about those other guys? My neighbours?' I asked, meaning the zombies. 'Do they understand?'

'They are not my friends,' he said. 'Business associates. And no, they do not.' He paused. 'Perhaps some of them do. But theirs was a different kind of empire.'

I looked at him, waiting for a less cryptic explanation, but it did not come.

'What was Srebrenica like?' I asked. I had wanted to ask him since I learned he had been there. The most terrible event of Bosnia's terrible civil war, and he had witnessed it.

'What was it like?' Sinisa thought the question over. 'It was difficult,' he said. 'Especially at the beginning. I understand that now it seems like it was evil Serbs against helpless Muslims, but in fact when the Serb advance began, we—the Dutch, I mean, the so-called peacekeepers—we were more worried about the Muslims. They threatened to murder us if we retreated from even a metre of their land, never mind the military realities. It was the Muslims who killed a Dutch soldier on the first day of the advance.

'From a military perspective it was hopeless. The Serbs did not have many men, but they had tanks and artillery. Our only real threat was air strikes, and once it became clear that the UN had no intention of bombing anyone, there was nothing we could do to stop them. So the Serbs advanced and the Muslims fled. Some of them fled to the UN base outside of town, but we did not allow them in. Thousands of them, desperate, weeping, old men who could barely walk, mothers carrying babies, and we watched the Serbs take them away. Oh, we made some pretence of ensuring that the trucks were going to Muslim territory, but it was only a pretence. The Muslims who gave up all hope in the UN at least had a chance. A very small chance. They had to cross eighty kilometres of fields, with Serb ambushes and patrols waiting for them at every step, but better some chance than none.

'In the end, all the men who got on those trucks, except the very old and very young, and all the men who were captured in those fields, they were taken to schools, or stadiums, or warehouses, and then in groups of fifteen or twenty they were taken outside, shot, and buried with bulldozers. Seven thousand dead.' Sinisa shrugged. 'We did not know this then. We heard rumours, we knew something terrible was happening, but we saw no actual evidence; the Serbs hid that very well. They were very efficient, very organized.

'You must understand, though, that the only exceptional thing about Srebrenica was the number of the dead. Every side did the same thing, Serbs and Croats and Muslims, throughout the war. In some ways Srebrenica was very tame. The cruelty of that war was amazing.'

I knew that already, from Talena's stories. When we had first begun dating, I started to do some reading about the Bosnian civil war, to learn more about where Talena had come from. I had soon stopped. It was too awful and depressing. I remembered pictures of thousands of emaciated, human stick-figure men penned behind barbed wire in concentration camps, descriptions of mass graves into which the remains of entire slaughtered villages had been bulldozed, nightmarish first-person stories written by women who had been taken by gunmen and tortured and gang-raped for weeks, tales of bodies that rotted on the streets of Sarajevo because no one dared to venture into the open to collect them for fear of falling victim to a sniper themselves. Organized campaigns of terror and torture and genocide, ordered and orchestrated by military and civilian commanders.

'The men and women who fought that war,' Sinisa said, 'the ones they call war criminals now, by the end they were entirely without moral limits, capable of anything, any kind of inhumanity. Not because they were inhuman. Because they had been shaped by the inhumanity around them. The UN wants to find them and put them on trial, as if the war was their fault, but the truth is it was they who were created by the war.'

He fell silent for a moment. I looked around at the amphitheatre and wondered if seven thousand men would fit in its terraces. Probably not.

'Enough,' Sinisa said. 'We have work to do, you and I.'

I followed him back to the mansion, wondering whether I admired him or thought he was crazy. Both, I decided. People talk about living their life to the fullest, but people like Sinisa who actually do it are crazy. Especially when they do it by building a criminal empire because they think getting shot at is cool. But even though his methods were questionable, and his associates were scary, what he was doing still seemed like a Good Thing. I thought of Zoltan and Zorana's unsubtle hints that maybe after I went back to America I could continue to help Sinisa's smuggling empire, courier packages, provide advice and the occasional bed for a night or two. I wondered if maybe I should. There was probably a lot I could do for Sinisa in America without ever breaking the law. My instinct was to disassociate myself from him as soon as humanly possible—*don't get involved,* again—but if I believed that what Sinisa was doing was good, shouldn't I stay involved? Shouldn't I do what I could to help him? My gut was telling me no, but I was no longer sure I trusted my gut.

'Saskia! Good news! I got you an English newspaper.' I waved the three-day-old copy of the *International Herald Tribune* proudly. 'Sinisa brought it back from Tirana.'

'Oh, good!' Saskia exclaimed. 'Excellent! Wonderful! Fantastic! Super!'

Both of us laughed at her imitation of a thesaurus. In only three weeks, Saskia's English had gone from infantile to conversational, a pretty amazing accomplishment. She had exhausted the thick ESL book Talena had bought her, and now she wanted new material, like the *Herald Trib*.

Saskia scanned the paper eagerly before folding it and putting it away. She looked very different since she had gotten her hair cut boy-short, even smaller, but somehow also stronger, wiry. I supposed cutting her hair was a symbolic way of severing ties with the past, kind of Samson in reverse.

'I will read this tomorrow,' she said. 'How was your work today?' A shadow of worry crept into her expression. 'You will finish in time?'

'I will finish in time,' I assured her. My coding skills, like her English, had returned with a vengeance, and I worked more efficiently with every passing day. 'What did you do today?'

'I went out. Zorana gave me a ride to the city. I wanted to go out again. I asked the woman across the street, but she said no. Her car was empty, but she said no, and she looked at me like . . . I do not know. I do not like her at all.'

I made a sympathetic noise. It wasn't the first time one of the zombies had given her the cold shoulder. Once we had gone for a walk at night, and the couple across the street had been sitting outside smoking. We had waved and Saskia had called out hello. They had scowled at us, stubbed out their cigarettes, pointedly turned their backs and gone into their house.

'I very much want to leave this place,' Saskia said. 'It is good of Sinisa to give us a home, but I want to leave and go to America. It is not, I am not frightened of, of him.' Her reluctance to speak Dragan's name said otherwise, but I pretended not to notice. 'If he had gone . . . no. If he was going to come and find me, he would come before now.'

'He would *have* come,' I corrected. 'I think you're right.'

'I just want to depart this place,' she said. 'There is nothing I can do, all day.'

'You're bored,' I said.

'Yes. I am bored. I am so very bored here. It is better being bored than being frightened, but it is best to be not bored and not frightened. To be neither. To be neither in America, that is what I want.'

'We're supposed to leave in ten days,' I said.

'Ten days. Paul, I am so excited! Today, in a store, I saw a . . . a plan.'

'A what?'

'A plan. Of America. Like you would make a plan of this room, or of Vlore.' She pretended to draw on a piece of paper. Yet another round of our endless and usually amusing game of Learning English Charades.

'A map,' I said.

'Of course! My vocabulary, that is the hardest thing; there are so many words. I saw a map, and I saw San Francisco in the map, and I thought, I am going to live there! In a place with buildings a hundred storeys high and that famous golden bridge and so many wonderful things! I have decided it will be like being born. When I enter America, it will be like being born from a new mother, it will be a new life, my old life will be dead.'

I considered telling her the sorry news that the Golden Gate Bridge was actually orange, and San Francisco didn't have any hundred-storey skyscrapers, but it wasn't the time for harsh reality, and besides, the Bay Area was full of enough genuine marvels and beautiful sights that she wasn't likely to be disappointed. 'You're going to love it there,' I told her. 'Everyone does.'

She smiled wistfully. After a moment she said, 'It would be nice, it would be so good if I really could be born again. I—what?'

'Nothing. Born again has a specific meaning in America. Doesn't matter. Go on.'

'If I could really be born again, then I could forget,' she said. 'It would be so easy if I could forget.'

'You'll put all that behind you,' I said, uneasily. Reassurance was not my strong suit, especially when I didn't really believe what I was saying.

'I do not know. It will be hard. I have . . . ' She hesitated. Another unknown word. 'When I am cut, and the skin grows back, there is a mark.'

'A scar,' I said.

'A scar. I have scars. On my body, my feet, but I mean here.' She raised her hands up and rubbed her temples with her fingers. 'I can feel them. When I think about certain things. I was trying to make myself think about being with other men. I mean to say, not like with you, as friends, but . . . being with a man. It was, I do not know what to say. I wanted not to think about it at all, not even to imagine it, it was frightening. I was so frightened, thinking of another man touching me, and it feeling like . . . I am sorry, Paul. I do not know how to say. I think even if I spoke English like you or Talena I still would not know how to say. It is like there are parts of me here'—she rubbed her temples again, fiercely—'that are like land-mines.'

I couldn't think of anything I could possibly say to that. I wanted to reach out and hug her, but I knew better. I had touched Saskia a couple of times, accidentally, and both times she had gasped and flinched away.

'I am sorry, Paul. I am very sorry.' She shook her head and forced a smile. 'I will talk happy talk. Maybe I can at least pretend to forget. I will think of good things. I will read books. So many books. I will make new friends. I will buy a bicycle. I will swim in the ocean.'

Not in San Francisco, not without a wet suit, I didn't say. She would have to find that out some time but this was the wrong time for discouraging news.

'I want to help people,' she said. 'When we get to America. If we get to America.'

'When,' I said.

She frowned. 'I am not a child, Paul. I know it is a long way. I know it is if.'

'Okay. Sorry. All right. If we get to America. Who do you want to help?'

'I do not yet know. But there are so many people who need help. Everywhere. I am sure even in America. Not just women like me with bad husbands. People who are sick, or lost, or, I do not know. But I know I want to help people. Like you and Talena have helped me. I owe you everything, Paul.'

'Saskia . . . '

'I know. You do not want me to say thank you. I understand. I know you do not like it when I talk like this, it makes you very uncomfortable.'

'No, no, Saskia, you can say anything you want to me, uh, I don't want you to feel—'

'Paul, you are a bad liar.'

I fell silent. It was true.

She smiled unexpectedly. 'Very bad. Awful. Terrible. Despicable. Appalling. Horrible.'

'All right,' I said, waving my hands mock-defensively. 'All right, I give in.'

'Come,' she said, standing. 'They listen to you. Make Arwin drive us to get ice cream.' I wasn't allowed to drive any of Sinisa's vehicles. 'We only have ten days and I hear American ice cream is loathsome and contemptible.'

'So this is the final game for the Italian league?' I asked.

'No, no, no,' Zoltan said, scandalized. 'This is Champions League.'

'That's not an Italian thing?'

'No. Is league for all best teams in Europe.' We had already had three beers apiece, except Sinisa who drank only water, and Zoltan's English was degrading.

'But both these teams are Italian, right?'

'They were lucky,' Sinisa said. 'Ajax should be playing tonight.'

'Ajax?' Zoltan snorted. 'Ajax very lucky to win Arsenal. Partisan Belgrade should be play tonight, but Champions League is cheat, cheat against poor countries, especially Serbia.'

It was nice to see that sports conspiracy theories were everywhere the same. I wasn't really that ignorant of European football, my many friends in London had seen to that, but it was fun playing the Stupid American. We sat in a bar on Vlore's waterfront festooned with satellite TVs. Sinisa had taken over the whole place. He, Zoltan, Zorana, Arwin and I sat at the best table. The zombies were clustered at three neighbouring tables, drinking heavily and maintaining their usual sour frowns and silence. Saskia had declined to come. I suspected the thought of so many people had spooked her.

'Everywhere in the world, football is very popular,' Zoltan announced. 'Everywhere but our new home in America. Because Americans are too stupid for football.'

'Oh, no, not at all,' I said politely. 'Everyone in Canada and America plays soccer. Until we're twelve. That's when we move on to sports for grown-ups.'

Zoltan stared at me. 'Grown-ups?'

Zorana translated. Zoltan frowned at me angrily and turned back to the game. I decided to turn down my snideness level. Zoltan seemed like a mean and confrontational drunk.

'Give me hockey any day,' Arwin said to me.

'Damn straight,' I agreed. We clinked our glasses together.

'Hockey?' Sinisa asked, pretending confusion. 'You mean the sport played on grass with little sticks? By women?'

'Ice hockey, you Dutch ditzdork,' Arwin said.

I blinked. Sometimes Arwin seemed to have not so much absorbed American slang as irradiated it and used the freakishly mutated results.

'Oh, yes. With skates. In Holland everyone skates until they are twelve.'

'Fastest, toughest game in the world,' I said. 'This game, you wink at one of the other players and they fall over. Some of them oughta get Oscars. When hockey players take dives the commentators say that they're acting like European soccer players.'

'Italians, yes, always they cheat. Always is how they play,' Zoltan agreed.

'It's how they do business too,' Sinisa said darkly.

We groused about Italians for a little while. When various ethnicities gather together it is always good to find a shared target without a representative present. The game went into sudden-death overtime, confusingly called 'golden goal extra time,' and was finally resolved by a penalty shootout. The somewhat slurred post-game consensus was that shootouts were a horribly unfair way to settle things.

'After extra time, more extra time,' Zoltan proposed. 'But only five players each side. Much better than shootout.'

'You must be happy, eh?' I asked Arwin. 'That Russian guy Shevchenko won it all.'

'Ukrainian,' Arwin corrected. 'They hate us down there.'

Zoltan launched into a speech in Serbian.

'Yo, Zoltan, English. Be civilized,' Arwin suggested.

Zoltan looked at Arwin, obviously amazed at the temerity of this little weaselly long-haired runt of a man.

'How you say in English,' Zoltan rumbled. 'Fuck you?'

Arwin didn't quail away like I expected. 'Fuck you very much back atcha,' he retorted. 'You want to sit at the grown-ups' table, you speak English so I can understand.'

Both of them, I realized, were go-out-and-pick-a-fight drunks. Zoltan clenched his beer stein and for a moment I thought he might use it as a club. Zorana put her hand on his shoulder and he cooled a little and took another swig instead, before muttering something in Serbian that I figured was probably an aspersion on Arwin's ancestry. Whatever it was it made Sinisa chuckle.

'You still haven't told me how we're getting to America,' I said to Sinisa, changing the subject.

'No,' he said absently. 'Come. You and Arwin. I want to stop by the pier before we go back. You can come and watch.'

'The pier? What's there?'

'Business. Unless you are not curious.'

Business. That meant there was a shipment of refugees going out to Italy tonight. Probably the same thing I would be doing soon enough.

'Oh no,' I said. 'I'm curious all right.'

Vlore's main street, the name of which I never learned due to the absence of any street signs in the city, ran straight up to the waterfront, through a chain-link fence, and through a little cluster of forklifts, small warehouses and cheap little administrative buildings, before continuing into the Adriatic, morphing from road into pier. The waterfront was guarded by two policemen with Dobermans and Kalashnikovs. They hustled to open the gate for Sinisa and treated him with reverential deference. I got the impression he didn't come down here for personal inspections very often.

The pier was as wide as the road and several hundred yards long. The lights from the dockside areas dwindled into darkness after a few dozen yards, but halfway along its length, to the left, a pool of dim light fell from the peak of the single moored fishing boat. Three rusty but functional loading cranes towered over us like gargantuan praying mantises. A tiny sliver of moon hung high in the sky. The sea lapped at the pilings of the pier and the wooden planks creaked beneath our feet. The air was salty and refreshingly cool.

The boat smelled of fish and unwashed humanity. It was smallish, maybe forty feet long. Two vanes descended in an inverted V from its peak, presumably used to hold the ends of a net. About sixty people huddled on its deck, most of them sitting, a few standing restlessly near the edges. A slight majority were Indian or Middle Eastern, single men, a few couples, two families. The youngest was a girl maybe ten years old. There were several black men, two of them dressed in geometrically patterned African robes which I knew meant they had come from south of the Sahara, and about fifteen white men. A half-dozen gauntly pretty white women stuck close together, like the ones I had seen in the factory near Sarajevo. Even in the dim forgiving light all of them looked filthy, beaten down, exhausted, their clothes tattered and crusted in dirt. Many of them clutched their pitifully small bags of possessions to their chests as they might a life-raft in a whirlpool.

They watched us, some with curiosity, some with trepidation, most with dull fatalism. They hardly spoke to each other. All were nervously waiting for their journey to begin and most of all for it to be over. Most of them had spent their life's savings to come to the West. Some of them had already spent months on a gruelling and perilous journey just to get this far. Tonight was the moment of truth. I wondered what their stories were. Some of them were no doubt fleeing torture and violence, but most of them, I suspected, were driven more by opportunity than oppression, and probably several of them were criminals on the run.

'Too bad they're going already,' Arwin murmured. 'I bet I could go up to those women and tell them I work for Sinisa and they'd line up on their knees to make me happy. Some of those lips could suck watermelons through garden hoses.'

I wondered what would happen to the people on the boat. They were going through a desperate struggle for just a taste of what I had been born with, travelling halfway around the world the hard way to be part of the poor, invisible underclass of the rich Western world I took for granted. Most of them were hard-working, motivated, smart, good planners, dedicated, just the kind of immigrant you want, or they wouldn't be here. Even if they weren't running for their lives, I couldn't help but think, watching them squat miserably in that stinking fishing boat, that they deserved to succeed.

Sinisa talked a little while with the crew of the boat, easily distinguishable from the passengers by their clean clothes and confident body language, who stood stiffly to attention while talking to their boss. Arwin and I hung a little way back near one of the cranes that towered unused over the smuggling vessel. I wondered if after unloading their passengers in Italy they would actually do some fishing before returning to Vlore.

There was a ticking sound at my feet and something seemed to jump up from the pier. I looked down, surprised, and instinctively crouched to investigate. It looked like something had harrowed a fresh gouge in the wooden pier below me. The pale jagged gorge of revealed wood looked so different from the tarred weather-beaten exterior that it seemed to be an entirely different substance, like flesh under skin. I heard a faint popping sound in the distance as I tried to work out what had happened to the pier. I actually thought of a meteorite.

Then there was an ear-splitting *clang!* of metal on metal above me. Something had struck the crane. I stood up, still driven purely by reflex wow-that-was-weird curiosity, and inspected the worm-shaped patch of newly shiny, indented metal, easily apparent against the yellow paint and rust that was the rest of the crane. I still didn't understand what was happening and when Arwin tackled me I barely got my hands up in time to break my fall. I heard another dim popping noise.

'What the hell?' I demanded, outraged. Splinters dug painfully into my palms.

I tried to get up to my feet and he pulled me back down, hard, shouting at me in Russian before realizing and switching to English, 'Someone's shooting at us, you fucking idiot! Stay the fuck down!'

I stayed down. The base of the crane was a solid metal platform about three feet high and I hugged the pier behind it as adrenaline and understanding finally began to course into me. Someone was shooting at us. A bullet had struck the pier, and then the crane, both of them missing me by only a couple of feet.

There were more popping noises and ticking sounds, and one splash. Then loud barking noises that I recognized as gunshots from the dockside area where pier met land.

A dissonant chorus of whimpering fear-noises rose from the ship. Arwin wiggled away from me and turned to peer around the corner of the crane, still prone. After a moment I did the same. If the gunmen were at the end of the pier there would be no way out other than jumping into the sea. I doubted all the refugees on the boat could swim.

'There,' Arwin said. We were facing back towards the land, and he was pointing at a big building on the waterfront just to the right of the chain-link fence that delimited the docks area. 'That building there.'

'It's a hotel,' I said. I had noticed it before, veteran traveller's reflex, instinctively filed it away as a possible place to stay in the extremely unlikely eventuality of a return to Vlore. 'Is that where they are?'

'I think so. I saw a flash up top—there!'

I saw it too, a brief white flicker, followed immediately by another *clang!* from the crane. Then the hollow pop of the gunshot, dawdling at the speed of sound and arriving a couple of seconds after the bullet. There followed a fusillade of a half-dozen shots from where the pier met the land.

'What about there?' I asked, pointing to the end of the pier.

'Those are our guys. Security. Shooting back.'

Another flash of light from the hotel. This one prompted a shocked cry of pain from the fishing boat. Someone had been hit. More shots came from the dockside. There was movement to my left and I twitched violently with panic but it was only Sinisa, elbow-crawling next to us, a small pistol in his hand. I hadn't realized he went around armed. He wore a disturbing grin, like he was actually enjoying this.

'I am so terribly insulted,' he said. 'How dare they not shoot at me?'

I decided he had gone crazy.

'If they are serious, they will come through the fence now,' Sinisa said. 'If they do, go into the water and swim north. Do not go towards the beach. Swim to the north end of the bay. Do not go back into Vlore. Go to the highway and get a *furgon* to Tirana. Leave a message at the English-language bookstore in Skandenberg Square.'

'Skandenberg Square,' I said, trying to burn his instructions into my memory.

'I should have told you these procedures before. But I did not think, nobody thought there would be a problem.'

'You think it's Mladen?' Arwin asked.

'No. Mladen would have shot at me first, not our Canadian friend.'

I stared at him, appalled. 'They were shooting at *me*?'

'That or they hired a blind sniper.'

'Your buddy from Bosnia,' Arwin said. 'Dragan.'

There were two more shots from the dockside, and men shouted at one another. I tensed up, waiting for a bulldozer or something to crash through the dimly visible chain-link fence. The low bleating from the ship rose into a horrific coruscating howl of pain.

'Shot in the stomach,' Sinisa said. 'The shock has worn off.'

We lay there for I don't know how long—your sense of time is massively dilated in a situation like that—but it felt like forever. Probably three or four minutes. The pier was cool and damp against my skin. My hands burned with the half-dozen splinters that had thrust into them when Arwin had tackled me to the ground. I was sweating like this was a boxing workout. The screams of the person who had been shot, I couldn't tell if it was a man or a woman, faded into gurgling coughing whimpers. My mind felt weirdly dissociated from my body. I felt half convinced that I was in some controlled environment, some Disney ride, Smugglers of the Adriatic, all the people around me were just animatrons and if I really needed to I could go through the emergency exit at any time. I wasn't really pressing myself against this damp pier jutting from a rotting Albanian city, fifty feet from a boat full of Third World refugees, one of them groaning from a gunshot wound, tensely waiting for a crowd of killers to swarm through the fence and come charging at us.

Headlights appeared outside the fence. I swallowed and measured the distance to the edge of the pier, tried to guess how far down the water was. Twenty or thirty feet. At least jumping into the ocean would clear my fear-fuzzed head.

The men inside the fence ran to the gate, opened it, and allowed a half-dozen figures with AK-47s inside. I recognized Zoltan and Zorana among them. Our people. We were safe.

'What an interesting development,' Sinisa said. He pressed his hands into the pier and vaulted upright like a yoga master. After a moment I climbed awkwardly to my feet and Arwin followed.

I looked over at the boat. The man who had been shot, Afghani if I guessed his ethnicity correctly, had been standing right at the edge of the crowd. Now he lay sprawled on deck, one foot hanging over the side of the boat, clutching his hands on his belly, lying in a pool of his own blood. He shuddered violently. Every breath was a battle and he seemed to have lost the strength to cry out. The rest of the passengers had moved away, cleared a semicircle of open deck around him as if he were contagious.

The ship's crew approached Sinisa. He directed a few curt words at them and they nodded and rushed back to the ship. One of them began to unwind the thick mooring rope.

'What's going on?' I asked. 'What are you doing?'

'They are leaving.'

'What about him?' I pointed at the wounded man.

Sinisa calmly aimed his gun at the fallen man and shot him in the head.

I jumped as if shocked with ten thousand volts, and gaped at Sinisa as he re-safetied his gun and tucked it into the back of his belt. Then I looked over to the boat and the dead man sprawled on its deck. The other refugees stared at Sinisa in frozen, terrified silence. My mind kept replaying the sledgehammer sound of the gunshot. I couldn't believe I had just seen him kill a man as casually as I might flick off a light switch.

'He was beyond saving,' Sinisa said. 'They will bury him at sea. Come. We have much to do.'

13 Back Doors

'You have brought a very large amount of trouble with you, Paul Wood,' Sinisa said.

I shrugged uneasily. 'Are you sure it's Dragan?'

'No. But I know the Mostar Tigers left Mostar a week ago, and have not been seen in Sarajevo.'

I said, 'I thought you would know if Dragan left Bosnia.'

'The fact I did not know tells us they were assisted.'

'Assisted?' I didn't like the sound of that. 'By who?'

'I do not know. It is the nature of my business that I have many enemies. I think one of my enemies helped the Tigers into the country, shelters them, uses them to attack me indirectly.'

'Right. So what's the bad news?'

He didn't get the joke and looked at me quizzically.

'Never mind. What's the plan?'

'You do not leave my compound, you or Saskia,' Sinisa said. 'Here there is no danger. They will not dare a frontal assault. I hope they do, but they will not. We are vulnerable only to ambush or a sniper, and if you remain in my compound neither can occur. You will be safe, I assure you.'

'That's a relief. For a moment there I was worried.'

Sarcasm was wasted on Sinisa, it just didn't compute. 'I am glad you are relieved. Furthermore, I am advancing our schedule. We leave for America in five days, not eight. Your system will be complete by then.' It wasn't a question.

'If we're so safe, why are you advancing our schedule?'

'That is an independent development,' he said smoothly.

Sure it was. 'If you say so. Anything else I should know?'

'Yes,' Sinisa said. 'There is one thing I want you to remember, Paul. When you are in America, safe in America, I want you to remember the risk I am taking for you. One day I may ask you to take risks for me.'

I was not in a good position to argue. 'I will remember,' I promised.

'Good. Go to work. Five days.'

From: balthazarwood@yahoo.com
To: talenar@lonelyplanet.com
Subject: Re: the albanian times
Date: 29 Apr 2003 01:50 GMT

Big trouble in little Albania. I got shot at
tonight. I'm okay. Everyone's okay except
some refugee who got hit by a stray bullet.
He didn't make it. I don't even know where
he came from.

S thinks D is in town and he's teamed up
with one of S's business enemies.

I wasn't going to tell you any of this, but
I guess you want to know, even though I know
it's going to stress you out and there isn't
anything you can do. Plus I figure you'd rip
my head off if I didn't tell you and you found
out later.

I'm not all that worried. We're going sooner,
now, and as long as we stay in S's compound,
we'll be fine. Don't go crazy worrying too
much about us, all right? We'll be okay.

Love,

Paul

When I left Sinisa's mansion that night, around midnight, I paused outside the gate and took a good look at the street on which I lived. I was seeing everything with new eyes that night: Sinisa's deck, the room in which I worked, the windows of our house. Believe me, you start viewing your surroundings in an entirely new manner when an invasion by armed men who badly want to kill you becomes a plausible near-future event.

The air outside was refreshingly cool, and I wondered if the heatwave was finally fading. Two dim lights mounted above the iron gates of Sinisa's mansion provided eerie, dreamlike illumination. I looked up and down the street and again wondered why it existed, why Sinisa had built a dozen houses for the zombies, how long the zombies had lived here, why they had come all the way from Serbia to live in Sinisa's compound. It must have cost a fortune. Sure, labour was cheap and the houses were slapped-together crap, but Sinisa still had to have paid for electricity, running water, septic tanks: all this for a couple of dozen middle-aged Serbians who spent their days doing fuck-all.

With the gate to my back, ours was the fourth house to the right. To the left, past the houses on that side, the ground fell steeply towards Vlore. To the right it sloped gently upwards into untamed land thick with bushes and clumps of trees. For the first time I understood the terrible appeal of land-mines. At that moment I would have liked nothing more than the knowledge that the land around Sinisa's compound was sown with lethal and undetectable explosives. But it wasn't, or he would have warned us when we first arrived.

I wasn't tired. I wanted to go for a walk, but of course I

had just been told not to leave the compound for any reason whatsoever. I wanted a cigarette, but Arwin was already asleep. I walked to our house, intending to try to sleep, but at the last second I changed my mind and went around the house, walked through our back yard of thigh-high weeds and into the forest.

I was violating Sinisa's direct order, and technically endangering myself, but that didn't really concern me. If the Tigers were waiting in the forest right behind our house then Saskia and I were pretty screwed anyhow. Leaves and branches clawed at my face and I pushed them aside. Once I was past the first screen of trees the forest was very dark. I began to wonder what the hell I was doing and why I hadn't stopped in my room to pick up my Maglite.

Then I stepped on something hard. I knelt and felt around, ran my hands over a cracked dome of concrete. Of course. A bunker, one of Hoxha's omnipresent mushrooms. Good enough, I decided. What I wanted was a quiet contemplative place to sit and think. This would do. I sat down at the apex of the bunker's six-foot-diameter dome, and I began to ponder.

I couldn't shake the image of Sinisa's callous execution of the Afghani man on the boat. Maybe he had been dying, but we could have taken him to the hospital or called a doctor, we could at least have tried to save him. The idea had not even crossed Sinisa's mind. So much for Robin Hood.

I shouldn't have been surprised. The man had a private army, he invited snipers to his business meetings, his closest assistants were Zoltan and Zorana, not exactly Central Casting's answer to Friar Tuck and Maid Marian. And yet I had somehow let him convince me with a few honeyed words that he was on the side of the angels. They call it the Stockholm Syndrome, when hostages begin to support and identify with the hostage-takers. When someone controls your life and the hour of your death, you desperately want to believe that they are good and noble. And Saskia and I had fallen completely into Sinisa's power the moment we crossed the border into Albania.

Sinisa didn't want to be Robin Hood. He had told me so himself. He wanted to be a CEO like Jeff Bezos or Gordon Moore. Maybe Pablo Escobar was a better analogy, cocaine emperor of the eighties, multibillionaire smuggler, at one point the eleventh wealthiest man in the world. Escobar had been assassinated, hunted down by American soldiers using advanced electronic surveillance techniques. I suspected Sinisa knew all about the killing of Pablo Escobar. I suspected his investment in Mycroft had something to do with that history lesson.

Illegal immigration wasn't exactly cocaine smuggling, but it was big business. I had read a lot about it in the last few weeks. At least ten billion dollars a year, estimated the *Economist,* spent in every corner of the globe. Mexican 'coyotes,' who escort hundreds of thousands of the undocumented over the US border every year, some of whom begin their journeys in Bolivia or Paraguay. Chinese 'snakeheads,' who fill shipping containers with people and send them from Shanghai to Long Beach, or buy old freighters, pack them to the gills with people, and sail them across the Pacific. Balkan gangs like Sinisa's who conduct their clients-slash-victims—Sri Lankan, Indian, Pakistani, Iranian, Kurdish, Arabian, Turkish, name your nationality—into Western Europe. Moroccans who cross the Straits of Gibraltar in rowboats overcrowded with Africans who might have come all the way from the Congo. Other Africans go south, hitch or jump trains or just walk, sometimes thousands of miles, all the way from their homes to Johannesburg or Cape Town. Haitians and Cubans take insane risks to come to Florida on rafts made of inner tubes. Indonesians come to Australia on stolen ships sold to them by the pirates who still ply the Straits of Malacca.

Like all crime, all smuggling, it was most rampant, most blatant, in failed or crippled states like Bosnia or Albania, places where corruption is so pervasive it almost isn't corruption any more, where money paid to government officials is not seen by either side of the transaction as a shameful bribe, but simply as a fee for services rendered, capitalism at its purest. I wondered how much of Sinisa's four million dollars a year went to various levels of the Albanian government in exchange for protection, for permission to build his own private enclave, for the blind eye turned as Sinisa openly ran his smuggling business out of the waterfront of one of the country's major ports. Albania had signed and ratified several international agreements binding it against the trade in human beings, but what did paper matter when Albania was so poor, and the Italian coast was only thirty miles away, and so many people would pay so much money to be conveyed to the legendary uttermost West?

I wondered what I would have done if I had grown up in Bangladesh or Afghanistan. I suspected I would have pestered the smugglers there from age twelve until they agreed to send me to London just to shut me up. Home had never meant much to me, had never been the necessary anchor it seemed to be for others. For years I had wanted only to wander, had dismissed the nesting instinct as an impulse of the weak and unadventurous. Now I was not so sure. I was twenty-nine years old. Did I really want to roam forever, dancing across the world like a water-spider on a stagnant pond, never making any impression?

I was a proud Canadian, but my ties to Canada were loose and distant. I had lived in San Francisco for five years, but it had never really felt like my home. Moving in with Talena had made me feel even more dissociated and detached. I was always acutely aware that it was her apartment, never ours.

Did I even want a home? What did 'home' mean? A mailing address, I supposed. That was a start. A place to lay your head. Mark Twain's definition: the place that, when you go there, they *have* to take you in. The place where your friends live. Whatever that means. My friends were scattered around the globe. Most of the people I was closest to, Hallam and Nicole and Steve and Lawrence, lived in London, where I couldn't reside without fighting my way through parsecs of red tape and visa paperwork.

My family, never close, had fragmented. Talena was family, sort of, except I was still on the brink of being dumped. That weird relationship paradox: is your girlfriend more like family, or your friends? You're far closer, much more intimate, with your girlfriend—but at the same time you both know, although you never speak of it, that this intimacy is probably temporary, that one day the relationship will be over.

In our first flush of falling in love we had called each other soul mates. But even before those chemicals wore off, our relationship, like about ninety-nine per cent of the world's human relationships (and those last one per cent generally involve the mentally damaged) was, if you looked at it from a certain perspective, about as romantic as a business partnership. Because the hard Darwinist truth is this: you only fall in love with people deemed worthy of your love.

When Talena and I had met, I had been heroic, adventurous, rich, free, someone she was proud to call her boyfriend. Sure, it helped that we liked each other so much, but that was what mathematicians call 'necessary but not sufficient.' After I had lost my attractive traits, I was no longer worthy of her. As simple as that, inevitable, mathematically inescapable. There was no reason to be angry or bitter if Talena broke up with me. The only surprising thing was that she hadn't dumped me months ago.

Maybe I wasn't meant to have a home. Maybe, if and when I got out of this Albanian mess, if and when Talena dumped me, I should go back on the road. Volunteer in Africa for a year, or use Sinisa's money to spend six months travelling overland from Panama to Tierra del Fuego. It didn't feel like a healthy idea. But what else was there for me to do?

'From the twilight's last gleaming,' Saskia sang from the bathtub, and paused. 'Paul,' she called out, 'what is a gleaming?'

I looked up from my cup of Nescafé. 'Like a little flash of light,' I said. 'But dimmer than a flash.'

'I see. Thank you.'

She went back to her idiosyncratic version of 'The Star-Spangled Banner.' I had taught it to her only yesterday and her melody was inventive. I considered draining the rest of my coffee and escaping to work. I wasn't looking forward to telling Saskia that her husband and his band of not-so-merry men were in town and heavily armed. But it had to be done.

'Over the land of the free,' Saskia sang, getting the melody right for this part, 'and the home of the brave.' I heard water splash and then begin to drain from the tub. After a few minutes she emerged from the bath, wearing a towel. When we had first moved into the house she had brought a change of clothes into the bathroom and dressed before exiting, but we were now so accustomed to each other's presence that she had stopped bothering.

She had lost weight since coming to Albania; she looked even smaller than before. I wondered how tall she was exactly, and how much she weighed. Five feet one, maybe, a full foot shorter than me, and certainly less than a hundred pounds. With her pale skin still gleamingly damp from the bath, she looked like a not-quite-life-sized doll.

'Lazy man,' she mock-scolded me when she returned from her room, dressed in a denim skirt and a white shirt, and found me still in the kitchen. 'Should you not go to work?'

'We need to talk,' I said.

She cocked her head at me, sensing from my tone that the topic was something more serious than the quality of the coffee she made, a running joke between us. She sat down opposite me. I looked across the cheap folding table at her and tried to find the right words. There didn't seem to be any, so I was blunt.

'We're pretty sure Dragan is here,' I said. 'And the Tigers. One of Sinisa's enemies is helping him. Somebody came after us on the pier in Vlore last night. They killed a man. One of Sinisa's refugees. They were shooting at me.'

She stared at me disbelievingly.

'Sinisa says we'll be fine,' I hurried to add. 'We'll be safe here. But you and I are not supposed to leave this neighbourhood any more, for any reason.'

For a while she didn't react. I started to wonder if she was in shock.

Then, to my considerable surprise, she said, 'I would like a gun.'

I mentally replayed the words I had just heard to ensure I had understood them correctly. 'A gun,' I said. 'I . . . a gun? Uh, jeez, I don't know. I can ask, but I don't know if Sinisa's going to want to give us any guns—'

'Sinisa took guns from us already,' she said. 'He should give them back.'

'I guess, but—'

'I know how to use them. I have killed men before. Did you know that?' Her voice was sharp, hard, angry. It was so unlike the voice of the timid, diffident Saskia I had come to know that if she had suddenly rotated her head three hundred and sixty degrees, *Exorcist*-style, I wouldn't have been entirely surprised.

'Uh, yes,' I said. 'Talena said.'

'Give me a gun, and if I see my husband I will kill him myself.'

'Well, good, that's a good attitude, I guess, and I'll ask Sinisa, but like I said—'

'He will never expect it. He thinks I am a frightened little bird. He thinks he has trained me. He thinks he has broken me, like I am a dog or a horse. He thinks all he has to do is show himself and then I will do whatever he says. I hope he does. I am glad he has come. I hope he comes to me and tries to tell me what I must do. He is the dog.' She finished with a few short sentences in Croatian. I was confident they weren't polite.

'You're angry,' I said.

'Angry? I am enraged. I am furious.'

'Good. Good. I'm glad. But don't get crazy, okay? It's good that you're angry, but I don't want you taking a gun and trying to go find Dragan yourself. It's fine if we just get out of here and leave him behind. You don't have to track him down and kill him, understand?'

'He should die a thousand times.'

'I don't doubt it. But the important thing here is your living, not his dying, okay?'

She thought about that for some time before grudgingly saying, 'Okay.'

We looked at each other.

'Wow,' I said. 'I thought you'd burst into tears and run into your room or something.'

For a moment I was afraid I shouldn't have said that. But it made her smile, one of her rare thousand-watt super-model smiles that surely brightened the mood of everyone within a five-mile radius.

'I was not always the woman you found in Mostar,' Saskia said. 'I am beginning to remember that. I am beginning to remember.'

From: talenar@lonelyplanet.com
To: balthazarwood@yahoo.com
Subject: Re: the albanian times

Date: 30 Apr 2003 13:22 GMT

Get out of there. Never mind Sinisa. Just
get the hell on to a boat and go to Italy.
I'll come meet you there and we'll work
things out. Seriously. Please. The email
you just sent sounded way too much like the
kind of email someone sends before they're
never heard from again.

If you can't, then just, I don't know, please
just stay alive. Write me every morning and
every night just to let me know you're okay.
Afternoons would be nice too.

Shit. I should be on the next flight out. Or
your friends, Hallam and Steven and Lawrence.
I'll get in touch with them. What can we do?
There has to be something.

Talena

PS You're right, I would have killed you
if you hadn't told me. PPS Give my love to
Saskia, and keep some for yourself.

From: balthazarwood@yahoo.com
To: talenar@lonelyplanet.com
Subject: Re: the albanian times
Date: 30 Apr 2003 23:09 GMT

Don't freak out overmuch here. Really, it's
much less bad than it sounds. I'd rather
have Sinisa protecting me than NATO.

We couldn't go even if we wanted to. And
we're safer here than trying to go on our
own. I'm sure of that. And I'm sorry, but
there's nothing you or Hallam or anyone
can do at this stage. Just hang in there.
It's just four more days. We'll be fine. I
promise.

Love,

Paul

Those last five days, when we were confined to Sinisa's
compound, I exorcised my daily bouts of restlessness by
roaming the nearby wilderness rather than the streets of
Vlore. The forest south-east of our back yard was replete
with interlacing trails, presumably laid by animals and three
thousand years of wandering Albanians.

On the second day, I went deep into the woods, listening to Linkin Park's *Hybrid Theory* on endless repeat as I
walked. The forest overlapped occasional east–west ridges
of stone that protruded ten feet from the ground like colossal ribs. The trail led up and over two of those ridges, then
turned eastwards and paralleled a third. After a few hundred
feet it bent around a shallow gulch, thick with fallen foli-
age, next to the ridge. Some kind of natural sewer, carved
by rainwater, now a place where storm debris collected.

I would have walked right past it if my presence hadn't caused an animal to scuttle out of the gulch, across the path maybe ten feet in front of me, and away into the forest.

It moved so fast I caught only a glimpse: lean, furry, maybe three feet long, somehow carnivorous in appearance. I couldn't tell if it was a fox or a bobcat or some strange-to-me native Balkan animal. I looked into the gulch, and I saw something pale, something out of place. I walked to the edge of the path and squinted. A bone. What I saw protruding from that loose scree of leaves and branches was the knobbed end of a large bone.

I advanced into the gulch, curious about what kind of animal had died here. The bottom of the gulch was uneven muddy gravel and dirt, and I had to be careful with my footing. Twigs snapped and leaves crackled as I walked through the fallen branches and undergrowth, shin-high and deepening, slippery and spongy. I stepped on something harder than a branch, something smoothly convex, and I stepped back and looked down. Whatever it was, it was pale and white, and still mostly concealed. Without thinking I reached down to pick it up.

It was a human skull.

I stood frozen for several long seconds, cupping the skull upside-down in my hand like a soccer ball, staring at its inverted leer. I was surprised, but not appalled. My pulse immediately began to pound, adrenaline flooded my system, but my mind stayed coolly detached, observing with interest my own primal involuntary reaction to the presence of human remains. I told myself that the skull was no threat, it meant nothing to me. It felt clinically clean to the touch, smooth and dry and slightly dusty in my hand. I figured it was years old, maybe decades, some victim of an internecine Albanian squabble.

The loud guitars screaming in my ears were suddenly oppressive. I fumbled for the Discman on my belt and switched it off with my free hand. The fingers of my other hand brushed a discontinuity. I rotated my hand and saw a small and neatly circular hole in the back of the skull.

After a moment I put the skull down and began rummaging through the underbrush, propelled by morbid curiosity. I wanted to unearth the rest of the skeleton, or clothes, jewellery, something that might hint at the victim's identity, why he or she had been murdered with a single bullet to the back of the brain. There was nothing around the skull. I returned to the bone that had first captured my attention and tried to pull it free from the brush. It shifted but wouldn't give. I braced my legs and pulled as hard as I could.

And most of a not fully decomposed human skeleton rattled out of the brush. Ragged leathery patches of dried skin still hung off its skull and ribcage. Sparse clumps of long desiccated hair dangled from its head. I held it by a shin bone.

Gagging, I released the carcass and leaped back, tripped and fell backwards but kept scrambling away, crablike, heedless of the branches scraping my palms, until I was a good ten feet away. The revulsion was almost overpowering. When I scrambled to my feet, my instincts screamed: *run, now, get away!*

But I didn't. Instead I looked at the remains I had just unearthed for a long time, thinking. Then I walked over, crouched down, and examined them as closely as I could without touching it. There was a faint but extremely rancid smell, and I had to fight a wave of nausea. Flies had already begun to buzz around.

I was no forensics expert, but I knew this victim had not died decades ago. More like months. Maybe weeks. The small size and long hair made me think it had been a woman. She too had been killed with a bullet to the back of the brain. Her arms were bound behind her with rusting wire.

I searched the rest of the gulch. There was no need; the implications of what I had found were immediately obvious, but I kept searching all the same. I found a third skull. Then another intact skeleton, this one old enough that there was no hair or skin. Then an even older skull, missing its jawbone. I kept going, breathing hard, my heart thumping, but working slowly and methodically, in some kind of psychotic archaeological frenzy, as if it were vitally important that I unearthed every man and woman who had been murdered and interred in this hidden charnel house.

I found eight human skulls in that gulch, but there were so many bones that at least a dozen bodies must have been disposed of there. Most of the remains were old and much gnawed, the bones randomly jumbled. I supposed many bones had been carried away by animals. Both intact skeletons had their wrists bound behind their back. All but one of the victims had been killed by a bullet to the back of the head. The odd skull out had been crushed with something so heavy that its top half had broken into triangular fragments, like broken pottery. When I saw that, my nausea rose again and I had to stop and sit down a while, breathing heavily, before I could continue.

Sinisa was responsible. That was obvious. It was not plausible that so many people had been killed over such a wide span of time, so near his headquarters, without Sinisa having given the orders.

Maybe he had his reasons. Maybe these had been Sinisa's rivals, employees who betrayed him, men who tried to kill him. It was easy to believe that. I wanted to believe that. Because the alternative was that Sinisa, my friendly charismatic CEO, whose lectures on morality and philosophy I found genuinely interesting, was a brutal mass murderer.

A dozen corpses, at least one of them very recent. The mysterious zombies. Months and tens of thousands of dollars, at least, spent on unbreakably secure communications. In our haste to flee from a pack of wolves, Saskia and I had taken refuge in a dragon's cave. Talena and I should have just put Saskia in the trunk of a car and tried to drive her to Italy ourselves.

Maybe I had just discovered my own grave. Maybe, instead of going to the time and expense of bringing Saskia and me to America, Sinisa would take us on this much shorter journey when my work was done. I didn't think so, not with all the hints that I would continue to assist Sinisa, be a tendril of his burgeoning empire, when I returned to California, but I couldn't rule out the possibility.

I went back to the mansion. There were four guards with machine-guns at its wrought-iron gate, and another two visible at the end of the road, new security posted since Dragan's attack. If that really had been Dragan. I wondered if the guards had orders to prevent Saskia and me from leaving the compound. Probably yes. Probably we were prisoners.

I returned to the glorified closet that was my office and sat down before my computer. I told myself to concentrate on my work. But it took a long time before I could focus on the lines of code that swam in front of me. For the rest of the day, if I wasn't careful, if I looked at the screen the wrong way, I saw the toothy grin and cavernous eye sockets of the skeleton I had unearthed.

I wanted to write Talena, tell her what I had found, have her call Hallam and get Major Botham to dig into Sinisa's recent activities, try to find out what was really going on. But my computer was bugged, the keyboard monitor and packet sniffer tracked every word I sent to her, and we were forbidden to leave the compound. There was no way I could get word of my suspicions to anyone else without Sinisa knowing about it. And even if we did, we were long past the point at which anyone could save us if he did decide to betray us. Nobody, not Talena, not Hallam and Lawrence and Steve, not Bond, James Bond, could help us now. We were on our own.

I left work early that night, unable to concentrate any longer. When I reached our house I stopped and looked at Saskia through the front window for a while. She sat at the kitchen table, reading my now battered copy of *Lonely Planet: Eastern Europe,* singing along to bits of something on the radio. As I watched her I seriously considered leaving her to travel to America by herself.

There were too many ways things could go fatally wrong. Even if Sinisa actually meant to take us to America, and not on a one-way journey to the body field deep in the forest, even if Dragan did not ambush us at the docks again, even if we made it on to that same fishing boat on which that Afghani man had died only four days before, it was still a long, long way to America. My best guess from online research was that we would then go across the Mediterranean to Libya, and overland to Morocco, before boarding a ship that would take us to Haiti, and finally, weeks later, from Haiti across the Caribbean to Florida. There was a reason why refugees rarely went from the Balkans to America: it was a desperate and dangerous journey.

I went into the house. Saskia was singing along with a staticky Mariah Carey. 'Baby if you give it to me, I'll give it to you, I know what you want,' she crooned. When I came into view, she smiled at me and kept singing.

I forced a return smile and went past her, up to my room, where I dug out my Eagle Creek travel pouch, sat on the plastic chair, opened the pouch, and stared at the passport and credit card within. Hard evidence that I did not need to endanger myself like Saskia. I could escape Sinisa's compound on foot, catch a *furgon* to Tirana, fly to London or Paris or Milan. It was a callous and cowardly notion, but it meant I would live, and I knew, I felt like snakes in my gut, that if I stayed with Saskia I might well die en route to America.

If I was going to move, then the sooner I got myself out of danger the better. Immediately would be best. Feign sleep, get up before dawn, walk into town and catch the first *furgon*, be at the airport before anyone even realized I was gone.

'Paul?' Saskia asked. I looked up. She stood in my doorway. 'Is everything okay?'

'Sure,' I lied. 'Just tired.'

She looked unconvinced.

'No,' I said. 'Everything's not okay. Come in. Sit.' I couldn't sneak out like a thief in the night, not without telling Saskia what I was doing, and why, and what I had discovered earlier that day.

She sat on my camp-bed, which creaked and shifted beneath her.

'How are you?' I asked.

She thought before answering. 'I am excited more and more, to go to America. I have so much hope. Only three more days we must pass safely through, and then we begin our journey, yes?'

'Three more days,' I agreed.

'Good. Because also I am frightened more and more.'

'Me too.'

Saskia said, 'I did not think you were frightened of anything.'

I snorted. 'Are you joking?'

'No.'

'Well. I'm sorry to disappoint you. But yeah. I'm scared. Terrified, actually.'

We looked at each other. I could tell there was something she wanted to say. 'What is it?' I asked.

Eventually she looked down. 'There is nothing,' she said. She sounded guilty. 'I am sorry. There is nothing. What is it you want to say? What is not okay?'

'Wait,' I said. 'Wait a minute. Were you just thinking of saying that you would be all right if I left you? To go on your own?'

She didn't answer, didn't look up.

'You were,' I said. 'But you didn't. And you shouldn't feel bad about it. Because, it, it . . . ' I hesitated, and in that half-second decided I couldn't sit here in this house we had shared for a month and tell Saskia, wounded vulnerable

Saskia with her quirky sense of humour and her newfound hope for the future, that I was leaving her. Abandoning her might save my life, but I would spend that life hating myself. 'Because it isn't true,' I finished. 'You wouldn't be all right. Not alone. It's still a long way there. You need my help.'

'I so much do not want anything bad to happen to you, Paul,' Saskia said.

'Well,' I said, 'that's how I feel about you too.'

'What is it you want to tell me? What is not okay?'

'Nothing,' I said. There was no point in frightening her further by telling her about the bodies in the forest. 'Just some stupid work headaches. Doesn't matter. Let's get some sleep. We only have to get through three more days here, like you say. Then at least we'll be on the move. Maybe that will be easier.'

Two days after finding Sinisa's personal cemetery, just before midnight on 2 May, two days before we were due to depart, I was still working. I had written all the code the system needed, but I still had to test it, then prove to Arwin and Sinisa that it worked. I had run enough tests that I was confident in the system, but I wasn't *certain*, and given the newfound possibility that my life was on the line, I intended to keep testing until the last possible minute.

I was running boundary tests, trying zero-length messages, messages that were too long, invalid public keys; situations that should never happen, but 'should never happen' is a phrase that makes programmers very wary indeed. I found what I thought was a bug with the way the system handled excessively long messages, in itself just a curious anomaly but one that might lead to a real problem. I spent twenty minutes tracking it to one of the Stegosaurus interface points, and from there into one of Arwin's many files of C code. I would have asked him about it, but he was sleeping.

I opened the file up and winced. This little program was short but incredibly hard to read, much more confusing than Arwin's usually intuitive code. I considered going to bed and asking Arwin about it in the morning, but my bug-hunt blood was up, so I sighed, resigned myself to a long night, and began to trace the convoluted logic of Arwin's program.

About an hour later I sat bolt upright. What I had found wasn't a bug. It was brilliant code, obfuscated so thoroughly that no one but an expert programmer could ever understand it. Definitely Arwin's. I recognized his style.

It was a back door.

In hacker parlance, a 'back door' is a security hole built into a system by its creator, usually a hidden password that grants complete access. The Stegosaurus, Arwin's program that converted a message into a picture hiding an unbreakable coded version of that message, actually had two back doors. One was there by design. Every message that went through the system was encrypted twice: once with the recipient's public key, and once, unbeknown to the user, with Sinisa's public key, so that Sinisa could read any message anyone sent. Arwin had written that back door for Sinisa, as requested; and then, secretly, he had added one for himself, programmed Stegosaurus to generate a hidden *third* copy of every message as well, encrypted with his own public key.

It might not indicate any ulterior motives on Arwin's part. He might have just decided that since he had written the damn system he had the moral right to read everything hidden within. But it was a massive, gaping security hole. Maybe Arwin planned to sell access to Sinisa's system to the highest bidder. Maybe Arwin was a KGB plant. Since the shootout on the pier, and my gruesome discovery in the forest, no speculation seemed too far-fetched. Selling access later on seemed most likely. I liked Arwin, but the idea was entirely in character.

I didn't even consider telling Sinisa. It seemed very likely that such a report would greatly truncate Arwin's lifespan. Despite his many flaws, I liked Arwin a lot, and he had arguably saved my life on the pier; as far as I was concerned he had earned himself a return to the USA.

I could do nothing, pretend I had never found anything. But that idea felt very wrong. I had spent a lot of time and effort building this secure system, and the notion of knowingly leaving a gargantuan hole in its defences offended every engineering instinct I had. And what if Arwin wasn't working alone? What if he was feeding information to someone else? If so, the most likely recipient was probably Sinisa's rival, the same one now supporting the Mostar Tigers. By doing nothing I might indirectly aid Dragan.

I could easily disable Arwin's code. But that didn't seem like the optimal solution either. I no longer trusted Sinisa any further than I could shot-put a cannonball. God only knew what exactly Stegosaurus might be used for down the road. Anyone, terrorist or paedophile or drug dealer, could use the system Arwin and I had written to elude the watchful eye of authority. Sinisa had said that there was nothing else like it in his business. I had found that odd; it hadn't been particularly hard to write, but what if it was true? Criminals tended to be pretty ignorant of technology, and good coders had enough lucrative licit opportunities that we didn't often write products like this. If we *were* the first, whoever got access to Stegosaurus would want to use it rather than going to the trouble of building their own version from scratch. Even if they already had an encryption infrastructure, they still might want to switch to ours, which was designed for ease of use. What if it caught on? What if Stegosaurus became the de facto industry standard for the criminal underworld, its eBay or Amazon, just as Sinisa had predicted?

A back door might some day be very useful. Maybe some day the world would need to break into Stegosaurus. I didn't think Sinisa would ever cooperate with the authorities, he was a tough character, but I suspected Arwin would fold under pressure like a Japanese fan.

What I could do, what I did, quickly and easily, with only a dozen additional lines of C code, was put a little lock on Arwin's back door. This way, when he tried to use his back door, when he opened a message, only gibberish would emerge. It would look like a bug in his code. Locking Arwin's back door wasn't as secure as getting rid of it entirely. He could, to extend the metaphor, quite possibly pick the lock. If he realized that the gibberish was actually a simple substitution cipher, he would be able to break the lock with the computing power of a digital watch. But that probably wouldn't occur to him.

At the time, it didn't seem like a big deal. I had more pressing things to worry about. Dragan's unknown whereabouts and ongoing hunt for my scalp, the non-zero chance that Sinisa intended to take Saskia and me on a one-way walk into the woods rather than to America, the very high probability that our journey to California would be long and hazardous, and what would happen to me and Talena if we ever did make it back, to name a few. Arwin's back door seemed almost irrelevant.

'Now you log in,' I explained, 'pick a message, and enter your pass phrase to read it.'

'I have to enter my pass phrase every time I wish to read a message?' Sinisa asked, as he followed my instructions. Arwin and I looked tensely over his shoulder, our mental fingers crossed. This was our formal demonstration of Mycroft, and despite the batteries of tests I had run, I was still worried that something might go wrong. Bugs often have a way of hiding until the first demo.

'Afraid so,' I said. 'Security thing. Otherwise it would be stored in memory and potentially vulnerable to attack.'

'I see.' He examined the screen. 'Yes, that is the correct original message, in full. Excellent. And the site is very simple. I think even my most stupid associates can learn how to use it. You have done well, Paul. And you, Arwin. I am very pleased.'

Arwin visibly relaxed. I probably did too. Mission accomplished: Mycroft was complete, successful and apparently bug-free. Unless you counted Arwin's built-in back door.

'I am extremely busy,' Sinisa said, 'but this calls for a quick celebratory drink. Come.'

We followed him out to the deck that overlooked the Adriatic, and cracked open three Pilsners and a pack of Marlboros. The sun shone in a cloudless sky and the sea glittered like chrome. We clinked our beers together and drank and smoked as if we were old friends.

'Tomorrow you begin the journey home,' Sinisa said. 'But if ever you wish to return here, Paul, Arwin, for a holiday, you will be most welcome. Or to any of my other houses, London or Amsterdam. *Mi casa, su casa,* as the Spanish say.'

I smiled and thanked him, pretending I was still an enthusiastic supporter of his noble cause, and did not have reason to believe he was a mass murderer. It was hard to reconcile this charismatic, avuncular Sinisa with the heap of human carcasses I had found in the forest.

Maybe he was just a psychopath who had learned to put on a human face. Possible. And if so, Saskia and I probably wouldn't make it out of Albania. But I didn't think so. There was nothing actually inconsistent in Sinisa's behaviour. Magnanimous to his friends, savage to his enemies—history books are full of leaders like that, many of them now revered as heroes and liberators, men who made stirring speeches about their noble cause of liberating the world's suffering peoples, then went out and killed anyone who got in their way, usually doing pretty well for themselves and their bank accounts while they were at it. The history of our species is a history of violence, and the notion that someone who has murdered a dozen people must necessarily be a brute is very Western and very recent.

At dawn the next day Saskia and I stood for the last time outside the building that had been our home for a month, bags packed with our pathetically few possessions, eyes red with sleeplessness, ready to begin a journey that would hopefully somehow carry us five thousand miles, across an ocean and two continents, undiscovered.

'There they are,' Saskia said.

Sinisa's decked-out bullet-proof Land Rover emerged from his mansion's driveway and pulled up in front of our house. Sinisa drove, Arwin rode shotgun. No Zoltan, no Zorana, which spoke well of Sinisa's intentions.

'All right, baby,' Arwin called out to me. 'Let's you and me get the hell out of this shithole.'

Saskia and I got into the back.

'Happiness,' Arwin intoned, 'is seeing Albania in your rear-view mirror.'

'Paul,' Sinisa said. 'Saskia. I have good news and bad news.'

I went cold.

'I have reason to believe that Dragan and my cordial enemy Mladen have prepared an ambush at the docks, many men, many guns. They plan to kill us all.' As he spoke, the Land Rover drove to the end of his private street, where the road began to descend in switchbacks to the Vlore waterfront.

I swallowed. 'That better not be the good news.' Why was Arwin so cheerful?

'No.'

Instead of making the tight left turn on to the first switchback, Sinisa turned to the right, where there was no road at all, just an uneven slope of dirt and weeds. The Land Rover, a fine specimen of four-wheel-drive engineering, didn't even slow down.

'Where are we going? What's the good news?' I asked.

'The good news is that we are not going to the docks. In fact it was never our intention to go to the docks. The good news, Mr Wood, is that we have a surprise for you.'

'What kind of surprise?'

'Today we transcend our situation,' Sinisa said.

I waited for a less Zen explanation, but it did not come. On the other side of the hill, we bounced and jostled down a rocky slope and then suddenly we were on dirt tracks leading east, into mainland Albania.

'I didn't know there was a road here,' Arwin said.

'Arwin, please, give me some respect,' Sinisa said. He was obviously enjoying himself immensely. 'I run a multi-million-dollar criminal organization. Do you really think I would build a home with only one exit?'

'Sinisa,' I said, 'please tell me, what the hell is going on?'

'The culmination of a plan of many years.'

'That's great. That's just great. Congratulations. Now where the fuck are we going?'

'You will see.'

The dirt became gravel, which became potholed pavement—a regression from gravel, if you ask me—which eventually merged with the smooth southbound highway towards Greece. Sinisa and Arwin refused to answer any questions. I wondered if we were driving to Athens; it was a major international port, maybe a freighter that would take us to America was waiting there for us? But after about half an hour we turned off the main highway and drove past farms for what felt like a long time.

I began to understand when an airplane passed over us, only a few thousand feet above ground.

'We're flying,' I said. 'You're flying us to Italy, aren't you?'

Sinisa grinned widely. I felt vaguely disappointed, anticlimactic. It was nice that he had fooled Dragan, but I had somehow expected more.

'I guess that's good,' I said. As long as we stayed under Italy's radar we should be fine. I had heard somewhere that despite America's decades-old war on drugs Colombian drug dealers still flew into Florida and Texas in small planes all the time. I expected the Italian radar shield was relatively porous. 'Then what? You want to tell me now? Some ship going to America? We live inside a shipping container for a couple of weeks?'

'It is a possible route,' Sinisa said. 'Some of my associates have spent considerable sums customizing shipping containers for such purposes. But no. That is not how you are getting to America.'

'Then how?'

'This is a business,' Sinisa said. 'Like any other business. Do you know how to grow a business? Increase profits?'

'What?'

'There are basically three techniques: increase margins, increase market share, or move into new markets. If you are moving into new markets, it is best to choose a market with high profit margins. Traditionally the highest profit margins are found in luxury goods, the more exclusive the better. Gucci, Louis Vuitton, Prada, those are the classic examples.'

'This is all very interesting,' I said, 'but I'm not following your point.'

'When people think of smuggling they think of filthy people sneaking over borders, hidden in back seats and shipping containers, riding underneath trains. It is a business whose clients are desperate, which is good, but poor, which is not. It occurred to me some time ago that I might be able to target an entirely separate market segment. One with a considerably greater profit margin and considerably wealthier clients.'

I paused. 'High-end refugee smuggling.' It sounded like a contradiction in terms.

'A market bigger than you might think. There is our airplane.'

It gleamed. I didn't know much about jets but I knew this was newish and expensive.

'You own that?' I asked, astonished. I was confident it was an order of magnitude beyond my previous estimate of Sinisa's wealth.

'At present I own one thirty-second of it.'

'What?'

'Fractional ownership. Very popular among corporations and wealthy individuals. Warren Buffett, the legendary American investor, he owns the company that operates this particular airplane. I purchased a fraction of a jet, one hundred hours of flight time a year. Mr Buffett keeps a huge fleet around the world, so I can use one whenever and wherever I like. His company provides the pilots, files flight plans, everything. You must forget the big public airlines. Their business models are unsustainable. Fractional ownership is the major profit centre of modern aviation.'

'You rented a private jet for us?' I was flabbergasted.

'Misdirection,' Sinisa said, enjoying my reaction. 'Nobody expects the people who step out of a ten-million-dollar jet to be missing any documents. Even if they are, it means only that there is a paperwork problem, not that they are filthy illegal immigrants.'

'You're flying us to Italy in a private jet.'

Sinisa said nothing.

'My God,' I said. 'You're flying us straight to America?'

'Sadly, no,' Sinisa said. 'We would need contacts in America, we would have to land illegally or influence the immigration officers, and we are still not yet there. No, we are flying to a place where influence and legal documentation are very easy to acquire, and where the road to America is wide and clear.'

'Where? Mexico? Wait a minute. *We?* You're coming with us?' I felt dizzy. All my imaginations and expectations of the near future had just been extinguished, replaced with a blank canvas.

'Mexico is too big, too important,' Sinisa said. 'Influence there is very expensive, easily compromised, tangled up with drug cartels. No, we go to a little country. A little country for which I have big plans. I think you will like it. The scuba diving is excellent.' He smiled. 'We will stop first in the Canary Islands, to refuel, and then, perhaps sixteen hours from now, we land in Belize.'

3 Latin America

14 Borderlands

The Gulfstream IV jet that carried us away from Albania was furnished with overstuffed leather chairs arranged in sixes around five mahogany tables. Original art hung on the walls. Two Filipino waitresses served us smoked salmon crêpes on fine china. The huge plasma television played the *Godfather* trilogy followed by *GoodFellas* and *Scarface*. I kept expecting to wake up. At one point I actually pinched myself.

The passenger list consisted of myself, Saskia, Sinisa, Arwin, Zoltan, Zorana—and the zombies, seventeen men and seven women, scowling and smoking up a storm. I was a little shocked when the first cigarette was lit. After realizing that smokers would not be keelhauled, I bummed one final Marlboro Light from Arwin. These days there is nothing quite so decadent as smoking at thirty thousand feet.

I looked at the zombies and wondered why Sinisa was going to so much trouble for them. Way back when, he had quoted fifty thousand dollars as his list price for American emigration. Multiply by twenty-four and you get 1.2 million dollars. The zombies sure didn't look like they were worth that much. Two of them stood out, their aristocratic leader and the little goateed bantamweight, but the other twenty-two were drab and lifeless. Slack, fleshy faces, tangled and/or thinning hair, cheap shoes, pot-bellies, sour frowns, grunts rather than words, fingers and uneven teeth stained chain-smoker yellow, dull eyes, drained expressions, colourless forgettable men and women the eye slid naturally away from: for them Sinisa had rented an intercontinental jet? Apparently so. It sure wasn't for me and Saskia. We were last-minute additions, surplus to requirements, not particularly wanted on the voyage. This journey—the 'culmination of a plan of many years,' Sinisa had said—was all about the zombies. I couldn't imagine why.

At least one of them proved useful. When we ascended to cruising altitude, Saskia's left ear refused to equalize to the lowered pressure. She tried to tough it out but within minutes she started to weep from the pain in her unnervingly silent way. Sinisa called on the white-haired zombie leader, who turned out to be a doctor and injected her with muscle relaxant. I was a little reluctant to let him stick her with a needle, but I couldn't think of any rational objection, and to my surprise it actually worked.

The Canary Islands refuelling stop took less than an hour. Sinisa spent the whole time looking out the window, expression taut, drumming his fingers on the mahogany. He smoked six cigarettes in those fifty minutes. I had never seen him nervous before. I understood that if we were going to be interdicted and arrested, it would be here. The zombies were nervous too, quiet and tense. It rubbed off on the rest of us, and when we finally lifted off, the Gulfstream's belly newly full of jet fuel, Arwin sighed with relief.

'Next stop,' Sinisa announced, 'paradise.'

'Sinisa,' I said. I couldn't resist any longer.

'Yes?'

I nodded at the zombies. 'Who are these guys?'

Silence fell. Sinisa exchanged a look with Zoltan and Zorana. Arwin leaned forward, interested. It seemed he too didn't know the whole story. Most of the zombies continued to pay no attention, but the white-haired man turned to look at us, and the goateed Napoleon glared at me as if I should be shot for even asking the question. Those two understood English, I could tell by the way they listened.

'In Kosovo,' Sinisa said slowly, 'after NATO drove the Serbian forces away, the Albanian rebels began to persecute the Serbians in the same way that they themselves, I am sorry to say, had been oppressed.' Zoltan started to say something but Sinisa held up his hand. 'I am sorry to say it but it is true,' he said firmly. 'Our friends here, they were important personages in Kosovo once. Mayors, military leaders, police chiefs. If they had stayed they would have been murdered. Four years ago I took them in. Today, finally, I take them to a place they are safe.'

'Out of the goodness of your heart,' I said.

Sinisa smiled. 'That I did not say.'

It was a plausible story. The life expectancy of a former Serb police chief in Kosovo, after the Serbian yoke had been lifted, was probably measured in minutes. Doubtless there were reasons for that, but I was in no position to pass judgement. There were few angels slumming in the Balkans, and even they had probably lost their haloes.

'So why Belize?' I asked.

Sinisa pretended not to have heard me. Clearly that was a question too far.

'Scuba diving,' Zoltan growled, frowning at me. 'All of them expert scuba divers.'

I looked at the squat, dumpy zombies, most of whom I wouldn't have trusted to tread water.

'Of course,' I agreed. 'Why else?'

We landed at dawn at the airstrip outside Punta Gordo, a small town in the south of Belize, on the coast between Mayan jungle and the luminous blue Caribbean, a town so distant that the only roads to the rest of the world remained unpaved and, at the height of the rainy season, unnavigable. From the sky, the thick jungle that began on the western edge of the airstrip and continued uninterrupted all the way to Guatemala looked like another kind of ocean, pervasive, all-encompassing. Belize clearly did not number overpopulation among its problems.

One of the pilots, a burly blond man, had to come back and help the Filipino stewardesses wrestle with the controls of the Gulfstream's staircase until it finally unfolded on to the cracked tarmac. A man with a complex ethnic background and a cheap polyester suit climbed aboard and shook Sinisa's hand. I gathered they had met before. After their brief conversation we all filed out of the airplane. Even at that hour, stepping on to the slightly jittery staircase and into Belize's damp tropical heat felt like entering a sauna. The landing strip, even to my untrained eye, seemed surprisingly long and well maintained for a remote jungle airfield. I wondered if it might be used by the military.

A van and bus waited for us on the grassy patch between the landing strip proper and the forbidding wall of jungle. The drivers wore airport uniforms. We moved slowly, half sedated by jet lag and by sixteen hours in an airplane; the brain-deadening effects of dry air, low pressure and cramped conditions are only partially cushioned by imperial luxury. Zorana directed traffic. The zombies and, to my surprise, Arwin, climbed on to the bus; the rest of us got in the van; and we drove off. That was it, no customs, no immigration, no security, no nothing. The simplicity was stunning. Just step into a private jet, effectively rented by the hour to anyone with enough money, and fly anywhere you want. All Sinisa had needed to do in order to smuggle thirty people into Belize was bribe the men who managed a small airport in a poor benighted Third World country. I doubted their price was anything more than a rounding error next to the cost of fractional Gulfstream ownership.

Our van went only as far as the other side of the airport. Sinisa, Zoltan, Zorana, Saskia and myself were scheduled to fly immediately to Belize City. I didn't know why, and I was too tiredly jubilant to care. Saskia and I were safe in North America. We had not been attacked, or arrested, or betrayed. We were not home yet, we were a long way from home, but we were at least on the right continent. It was a heck of a start.

And we were safe from Dragan. After weeks of imagining him around every corner, it was hard to believe this, but it was true. This single drastic stroke had left the Mostar Tigers so far behind us they effectively no longer existed. They were doggedly persistent, fuelled by a blood vendetta, but they were small-minded men, constitutionally incapable of crossing oceans and spanning continents, entirely without Sinisa's ability to think big and act globally. I was certain they would follow us no further. As far as Dragan was concerned we might as well have escaped to Mars.

Our flight to Belize City allowed me to chalk up another entry on my list of Obscure Third World Airlines I Have Flown. In this case, Maya Island Air, with service several times daily from Punta Gordo. Tickets were cheap, twenty-five cash US dollars a pop, and nobody asked for a passport. The other passengers were a bewilderingly diverse human menagerie: elderly Mayan women in traditional dress, a dreadlocked black man in a business suit, a gang of heavily tattooed Latino men, four young Austrian backpackers, three elderly American expats, and a clutch of blond leather-faced Mennonites in suspenders and straw hats who looked like they had just stepped out of the eighteenth century, plus the five of us. I hadn't even realized that Belize was an English-speaking nation until I heard the other passengers talking.

The prop plane was small, very loud, and shuddered like the pilot had Parkinson's. Nonetheless I managed to doze through the one-hour flight. A van-taxi carried all five of us from the Municipal Airport to the Radisson Fort George, Belize's finest and only four-star hotel. We drove through the ugly sunbaked ghetto that was Belize City, cracked and grimy streets with open sewers carved roughly into either edge, lined with buildings that were either cheap concrete carcasses or ramshackle wood-frame and corrugated-aluminium houses, all worn and dull and faded, any bright colours long since bleached and pounded flat by the relentless tropical sun. Only a few elegant colonial buildings leavened the oppressive shantytown feel.

The Radisson Fort George was objectively a little shabby, but compared to the city outside it was the Taj Mahal. Sinisa strode to the front desk like he owned the place and said, 'Obradovic, a suite and a double room, and quickly please, we are quite tired.'

The receptionist scurried to make arrangements. When asked for identification, Sinisa, to my surprise, passed over not a Dutch passport but a green and gold one emblazoned BELIZE, along with an American Express Platinum card. Nobody else had to show any ID.

'I didn't know you were a citizen,' I said, on the way up.

'Until last year,' Sinisa said, 'anybody with fifty thousand dollars could purchase Belizean citizenship. The Economic Citizenship Program. Last year, because of American pressure, it was cancelled.' He smiled. 'Do you know what then happened to the price of a fully valid Belize passport, if you know the right people?'

'Surprise me.'

'It plummeted. Adam Smith would be proud. The capitalism of the black market is far more ruthless than any bureaucratic initiative. For thirty-five thousand dollars each I can arrange for both you and she to become citizens of this nation.'

An interesting idea, but, 'I think that's out of our price range,' I said, as we stepped out of the elevator. 'And we'd still need a visa for the States. Is that what you're doing for all the zombies?'

'The *what*?'

I had forgotten that Arwin's pet name for them was not universal. 'Your friends who got on the bus.'

'Never mind them,' Sinisa said, and his voice had an edge to it. 'You will not see them again. They have nothing to do with you. Forget them. Here is your room, next to ours. Sleep. We are all tired. Sleep and I will see you tonight.'

After a month on a cheap camp-bed, the bed of a four-star hotel felt like heaven. I disappeared into it like it was a black hole.

I woke to terrifying disorientation. For a long moment I didn't know where I was or what I was doing. I couldn't have told you what the last thing I remembered was. I had lost all sense of chronological order.

I looked over, beginning to panic, and when I saw Saskia sleeping peacefully in the other bed, the spark of recognition caused the rest of my memory to assemble. Belize City. Of course. I stood up, padded to our window, and looked out over the Caribbean and the long strips of mangrove-covered cayes that paralleled the shoreline a few miles from the mainland. It was hard to believe that only twenty-four hours ago I had been in Albania. My new surroundings were so different that my month in Vlore felt like a fleeting and insubstantial dream.

It was mid-afternoon. I was wide awake, ready for action, eager to explore. I dug a pair of jeans from the battered Adidas bag that still contained all my worldly possessions, brushed my teeth, and sallied forth, down the stairs, through the empty lobby, and out into Belize City.

The heat outside was like a physical weight on my shoulders, as bad as the worst of the Balkan heatwave but much more humid. The area around the hotel was quiet, but a block away the streets buzzed with cars, trucks, businessmen in suits, dreadlocked rastamen, women carrying plastic shopping bags, blond Mennonites in overalls, schoolchildren in green and white uniforms. Belize's ethnic demography seemed equally split between black and Latino, plus a small native minority and a smattering of whites. An ad on the side of a passing truck advertised 'Belize's Best Buy!'— beans, apparently. I passed a company with the disturbing name of The Pathology Laboratory. Signs adorned with

Pepsi or Coke logos headlined almost all storefront windows; those two companies gave Third World proprietors free signs in exchange for the advertising space.

My usual first-day-in-the-country priorities: money and information. Belize Bank's ATM rejected my Citibank card, but its tellers happily converted a hundred euros to two hundred and ten Belize dollars, and the window Visa and MasterCard stickers indicated I could get credit card advances if necessary. I wandered until I found an Internet café, which didn't take long. Belize City's population was a meagre fifty thousand, its downtown very compact. The Net cost only four Belizean dollars an hour. I emailed Talena the grand news that we were safe and sound in an English-speaking nation halfway across the world from the Mostar Tigers, and cc'd Hallam and Lawrence and Steve.

When I finished I was hungry. I have a steel stomach, but long experience has taught me not to dive straight into street food on my first day in a Third World country. After a week or two, then maybe. I bought bread and cheese and a Snickers bar and a Coke at a little market, warily noting the rusted iron cage from behind which the proprietor operated, a telling indicator that crime is or has recently been a serious local problem. I had my picnic lunch sitting by the busy Swing Bridge next to the Marine Terminal, where a wide creek or small river, depending on your point of view, runs into the Caribbean. While I was there a team of burly men turned a series of cranks and wheels next to the bridge, operating a gears and pulley system straight out of the Industrial Revolution that rotated the bridge so its length ran parallel to the river, allowing the many boats on either side to pass what had been a barrier.

When the show was over and the bridge had been returned to its original alignment, I crossed over, explored further, haggled for a counterfeit New York Yankees baseball cap, found the old British cemetery and marvelled at how lethal the colonial era had been to its young settlers, discovered a very pleasant bookstore called the Book Center, and spent thirty more local dollars on *Lonely Planet: Belize*. I walked over to the mortared-stone breakwater that overlooked the Caribbean, sat in the shadow of a tall tree, and began to read, occasionally looking up at the ocean or the enormous frigate birds hovering in the postcard-blue sky.

For the first time in six weeks I started to relax a little. Exploring new cities in new countries was one of my favourite pastimes. And here in Belize I didn't need to rely on anyone else. Nobody was chasing me. I spoke the language. Sinisa was still a worrisome enigma, but he was living up to his end of our agreement, and while I still might need his help to get Saskia into Mexico and thence America, I no longer relied entirely on his patronage for my day-to-day existence.

I was very glad about that last. Sinisa was an interesting character, and maybe perversely admirable, but he was still a killer, a criminal, and a dangerous man to know. I did not want to associate with him any longer than necessary. And I was beginning to suspect that whatever Sinisa was doing here had little to do with his oft-proclaimed mission to convey the poor and weak and oppressed to their noble aspirations in the West. A little voice in my head had started telling me that something, something to do with the zombies, was very, very wrong.

Even if that maddeningly unspecific voice was incorrect, this felt like a good time to start detaching myself from Sinisa and Zoltan and Zorana and . . . well, maybe not Arwin. Arwin wasn't a mass murderer hip-deep in nefarious conspiracies. His situation was more like mine, and if Arwin made it to San Francisco, I would adopt him as a friend despite his many warts. But it was high time to say goodbye to the others. My month in Albania had been enough work experience in the dark alleys of the criminal world for a lifetime.

It occurred to me that maybe a physical detachment would be a good way to start. It would be hard to get out from under Sinisa's thumb when we were living right next door. I flipped to Lonely Planet's 'Places to Stay' section and began to read with an eye towards immediate action.

'Just a moment,' I said to Saskia, as we passed the front desk, Adidas bags over our shoulders. 'I want to write them a note.'

I felt a little uneasy about our furtive escape from the Radisson. I had not knocked on Sinisa's door to announce what we were doing; instead, Saskia and I had scurried into the elevator like we feared discovery. I wanted to distance myself from Sinisa's influence, not anger him by fleeing like a thief. I had seen what he did to his enemies. Besides, down the road, he might be a very useful friend to have.

'I'd like to leave a message for Mr Obradovic,' I said to the receptionist.

'Certainly,' she said brightly.

She turned to the cubby-holes behind her and passed me a slip of paper. On it, neatly printed in pencil, was the message: MR CHANG AND MR LEE WISH TO INFORM YOU THEY HAVE BEEN DELAYED IN TAIWAN AND WILL NOT ARRIVE IN BELIZE UNTIL 8 MAY.

'No, I'd like to *leave* a message,' I said, making a scribbling motion.

'Oh, I am sorry,' she said, and gave me a blank piece of paper. I wrote: SASKIA AND I DECIDED TO MOVE TO HOTEL MOPAN JUST ACROSS THE RIVER. MORE MY STYLE. WE'LL BE THERE IF YOU WANT TO FIND US. MEET YOU BACK HERE FOR BEERS AT 7? LET ME KNOW IF THAT'S NOT OK. PAUL.

May 8 was the day after tomorrow. I wondered, as we walked out of the Radisson and into the thick tropical heat, why Sinisa was entertaining visitors from Taiwan in Belize City. He appeared to move in ways more mysterious than God.

'I do not understand,' Sinisa said. 'It is not a problem, I just do not understand. Why would you leave this hotel? It is the finest hotel in Belize! Do you think I will not pay for your room?'

'It's not that,' I said. 'It's just, the backpacker place we moved to, it's just more my style. There's American backpackers there, and a common room, and . . . this place is all formal and, I don't know, like a morgue.'

'Morgue?' Zoltan asked. 'What is morgue?'

I wished I had chosen a different word. 'A place for dead people.'

All three of them frowned at me sternly. I pretended I wasn't nervous. I felt a bit like a teenager who wanted his own place but whose parents weren't ready for him to leave the nest. The thought of Sinisa, Zoltan and Zorana as anyone's joint parents would have sent me into slightly panicky hysterics if I hadn't squelched the urge.

'Dead people,' Zoltan rumbled. 'Yes. Exactly. That is

why best you come back here. You no understand. This is very dangerous city.'

I blinked. This was not the conversational tack I had expected. 'It's not that bad.'

'Paul, this entire country is highly insecure,' Sinisa said. 'Violent crime, drug abuse, robbery, all of them are rampant, and the police are not to be trusted. I think it best that we all stay here in safety. This hotel has private security. You are a valuable asset and I do not want to lose you to some addict with a gun.'

'Come on, guys, it's not like we're in Baghdad,' I said, perplexed by their excessive caution. 'I've stayed in worse places than the Hotel Mopan, in worse cities than this.'

'Don't be so *stupid*, Paul,' Zorana said, as if I wanted to run with scissors through a crystal meth lab. 'There are guns everywhere here, like Bosnia, but here we hardly know anyone, and you must have seen all the blacks on drugs here. There is no organization. These blacks cannot be trusted. They might smoke crack and go crazy and shoot anyone right in the middle of the street. They might break into your hotel and shoot you in your bed. Don't pretend you are so brave and tough. This city is far more dangerous than Sarajevo. Come back here and be safe.'

The other two Bosnians nodded sympathetically. I stared at the three of them for a moment, bewildered, and then understanding dawned and I chuckled.

'Why do you laugh?' Zoltan asked, annoyed.

I didn't dare tell him, but it was pretty funny. Sure, Sinisa and Zoltan and Zorana were tough and dangerous people, no strangers to violence—but they weren't travellers. They weren't used to dealing with new places. They were accustomed to controlling every aspect of their environment, and now, like any novice travellers in an edgy Third World country, they were assuming the worst, reacting like Belize City was a den of rattlesnakes rather than a normal city like many others. It was funny how the tables had turned. The dangerous criminals stayed in their four-star hotel, cautiously avoiding the gun-wielding crackheads they were sure roamed the streets like rabid dogs, while I, the mild-mannered computer programmer, was ready to saunter casually through those same streets to and from my cheap guest-house, unprotected by security guards or razor wire. This was my element. Belize City was no worse than Port Moresby or Treichville or Calcutta or any of a dozen other edgy but fun Third World cities I had visited in my years of backpacking.

'I appreciate your concern,' I said casually, revelling for a moment in the new power dynamic, enjoying my moment as the tough-talking daredevil. 'But really. Believe me. I'll be fine. This is my kind of town.'

The three of them looked at one another and conferred in Serbian for at least a minute. Zoltan seemed angry. I sipped my beer and pretended not to care about their conversation.

'Fine,' Sinisa said in the end, after overruling Zoltan. 'If you wish to take this risk, Paul, then stay wherever it makes you happiest. I sincerely hope you and Saskia do not suffer from this decision. Let us move on.' They were obviously unhappy with our sudden exodus from their embrace, but not quite unhappy enough to order me back to the Radisson. Though judging from Zoltan's expression I had come pretty close.

'Great. Thanks.'

'Saskia is not joining us?' Zorana asked.

'No, she's still tired,' I lied. Actually I had known this meeting might verge on confrontation, and I didn't want to expose her to that.

'I imagine you are eager to return to America as quickly as possible,' Sinisa said.

'As safely as possible,' I corrected.

'Of course. To that end I have made some arrangements. My connections in this area are presently somewhat tenuous, but I have great confidence in them. They come with glowing recommendations. The rest of us will be remaining in Belize for some time, but I have made arrangements for you and Saskia to be transported into Mexico and then to California in the very near future.'

I wasn't sure I liked the sound of that. 'Just the two of us?'

'Yes.'

'What arrangements?'

'It is extremely simple. From Belize to Mexico, you will go by boat. There is no risk; if you are found you will claim that you were out fishing at night. Many Americans come to Belize to fish, and you will claim that your foolish Belizean crew ran out of fuel and you drifted in towards Mexico. Once in Mexico you will be taken to the town of Chetumal. I will give you a name and a phone number in Mexico. That number will connect you to an organization in Tijuana which conveys thousands of people across the American border every year.'

'And this is a safe route? Tried and tested?'

'I assure you it is safe,' Sinisa said. 'I would not send you on this route if I was not sure it was safe. Because I would like you to carry something into America for me, and once you are in America, to deliver it to a friend of mine.'

I looked at him.

'Furthermore,' he said, 'I want you to understand that this is not the last favour I will ask of you. I do understand that once you reach America, our agreement is complete. In fact the rest of your fifteen thousand dollars has already been paid. Your work for me is done. But someone like you, a man with a Canadian passport, living legally in California, you are not just my friend, Paul, you are an important asset. Not just for your brilliant computer programming. To have someone like you there, someone I can trust, someone with a good heart, I will find that reassuring. From time to time I will ask you for favours. And I want you to know that I consider you my friend, and if ever you need my assistance, I will feel obligated to give it.'

I didn't know what to say.

'Us also,' Zorana said, leaning forward and taking my hand. 'Zoltan and I, we are your friends too, Paul. I want you to remember that.'

Zoltan nodded, somewhat reluctantly.

'Huh,' I said, fumbling for words that wouldn't commit me to anything. 'I, thanks, yes, we're all friends here, but, but I wasn't expecting this.'

'It is nothing to worry about,' Sinisa said. 'A small package for you to carry, that is all.'

'It's just I didn't think this was our agreement.'

Wrong thing to say. 'Are you suggesting I am violating the terms of our agreement?' Sinisa demanded, his voice low and dangerous, as if the never-codified 'terms of our agreement' were as sacrosanct as the Ten Commandments. I realized I was insulting his personal honour; he saw himself as a man who never reneged on a deal.

'No,' I said. 'It's just I don't remember anything about carrying a package for you.'

'Ah,' Sinisa said. 'You understand, this is not part of our agreement. This is merely a favour I am asking you. You are absolutely free to say no, and this will not affect our agreement in the slightest.'

Zoltan and Zorana nodded eagerly, as if on cue. I opened my mouth to politely decline his request. Then I coughed and shut my mouth again, realizing that I really needed to think about this, needed about six hours to think through all the ramifications. Just because Sinisa said I could say no without repercussion didn't make it necessarily so. I thought of the bodies I had found in the Albanian forest. Maybe they too had been asked for favours and said no. Saskia and I were still in a Third World country where we knew no one and where Sinisa had powerful friends. He could probably disappear us without breaking a sweat, and there was no doubt he would if he thought he had reason enough.

'What's in the package?' I asked, stalling for time.

'I am afraid I cannot answer that question,' he said blandly. 'A briefcase, I can tell you that much. But I have promised the intended recipient that no one will know its contents.'

My stomach clenched. Drugs. Almost certainly. Sinisa wanted me to be a drug mule, to commit the classic and classically stupid traveller's crime, reach for a pot of gold and find yourself in handcuffs instead, staring at fifteen years in a Third World jail. And there wasn't even a pot of gold at the end of this particular rainbow. He had already paid me the rest of my money. His offer was all stick and no carrot.

'Just as a favour,' I said.

'Just as a favour.'

Sinisa wanted me to smuggle drugs into America and he wasn't even offering to pay me for it. I was almost insulted. What kind of offer was that? A Don Corleone offer, an offer that can't be refused? If I said no, would he really have me killed? The notion sounded so ridiculous I could barely even articulate it to myself. I had just spent a month living and working with Sinisa. We were friends, he had just said so himself. He was certainly capable of murder, but of me? He liked me. He had approvingly said that I was one of the rare people who understood him. Surely the smiling Gucci-clad man sitting across from me wouldn't really have me killed for refusing to carry a briefcase.

But why he was offering me no reward for this so-called favour? He actually seemed to be going out of his way to motivate me to say no. The only reasons to say yes were self-preservation and loyalty. And he didn't know that I knew that self-preservation was an issue. He thought I still thought he was Robin Hood.

I understood. This was no favour. This was his acid loyalty test.

If I passed, it meant I was a valuable asset. But if I failed, I was disloyal, and disloyal, that's not so different from being a traitor, right? And Sinisa was good to his friends, but if he considered me a traitor, he would quite calmly kill me. Probably not personally, not with his own hands, that was beneath his station. No, he would murmur a few words to Zoltan and Zorana, and within the hour Saskia and I would be dead.

Maybe I was wrong. But that did not feel like a chance I could take. I was talking to three ruthless killers. Turning down their request was not a good way to extend my lifespan. Neither was smuggling drugs across Mexico and into America, but my life had somehow gotten to the point where that terrifying prospect seemed the lesser of two evils.

'All right,' I said. 'That's fair. You saved my life, you saved Saskia's life. I owe you. Carrying a briefcase for you is the least I can do.'

I immediately wished I hadn't phrased it in that way. Not that it really mattered. It was already clear that there would be more favours asked of me. So much for painlessly extricating myself from Sinisa's web. I understood then that this smuggler's-aide experience, which I had thought of as an isolated and self-contained period, might infect the rest of my life.

'I am very glad to hear you say that,' Sinisa said sincerely. 'Very glad. I will have details of the arrangements for you tomorrow.'

I nodded. We sipped our drinks, smiled genially at one another, and pretended that we were one big happy family.

Out of Albania, into Belize, I thought. Out of the frying pan, into the fire.

15 Overhead Environment

Two mornings later, Saskia and I sat, ate banana pancakes, and drank coffee in the Hotel Mopan's flagstoned courtyard, walled by bushes and shaded by two tall trees. Three German-speaking girls in their twenties sat at another table, quietly hung over. I suspected they were the ones who had barged loudly into the Hotel Mopan at 2 a.m. I thought wistfully of the thick walls and three-hundred-thread-count sheets of the Radisson.

I was torn from my reverie by an unexpected and very familiar voice.

'Paul!' Talena cried. 'Saskia!' She bounded out of the cab outside the gate, wearing shorts and a T-shirt and a huge relieved smile. I was so surprised I started out of my seat and gaped. She ran to me, wrapped her arms around me, and gave me a long kiss hello. I hugged her back so hard that her feet left the ground.

The taxi driver interrupted us with a slight cough. I forked over the twenty US dollars it cost to ride in from the airport, sheer extortion but this time cheap at the price, as Talena and Saskia hugged and laughed.

'I can't believe you did it!' Talena said, her voice giddily childlike. 'I can't believe you're here! I can't believe you're both here! I can't believe I'm here! This is wonderful! This is so fucking great!'

I found my voice. 'What are you—how did you—I mean, whoa! Wow! Welcome to Belize! What the hell are you doing here?' Talena's giddiness was infectious. Seeing her in the flesh again, unexpectedly, was pure joy. It had not occurred to me that mentioning our location in a recent email would prompt her to join us for a surprise weekend visit.

'How could I stay away when you were just around the corner? You're almost home! I can't believe you're almost home!'

'We're not out of the jungle yet,' I said cautiously.

'But like you say, the hard part, we have done that,' Saskia suggested.

'Saskia! You can speak English! Paul, you taught her English!'

'She taught herself,' I said, laughing. 'Come on. Sit. Have a coffee. The coffee here's pretty good. How did you get here? How'd you get off work?'

'I didn't. I'm going to IM in sick today and tomorrow. I probably have to go back Monday. Didn't you get my email? I guess I just sent it, what, ten hours ago? Oh, my God, this is *so great!* What are you laughing at?'

'I've never heard you sound so sorority Valley Girl before,' I said, smiling.

'And you never will again so enjoy it while it lasts. Now tell me everything! And Saskia, how are you? You cut your hair! Is everything okay? Tell me everything!'

Saskia and I took turns talking. I left out only my discovery of the body field and my recent agreement to play mule for Sinisa. I didn't want to talk about either of those things in front of Saskia and worry her unduly.

Saskia switched to Croatian sometimes when her English failed her. She was far more animated in her native tongue. In English she was always a little hesitant, but in Croatian she was passionate, gesticulating with her hands, laughing and cracking jokes, almost as if she had a split personality, as if when she switched languages she was possessed by a different soul. I guess this was true for a lot of people, that the struggle of speaking in a second language hid their real selves, made them seem dull and reserved.

'I guess I should check in,' Talena said, after she finished her coffee.

'Oh, yeah,' I said.

Both of us went silent. Now that the first flush of our reunion had worn off, we looked at each other and remembered that things between us were still uncertain and confusing. I didn't know what our sleeping arrangements would be. Neither did Talena, judging from the expression on her face.

'I will get a room for myself,' Saskia said, apparently insensate to the sudden tension. 'Talking to the hotel woman will be good English practice. Then you and Talena take the room we have now.' She nodded, satisfied with her plan, and walked into the Hotel Mopan.

Talena and I looked at one another.

'Hi,' I said.

'Hi.'

'It's good to see you.'

'Good to see you too.'

For a moment it seemed that neither of us had anything else to say.

'Come here,' she said, standing up, her voice soft, and I came to her and we held each other tightly enough to crack ribs, her head against my chest, her hair soft on my chin, both of us breathing hard.

'Good to see you,' she whispered. 'Understatement of the century.'

'Oh,' Saskia said, behind me. 'Excuse me, I am sorry—'

'It's okay,' Talena and I said in unison, releasing each other and turning to her. Saskia stood holding her new room key, embarrassed that she had intruded.

'Don't worry about it,' Talena said. 'We're all here and it's so great. Now what's on the schedule for today? What are the plans?'

'You're just in time. We've got a meeting with the guys who are supposed to take us into Mexico this afternoon,' I said.

'How exciting.'

'Yeah. Smuggler tourism. You should have brought a camera.'

'They'd probably get all Sean Penn on my ass,' she said. 'I'm hungry. For food, not breakfast. What do they serve around here?'

'Oh, they serve both kinds. Rice and beans or beans and rice. You'll love it.'

'I can't wait. Maybe after I eat we can all go walk around town. You can show me the sights before we meet the smugglers.'

'All the fabulous sights of Belize City,' I said. 'Don't blink.'

We met the Belizean smugglers at the tomb of Baron Bliss, an eccentric and wonderfully named nineteenth-century Englishman who, despite never having actually set foot on Belize's mainland, had willed most of his considerable fortune to its people. His tomb was a slab of black basalt beneath the lighthouse that marked the easternmost point of Belize City. The view east was stunning, across the luminescent ocean to long bands of mangrove cayes, intensely green and blue beneath the blazing tropical sun that hyperintensified every colour. The view west was of a ratty, weed-choked park, infested by plastic bags and bottles and a few rusting benches, surrounded by cheap, dull grey buildings.

The smugglers were fifteen minutes late. Two black men

in their mid-twenties, one short-haired, clean-cut, and relatively conservatively dressed in jeans and a tank top, the other dreadlocked with a rasta hat and a flashy rainbow coat he must have stolen from the biblical Joseph.

'You Paul?' the big clean-cut one asked, his voice low and gravelly. 'You here to meet some people?'

'That's me.'

'Yo, howyadoin?' the little rasta one said. 'Good to meet you. You can call me Abel. This is my brother Cain.'

'Um . . . okay. Hi. This is Talena and Saskia.'

We all shook hands.

'Now, you don't have to worry none about money, your man Sinisa, he already taking care of that,' Abel said. Despite his dreads and Jah-Love look, Abel sounded a lot more American and less Caribbean than clean-cut Cain. 'We just here to set up a time and a place.'

I shrugged. 'You're the experts. Soon is good, but, you know, whenever you're sure we'll be safe.'

'No such thing as sure of safe,' Cain said. 'Not in Belize. Not in my work.'

'Don't you worry about him none,' Abel quickly intervened. 'He just a hardass. You safe as houses with us. Me and Cain, money in the bank, promise you that. Easiest thing since sliced bread. We just gonna take you for a thirty-minute boat ride, that's all. I thinking day after tomorrow, Saturday night.'

The more I heard the more I suspected that Abel was from somewhere in the Midwest, his lilting singsong voice and reggae talk just an act. I wondered what had brought him here. Took a holiday and fell in love with the place? Unlikely. Skipped bail in America and ran for Central

America's only English-speaking country? That sounded a lot more convincing.

'Saturday night from where?' Talena asked.

'Caye Caulker,' Abel said. 'Caye' sounded like 'key.' 'You want to go there tomorrow. You like it there. Just take a water taxi from by the Swing Bridge, just down this road. You want to stay at a place called Popeye's. It got a big sign, it say "De Place To Be On De Caye." Saturday night, eight o'clock, we put you on a boat, we say we going night-fishing, we take a little ride to Mexico, and our friends there, they pick you up. Easiest thing there ever did be.'

'A boat across the ocean in the middle of the night?' I asked, sceptically.

'Not a problem. Not a problem. Cain here, he knows the cayes like no one else, his momma gave him birth in the ocean there, no lie.'

'I can get you to Mexico,' Cain said. 'For sure.'

We looked at each other silently, as if we had all run out of words.

'Okay,' I said. I wasn't sure I trusted these guys, but I also wasn't sure I didn't. I was beginning to realize that when you deal with criminals on a regular basis, 'trust' becomes a highly fungible concept. 'Caye Caulker, Popeye's, Saturday night at eight.'

'That right,' Abel said. 'No problem.'

We went back to the Hotel Mopan and informed them we would be checking out tomorrow. Saskia, saying she was tired, quickly retired to her room. I suspected she was just trying to give Talena and me some privacy. I almost wished she hadn't. Talena and I were skittishly awkward around one another and Saskia's chaperoning presence had made the day easier for both of us.

'Let's get a drink,' Talena said.

'Good idea,' I agreed.

We went into the bar, ordered two bottles of Belikin beer, and sat as far away from the noisy German girls as we could. We clinked our dark bottles together and smiled and drank. I searched for something to say. Nothing came to mind.

'What did you leave out?' Talena asked.

'Leave out?' Then I understood. I thought of the briefcase that lay hidden beneath my bed. Sinisa's briefcase. I was almost grateful that we had a crisis to discuss, to distract ourselves from the subject of ourselves. 'Right. Well. I didn't want to say anything in front of Saskia. We've got a problem. Actually a couple of problems. Not small ones, either.'

'Tell me.'

'First of all,' I said, 'Sinisa gave me something he wants me to carry into America.'

Her eyes narrowed. 'What is it?'

'A briefcase. It's locked. Weighs about ten pounds. He won't tell me what's in it.'

'He won't . . . Why didn't you just say no?'

'That's not as easy as Nancy Reagan claims,' I said. 'Let me tell you about Sinisa's version of peer pressure.' I briefly recounted my discovery of human remains near his mansion, and his casual murder of the Afghani man on the boat. She listened intently.

'Great,' she said. 'Well, that's just fucking great.'

'Isn't it though?'

'We could leave tonight,' she said. 'Right now. Get a taxi

to the border and try to walk across or bribe the guards there or . . . shit. I don't know.'

'We could,' I said. 'But if we don't make it, then we're really fucked. Sinisa has big friends here, and we don't know anyone.'

'We could go to the American embassy and . . . ' Her voice trailed off.

'Yeah. Tell them we have this illegal Bosnian refugee who needs their help. They'd be all over that.'

'Shit.'

'Exactly,' I agreed.

'What are we going to do?'

I shrugged. 'I'm going to let Sinisa's smuggler buddies carry me and Saskia and this briefcase into Mexico. If we get caught, we're in trouble anyways, briefcase or no briefcase. This just means I'll be in a little more trouble if it goes wrong.'

'A little more trouble. If my guess is even in shouting distance of correct, you'll be in a Mexican jail for twenty years. Where I come from we call that a huge life-wrecking disaster, not a little more trouble.'

'Whatever. We rolls the dice and we takes our chances.'

'Jesus Christ, Paul, how can you act so fucking *casual* about this?' she asked. 'You do understand that this is an immensely dangerous situation that could destroy the entire rest of your life, right?'

I snorted. 'So what else is new? Welcome to the last six weeks of my life.'

Talena looked at me like she didn't quite recognize me. I remembered that, unlike me, she had come to Belize from a month at a peaceful office job in America, where smugglers and guns and volatile negotiations and the ongoing threat of violent death were appalling horrors rather than the stuff of everyday life. I was terribly frightened, but I had been frightened for so long I had learned to wall it off a little with sarcastic fatalism. She couldn't share that, at least not yet.

'There has to be some other way,' she said.

'The sad thing I have discovered is, there doesn't,' I said. 'Just because all the choices are really bad doesn't mean there's a good one hidden somewhere.'

'Don't give me a philosophy lecture, okay? Jesus. You really think that if you said no they'd come here and kill us all? That sounds so . . . I don't know. Melodramatic.'

'Sinisa and friends are a seriously melodramatic crew. Ask all those dead people I found in the forest. I'm sure they'll back me up.'

'What if you do get it into Mexico? Are you actually going to bring it into America?'

'I don't know,' I said. 'I'll worry about that in Mexico.'

'I'll take it,' she said.

I sat quietly for a moment. Then I said, 'What?'

'This is all for Saskia. If it wasn't for Saskia you could fly home tonight. You already went through Albania for her. She's my sister. You've done enough. It's my turn. You fly home. I'll take things from here.'

'No,' I said.

'What? Why not?'

'Well . . . for one thing, you know, she feels like my sister too,' I said. 'We just spent a month living together. She's . . . I want to see her safe as much as you do. And Sinisa would see it as some kind of bait and switch. I will not get an A grade on this loyalty test if I subcontract it out.' I paused. 'And because I'm just not going to let you endanger yourself like that. End of story.'

'But I'm supposed to sit idly by while you endanger *your* self, is that it? Fuck you.'

She glared at me. I stared calmly back into her electric-blue eyes. I was a little surprised at myself, at the detached cool I was maintaining. Being alone with her made me feel a little bit like I had on the pier when the sniper was shooting at me, hyperaware and adrenalinized and afraid. Afraid that something I might do or say, a single wrong word or action, would lose her. But at least I could speak to her without the guilt at being her contemptible loser boyfriend that had tinged my every word to her in the year before Bosnia. For a whole year I had not dared to meet her gaze when she looked at me angrily. No longer.

'I'm coming with you into Mexico,' she said eventually.

I knew from her tone there was no point in arguing. 'All right.'

She nodded, satisfied that she had gotten at least one concession. We fell silent, but it was the most comfortable silence we had enjoyed since her arrival. Our dispute seemed to have broken some ice. I wondered if this was a good time to bring up the subject of Us. Sooner or later we had to have a serious talk. But this, I decided, was too soon.

'So how's sunny California been?' I asked.

She looked relieved. I think she knew I had been considering a Serious Conversation and dreaded the prospect. 'Bring me another beer and I'll tell you all about it,' she said.

The two-beer drowsiness hit us at about the same time our conversation began to falter. We went up to our room and I followed her in. There were two twin beds. Talena sat on the bed to the left. After a moment I took my cue from her constricted body language and sat on the other. We looked at one another.

'Okay,' she said. 'Um. Goodnight?'

'Goodnight.'

'I'm sorry I can't be—' She stopped.

'Don't be sorry,' I said. 'I understand.'

We stared at each other a little longer. Then she sighed, shrugged, smiled wryly, and wordlessly began to remove her outer layer of clothes. I did the same. We crawled under the covers of our beds and I reached up to switch out the light.

'Sleep tight,' I said. 'Sweet dreams.'

She smiled at me and my heart thumped.

'Back atcha,' she said.

It took me a long time to get to sleep that night. I couldn't help but think of our last reunion, six months earlier, the day Talena had come home from Melbourne, and every time I did, I squirmed with guilt.

Talena had been gone for two weeks, for work. The day she returned home, she found me sitting on her couch, amid stacked pizza boxes and crushed beer cans, in an apartment that stank of unwashed dishes and old laundry, playing video games on her XBox. Her smile wilted. She dropped her bags, shut the door, and looked at me.

'Love what you've done with the place,' she said.

'Sorry,' I shrugged disinterestedly. 'I meant to clean up. I thought you were coming later. How was the trip?'

'It was fun. Met some cool people. What have you been doing?'

'I don't know. I had a couple interviews, but they didn't go too well.'

'A couple interviews,' she said. 'Okay. Paul, what are you doing?'

'I'm playing Halo.'

'You want to get off the couch and maybe come say hello to your girlfriend who just got home from halfway around the world?'

'Sure. Yeah. Sorry.'

I paused the game, came to her, and gave her an awkward welcome-home kiss.

'You've just been sitting here playing video games the whole time?' she asked incredulously.

'Not always,' I said, stung. 'But what else do you want me to do? I'm pretty much out of money. I went walking around earlier.'

'If you needed more money you should have just called me.'

I shook my head, avoiding her gaze.

'Come on, Neanderthal man.' She said it fondly. 'I know you hate me supporting you. But that's just how we live right now. You have to try to get used to it. At least until you get a job.'

'Get a job,' I said bitterly. 'You think I haven't been trying? Maybe you lost track of reality down under, but we're in the middle of the worst depression the tech industry has ever seen, and I'm not even allowed to flip burgers on my visa, and even if I tried there's eight million illegal Mexicans in line ahead of me. Get a job? Did you bring a fucking job home from Australia with you?'

'Easy,' she said. 'Easy. I wasn't accusing. Honest. But,

Jesus, Paul, you've got to do something. I don't know what, but look around. No wonder you're depressed if you sit around here all day.'

'Depressed? I'm not depressed. There's nothing wrong with my brain chemicals. I'm unemployed. You know what happened when you were gone? I hit my anniversary. It's a been a year since I had a job. It's been a whole year. That's my only problem.'

'Other people,' she said softly, 'seem to manage it better.'

'Other people. Easy for you to say. Didn't you go scuba diving in Australia? Weren't you going on some corporate feelgood camping trip along the Great Ocean Road? You come back from that and tell me it's my fault I'm no good at being poor?'

'No,' she said. 'No, I come back all excited to see my boyfriend again because I missed him so much, and I walk in here and he doesn't even get up to come to the door. And all I feel is disappointed. Two weeks, Paul. You could have, I don't know. You could have done *something*.'

I just looked at her, feeling gut-punched. I'd been ready for anger. Disappointment was a hundred times worse. I knew it was only a short hop from there to pity.

'Never mind. Never mind. I don't want to fight. Let's,' she looked around the apartment, 'let's go out for dinner. Get a bottle of wine or something. I've got a few more hours in me before I pass out. Let's start this great return home all over again, what do you say?'

'Oh, for Christ's sake,' I said, angry now, at myself more than her. 'It's always the same way. You get your digs in and then you say "I don't want to fight" so all of a sudden I'm the bad guy if I don't leave it alone. I have a better idea. You go have dinner. I'll stay here and clean your fucking apartment. At least I can be good for that.'

She had looked at me silently for a moment, on the verge of tears, and then she had turned and walked out without a word. And I had been glad. That was what made my stomach writhe with guilt, looking back on it, that some sick corner of my mind had counted driving her away as a victory.

We had made up, eventually. We had always made up. But as I looked over to Talena, sleeping peacefully in our shared Hotel Mopan room, I knew it was amazing she hadn't dumped me already. I couldn't blame her if she decided she didn't want me back.

The boat trip from the mainland was gorgeous. Our open-topped motorboat, its passenger demographic split about 50–50 between backpacker tourists and Belizeans, crossed ocean water calmed by Belize's barrier reef, went through a narrow gap between two uninhabited cayes dense with mangrove forest, and half an hour later reached the east coast of Caye Caulker, a strip of land three miles long and a thousand feet wide, built up with one- and two-storey clapboard buildings. Dozens of rickety wooden docks protruded into the ocean, a small one for each beachfront hotel and a larger pier where the mainland boats stopped. A dozen muscular touts waited for our boat, eager to carry backpacks to hostels that gave them kickbacks in exchange for new customers. We ignored their entreaties and walked to Popeye's, past restaurants, stores, guest-houses, dive shops, Internet cafés, all the comforts of home for the thousand or so backpackers who inhabited Caye Caulker at any given moment and formed the majority of its population. Ambergris Caye to the north was where the wealthy package-tour vacationers went. Caye Caulker was one of the world's cosy backpacker paradises, like Pokhara in Nepal, Dahab in Egypt, Goa in India, Yangshuo in China, Essouaira in Morocco, Krabi in Thailand, or any of dozens of other once sleepy small towns that in the last few decades had morphed into mainstays on the international backpacker trail, places where rooms were cheap, pot was ubiquitous, government oversight was minimal, and half the population was young, white, relatively rich, extremely transient and often intoxicated. Fun, laid-back places where you could easily spend a couple of weeks, day-tripping to the local ecotourism adventures or dive sites, passing the nights drinking and smoking with all your newfound temporary friends. I had not previously realized that their transient population, well-established transport links, and no-questions-asked attitude also made them ideal havens for smugglers.

Popeye's, welcoming and air-conditioned and cheap, was on Front Street. The caye had only three streets with names: Front, Middle and Back, all of them hard-packed sand. The only vehicles permitted on Caye Caulker were golf carts. Lonely Planet reported that old-timers lamented about the good old days when Middle had been Back. I wondered how long it had been since Caye Caulker was little more than sand and palm trees and thick mangrove bush.

We spent most of that afternoon and night and the next day on the patio at Café Rasta Pasta, a pleasant place with a cool ocean breeze and good food, relaxing as best we could, reading and drinking beer and chatting with various other backpackers, mostly European but a few Americans and

Canadians. We bought bathing suits and went swimming a few times. The water was warm and buoyant but the shallows were thick with seaweed. Talena and I were amused, and Saskia a bit scandalized, by the envious looks I got from male backpackers who did not have the good fortune to be escorted by two pretty bikini-clad women.

The evening we arrived, Saskia, overcome by too much Belikin, retreated back to Popeye's to sleep, and Talena and I stayed to chat with a Norwegian dive instructor named Torsten, a man built like a barrel, with a constant infectious grin plastered on his face.

'Tomorrow's dive is the Blue Hole,' Torsten said. 'The most famous dive site in North America. One of the most famous dive sites in the whole world.' His grin widened. 'Of course it helps that every dive country has its own famous dive site called the Blue Hole. Australia, Egypt, Thailand, everywhere. Sometimes, when I dive a Blue Hole, I ascend and it takes me a minute to think, what country am I in? Where is this Blue Hole?'

'Have you worked in all those places?' Talena asked.

Torsten nodded and began ticking names off on his fingers. 'Australia. Thailand. Malaysia. Mauritius. Egypt, for almost six months; that was where I qualified to teach new instructors. They called me Torsten the Torturer.' He chuckled. 'Greece, but only for a week, a bad company. The Andaman Islands. Papua New Guinea. Micronesia, Truk Lagoon, the greatest dive site in the world; I worked there for only one month, not long enough. Then the Galapagos, then Costa Rica, and then here.' His grin stretched even further, its corners reaching towards his skull earrings. 'And three years ago, only three years, I was an accountant in Trondheim. An accountant!' He raised his black bottle of Belikin high into the air. 'To the death of accounting! *Skaal!*'

We drank. He drained his bottle, called for another, and lit up a Colonial cigarette, cheap local filth but Marlboros and Camels were nearly impossible to find, as with all former British colonies. I wanted to bum a smoke but remembered Talena's presence and refrained.

You hear stories like Torsten's at all the world's diving meccas. Scuba diving grows more popular every year and the demand for instructors always outstrips supply. Qualified dive instructors can show up in any of a wide variety of exotic tropical places and easily find work for cash under the table; the laid-back counter-culture types you find running dive shops in backpacker havens such as Caye Caulker, Dahab, Krabi, even Cairns, are rarely interested in immigration paperwork. A dive instructor can travel around the world, living a frugal but decadent existence, for however long he or she wants. It's the next best thing to being paid to travel, that oft-cited ultimate goal of the backpacker set.

'Doesn't it bother you not having a home?' Talena asked.

'Home?' Torsten asked. 'What is a home? People tell me Norway is my home. I say, yes, maybe it was, but not is. Do you know what we say about our country? It is a place where a man gets on an empty bus, he sits in the back left corner. Another man gets on, and he sits in the front right corner, as far away from the first man as possible. Another man gets on, and he sits in the middle, as far away from all the others as possible. Norwegians are cold people in a cold country. I am a warm person, I belong in a warm country. So I ask you, how is Norway my home?'

'You've never thought of basing yourself somewhere? Buying a home here on Caye Caulker or something?'

'Why would I do that? I ask you, in all seriousness, who needs homes? A serious question. For what kind of person do homes exist?' He paused dramatically. 'I will tell you. Homes are for children. If you have a child, yes, absolutely, they must have a home, they must grow up in a home. But for me? I am not a child, not for a long time. And no children for me, not for Torsten Klug, not ever if I have a choice. There are too many people on this little ball of dirt already, any fool can see that. Why should I need a home? A good money investment? No, money is a drug, worse than heroin, and I am not addicted, not yet, I hope never. For staying in one place with one group of friends? All my friends today, they do the same thing I do, they move and move and move, we know where each other are from email. If I made a home somewhere most of them I would see less not more. I ask you in all seriousness, what good is a home for Torsten Klug?'

We had no answer for him.

'My home is anywhere, everywhere. Wherever I may roam, wherever I lay my head is home.' He chuckled. 'Just like Metallica sings. To Metallica. *Skaal!*'

'Do you think he was right about homes?' Talena asked, after he left.

I thought about it. 'I don't know,' I said. 'These days I feel pretty homeless. I guess, you know, I have for years. Never really felt rooted. I used to be like him, you know, I never used to care, but these days . . . I think I'd like a home. Maybe I'm getting old.'

'You've felt pretty homeless for years? I kind of thought you lived in my apartment.'

'Exactly. *Your* apartment.'

'What—what are you saying? Are you saying you feel like you haven't been welcome?'

'No,' I said. 'Not at all. I'm just saying that it's always been your apartment and it's never felt the slightest like my place. Also—let me finish—also I lived there during the most miserable period of my life, which has nothing to do with you or your apartment; it would have been a lot worse without you.'

'Well,' she said. 'I'm sorry my home never felt like your home. I never knew that.'

We stared at one another.

'Maybe we should go have a nap,' Talena said.

I took a deep breath. My heart was pounding. I felt like I was about to jump out of an airplane without knowing whether the backpack I wore was a parachute or a load of bricks. 'No,' I said, looking straight into her electric-blue eyes. 'I think we should talk.'

'I don't know if now is the—'

'I think we should talk.'

We looked at one another silently for a little while, both of us breathing hard.

'Okay,' Talena said. 'Okay. Um, anything you want to say, or . . . ?'

'Yeah. You wanna break up or what?'

She looked at me. I swallowed.

'I don't know,' she said. 'I know that's, like, the worst possible answer, and I'm sorry, but I still don't know.'

'It's not the worst possible answer,' I said.

'No?'

'Definitely not. Definitely not.'

'Things have been so fucked between us for so long,' she said. 'I don't even know how long, that's how long. I don't know if we can fix that. Maybe I want to try, but . . . but not if it's impossible, you know? If it's inevitable we may as well get it over with, right? I know that sounds, I don't know, cruel, but, God, Paul, I don't want to go through it all again. It hurt too much the first time.'

'Aw,' I said. 'Jesus. Talena. I'm sorry. I'm so sorry. I never wanted to hurt you.'

'I think sometimes you did,' she said very quietly. She was trembling. So was I. I wanted to reach out and take her in my arms but I didn't dare move. 'You treated me so badly, Paul. You have been such a total shit. I have tried so fucking hard, so many times, and for the last year you have been such a self-obsessed, self-torturing, fucked-up asshole, lashing out at me so many times for such no-good reasons . . . I'm sorry but I get livid just thinking about how you treated me. For a *year*, Paul, for a whole fucking *year*. I didn't even realize, you know, it was so, like, just accepted that that was how you were, until I got back from Bosnia and you weren't there and I started to think. You behaved so badly for so long I don't know if I can forgive you.'

I didn't say anything.

'I guess that's not how you see it, huh?' she asked. 'Well, that's how I see it.'

I closed my eyes for a moment.

'All right,' I said when I opened them. I was angry. Not with her. Not at myself, not exactly. Angry at the universe, I guess. Maybe I just needed to be angry right then even if there was nothing or no one to be angry at. 'Okay. Yes, I was a shit. You know how it feels to me? It feels like I fell into . . . I don't even know what to call it. A pit. A fucking abyss, whatever. And this last couple of months I fell out of it again. I guess you can see that much. And I will not be going back in. There is nothing I am more sure of in all this world. And I am sorry, I am so sorry, I am . . . I'm as sorry as the ocean is deep, I really am, for however much I hurt you when I was there. I love you, Talena, it rips my guts up to think that I hurt you at all, ever. I love you. But here we are. And, and, and you know what? I'm not even going to ask you to stay. I hope you do. And if you do I will try so hard to be the man you deserve. And I will never, ever, ever, do anything to hurt you again. But I'm not even going to ask. Do what you need to do. That's all I have to say. I mean it. That's what I want for you, that's what I want for both of us, that's all. Do what you need to do. But don't say it's inevitable. Please don't say that. Nothing is inevitable.'

I realized my speech was finished and fell back in my chair, panting like I had just sparred five full-contact rounds with Zoltan.

Talena stared at me wide-eyed.

'Okay,' she said quietly. 'Okay. I hear you. Okay.'

16 Night Flight

'One more night,' I said. 'We'll give them one more night and then try our luck ourselves.' Cain and Abel were more than half an hour late.

'Maybe we should call Sinisa?' Saskia suggested.

I shook my head. 'If these guys don't work out, I don't know. He's new around here too. I don't think he knows anybody else.'

'For fuck's sake,' Talena said. 'I'm supposed to work on Monday. If I don't show up at least on Tuesday they're going to start asking some seriously pointed questions about how exactly I got so sick.'

Not for the first time I considered abandoning Sinisa's plan and going overland as Talena had suggested. We could rent a car in Belize City, hide Saskia in the trunk, and just drive into Mexico. What were the odds of them searching a car driven by two wealthy gringos?

Unfortunately the more I thought about that question the higher those odds seemed. Belize, like Bosnia, was more placid than it had been ten years ago, but was still a classic smuggling nexus: loose borders, lax and/or corrupt government, a scofflaw culture. I didn't need Sinisa to tell me that. His security concerns, while overblown, had not been entirely delusional. You could see it in the wild-eyed crackheads who roamed the grimy streets of Belize City, the rusted grids of iron bars from behind which many shopkeepers sold their wares, the lengthy 'Dangers and Annoyances' section of the local *Lonely Planet*, the lost-generation lamentations of the local newspapers. The Mexican border guards wouldn't expect to find a battered Bosnian refugee in the trunk of our car, but they just might look for a hidden stash of coke or pot or heroin. Talena and I fitted the Big Score gringo-drug-mule profile to the proverbial T. Being Sinisa's guinea pigs was risky, but less risky than simultaneously braving the border ourselves and earning Sinisa's undying enmity.

'They are here,' Saskia said.

Indeed they were. Cain and Abel, big and small, crew cut and dreadlocks. They walked up to our table and surveyed us for a moment. I couldn't think of anything to say. 'Hello' seemed too trivial for what we were about to do.

'Let's go,' Abel said. 'Time be a-wasting.'

Hurry up and wait. Not my favourite game. We shouldered our bags, I hefted Sinisa's briefcase, and we followed them out of Popeye's and on to Front Street.

It was dark out, the moon had not yet risen, and when we got to Back Street there were few lights and we had to follow Cain's flashlight down the sandy streets. He led us around a ramshackle clapboard house, where we had to push our way past the encroaching palm trees, and suddenly the ocean was before us. Not much of it. The thin western passage between Caye Caulker and mainland Belize was maybe five miles wide. We could see lights on the mainland shore. Their boat was attached to a rotting wooden dock that jutted into the water behind the house. It was only a little bigger than the aluminium boats I had spent much of my teenage summers on, bombing around the lakes of northern Ontario. But it didn't need to be big. We were going to spend our whole journey behind Belize's mighty barrier reef, second largest in the world after Australia's, and the ocean behind that protective shield didn't get any rougher than the windy lakes of my youth unless a hurricane paid a visit.

'Go on, get in,' Cain said, illuminating the front of the boat with his light.

I felt perfectly calm and collected until I actually stepped into the boat. It bobbed in response to my weight transfer, and though I righted myself automatically something about the motion made me uneasy. My gut tautened with anxiety. I sat down on the bench, put the briefcase on my lap, and tried not to think about the fact that we were trusting these two men we had met only days ago to carry us illegally from Belize into Mexico, us and the mysterious cargo in my briefcase, on nothing more than Sinisa's inexperienced say-so. Even if Cain and Abel were reliable we still might be intercepted by the police. A boat engine carried a long way over water at night.

• The night air was warm and damp and full of mosquitoes. The smell of the sea was pungent; the ocean here was unusually briny, maybe something to do with the reef. There was a slight offshore breeze. Talena sat beside me, and Saskia beside her. The disc of light cast by Cain's flashlight illuminated a pair of fishing rods and an ancient tackle box made of cracked green plastic. Our cover story. I doubted the police would believe it for a minute. Maybe they were bribable. I hoped so. At least I could throw the briefcase overboard if we were intercepted on the open sea.

Cain and Abel sat on the back, on the other side of the boat, equalizing the weight. Abel took the flashlight and Cain started the engine. He had to yank the starter six times before the engine caught. I noticed there were no paddles and no life jackets. Abel jumped out, untied the boat from the dock, and stepped back in just before Cain switched off the flashlight and gunned the engine. The boat leaped out into the Caribbean.

It was so dark that without the electric lights on Caye Caulker, Ambergris Caye, and the mainland, I wouldn't have known that there was any land at all nearby. The howl of the engine sounded unhealthy. Between that, the wind shrieking past my ears, and the rapid-fire thumping of bow against waves, I would have had to scream for anyone to hear me. I wondered how Cain could possibly navigate in this darkness. I envisioned him taking a wrong turn and driving straight into the dense mangrove swamps that fringed all the undeveloped land here, hurtling the three of us face-first into the jungle. I reached out and took Talena's hand. Her heart was pulsing almost as fast as mine. I tried to focus on breathing deeply and not thinking at all, rather than imagining everything that might go wrong.

We moved north. The lights of Caye Caulker dwindled and vanished. We passed Ambergris Caye and then its lights too began to dissipate. There were no lights on the water. I began to suspect my fears of the Belizean border police had been unfounded. Belize didn't even have enough money to keep order in its capital city. Patrolling the ocean at night was off the bottom of the country's priority list. Mexico had more resources, but its coastguard probably wasn't in a position to mount a twenty-four-hour watch on its coastline either. If Mexico even had a coastguard.

About twenty minutes after leaving Caye Caulker, the engine noise dwindled to a low grumble. For a moment I was afraid that it had broken down or we were out of gas. I looked towards the back of the boat. My eyes had adjusted enough to the starlight to have an idea that Cain was looking to our left. I couldn't tell if we were near land or not, but then I saw a flash of light to our left, and another, and the boat yawed over to head straight for that light. As we neared shore Abel switched on our flashlight.

A little inlet led between many-branched mangrove trees, their leafy limbs reaching ten feet out from where land met sea. Cain threaded our boat through the narrow passage. It veered a little to the right and led us up to a clearing hacked roughly out of the swamp, mangrove stumps still visible amid the dirt. Big furrows that led from the clearing down into the sea told me that this place had been used for launching and unlaunching boats, at least one of them considerably bigger than Cain's. A Toyota Land Cruiser was parked in the clearing, by the mouth of a trail maybe six feet wide and overgrown with waist-high grass. Two men sat cross-legged on its hood, smoking and playing flashlights over our boat. Shielding my eyes against their bright halogen beams, I looked back and saw that the inlet trail had curved enough that the Land Cruiser was invisible from the open sea. I wondered how much cocaine had passed through this makeshift landing. My best guess was 'a whole lot.'

Cain drove the boat right up on to land until four feet of it protruded on to the muddy shore of the clearing. We had to hold on tightly to avoid falling off as it rolled to the left and came to a stop. Cain switched off the engine, and Talena and Saskia and I stepped out into wet mud.

'Hey man, wha's going on?' Abel asked brightly.

The guys on the Land Cruiser dismounted but didn't answer his question. In the light of Abel's flashlight they looked pretty creepy. Both of them were short but so heavily muscled that steroids had to be one of their four basic food groups, and both were tattooed with vivid murals featuring heavy use of jaguars, eagles, guns, knives and skulls. They weren't actually twins but looked similar enough that they could easily have been brothers.

Talena and Saskia and I squelched our way up to the Land Cruiser, which was parked on slightly more solid land.

'Hi,' I said, trying to sound bright and chirpy and unafraid. 'I'm Paul.'

I held out my hand to shake but they ignored it and looked past me to the boat. I couldn't really blame them since their hands were full of flashlights and cigarettes. After a moment I dropped my hand and looked back. I nearly gasped at the sight of the Uzi now hanging around Cain's shoulder on what looked like a guitar strap. An unexpected gun always looks obscene and unreal, like a movie prop. Cain followed Abel off the boat. Abel was holding two stapled-shut sacks about the size of pillow cases.

'Not just us being smuggled tonight,' Talena muttered.

I nodded uneasily. I was guessing it was just pot, from the way the sacks bulged, full of something loosely packed instead of some kind of dense powdered drug. But I didn't want to be part of any drug deal at all, especially one with guns involved. And when the Mexicans walked towards Cain and Abel, ignoring us completely, I saw that they carried pistols tucked behind their backs.

A long and frequently hostile discussion followed, in Spanish, between Cain and the Mexicans. We leaned against the Land Cruiser and watched nervously. I hoped they weren't arguing about money. If things went terribly wrong there wasn't much we could do. The mangrove jungle was too thick to flee into. The only bargaining chips we had were the threat of Sinisa's wrath, which might not count for much down here, at least not yet, and the fact that being white Americans our deaths would presumably not go uninvestigated. I wondered what would happen if the Latinos did suddenly turn on us and kill us. We would probably just vanish. Our bodies would never be discovered. Sinisa would regretfully write us off as a business expense. No governmental body would ever investigate.

But Hallam, Nicole, Lawrence, Steve, my friends in London, they would come to find out what had happened to us. I was sure of that. They knew we were here, I had kept them posted via email. It was somehow reassuring, knowing that even if these men betrayed us, even if we died here on this lonely smugglers' trail, I had friends who would turn over every stone in this country to find out what had happened to me.

The mellifluous flow of Spanish finally dried up. One of the muscle-bound Mexicans dug into a shoulder bag and came up with a shopping bag wrapped around what looked like a small brick. Money, I realized, US dollars. I couldn't tell the denomination but if it was twenties then the total had to be four or five thousand. He opened it up and partitioned it, keeping the smaller chunk and passing the larger to Cain. Cain counted his money, which took some time, and in the end he grunted his approval. I worked out what was happening. The Mexicans owed Cain for the pot, but Cain owed them for smuggling us. It looked like we were less valuable than the pot. I wondered if we should be insulted.

Then, the deal complete, big smiles broke out on all four smugglers' faces and they started laughing and joking and talking mile-a-second Spanish and clapping one another on the shoulder, like old friends at a party. A few minutes later, Cain and Abel returned to the boat, restarted the engine, and reversed out of the little inlet and into the darkness of the sea.

The Mexican steroid twins motioned us into the back seat of the Land Cruiser. The seats were torn and smelled powerfully of fish. I wondered if this was to confuse drug-sniffing dogs, or if the Mexicans were just keen fishermen.

The road through the mangrove jungle was a pair of pitted dirt tracks that crawled over extremely uneven terrain, but the Land Cruiser was equal to the task. Eventually we emerged from the jungle and turned on to a paved road. A half-hour later the three of us were in Chetumal's bus station, waiting for the last bus to Cancun.

'Only one border to go,' I said, later that night. We sat in one of Cancun's hundreds of hotels, cheaper and tawdrier than most, but the water pressure was good and the sheets tattered but clean. The clerk had copied information from my passport without looking up to see if I matched the picture. I had already forgotten the name of the place. Cancun was an awful town, all neon faux-glitz and cheesy dance clubs targeted at mindless hard-partying American college students, but it was a major transit nexus and a town where three white people could stay in complete anonymity as long as they liked.

'If it's even remotely like that last border you should stay in Mexico,' Talena said.

'We're here, aren't we?'

'Sure. Because the drug smugglers happened to be in a good mood and didn't screw each other over for once. This is fucked up, Paul. You're guinea pigs, you got that right, but not for people who are going to come after you. For drugs. That briefcase is the tip of the iceberg. Sinisa brought a boatload of something over in that private jet and he wants to get it into America and sell it. You two are here to make sure the road is open.'

'You're probably right,' I said. 'I bet when I call the number Sinisa gave us it'll be a drug smuggler who answers.

But that's not the point. We have to focus on getting Saskia over the border.'

'Yes. But we don't go with drug smugglers. That's way more dangerous than it needs to be. We dump that briefcase in a trash can somewhere and do it ourselves. There's what, a quarter of a million people who go across this border every year? Paul, this should be *easy*.'

That was true. Hundreds of would-be migrants died in the searing heat of the borderland desert every year, thousands more were intercepted by America's Border Guard, and there were plenty of stories of *coyotes*, professional smugglers, imprisoning their clients in so-called safe houses until their families ransomed them; but Talena was right, the vast majority of would-be Mexican illegals made it safely into America. Turning to drug smugglers for help getting across the border did sound a bit like using high explosives to landscape your garden.

'But what will Sinisa do if we leave his briefcase?' Saskia asked.

I looked at the nondescript briefcase and the small lock that sealed it shut. I felt like I was starring in the prequel to *Pulp Fiction*. Sinisa's briefcase looked a lot like that one. It didn't seem fair that my life revolved around this battered article of luggage and its unknowable contents.

'Depends on what's in there,' I said.

Talena said, 'Let's assume for the moment that it's drugs.'

'Fair enough.' I considered. 'Then I think we can also assume that if we and the briefcase just plain disappear, Sinisa figures we stole it and tracks us down and kills us.'

'In San Francisco? In America?' Saskia asked, shocked

at the thought that such things could happen in our golden end-of-the-rainbow destination.

'I hate to disappoint you,' I said, 'but America is not exactly a murder-free zone.'

'Then we should not leave the briefcase,' Saskia said. 'I am sorry, Talena, but I think Sinisa is very dangerous.'

'You and me both,' I agreed. 'But that still doesn't mean we have to use Sinisa's guys. We could still cross the border ourselves. But it's a big risk.'

'Big risk?' Talena asked. 'It's crazy. It's fucking insane. You understand that if we get caught driving a suitcase full of drugs across the border, our lives are *over*, right?'

'Metaphorically over,' I said. 'But if we don't get that suitcase over the border, our lives are *literally* over.'

'If you do this for Sinisa he'll just turn around and ask you to do something else.'

'But by then we'll be in America,' I said. 'In America we can say no. I'll be very happy to say no. But not until we get there.'

'I can't believe how fucked up this is,' Talena said.

Neither Saskia nor I had anything to say to that.

'All right,' she said. 'Fine. We take Sinisa's briefcase into America for him. But we get there by ourselves. No getting involved with more drug smugglers. Right?'

I nodded. We both looked at Saskia.

'Whatever you think is best,' she said, obviously still a little reluctant.

'Trust us,' I said. I hoped I wouldn't regret it.

'You want to go for a walk?' Talena asked later that night.

I looked at her, surprised. Saskia had just gone to her

room to sleep, and I had been on the verge of doing the same.

'Where?' I asked.

'The beach,' she said.

I shrugged. 'Sure.'

Cancun's beach, despite the best efforts of the vile high-rises and gated tourist complexes that polluted it, was very pretty, a pale endless arc of sand. The rushing sounds of the ocean drowned out most of the thumping techno from the waterfront discos. A warm sea breeze plucked at Talena's long hair as we walked, and the sand was cool and damp against our bare feet. I was in shorts, she in a green patterned sarong and blue bikini top. We walked hand in hand, silently, but comfortably so, for a long time.

'I wish we could walk forever,' Talena said. 'Somewhere the sun would never come up, and the beach would never end, and we would never get tired, we could just go on and on and never go back to real life.'

'This is real life too,' I said.

She nodded thoughtfully.

A little while later she said, 'Let's sit down for a bit, okay?'

We sat next to one another and faced the ocean, watched the white-capped waves surge and ripple in the moonlight, then lay back and stared up at the stars. I reached out for her without thinking about it, natural as breathing, and she rolled towards me and we lay together on the damp sand, my arm around her, her head on my chest. I felt her whole slender body quiver a little with each heartbeat. Her breath was warm against the hollow of my throat. She closed her eyes, and so did I, and we slept a little.

When I woke up I didn't know how much time had passed. Talena was motionless but I could tell by her breathing that she was awake. My arm around her ached slightly.

'Paul?' she whispered, after a little while.

'Yes?'

'If we try again?'

I swallowed. 'Yes?'

'You have to be nicer and better to me—'

'I know,' I said hastily, 'I know, I've been—'

'Wait,' she said. She wasn't whispering any more but her voice was low and soft and thick with sleep. 'Please. I'm not finished. I have to be nicer and better to you too. I've been vicious sometimes. I know you're sorry for how you've been. Well, I'm sorry too.'

I reached to her with my free hand and took her chin and tilted her face towards mine. There were tears on her cheeks. I kissed her very softly. We held each other for a long time.

'We don't have to live in the same apartment any more if you don't want,' she said. 'You can get your own place and we can date like before. But I was thinking, I mean, if you want to, maybe we could find a new place together. So it would feel more like home for both of us. Just if you want to. The other way is fine too.'

'I'd like that,' I said. 'Us finding a new place together. That would be fun.'

She smiled and kissed me.

'Silver lining department,' I said. 'You know how great normal life is going to seem when we get back? I swear, I'll whistle on the way to work every morning. You will too. All the crap that pisses people off, Muni and money and taxes and, I don't know, bad waiters, we're going to be fucking overjoyed to be so lucky as to experience them. People will think we're on happy drugs.'

'Yeah,' Talena said. 'You know what I've decided? Adventure sucks. Boring is good. Boring is the new black. From three days from now on, you and me are going to be as boring as boring can be.'

'Deal,' I agreed.

Her smile grew strained. 'Unless of course we both get arrested and thrown in jail for ten years tomorrow. That would be very unboring. Let's not do that.'

We laughed nervously.

17 Imperial Desert

Cancun to Ciudad Juárez via Mexico City by bus is an epic journey of suffering and endurance, one that would be worthy of television specials and ballads and Shakespearean plays, except the suffering consists of boredom and jackhammer headaches. You try spending twenty-eight consecutive hours on buses in a country where mass transit entertainment consists of dangling a dozen TVs from the bus ceiling, turning their collective volume all the way up to eleven, and showing an endless stream of amazingly low-production-value ninja action shoot-em-ups. My advice is to bring lots of aspirin, or a baseball bat to knock yourself out with. Especially if you happen to be in a position where your tedium turns to gut-wrenching dread every time you think of the next day's border crossing.

I learned on that bus that fear and boredom reinforce one another in a vicious spiral. Boredom gave me plenty of time to brood, the more I brooded the more scared I got, and the more scared I got, the slower time seemed to pass. I fluctuated between periods of being nervous but confident that the odds were in our favour, when I just wanted the crossing to be over with, and periods of abject gasping terror, when I wanted to turn around and stay in Mexico as long as possible, rather than dare the border.

It was Moby who saved my sanity, Moby and his buddies Radiohead, Fleetwood Mac, and the Sex Pistols, powered by the twenty-pack of batteries I had wisely purchased for my Discman. Saskia and Talena and I passed the Discman and the Harry Potter books we had bought in Cancun back and forth, when we weren't dozing. It was hard to read, with the constant jostling of the bus and the sounds that kept trying to batter their way into our consciousness, mostly movie gunfights and chop-socky ninja battles but sometimes car horns or passenger arguments.

Our only respite was in Mexico City, where we traded boredom and dread for hassle. We arrived at the southern bus station, hopped a shuttle bus to the northern bus station, and promptly got stuck in traffic. It was night, which I regretted; I wanted to get a sense of Mexico City's vast megalopolis, which contains in its greater urban area more people than the entire population of Canada, but all I saw was an endless ocean of roads, cars, street lights, neon signs, brightly lit storefronts, and occasional glimpses of mobs of people that reminded me of Hong Kong. Thankfully Mexico's bus stations were considerably more efficient and less chaotic than I had expected, and we made it on to the northbound bus to Ciudad Juárez.

'Talk about a good walk spoiled,' Talena said, as the TV ninja slaughtered a golfing foursome for poorly explained reasons.

'He forgot to yell "fore" before he threw the throwing star!' I said. 'Two-stroke penalty!'

'I bet the ninja is really a member of the fashion police,' she said. 'The fashion assassin. Look, my God, that guy's wearing a paisley jacket over a striped shirt, he better not get away!' He didn't.

'I bet he's just jealous,' I said. 'Sure, he knows eighty silent ways to kill a man, but he's still a thirty handicap.'

'Maybe the country club has a no ninjas policy,' Talena suggested. 'But look, do they ever have heavily armed security! In golf carts!'

'I bet they're Humvee golf carts,' I said. 'The Pentagon paid a million dollars each for those. Thirty gallons a mile.'

'Now they're chasing him! It's a low-speed pursuit!'

'The ninja is down!' I announced. 'I repeat, the ninja is—oh, wait, he's hiding in the water hazard. He's going to catch a cold.'

'Maybe he's looking for golf balls,' Talena said. 'Even ninjas have to make ends meet.'

'Where's he going to dry that ninja suit?' I asked. 'Where do ninjas do laundry?'

'They sneak in late at night and hotwire the machines,' she explained. 'It's one of the lesser known secret ninja tricks, along with sneaking to the front of the line at the bank.'

'I wondered how it was the damn ninjas always beat me to the tellers.'

'Look, he's making a reed into a blowgun! He's a ninja *and* a Boy Scout! Now—'

The old woman in front of Talena turned and furiously shushed us. I looked around and realized that every Mexican on the bus, which meant everyone but the three of us, was glaring in our general direction. I smiled weakly. 'Sorry,' I said, and Talena and I shrank back down into our seats, chastened, until we looked at one another and started giggling wildly again, like children.

Saskia leaned over and whispered, 'I think we should not make so much noise. I think maybe this is a very important movie for them.'

Then we really started laughing, heedless of the angry Mexicans.

'Ninja III: The Domination—' I said, but I was laughing too hard to finish.

'It's the *Schindler's List* of Mexico!' Talena howled, and we whooped with laughter until it hurt. The Mexicans, writing us off as crazy or drug-addled, sighed and turned back to their own devices.

We were a little crazy. We were frightened of the upcoming border crossing, and punch-drunk from non-stop bus travel, and our laughter was a little hysterical. But more than that, Talena and I were just giddily happy with one another again, silly and childish and wonderfully unself-conscious together for the first time in more than a year. I wouldn't have traded that feeling for anything.

When we settled back down I noticed that a score of our fellow passengers were in a single tight group: mostly men in jeans and T-shirts, small and dark-skinned, but a few women in home-made dresses and blue and white shawls. They were . . . Indians? Native Mexicans? First Nations? I didn't know what the culturally sensitive descriptor was in Mexico. The leader of the group was a pretty young woman just out of her teens, with considerably paler skin than those she led, wearing Juicy Couture sweat pants and an expensive-looking denim jacket. I couldn't understand a word she said, but when she lectured her followers, many of whom were much older than her, I could tell she had all the usual petulance and know-it-all impatience of youth, and then some. I had imagined coyotes as tough-looking middle-aged hombres, the kind of men who smoked cigarillos and wore fringed leather jackets. This girl would have looked right at home in Beverly Hills. I supposed in a way that was the point. I wonder if she would actually lead this pack of would-be farm workers right over the border and across the desert in those Juicy Couture sweat pants, or if she was just a recruiter who took them to Ciudad Juárez, somebody else handled the actual crossing.

As we advanced northward the landscape changed from green hills to rocky scrub tufted with thorn bushes, and then the kind of arid desert I always imagined when I thought of Mexico, thanks to the thousand Hollywood depictions deep in my cultural DNA. We passed dozens of twenty-four-hour tyre-repair shops, which said a lot about Mexican roads, their presence indicated by huge truck tyres with naked light bulbs burning within like bull's-eyes.

Around midnight Talena curled up against me and fell asleep, her head on my shoulder, my arm around her neck. I watched her sleep for a little while, luminously beautiful. I felt like I cradled something invaluably precious and terribly fragile in my arm. I didn't move a muscle for fear of waking her. She occasionally muttered a few garbled words of Croatian. I knew that even though for years now she had thought only in English, she often still dreamed in Croatian.

I was uneasy when we finally entered the outskirts of Ciudad Juárez the next morning. I knew from Internet research that this was a city of dire reputation, the hunting ground of one or more extremely busy serial killers. Given the numbers it almost had to be a group. Over the last decade, the bodies of at least a hundred young women had been found abandoned in the desert, raped and strangled and mutilated. The one thing every source agreed on was that the true number of victims was far larger. Estimates of the real body count varied from three hundred to over a thousand, but nobody really knew how many more might lie undiscovered by the Ciudad Juárez police. Or perhaps outright hidden by them. Site after site excoriated the catalogue of police idiocy, corruption and laziness in connection with this case. Their hunt for the most prolific murderers in the history of the continent was at best lacklustre. Several commentators had suggested that the police were somehow involved or actively trying to protect the killers. True or not, it underscored that this was not a good place to get into any kind of trouble.

Serial killers aside, Ciudad Juárez was a terrible city, one that had obviously grown too far too fast, a wasteland of rotted streets, crumbling walls, broken traffic lights, rusted skeletal automotive remains abandoned on the street, masses of beaten-down people shambling from place to place like they were in a George Romero movie. I splurged on the Holiday Inn, rather than one of Ciudad Juárez's several backpacker hostels. I wondered, as I passed my credit card to the receptionista, if this was a sign I was getting old. The full-on sensory overload of backpacker hostels nowadays seemed frenetic and draining. Somehow, while my back was turned, the inhabitants of such places had become young, callow and loudly alcoholized, people I would rather avoid. Once they had been full of people just like me. These days, especially after a long bus ride, the relative peace and serenity of the Holiday Inn was extremely inviting.

Our plan was idiot-simple. Saskia and I would spend the night in Ciudad Juárez. Talena would cross the border to El Paso. Tomorrow she would rent a car, drive down here, pick us up, and drive back, with me in the passenger seat and Saskia and the briefcase in the trunk. We would simply hope that ours was one of the cars not selected for further inspection. The odds were pretty good. About one in fifty was pulled aside, said the all-knowing Internet. A ninety-eight per cent chance of success. Who wouldn't take that? But those last two per cent loomed Tyrannosaurus Rex large in our minds.

Talena came up with Saskia and me to our Holiday Inn room. I thought she was just saying goodbye before hopping a cab to the border. But instead she said something to Saskia in Croatian. Saskia fell silent for a moment, and then smiled widely, said something back, and quickly exited the room.

I looked at Talena. 'What was that all about?'

'I told her to stay down there with her magazine and give us an hour of privacy.'

'Oh.' I turned and looked at her as she closed and locked the door.

'Don't just stand there,' she said. 'Clock's ticking.'

'Are you scared?' Talena asked.

'Yeah,' I said.

She raised herself up to kiss me and lowered her head back to my sweat-soaked chest.

'Are you?' I asked.

'Sure. But not like I was before. Now the worst that can happen is getting arrested. Which would really suck but isn't as bad as finding out Dragan found you and tortured you to death. I'd catch myself imagining that sometimes. The things the back alleys of my brain can come up with, God, you have no idea. Anyways, never mind, never happened. It's all good.'

'It's all good,' I echoed, closing my eyes.

She snorted. 'I almost forgot how little you like to talk after sex.'

'No, I like it,' I protested. 'I always like talking to you. I'm just kind of dreamy. Especially this time. This was, yeah. Wow.'

'Yeah. I could tell. You're not usually so noisy.'

'Was I noisy?'

She giggled.

'Oh,' I said, embarrassed.

'Sorry about the bite marks,' she said, inspecting my shoulder. 'They, um, seemed like the thing to do at the time. I don't think they'll bruise. I'm sure glad this cheap-ass Third World bed held up. You'd think Holiday Inn could afford better. I was getting a little worried about it while I was still, you know, able to think.'

'Yeah. If Saskia came up here and found out we broke the bed I bet she wouldn't stop blushing for weeks.'

'She's not so shy and innocent as all that, believe me,'

Talena said. She paused. 'How is she? How do you think she's doing?'

'She seems okay,' I said. 'I guess. I don't know. She has a lot of nightmares. I guess when someone tells you she has a head full of land-mines you can't really say she's okay. But I think she will be eventually. She's getting better. I really like her. We get along really well. She's funny. And she's so smart; can you believe how good her English is already? Give her a year or two, and the whole total new environment thing, and I think she'll be okay.'

'I hope so,' Talena said. 'I bet being around you has been good for her. I don't know if she would have been able to be friends with a guy for a long time otherwise.'

'Yeah.'

'You're a good man, Balthazar Wood.'

'You're a good woman, Talena Radovich.'

'I bet you say that to all the girls.'

I laughed.

'All right,' Talena said. 'Let's get this show on the road.'

On Wednesday, 14 May 2003, at 4.15 p.m., we approached the border between Mexico and America. Borders are fuzzy things but this one was pretty clearly marked. The real border here was the US immigration post.

Talena drove. I sat in the passenger seat. Saskia was curled up in the trunk with Sinisa's briefcase. There was nobody else, there was no elaborate plan. DIY smuggling. It had seemed like a good idea. But as we approached, I was visibly sweating, my heart was thundering like I had contracted malaria and then snorted a line of coke, and I was silently but desperately wishing we had used Sinisa's connection after all.

I tried to emanate vibes of being nothing more suspicious than a pleasant young couple who had come down to Ciudad Juárez for a weekend of fun. Not exactly a perfect cover. For one thing, I wasn't sure there was any fun within a fifty-mile radius of Ciudad Juárez. And the whole drug-mule thing was still an issue. Be cool, I told myself. Be cool.

I did not feel cool. All this anticipation, stop-and-go as car after car filed through the border, was slowly driving me insane. And I hadn't seen a vehicle pulled aside for further inspection for a long time. I thought it was about due to happen again.

The car in front of us pulled away from the border station, and it was officially too late to back out. The bar swung back down to block our entry and Talena eased the car up to the booth in which the bored immigration officer stood. My heart sank when I saw it was a man. I had hoped for a woman. Women are more sympathetic.

The man was big and white, obviously a gym rat, with a nearly shaved layer of dyed-blond hair on his head and a single earring, standard current American-cool look. His eyes held no spark of intelligence. And this Eminem wannabe, who probably didn't even have a college education, hadn't read a book since high school, and had never been out of the country himself, was about to decide the course of my life, and Talena's and Saskia's. I swallowed, told myself not to be such an intellectual snob, and put on my best shit-eating smile.

'Are you US citizens?' he asked.

'I am,' Talena said. 'He's Canadian.'

'Passports.'

We passed ours over. He glanced at Talena's American passport and immediately passed it back. 'What is the purpose of your travel?' he asked me.

'I'm . . . purpose? In the States? Oh. I'm visiting her. She's my girlfriend.'

Talena gave me a steady-yourself look. I was sure he could see that I was visibly nervous. But then he was probably used to that, I thought wildly, he probably knew that lots of innocent people got nervous when facing immigration, including me. I actually wasn't that much more nervous than I was when entering America without an illegal Bosnian refugee and a briefcase probably full of drugs tucked into the trunk of my car.

'Where is your place of residence?'

'Toronto,' I lied. I couldn't answer "San Francisco" because I wasn't legally allowed to live there indefinitely without a job.

'What do you do there?'

'I'm a computer programmer.'

I tried to think of a Toronto company I could claim to work for, but he didn't ask. He flipped through my passport, and his eyes narrowed. A common reaction. My passport was double-wide, forty-eight pages rather than the usual twenty-four, and was decorated with the stamps of more than thirty countries. Some of those countries were Indonesia, Morocco, Mauritania and Egypt, Islamic-majority nations, my visits to which could well cause suspicion in post-World-Trade-Center America. Even without those four stamps, the fact that I travelled so much might alone make him decide to pull us over and open the trunk. I kicked myself for not having realized that I was the risk. I should have gone over the border by myself and allowed Talena to shuttle Saskia and the briefcase alone.

'Where's your entry stamp?'

I blinked. 'Excuse me?'

'Your entry stamp. Into Mexico. When you come in, they're supposed to stamp your passport.'

Not the way I came in, I almost said. Instead I shrugged.

'Why don't you have an entry stamp?' he demanded, looking straight at me.

I tried to think of a good reason but couldn't. My throat was so tensely constricted that I could barely breathe. I thought it was obvious that I was panicking but later Talena told me that I just looked very confused.

'I don't know,' I croaked.

The immigration officer shook his head.

'They're so unprofessional over there,' he said, looking to the Mexican side of the border. 'They make our job twice as hard as it needs to be.'

He stamped my passport and passed it back.

'Enjoy your visit,' he said to me, and to Talena, 'Welcome home.'

We thanked him. He pushed a button and the bar before us went up like a *Sieg heil* salute. Talena stepped on the gas and we drove forward, away from the border, into the Promised Land, into America. Into America, free and clear.

We called the number Sinisa had given us from an El Paso pay phone. It rang three times, then, after a brief pause, rang again. Some kind of automatic forwarding system.

'Yes?' Sinisa answered.

'Sinisa,' I said. I felt nervous, like I was about to quit a job. Which in a way I was. 'This is Paul.'

'Paul. Good. I was worried about you. My associates told me you had not yet contacted them. Where are you?'

'El Paso, Texas.'

'Texas,' he said. 'I am glad to hear that. Were my associates mistaken or did you elect not to employ their services?'

'We decided it would be easier to cross by ourselves.'

'Did you lose anything on the journey?'

'No,' I said. 'We have the briefcase. We want to know what you want done with it.'

'Did you lose the address?' Sinisa asked. He had given us a Los Angeles address where we were meant to drop off the briefcase, en route to San Francisco. Talena and I had discussed actually going there, but it sounded too much like making a delivery to a crack house.

'No,' I said.

After a moment Sinisa said, 'Paul, I do not understand why you are calling me.'

'All right,' I said. I swallowed. 'Listen. I'm very sorry. I have the greatest respect for you and for your vision. And I want you to know that I will never tell anyone about you, or what you are doing, or the work I did for you. But I don't wish to continue our relationship any more, on a business or a personal level, as of today. I'll mail the briefcase wherever you like, but one way or another, it leaves my possession today.'

I waited, holding my breath, for what felt like a long time.

Finally he spoke. 'I am very disappointed, Paul. Surprised and very disappointed. I had high hopes for you.'

'I'm sorry,' I mumbled. 'I guess I'm not cut out for living your kind of life.'

'Do you know what was in that briefcase?' he asked.

I didn't want to get drawn into a guessing game. 'No.'

'Sand. Four kilograms of sand. Do what you like with it. You thought it was drugs? You thought I might give you drugs? Foolish, Paul, very foolish. I am a businessman. Illicit drugs, I assure you, are bad business. The profits are very high, but the risks even higher. Even if I did wish to send drugs to America, do you really think I would send so much, a briefcase full, perhaps a million dollars' worth, with a man I had met only six weeks ago, with no escort, no security, no certainty? When I have Zoltan and Zorana here, who I trust implicitly, ready to do such things for me?'

He raised a good point. After a moment I said, 'Why?'

'To see if I could trust you. To see if you would trust me. That is all. I thought you were a friend, Paul. I had high hopes for you. I am building an empire, an empire that will carry the weak people of this world to places where they can become strong, and I had a high place in it reserved for you. You are so stupid it makes me angry. I give you a chance to be part of something important, something noble, I give you a chance to change the world for the better, and you spit it back in my face.'

'I'm sorry you feel that way,' I said. And I did feel bad about it. I knew it was the right thing to do, but I still felt a little like I was throwing away something wonderful, abandoning a chance at an extraordinary life in favour of that endless monotony called safety.

'Zoltan and Zorana were right,' Sinisa said. 'They told me you were weak, fearful, a little man. I thought there was more to you. But they were right. I pity you, Paul. I pity your little life. I think we will not speak again. Goodbye.'

He hung up. I looked at the phone for a long moment before I did the same. I wondered if some day, years or decades from now, I might bitterly regret this phone call.

'Well?' Talena asked, when I emerged from the pay phone.

'Maybe he's not such a bad guy after all,' I said.

'Maybe *what?*'

'Never mind,' I said. 'He won't bother us any more, that's what's important. We're clear.' I sighed. 'So let's go home.'

Three months passed.

4 California, August 2003

18 Satori

'Christ, I'm a *sidewinder*, I'm a *California king*,' I sang along with Anthony Kiedis. 'I swear it's *everywhere* now, it's *every*—oh. Oh. Hi. You're home.'

'You were expecting someone else?' Talena asked, laughing as I sheepishly unhooked my Discman. She was at the computer, looking at pictures, probably some kind of research or fact-checking for a new Lonely Planet guide.

'I thought you were out at the poetry reading,' I said.

'I thought it would be more fun to stay home and listen to karaoke Chili Peppers. No, the reading was cancelled, three of the poets couldn't make it. I was going to go to yoga but the time got away from me. How was boxing?'

'Fun. Tough. But it's not making me sweat as much as it used to.'

'Yeah. Your shirt just looks sweaty. Not soaked. You know something, Mr Wood, you look pretty good these days. All this running and boxing is making you downright athletic.'

'Yeah?' I asked, smiling. I smiled a lot these days, and it wasn't just the post-workout endorphins. I had money in the bank, I was semi-gainfully employed at an interesting job, and I had just moved into a comfortable new apartment with the World's Most Perfect Girlfriend.

'Yeah.' She reached her arms up and stretched. 'I should exercise more too. Stupid time-eating computer. And I meant to go grocery shopping. I think we have to eat out tonight. How does Thai sound?'

'Sounds good to—' I began, and then the recognition centre of my brain fired off a lightning bolt, and I stopped talking and looked at the computer screen. There were about a dozen passport-sized photos on screen, each with a little blurb of information beneath. I knew the man on the upper left.

'What the hell?' I said.

Talena blinked and followed my gaze. 'What?'

'What . . . that . . . what are you doing?'

'Oh.' She shook her head. 'Just, I don't know, checking up. No progress, not really. They caught some minnow guy who shelled Dubrovnik and they unsealed a bunch more warrants and indictments, that's all.'

'You were checking up on Zoltan?'

She looked up at me, confused. 'On who?'

'Zoltan,' I said. 'That's Zoltan.' I pointed at his picture. 'The guy I told you about, who was with Sinisa. You met him, remember? For like ten seconds. Him and his wife Zorana. What are you looking at? What is this site?'

I peered at the picture, which was captioned 'Zoltan Knezevic, born 26.07.69 Vojvodina, warrant date 13.08.03, no known alias.' The photo was black and white, taken from his left side. It was a few years old but there was no doubt it was him.

'The guy who was with Sinisa,' Talena repeated slowly. She stared up at me as if I had spoken in some foreign language that she barely knew, and she had to slowly mentally translate. 'You knew him. He was with Sinisa. This man right here'—she pointed at the screen—'you're saying he was with Sinisa.'

'Yeah. What is this? How did you get this picture?'

'Oh, my God.' She stared up at me with her mouth half open.

'What . . . ' I looked at the page address, which started with 'www.un.org/icty/.' 'The UN? What does Zoltan have to do with the UN?'

She just looked at me.

A cloud of horrible comprehension began to congeal inside my skull.

'Warrant date? What the fuck is ICTY?' I demanded.

Her voice was very quiet, almost a whisper. 'The International Criminal Tribunal for the former Yugoslavia,' she said. 'The war crimes tribunal. This is their list of wanted war criminals they've issued arrest warrants for. They just, he just, he's on the list. He's a war criminal. Three times over. I was just reading about him. He was at Omarska and at Keraterm and, Jesus, Paul, he was at Srebrenica, he helped *organize* Srebrenica.'

'The doctor,' I said, pointing at another face, a row below. I felt cold and dizzy, like all the blood was draining from my body. 'That's the doctor. That's the one who helped Saskia on the plane when she had that ear problem.'

'Veselin Mrksic,' Talena said. 'Oh, my fucking God. He was on the plane too? He helped Saskia?' She shook her head disbelievingly.

'What did he do? Why is he there?'

'He was at Vukovar Hospital. He was a doctor there, but he helped. There was a massacre. He murdered his own patients. Dozens of them. After that he was Mladic's personal doctor. Ratko Mladic. The Serb general. King of the monsters.'

I scanned the rest of the pictures. 'Oh, shit. I think those two too. I think they came to Belize with us too.'

We stared at each other.

'War criminals,' she said. 'You're saying your friend Sinisa flew a planeload of war criminals over the Atlantic with you. Not just, I mean, criminals, that's such a, that's not the right word, I don't think there is a right word, not for what they did. Evil. That's the only word. These people on this page, they were the worst of the worst, they could have given lessons to the Nazis. Jesus, Paul, do you have any idea what these people *did*? Do you have any fucking idea?'

'I guess. I've read some books about it.'

'You guess. No, you don't. You don't. Neither do I. You had to be there to have any idea. You know what Zoltan is wanted for? I was just fucking reading about him. For pushing a prisoner's face against a red-hot stove until half his face was burned off, then doing the other half. For smashing a prisoner in the face with a big chain until he didn't have any teeth left and every bone in his face, every single bone, was broken and one eye was burst. For wrapping wire around a prisoner's testicles, then tying the other end of the wire to his motorcycle and driving off. He had an office. It sounds like a sick joke, but he had an office. Omarska was an old mining complex and there were offices in the administrative building. Every day he would torture men in his office, then at night he'd take a woman into this office, high-school girls a lot of the time, with the men's blood and shit and bones and brains all over the place, and he and his friends would make her clean it up, sometimes they made her eat it, and then they would bend her over the desk and gang-rape her and stick things in her until at least once a girl died of blood loss because she was haemorrhaging from everywhere. There's more. There's a lot more. That's just his greatest hits, just Omarska. That doesn't count Keraterm. That doesn't count Srebrenica. Jesus, Paul, Srebrenica, seven thousand people slaughtered, fucking genocide, Zoltan was *there,* he helped *organize* it.'

'He's here.'

'He *what?*'

'I told you. I think I told you. Last month, when I met up with Arwin, he said Zoltan and Zorana came with him to San Francisco.'

'Yeah,' she said. 'Yeah. I remember. You told me.'

We stared at each other.

I sat down, hard. The enormity of it all was beginning to hit.

Zoltan and the zombies were war criminals. Not smugglers, not drug dealers. They made murderers and arms dealers and child pornographers look like Mother Teresa. The things they had done were called *crimes against humanity,* and with reason. The other passengers on the Gulfstream that had carried Saskia and me to safety were two dozen of the worst people in the world. No hyperbole, no exaggeration, cold hard fact, up there in the pantheon of modern evil with the architects of the Rwandan genocide, the brutal SLORC generals who ran Myanmar, or the late unlamented Uday Hussein, to name a few. And Sinisa, ponytailed self-proclaimed idealist Sinisa, had smuggled them out of the Balkans, away from the scene of their crimes, into the relative safety of Belize. Some of them had since come to America. Maybe all of them.

And I had helped them.

He had known. Sinisa must have known. He had known all along who they were. He had told me he was helping the poor and downtrodden, setting the world to rights, and I had taken his blood money and shrouded his operation in a cloak of absolute secrecy. It was like I had helped Goebbels and Eichmann escape Nazi Germany.

They would be almost impossible to catch now. In part because of me.

'What are we going to do?' Talena asked. 'What in God's name are we going to *do*?'

What we were going to do was, we were going to call the FBI.

It was a pretty stark choice. Stay quiet or go to the cops. There were a lot of reasons to stay quiet. Saskia, for one. Arwin, probably. I didn't think he knew who the zombies were, I thought he was relatively innocent. In this newly paranoid America they could both easily get sucked in and chewed up by the vortex of an official FBI investigation. For all I knew they might wind up in Guantánamo Bay. Hell, *I* might wind up in Guantánamo Bay; it was far-fetched but it didn't seem impossible. I had been complicit in what Sinisa had done, ignorant or not I was probably culpable of something, aiding or abetting or who knows what. God knew it *felt* like I had committed a terrible crime. I had provided tangible assistance to some of the most horrific torturers and mass murderers in recent planetary history.

We never really seriously considered keeping our mouths shut. We wouldn't have been able to live with ourselves. Talena had been slightly obsessed with the hunt for Bosnia's war criminals ever since she first escaped to America. I felt crippling guilt about what I had done, but at least I had the excuse of honest ignorance. Now that I knew the truth, doing nothing would be far worse than what I had already done. Saskia or no, Arwin or no, even me or no, silence was not an option.

'It's here somewhere,' I said absent-mindedly, digging through my NATO ammunition box, a gift from Hallam that contained all of my potentially important but rarely needed documents. 'What happened to the one she gave you?'

'I lost it. Didn't she send you email? Can't you get her name from that?'

'That's right. She did. I don't—oh, here it is.' I dug a business card from the box. The FBI logo was embossed on the upper left-hand corner. 'Turner,' I read. 'Of course. I can't believe I forgot. Must be getting old or something. Special Agent Anita Turner. Pass me my phone.'

It was almost 9 p.m. but I dialled the number anyway on the off chance she was still in the office. The receiving telephone rang once.

'Special Agent Turner,' she answered briskly.

'Ms Turner. Oh. Uh. Hi.' I had expected voice-mail. 'Uh, yeah, um, good to talk to you again. My name is Balthazar Wood. I don't know if you remember me, but, um, we met a few years ago, about, uh . . . ' I didn't know how to describe it. I didn't really want to talk about our previous encounter.

'I remember you well, Mr Wood.'

'Oh. Good. I hope. Anyway, something's happened, um, not at all related to what was going on back then, something else entirely, and the FBI needs to know about it. You really do. So, it's complicated. I'd like to meet you if that's possible, tomorrow if that's possible, and I'll tell you all about it.'

'Is that so.'

'Yes, ma'am.' Ma'am was not part of my usual conversational repertoire but it seemed appropriate. Agent Turner, if I recalled correctly, was very proper and 1950s.

'What I remember most about you, Mr Wood, is that less than a week after our last conversation, the subject of that conversation was found in Morocco, dead.'

There wasn't anything I wanted to say to that.

'What is the subject you want to discuss?' she asked.

'War criminals,' I said.

'Excuse me?'

'War criminals. Bosnian war criminals. They've been smuggled into America.'

'Mr Wood, this sounds a lot like a crank call.'

'I know. That's why I'm calling you. Because you know from our last conversation that I'm a serious person. You can probably also guess that I wouldn't be calling you at all if I didn't think it was absolutely necessary.'

After a pause she said, 'True. My office, oh eight hundred Friday.'

'What?'

'Oh eight hundred,' she said impatiently. 'Be in my office at that time the day after tomorrow.'

'Right.' I had forgotten that she talked in military time. 'I'll be there.'

She hung up without another word. I supposed it was efficiency rather than rudeness.

I looked over to Talena. 'I hope this is the right thing to do.'

'Me too. Me too. We better practise your lies before you go.'

'Yeah,' I said.

'She's going to know you're lying. She's really fucking smart. I remember that.'

'I know. I hope she's smart enough to see I'm not lying about the important parts.'

Talena nodded.

'It all makes sense now,' I said. 'Fucking war criminals. Fuck. That was so *stupid*. I should have known. I knew something was wrong with them, the zombies, but I didn't know what. It was all so weird, I figured I was just being paranoid.'

'Stop it. There will be no blaming yourself, understand?'

'Easy for you to say,' I muttered.

'Shut up. I don't want to hear it. You were not stupid. You were in a desperate situation in an alien country and there is no way you could have known. You were lucky the warrants weren't unsealed while you were there or they would have killed both of you. Now what about the Russian guy? Arwin?'

'I don't know.' I considered. 'I don't think he knew the whole story. He knew we were going to Belize, but he didn't know much about the zombies. He acted more like he thought they were total losers, not scary war criminals. I hope he didn't know. I like Arwin. You know, him I can get in touch with, he gave me his email—holy shit.'

'What?'

'His back door. Arwin put a back door into the system. I scrambled it but it's still there.'

Talena regarded me warily.

'Basically,' I said, 'if Arwin and I got together, we could break into Mycroft. That website I built for them. Arwin put a back door in. All the messages there are supposed to be secret but if Arwin and I got together we could read them.'

'Good. That's good. You should tell the FBI that.'

'Yeah. But. If I tell the FBI about Arwin they'll probably lock him up. He was already deported, at least once, and now they'll probably figure he's some kind of dangerous hacker on top of that.'

'Can't make an omelette.'

'Yeah, but . . . probably the one guy who doesn't deserve to get screwed over is Arwin.'

'Life is harsh,' Talena said curtly.

'Okay, point taken, getting Sinisa and Zoltan and the rest is more important. But still. We don't actually need Arwin, we just need . . . basically we just need him to give us a password. If I can get him to give me that then we won't have to sic the FBI on him.'

'So now you're going to lie about both Saskia and Arwin? And you're still going to pretend that what you're lying about isn't important? Arwin's password thing is probably the most important thing you can tell them. And he's the one who told you that Zoltan and Zorana were here in the USA. All the important stuff is all about him.'

'I think I owe him one chance,' I said. She was right, but I didn't want to turn around and rat on Arwin without at least giving him a chance. 'Tell you what. I'll send him an email and tell him I have to talk to him tomorrow. Then I'll give him one chance to give me the password. If he does then I won't have to tell the FBI about him.'

'You're going to threaten him,' Talena said sceptically.

'What, now you think I'm going too hard on him?'

'You're not thinking this through, Paul.'

'What do you mean?' I asked.

'I mean if you go to Arwin and threaten him and tell him you're about to go to the FBI, he just might turn around, call your friend Zoltan—'

'Please stop referring to him as my friend.'

'Okay. Sorry. But he just might call Zoltan and tell him he better make sure we never make it to Agent Turner's office. You understand? This isn't a game. Please wake the fuck up. Just because we're back in America doesn't mean we're safe. If they find out that we know, we'll be in very deep, very serious shit. Even after we tell the FBI, we'll be witnesses. You know what happens to witnesses a lot of the time? Their corpses wind up face-down in large bodies of water. Not the final resting place I had in mind, you know. I was kind of planning on a big funeral when I'm eighty, lots of sobbing grandchildren and a nice mausoleum and all the bells and whistles. So wake up and stop worrying about your Russian friend and start worrying about us. We could be in danger here. Seriously. A lot of it. You understand?'

I looked at her. After a moment I nodded. 'Yeah,' I said quietly. 'Yeah. I understand.'

The FBI's San Francisco headquarters is on the thirteenth floor of 450 Golden Gate Avenue, the Philip Burton Federal Building and US Courthouse, a twenty-two-storey sheer-walled monstrosity near City Hall that looks a bit like a gigantic radiator grille. The Stars and Stripes waved over a few small trees struggling to emerge from tiny portholes in the concrete plaza that led up to the entrance. The general architectural intent seemed to be Abandon All Hope And Be Intimidated And Dehumanized, Ye Who Enter Here. I felt a bit like a Catholic schoolboy about to go to his first confession, afraid that he would be damned to hell forever.

Agent Turner hadn't changed a bit. Middle-aged, dressed in a conservative dark business suit, a face wrinkled like her skull had shrunk beneath it, sharp eyes that studied rather than observed everything they encountered. Her desk was frighteningly clean, decorated only by the picture of a pretty blonde girl maybe eighteen years old holding a swimming trophy. Her daughter, I supposed. Maybe her niece. It was hard to imagine Agent Turner with a family or any kind of human existence at all outside the FBI.

She shook our hands from behind her desk and had us sit down.

'Begin recording,' Agent Turner said, presumably to some voice-activated digital recorder lurking in her desk. 'August fifteenth, two thousand and three, oh eight oh four Pacific time. Special Agent Anita Turner.' She looked at us. 'Please introduce yourselves with your names, ages, addresses and occupations.'

I swallowed and said, 'Balthazar Wood, twenty-nine, 1256 Rhode Island Street, San Francisco, software consultant, self-employed.'

After a moment Talena said, 'Talena Radovich, twenty-nine, 880 Kansas Street, San Francisco, Web editor, Lonely Planet Publications.'

Which was already something of a lie. Talena paid the rent on 880 Kansas, but it was occupied by Saskia. Talena lived with me in our new place on Rhode Island. If she had given my address it might have looked suspicious that she was the tenant of record at Kansas Street. On the other hand now that they had both addresses maybe they would come to 880 Kansas looking for Talena and find Saskia there. What a tangled web we weave.

'Subjects have alleged that they have personal knowledge of Balkan war criminals at large in America,' Agent Turner said. She turned to me. 'Please tell me everything in your own words, from the start. Then I'll ask whatever questions I need answered.'

'All right,' I said. 'Well. I guess it all started with the little boy . . .'

I talked long enough that my voice grew hoarse. Mostly I told the truth. Omitting any mention whatsoever of Saskia was surprisingly easy. I simply claimed that after I took the little boy to the warehouse, Sinisa had asked to meet me, and when we met he offered me a job, and I needed the money so I took it. The lie depicted me as pretty damn mercenary, eagerly selling my services to highly suspicious people while being at best wilfully ignorant that they were a criminal refugee-smuggling syndicate, but as long as I shielded Saskia I didn't mind being misunderstood.

I told Agent Turner all about meeting Arwin in San Francisco, and him telling me that Zoltan and Zorana had arrived in the country, and, although I felt terrible about it, I told her about Arwin's back door. As I spoke I was convinced that I was initiating a massive FBI investigation, the full brunt of which was about to fall on Arwin's rodentlike shoulders, and I felt horribly guilty about ratting out a friend.

It turned out I didn't need to be quite so concerned about what the FBI might do to him.

'So that's it,' I finished. 'That's the story.'

'That's everything,' Agent Turner said.

'Yes, ma'am.'

I figured she knew that there were gaps in my story. I expected her to start probing for as many details as possible, begin an exhaustive interrogation.

Instead she asked, annoyed, 'And what do you expect me to do?'

Talena and I exchanged bewildered glances.

'Are you kidding?' I asked. 'I'm telling you that there are wanted war criminals here on American soil.'

'No. You told me that an illegal immigrant and known criminal told you this. You have not actually personally seen any of the alleged war criminals here in America, correct?'

'I . . . well . . . no, not personally. But Arwin wouldn't have lied about it. And, regardless, I'm telling you about an international war criminal smuggling ring.'

'Mr Wood, the FBI's jurisdiction ends at the American border. Since 9/11 we have obviously grown more interested in international crime, but Bosnian war criminals, however terrible their previous deeds may be, are not an obvious threat to our homeland security. The system you helped build for them is a disturbing development, and frankly I think you ought to be ashamed for what you have done, but it's also nothing new; the genie of strong cryptography has been out of its bottle for years. If you had seen them here in person, that would be something. Then, in consultation with the war crimes tribunal, I could launch an official investigation with an eye towards serving the tribunal's warrant and arresting these persons. But all you have, Mr Wood, is a colourful story, all of which took place outside of America, and no supporting evidence. I am a federal agent, not Glinda the Good Witch.'

'Mycroft. The website. That's evidence.'

'A website which, if your claim is correct, contains pictures that contain undecryptable messages. Even if your friend cooperates with us and opens his back door, which you admit is unlikely, it is an untrustworthy website full of uncorroborated information, hosted in Albania, again very far indeed from our jurisdiction, and extremely unlikely to contain actionable evidence. Honestly, Mr Wood, what did you expect? SWAT teams and all-points bulletins and a slot on the Ten Most Wanted list?'

'Something like that,' I admitted.

She shook her head. 'On a personal level obviously I deplore what these people have done. But there is nothing I can do in the way of initiating an investigation and pursuing them. Not without real physical evidence that war criminals are on American soil.'

'Then who else?' Talena asked angrily. 'Should we go to the Secret Service or CIA or *who*? You can't just blow us off like this. We'll go to the media if we have to.'

'With what?' Agent Turner asked. 'I do understand your frustration, Miss Radovich, but once again, you have *no evidence*. Believe me, CNN won't receive you with any more warmth than I have. I suspect considerably less.'

Talena shook her head disbelievingly. 'This is crazy.'

'I'll tell you what I am going to do,' Agent Turner said. 'I will file a report on Sinisa and his smuggling network with the CIA. That is of some interest because like all smuggling networks it is a potential threat to national security. In that report I will mention Zoltan Knezevic and Veselin Mrksic and the others, and Zoltan's alleged presence in the United States. I have no idea what, if anything, the CIA will do with this information. I suspect very little.'

'This is so fucked,' I said. 'That's all? That's all you're going to do? You're going to file a report and forget about it?'

'That's all I *can* do for the moment,' Agent Turner said sharply. 'Until and unless you can come to me and tell me that you are willing to testify under oath that with your own eyes you have seen one of these war criminals here in America. I would consider either or both of you to be a credible eyewitness. Or you can bring me Arwin and convince me of his credibility. But judging from his history and your depiction of him that will be something of a challenge.'

'Oh,' I said, beginning to understand. 'You want me to arrange a meeting with them. So I can come and tell you I've seen them here personally.'

Agent Turner paused, and said very carefully, 'I am not suggesting that. It would be unethical for me to do so. Such an action could expose both of you to considerable danger.'

'Uh-huh. Suppose I do come to you and tell you I've seen them. What happens then?'

'If that were to happen, then I could begin communications with the war crimes tribunal which should, after several weeks, culminate with the initiation of an official investigation.'

'After several *weeks?*' Talena asked, disbelievingly.

'If we're lucky. The wheels of international justice grind exceedingly slow. And of course after we serve the warrant the subjects will have various levels of legal appeals before we actually turn them over to the tribunal. If everything goes smoothly it will probably still be years before they make it to The Hague. Hypothetically speaking of course.'

'That's insane,' I said.

'Yes, it is,' Agent Turner agreed. 'That's international law.'

Talena and I stopped for a coffee at Steven's Café on Market en route to the BART station. We had plenty of time. Expecting a lengthy interrogation, both of us had phoned our workplaces and told them we wouldn't be in until noon.

'I should have known,' I said. 'It was all too perfect. We find an apartment and move in, Saskia gets your old place, Saskia gets a job, I get, well, at least half a job, summer is wonderful, we've got money in the bank, Steve and Lawrence are coming to visit, everyone's happy, life is perfect, and then boom. I should have seen it coming.'

Talena nodded. She hadn't spoken a word since leaving Agent Turner's office.

'I've still got about four thousand dollars of Sinisa's money in the bank,' I said.

'Blood money,' she said dully. 'They stole it from the Muslims and Croats they murdered. Or from smuggling during the war. We can't spend it any more. Not on ourselves.'

'I know.'

We sipped our coffees, dejected.

'Sinisa was in the Dutch army at Srebrenica,' I said. 'He was there. Seven thousand people massacred. How could he turn around and help the same people who did it?'

'Money,' Talena said.

'Money. Yeah. Market fucking share. To grow his business. To be the Amazon and the eBay of international crime. I should have known. I should have fucking known.'

'Stop that,' Talena said sharply. 'Let's focus on what we're going to do. Not what you think you should have done or known or telepathically intuited.'

'Okay.' I sighed. 'I guess I'll email Arwin and try to set up a meeting. Except I can't think of any good excuse to want to see them. Maybe I can check out the area boxing gyms. They might be working out at one of them.' It sounded feeble even as I said it.

'Arwin's back door,' Talena said. 'If he gave you his password. Then maybe you could read the messages and find out where they are.'

'Maybe,' I said. 'If he just up and gave it to me.'

We looked at each other.

'They're going to get away, aren't they?' Talena asked. 'They'll find out we're looking for them and they'll disappear. Just like that. Take a bus to Columbus, somewhere nobody knows them. They've got all kinds of money, they'll help each other out, they could die of old age here. Just like a lot of Nazis did. They're going to get away.'

'Not if I can help it,' I promised. But right then it felt like a pretty empty promise.

I went from the FBI to my job at Autarch Software, where I wrote billing-management software for cellphones. It was only twenty hours per week, but it paid forty dollars an hour, a sum I would have sneered at during the dot-com boom but which seemed a godsend in this post-crash era. A painful era which at long last seemed to be ending. Most of my qualified techie friends now had jobs, and it took reassuringly longer every week to browse the coder-help-wanted ads on Craigslist, Monster, and HotJobs. I was still worried that in the long term all the world's programming jobs would be outsourced to Bangalore, but in the medium term my professional future looked brighter than it had for years.

I sent Arwin an email from work. I hoped to get him to set up a meeting with Zoltan, and maybe wheedle his back door's private key from him, using the carrot of a job along with the implied stick of an FBI investigation.

```
From:     balthazarwood@yahoo.com
To:       raskolnikov@hushmail.com
Subject:  what up?
Date:     15 Aug 2003 19:11 GMT

Hey, Arwin, what's going on?

Wanna meet for a beer tonight or tomorrow?
I'm working a contract job now and I've got
some leads you might be interested in. Say,
Noc Noc, 7 tonight, if you're free?

Paul
```

Arwin called me just before I left work.

'Hey hey hey, my main man Paul!' he greeted me.

'Arwin, hey, what's up? Got time for a beer?'

'Tomorrow. Tonight I got a date. You should see this girl. She's like a fucking miracle freak of nature. Her tits, man, they're beyond good, they're fucking *hypnotic*.'

'What's her name?'

'How the fuck should I know?' He laughed. 'Just kidding. Her name's Oksana. She acts like she's a good girl, but she's a nasty freaky ho, I can tell it, I can smell it. But she's playing good girl so I'm playing romantic Russian criminal.'

'You are, technically, a Russian criminal,' I said. 'But romantic?'

'Fuck, man, I don't know. Chicks see what they want to see.'

'True.'

'True dat. What about these jobs?'

I described the openings that did more or less exist at Autarch Software. 'They're a small start-up company,' I warned him. 'So this depends on financing. Right now I'm only working twenty hours a week. Ian, my friend who got me the job, he says it's a slamdunk, but you know how it is. Not until the ink dries on the paper.'

'All right. But they sound pretty good. I could do them. You know that.' He sounded like it was important I believe him.

'Yeah,' I agreed. 'I know that.'

'They pay cash?'

'You don't have to worry about it. You tell them you're a self-employed sole proprietorship. There's a massive enforcement loophole there. Then they wash their hands and pay you like you're a business, and that means it's your responsibility, not theirs, to check whether you're legal or not.'

'Cool. That's fucking great, man. I got to get a new job. Right now I'm working for this Chink fuck who's got this online porn site. At first I thought, hey, cool, he pays fuck-all but it's still the greatest job ever, right? But mother of fucking God, man. This shit he does, it is *fucked up*. This shoot they were doing yesterday, you shoulda seen it—'

I definitely did not want to know a single thing about pornography so extreme that even Arwin found it disturbing. 'Listen,' I said quickly, 'you seen Zoltan or Zorana?'

'Actually, yeah,' he said. 'Zoltan called me like an hour ago. Asking about you and if I had your phone number. He sounded, I dunno, weird. I wasn't sure you wanted to talk to him, so I told him I just had your email. He didn't even want that.'

I sat for a second, trying to make sense out of what I had just heard. Zoltan had called Arwin to ask about me. Why would Zoltan want to get in touch with me?

'Sounded weird how?' I asked.

'I dunno. Just like something had gone wrong.'

For a bad moment I wondered if Zoltan somehow knew I had gone to the FBI. But he couldn't. No one knew but me, Talena and Agent Turner herself. It had to be just coincidence that he was asking about me now.

There had been that conversation in Albania, when Zoltan and Zorana had pumped me for information on living in California, and I had told them they could call me if anything went wrong. That could explain why they were trying to find me. If so, it was perfect. I would meet them, give them advice on whatever their problem was, maybe even find out exactly where they were living, and then I would go to Agent Turner and topple the first domino in a chain that hopefully led from her office all the way to The Hague and the international war crimes tribunal.

'Do you have his number?' I asked.

'No. I think he called from a pay phone.'

'All right,' I said. 'If he calls again, give him my cell number, and tell him I'll be happy to meet him and help him out if he's having any trouble.'

'Really? Okay, you want to play nice with those two crazies, that's your problem. You want to meet for a beer tomorrow? Noc Noc is good, that place rocks. Buy me a beer and I'll tell you all about the freaky Oksana.'

'I can't wait,' I said, amused. 'Sounds good. See you then.'

19 Spy in the House of Love

The number 19 bus took me to the corner of 16th Street and Rhode Island. From there I walked a steep seven blocks to our house. I could have waited for another bus, but after six hours staring at a computer screen while performing intense mental abstractions, any physical strain was refreshing. I didn't pay attention to my surroundings. My thoughts alternated between work problems and how I might convince Arwin to give up his password.

Talena had just gotten home, was shrugging off her jacket as I walked in.

'Hi, honey, I'm home, what's for dinner?' I mock-demanded. I swung the door shut behind me, walked up to her, and kissed her hello. I did not notice that the door did not thunk into place.

'I was just wondering that,' she said. 'We could make fajitas, or—'

She stiffened and looked over my shoulder. I released her and turned around, perplexed. Then I gasped with surprise and horror. Zoltan and Zorana stood in the doorway.

'Paul,' Zoltan said, as Zorana closed the door behind them. 'So good to see you.'

'Uh,' I said. *Play it cool.* 'Yeah. Hi. Good to see you too.' I approached his outstretched hand and reached to shake it. 'How did you find out—'

But I never finished asking him how he found where I lived, because he punched me in the stomach so hard that I blacked out for a moment.

It was a perfect punch, just what he had taught me in Sinisa's basement boxing gym, a low right cross, powered from the hips, connecting just under my ribcage and exploding into my solar plexus. When I came to I was curled up on the floor, clutching my gut and retching for breath. He had knocked the wind out of me. I hurt so badly my first coherent thought was that he had damaged some organ and I must be bleeding internally. All strength had drained from my limbs. I felt like a marionette whose strings had been cut. I looked up, still gasping ineffectually like a landed fish, still not really understanding what was going on. Everything seemed to be happening in slow motion. Talena looked down at me, shocked, her mouth open, and her hands fluttered ineffectually in front of her as Zorana, behind her, grabbed Talena's long dark hair and yanked. Talena's head flew back and hit the wall with a sickening crack. As she fought for balance Zoltan hit her in the gut with a textbook left hook and Talena folded over gracefully, like it was deliberate, some sort of gymnastics move, and fell near me on the floor. I tried to scramble over on top of her, to shield her body with mine, but I couldn't breathe, I was too weak to move fast, and before I made it to her Zorana stepped behind me and unleashed a perfect kick into my testicles. The pain was incredible, brain-erasing, a nuclear detonation. It reduced me to an animal. For a moment I stopped thinking about Talena. I no longer knew that Talena was in the room. I no longer knew where or maybe even who I was. All I knew was that I was in unbelievable agony and I couldn't breathe.

By the time I finally forced oxygen back into my wheezing, pain-wracked body, my wrists had been handcuffed behind my back and a filthy dishrag had been stuffed into my mouth and tied around my head. From where I lay on the floor I could see that Talena too had been cuffed and gagged. Blood seeped down the side of her head and on to her right ear and the side of her face, and she coughed and choked against her gag. It was almost unbearable, watching her like that, unable to do anything to help her. I still didn't really comprehend what was going on, it had all happened too suddenly, but when I came to enough of my senses to understand that Talena was badly hurt and in terrible danger, that hurt worse than any physical pain I could possibly suffer.

Zoltan barked something in Serbian and then he was behind me, lifting me up by the arms. I scrambled to get to my feet before he dislocated both of my shoulders. He marched me over into the kitchen, spun one of the wooden chairs around, and sat me down, threading the back of the chair between my back and my cuffed arms. My shoulders immediately began to ache. Zorana, after closing all the curtains, forced Talena on to a chair next to me. Zoltan shoved her chair next to mine so we sat side by side, our backs to the kitchen table. Then he took another chair and sat in front of us. There wasn't much room and his knees almost touched mine.

'From the beginning I wanted to kill you,' he said. 'From the beginning.'

I tried to talk through my gag, to ask him what was going on, to feign indignation, but the noises that came out were incoherent and so quiet I don't know if he heard anything at all. I was so weak and nauseous with pain that I don't think he would have understood me even without the gag. My lungs and shoulders ached, my stomach where he had hit me felt like it was on fire, and worst of all a huge, cold, sickening knot of agony had formed deep inside my gut and seemed to tighten with every breath. I breathed as fast and shallowly as I could and told myself not to throw up, whatever happened, or with this gag on I might easily suffocate myself.

'We were so good to you,' Zorana said. She sounded disappointed, like she was scolding a wayward child. 'We helped your little friend Saskia, we paid you well, we fed you, we sheltered you, we drank beer with you. I thought we were friends, Paul. And now you go to the FBI, you try to have us arrested? You betrayed us. There is nothing worse than a person who betrays his friends. Nothing worse.'

I winced with understanding. How could they know? How could they possibly know we had gone to the FBI?

'You deserve everything we do to you,' Zorana concluded.

Zoltan reached into his jacket and his hand came out holding a combat knife, its blade at least six inches long. I moaned involuntarily with fear.

'You will keep your voice quiet,' Zoltan advised me, 'or your girlfriend, I will cut her throat like a pig.' He reached out and pulled the gag from my mouth down to my neck.

'You understand me?' he asked.

'Yes,' I managed. 'Yes. I understand. Please don't, please, please I'll do anything. I'll do anything you want.'

My whimpering pleas were heartfelt, but they were also very deliberate. I was terrified, I was in shock and agony, but one tiny corner of my mind was cool and calm and analytic, racing to calculate how I might possibly improve our odds of survival. Stoke Zoltan's vanity, accelerate his power trip, seem as frightened and harmless and beneath contempt as possible. If there was any chance of us getting out of this alive, it lay in him believing we would be too terrified to ever so much as speak his name again.

'Of course you will,' he said. 'Who else did you tell?'

'No one,' I said. 'I swear.' For a moment I considered denying that we had ever gone to the FBI, but there was no point. I couldn't imagine how he knew but given that he did his proof was probably pretty decisive, and, besides, the idea was to show him that he had already broken my will completely; lying to him would indicate resistance. 'We just went to the FBI. I knew an agent there. I know an agent. We just went to her. No one else, they don't know anything. Not even Saskia, we didn't tell her.'

'You fucking liar,' Zoltan said. 'Who else did you tell?'

'No one!' I said desperately. 'No one else! Oh, God, no, *no, don't!*' as he rose and stood over Talena with the knife.

'Be quiet or her blood will fall like fucking rain,' he said to me.

Over his shoulder, to Zorana, he said something in Serbian. Zorana came over, took his place on the folding chair in front of me. She watched me very carefully, fascinated, as if I were a particularly good television programme, while Zoltan roughly pulled Talena's T-shirt up over her head, prompting a grunt of pain from her, and cut her bra off.

'Please no,' I breathed. 'Please, we didn't tell anyone else. I'm telling the truth. Please.'

Zoltan dragged Talena up from the chair with a hand in her hair, turned her around, bent her over the table, undid her jeans, which took a little while, and pulled her jeans and underwear down below her knees. Talena was grunting through her gag and shivering and her eyes were closed. The wet blood on the side of her head smeared the pale wood of our kitchen table. I decided that if I got out of this room alive then some day Zoltan would die at my hands. Some day very soon.

'No. Zoltan. No. Please.' I begged, keeping the fury out of my voice with an effort. 'Please don't. Please no. Please no.'

'Tell me everything. Tell me who else knows.'

'No one knows!' I was almost sobbing with rage and fear. 'We didn't tell anyone! No one else!'

'How did you find out?'

'She was looking at a website. The war tribunal. Your picture was there.'

'The tribunal,' Zorana said. 'I knew it.'

'We know you told others,' Zoltan said. 'Tell me who else and I'll let her live.'

'No one! There wasn't anyone else! We went to the fucking *FBI!* Why would we tell anyone else after that?' My voice was hoarse.

Zoltan nodded, satisfied, and stood back from Talena. 'Get up,' he told her. 'Sit.'

After a moment she did, awkwardly. He approached her again, this time holding the knife. I could tell he intended to use it on her.

'Not her,' I gasped. 'No, Zoltan, not her, me, not her, don't, *don't*—'

Zoltan spoke a few Serbian words that prompted Zorana to punch me in the stomach again. She was sitting down and couldn't punch as hard as Zoltan, but the pain erupted anew, even worse this time, like pouring gasoline on a fire. It hurt so much that the world blurred and for a moment I thought I might pass out. I felt vaguely dissociated from my body, as if I were observing rather than experiencing its suffering, watching myself writhe in agony, choke and gasp and make low dying noises. Then the moment passed and I was back inside my skin, desperately trying not to throw up.

'She's pretty,' Zoltan said, staring at Talena's nakedness. 'Isn't she pretty.' He lowered the tip of his knife to her skin, hard enough to dimple her skin but not hard enough to cut her, and began to trace it up and down the contours of her body. Talena shuddered. I snarled like an animal but it made the knot of agony worse and I began to choke and whimper again as Zorana laughed at me. Tears began to leak from Talena's eyes, mixing with the blood on one side of her face, but her body stayed ramrod straight.

'It would almost be worth it, to keep her, finish her,'

Zoltan said. He was talking to Zorana. 'Finish both of them. It would be so good.'

'No,' Zorana said sharply. 'It's not worth it. They're not worth America.'

'America.' Zoltan tasted the word. He thought about it a moment. 'No,' he said decisively. 'Not worth America.'

He turned to me. 'You will never speak of us again. Not to the police, not even to Arwin or Sinisa, not to anyone. You will never even think of us. If the police or FBI ever ask, you will tell them we stayed in Belize. Or we will find you. We have friends. We have such friends. You will never escape. We will find you. I think you know what we will do to you then, don't you? You know what will happen to you, and your pretty girlfriend, and your little friend Saskia?' He lightly trailed a figure of eight around Talena's nipples with the point of his knife. 'I hope you do speak of us again. But you won't. I know. I see it in your eyes. Am I right?'

'Yes,' I said. Maybe we were going to live. Unless he was just teasing us. 'Yes. We'll never say anything to anyone about you. Please don't hurt her. We'll never say anything. Nothing ever. Please don't hurt her, please. *Please.*' I somehow knew from his grin and his body language that he was still going to use the knife. I started to cry.

Zoltan pulled Talena's gag down. 'And you as well? You will say nothing?'

Talena took a breath. 'I will say nothing,' she said, her voice trembling.

'Good,' Zoltan said. 'Now here is something to remember your promises with.' He turned to me. 'Every time you see her naked, from now on, you will think of me. You will remember.'

Then he cut Talena: he drew a short bloody vertical line about three inches long between her breasts, cutting her right down to her breastbone. Talena shook but didn't make a sound. I opened my mouth to cry out and Zorana lifted her right leg up and jammed her foot into my crotch, grinding her heel into me. My scream turned into a tortured groan. I had not known it was possible to hurt so much. When she pulled her leg away I couldn't hold back the nausea any longer. I began to throw up. I tried to lean over but all I could do was bend my head and vomit on to my shirt and my lap.

'It will scar, I think,' Zoltan said, inspecting his work clinically.

Blood flowed down Talena's quivering belly, began to pool in her pubic hair.

You will die, I told him silently, a supernova of wrath blotting out most of my pain for a single blessed moment. I will see you dead. That's a promise.

'Do not take her to hospital,' he said to me. 'They will ask questions. If you take her to hospital, we will find out.'

I didn't say anything. I stared at the floor. I didn't dare look at him.

Zoltan looked at Zorana and said, 'Enough. It is enough.'

Zorana smiled at him and stood. She reached into her pocket and put something metal next to the sink. 'Handcuff keys,' she said brightly, like she was giving us a Christmas gift. 'Goodbye, Paul.' She leaned over and kissed my forehead. Then she followed Zoltan outside, and the door slammed, and we were alone in our home, alone and wounded but alive.

'Maybe we should go to the hospital,' I whispered.

'No,' she whispered back. 'No. It's not worth it. I'll be fine. I think it's clotted over already. You're more hurt than I am.'

We had no reason to whisper. The door was locked, Zoltan and Zorana were long gone. But we felt a long, long way from safe and sound. Not here, where we had been attacked. Not in what had been our home, but didn't feel like a home any more, and I thought maybe never would again.

It had taken us a long time to free ourselves. We had awkwardly, painfully contorted ourselves, standing back to back, until Talena was able to insert the key into my handcuffs and free me. My hands were shaking so much it took me five attempts before I could do the same for her. We held each other, then, for a long time; we made it to our couch and fell on it and held each other and wept, before we cleaned up as best we could.

We didn't call the police. Neither of us even suggested it as a possibility.

'What about your head?' I asked, deliberately using a normal voice.

'It hurts,' she said. 'I think maybe a concussion. I don't really remember it hitting. Or you getting home. I've got a headache, it's not blinding or anything but it's not going away any time soon.'

'We should take you to the hospital. It's just down the street.'

'Don't be an idiot. He wasn't making empty threats. He'll *kill* us. He'll find us and rape me and torture you and kill us both. Do you not get it?'

'I get it,' I said. 'But I think he was lying about knowing about hospitals.'

'If he can find out we went to the FBI, he can find out we went to a hospital.'

'I'm not so sure. But okay. I think for concussions they just keep you under observation anyway.'

I had cleaned Talena's wounds with soap as she hissed with pain, smeared antibiotic cream all over them, then wadded an old T-shirt on Talena's chest and taped it down firmly. It seemed to have stanched the bleeding. We took three ibuprofen each. There wasn't much else we could do for her headache, or the gargantuan yellowing bruise beneath my breastbone, or my hugely swollen gonads. Now we lay on the couch, each of us slumped on one end, our legs crossing in the middle. I had turned the TV on, volume low, to create the illusion of warmth and company. It wasn't much but at this point we were ready to take whatever comforting delusions we could find.

'What about you?' she asked. 'Do you think you're okay?'

I shrugged. 'I'll be okay. I'm not coughing blood or anything.'

'But, Jesus, Paul, your balls, they . . . they don't look so good.'

'Normal,' I assured her. 'Just like when Jeff Koller kicked me in the nuts in fourth grade. I'll be okay as long as I walk slow and careful. They'll be fine in a few days. Probably no sex for a week, but fine.' I still felt nauseous, and every breath caused pain to blossom anew in my stomach, but I didn't want to worry her. It wasn't like I was coughing up blood. At least not yet.

'I'm not going to be Miss Sex-Positive any time soon either,' Talena said bitterly. 'I thought he was going to rape me. I was, I always thought, it would be awful but just physical, you know? I figured if it ever happened I'd deal with it okay, I figured I survived the siege of Sarajevo, I could survive rape. But when I thought he was going to do it, in front of you, that was the worst part, I felt like I was about to have the worst thing in the world happen to me. Like the worst thing in the world that could ever happen was really about to happen.' She started to shiver.

'It's okay,' I tried to soothe her. 'It's okay. We're all right. Nothing awful happened. Well, nothing too awful, nothing, nothing irrevocable. We're okay. We're fine.'

'We're not fine,' she said bitterly.

'No,' I said. 'No, we're not. But we will be.'

'You think so? I don't think so. We're fucking trauma-tized. Don't pretend we're not. And now if we say nothing then we let one of the most evil fucking monsters on the planet go ahead and live. In our city. Our home. But if we say something he'll find out and find us and him and his witch wife will fucking torture us to death for real. You call that fine? You tell me just what's going to be so fucking fine about that.'

I didn't have an answer.

'How did they know?' Talena asked. 'How could they possibly have known? Did they put some kind of bug on you in Belize? Or Agent Turner, did you ever talk about her? We told one person, a fucking FBI agent, and they knew fucking everything.'

'I don't know. Not a bug, the battery would have died a long time ago. Maybe they hired some Romanian hackers who cracked the FBI's computers or something. Not likely, but neither is anything else. But not Agent Turner. She wouldn't have . . . We can trust her, I'm sure.'

'Yeah. So am I. She's safe.' Talena took a deep breath. 'Maybe . . . Paul, I think we should talk about this now. Right away. The longer we wait the more scared we're going to get, and . . . Shit. I'm already scared to even say this. Paul, I think we should go to her again. I think we should tell her everything, everything, and ask her for protection. We can't say nothing and let them get away. We just can't.'

I looked at her and didn't answer.

'We can't let them go,' Talena said. 'Getting them, I don't know, some kind of justice, that's bigger than us. You know that, don't you? It's more important than we are.'

'I don't want to go to Agent Turner,' I said.

'Paul . . . ' She hesitated. 'I understand. I do. You're frightened for me, aren't you? Don't be. Not that, I know you can't not be, but you can't let it paralyze you, that's what he's counting on, we have to—'

'No. You don't understand. I don't want to go to the FBI because I don't want them arrested.'

'What?'

'I don't want them arrested. I want them dead.'

Talena looked at me incredulously.

'Fuck the FBI,' I said. 'Weeks to get a warrant and then years to extradite them, if they can find them in the first place, which is probably impossible, since they'll probably know when the FBI's investigating them. I want them dead. I'll do it myself. With not a second's hesitation, believe me. Not a fucking second.'

'Paul . . . okay . . . Paul, being too macho is just as bad

as being too frightened here. You're not, you're just not a killer, okay?'

'Yeah? Remember what happened the last time I wanted somebody dead?'

'I thought you didn't actually do that yourself,' Talena said.

'No, fine, not physically me, it was Hallam who physically did it, but I was willing. And right now, believe me, I am extra willing. I am fucking eager.'

'Well.' She looked at me for a moment like she didn't quite recognize me. 'I'm glad you're angry. It's good. You should be. We should both be fucking furious, and we are. I am too, that's good, it's healthy, but, Paul, we have to channel it in a halfway constructive way, not in some crazy revenge mission. It would be good enough to turn them over to the FBI. You understand? It would be good enough. And it would be a whole fuck of a lot easier. And it would be a whole lot less likely to end up in one of us weeping on top of the other's grave or spending our whole lives waiting for next month's conjugal prison visit.'

'True,' I said reluctantly.

'Good,' Talena said. 'Good. So we're agreed? We'll go to Agent Turner tomorrow?'

'Fuck tomorrow,' I said. 'Let's call her right now.'

'Good idea. They won't expect that.'

'They don't expect us to do anything. Or we wouldn't be breathing. Zoltan thinks we're like, I don't know, mice. He thinks we're going to spend the rest of our lives being paralyzed we're so scared of him. He thinks we're pathetic.'

'That's good,' she said. 'Don't be angry about that. It's good. Overconfidence is good.'

'Yeah,' I said. 'It's good. With any luck it will be the fucking death of him.'

I reached for the phone, lifted it up, and replaced it on its hook.

'What is it?' she asked.

'We should use a pay phone,' I said.

'Oh. Right.'

'From now on,' I said, 'there is no such thing as too paranoid.'

20 True Confessions

The BART trip to Agent Turner's home was nightmarish. Walking hurt, the bright lights and other people's loud conversations were hard to cope with, our bodies only wanted to lie down somewhere and heal, and the pressure change when the train went under the San Francisco Bay exacerbated Talena's headache and provoked my own, a throbbing pain right behind my eyes.

'Wait a minute,' I said, at the West Oakland station. 'Wait. Come on. We have to get off for a minute.'

I took Talena's pale unresisting hand and led her out of the train.

'It's okay,' Talena said weakly, as we exited. 'It's just a headache. I'll be fine.'

'No offence, but it's not that.'

'What is it?'

'Arwin,' I said. 'If they know we went to the FBI, they know about his back door.'

'Shit.'

'Yeah. I gotta warn him.'

I tried three pay phones before I found one that worked. Typical Oakland. I called Arwin's Virgin Mobile cellphone—Virgin, answering the prayers of undocumented immigrants everywhere, sold pay-as-you-go cellphones that required no customer information—and got kicked to his voice-mail. Of course, I remembered, he had a date with some Ukrainian girl.

'Arwin,' I said. 'Listen. This is serious. Zoltan and Zorana know about the back door you put into Mycroft. And they're not fucking around. You're in serious danger. I mean it. If you think they might know where you live, get the fuck out of there, and stay out. Email me. We have to meet up and talk.'

I hung up, hoping I had impressed the seriousness of the situation on him, hoping that Zoltan and Zorana didn't already know where he lived, that he wouldn't bring the Ukrainian girl home to find that violently unwelcoming committee waiting for him. Hoping he wasn't dead already. Only he could open that back door. That put his name well above mine on any People We Must Kill Right Away list.

'Okay,' I said. 'Onwards.'

Agent Turner lived in a small house in Emeryville, just east of Oakland, not too far from the BART station. We arrived around 9 p.m. It was hard to believe that only three hours ago I had walked happily and confidently back into my home and kissed Talena hello. It felt like weeks had passed. The whole world seemed to have gone through some fundamental change in the last few hours, grown darker, more threatening, less comprehensible. It felt a lot like the day the World Trade Center fell.

'Come in,' Agent Turner said, greeting us at the front door. 'Come in. Sit.'

Her tiny living room really was straight out of the 1950s, down to the old-fashioned furniture and a print of Rockwell's *American Gothic* on the wall. We sat on her couch gingerly. Both of us now had headaches.

'Do you want some tea?' Agent Turner asked.

'Something stronger,' Talena said. 'Vodka? Orange juice?'

I nodded my agreement. I half expected Agent Turner to say that she didn't drink, but she disappeared into her kitchen and quickly returned with two tall screwdrivers that were half vodka.

'I hardly know what to say,' Agent Turner said. 'I regret very much what happened to you tonight. That's one thing. And I want you to understand that this is very serious to me. The leak especially. I believe that only someone who works in the Bureau could have read my report today. Only someone who is an agent themselves. Or even more senior.'

'They said they had a big friend in America,' I remembered. 'Jesus. You're saying they've got a fucking FBI agent on their side?'

'Please remember this is still just a hypothesis,' Agent Turner cautioned. 'It fits all the available evidence, but I don't want to rely on it yet. Your lives are at risk here. Very serious risk. But you have done the right thing. If there is one silver lining to what happened to you, it is that if we capture them we now have enough to incarcerate them here in America for a very long time.'

'It's an ill wind,' Talena said bitterly. 'So what are we going to do?'

'I don't know,' Agent Turner said.

That wasn't what we wanted to hear.

'I can't do what I want to do,' she said. 'What I want is for both of you to see a doctor tonight, for evidence of what happened to you. I want a crime scene team in your house. But if someone inside the Bureau is reporting to Zoltan . . . to me, that is the most serious and most dangerous thing. If word gets out that you came here—'

The door to the house swung open, and Talena and I both flinched. But it was not Zoltan or Zorana who walked in, it was the blonde girl whose picture was on Agent Turner's desk, maybe a few years older now, her hair longer, dressed in jeans with various peace and Om symbols painted on, wearing a similarly decorated backpack over a tie-dye jacket. She stopped in her tracks and stared at us.

'Uh . . . hi,' the girl said, confused.

'Danielle,' Agent Turner said. For the first time since I had met her she looked awkward and unprofessional. 'I, I didn't expect you home so soon. Yes. This is my daughter Danielle. These are . . . Dani, I'm sorry, there's a bit of a work emergency, can you leave us alone for a little while?'

Danielle's expression grew sour. 'Fine,' she said shortly. She kicked off her shoes and disappeared upstairs.

'Sorry about that,' Agent Turner said. 'I, yes, I was saying. There are a lot of things I don't dare do. I need to think a little while. I want you to know that I am going to make *damn* certain that no one finds out you called me tonight. There will be no repeat of the leak. You absolutely need not worry about that. But right now I cannot give you any formal protection. What I need you to do is go about your lives normally. Cautiously but normally.'

'You have to be kidding,' I said.

'I'm sorry. Paul, Talena, I am very sorry. But anything I do officially could and would be compromised by Zoltan's source inside the Bureau. This kind of investigation has to be slow and careful. I've never done this before. I promise you I will devote every waking hour to it, but at the same time I have to move slow. I don't even know where to begin yet. I can't *imagine* how Zoltan compromised a federal agent. He—'

'Bosnia,' Talena said suddenly.

'What?'

'The mole. Bosnia. And not Zoltan. Sinisa.'

Agent Turner and I looked at her curiously.

'The US has had peacekeepers in Bosnia for eight years now,' Talena said. 'I bet the mole was there as a peacekeeper. I bet he met Sinisa then. Not Zoltan, he's just an animal. Sinisa fooled Paul, and Paul's a lot smarter than your average bear. Sinisa plans long term. I bet the mole and Sinisa met and teamed up back then. I bet he came back from his tour and right away applied for the FBI.'

Agent Turner and I nodded.

'A compelling theory,' Agent Turner said. 'It will be at the top of my list. But you need to understand, this will still be a slow process. Unless . . . '

'Unless what?' I asked.

'Unless you can get your friend Arwin to open his back door. I may have been wrong about its importance. If we're right, if there is a . . . I'll say it, a mole . . . he or she may be communicating with Sinisa and Zoltan using the Mycroft site you built. That may be a way to find them.' She sighed. 'I hope so. I can't think of many other ways.'

'Saskia,' Talena said, on the BART ride back from Agent Turner's. 'They've got her address. My old address. We need to get her out of there.'

'Shit. Yeah.'

We sat in silence for a moment as the train passed beneath the bay.

'We're in deep shit,' I said.

'No kidding. If they find out Agent Turner is looking for the mole . . . '

'Yeah. I thought she'd put us under police protection or something.'

'Then the mole would know. We're on our own,' Talena said.

I put my arm around her and we held each other tightly.

Two stops later, I said, 'I'm going to call Steve and Lawrence and ask them to fly over. We might need back-up. If they can get here, I'll feel a lot better with them around.'

'Paul, Talena, hello,' Saskia said, surprised. 'Come in, please.'

We entered Saskia's apartment, Talena's old apartment. I felt instinctive foreboding as I crossed the threshold. This was the place where I had spent my year of miserable poverty, and I associated it with frustration and self-loathing. But Saskia had repainted it with swirls of bright green and purple, the apartment's distinctive sour smell was gone, and the kitchen table was decorated with freshly picked flowers.

Food Not Bombs pamphlets, stickers and buttons were stacked on the counter.

Saskia was so busy we had hardly seen her in the last month. She worked six days a week, cleaning houses for cash, and spent the rest of her time volunteering with Food Not Bombs and other activist groups. I admired her for it, was glad she was making friends and building a new life, but I was a little worried about her predilection for San Francisco's loudest and most uncompromising activists. I feared she might start attending demonstrations and get arrested at one that turned violent.

'Is something wrong?' Saskia asked, after we sat down.

'Yes,' I said. 'I'm sorry. Something is very wrong.'

'I believed it was over,' Saskia said, when we finished telling her. 'I believed Bosnia was behind me. I believed America was a place to forget.'

'I'm sorry,' I said. I wondered if maybe we shouldn't have told her, left her in the bliss of ignorance. But she was in danger too, she was a witness, she deserved to know what was happening.

'What can I do to help?' she asked.

I paused. I hadn't expected that. 'Nothing, I don't think,' I said.

'No. Paul, Talena, that is not good enough. It is because of me you were attacked. If not for me, you would never have become involved. You must allow me to help. You have done so much for me. It is time for me to help you.'

'There is one thing we would like you to do,' Talena said. 'Move out of this apartment. Zoltan and Zorana have this address. I think Paul and I make for pretty good evidence that you don't want to still be here if they come to check the place out.'

'You think they will come here?' Saskia asked.

'It's possible,' I said. 'Not likely, but possible.'

She thought about it for maybe thirty seconds. Then she said, 'No. No, never again. Let them come. Let them come to me. I will wait for them.'

I stared at Saskia like she had spoken in incomprehensible Croatian.

Talena recovered first. 'Remind me again exactly how them killing you will help us?'

'It is not only I who is in danger if they come,' she said defiantly. 'I have killed Serbs before.'

Talena said something in Croatian. Saskia said something back. I sighed. My headache had returned and I wasn't in any mood to argue. I almost missed the wounded and pliable Saskia we had first met.

'Saskia,' I said, trying to work with her as best I could, 'I know you're a veteran. I know you're dangerous. But, how should I put this, you're dangerous like a vicious little terrier, and Zoltan and Zorana are dangerous like big fucking wolves. Terriers who want to live run away from wolves.'

My offbeat analogy prompted a weird look from Talena. I gave her a shrug intended as 'best I could do on the spur of the moment with a bad headache.'

Apparently it hadn't been good enough. 'No more running away,' Saskia declared. 'No more being a victim. I was a victim long enough. This is my home now, I will stay, and no one will drive me away.'

I considered pointing out that we still paid most of her rent, but it seemed like an unfair tactic. God knew she worked harder than I did, scrubbing and mopping and breathing air thick with cleaning fluids for fifty dollars a day, while I groused about making only forty dollars an *hour* for Autarch in exchange for sitting in front of a computer and writing programs that would probably never improve anybody's life in any measurable way.

'That's just great,' Talena said. 'So you're going to help us by stubbornly refusing to do the one thing we ask you, is that it? Thank you so much.'

'Ask me to fight. I will fight. Do not ask me to run away. I will never run away again.'

'Stop being such an idiot. You go to a safe place as of tomorrow,' Talena said.

'I do not think you have been listening to me. I will do no such thing. I have hidden from these Serbs enough for one lifetime. Do you not remember what they did to us? Three years of snipers and mortars and eating charity food, winter months with no electricity, just enough fuel to live without quite freezing to death, living in our own filth because water was too cold and precious for bathing, watching my friends die in the streets, watching men who had been professors and lawyers beg in the streets for a single egg to feed their family. And we were the lucky people. In the country they were killing whole villages, murdering children in front of their parents, capturing women and raping them for months until they died of it. Do you not remember? I remember you stopped running, Talena. I remember you started walking slowly across sniper streets, you dared them to shoot you. And now you ask me to run from Serbs again? No. Never again. I am glad they have come. I welcome them.'

I was deeply uncomfortable with her depiction of all Serbs as inhuman killing machines, but decided it wasn't the right time for a lecture on the evils of cultural stereotypes. One battle at a time.

'Face it,' I said to Talena. 'If she doesn't want to go, we can't very well kick her out.'

'She is being so, fucking, pigheaded!' Talena said, to me but intended for Saskia.

'Yeah, well, it runs in the family,' I muttered before I could stop myself. Talena looked at me darkly. I hurried on, 'If she wants to risk her life for no good reason, and endanger our lives in the process, if she wants to be that selfish, that's her right.'

'Thank you, Paul,' Saskia said, satisfied. So much for my guilt-trip tactic.

'We can't protect you here,' Talena said. 'Nobody can protect you.'

'I do not want your protection. I want to protect you.'

I sat up, wincing as the sudden movement intensified my headache. 'Wait a minute. You're thinking about going after them, aren't you? I bet you're almost glad they're here. Now you can make up for that huge unpayable debt that only you think you owe us. Is that it? Am I right?'

Saskia did not answer.

'Oh, for God's sake,' Talena said, disgusted.

'I will do what I feel I need to do,' Saskia said.

I sighed. But I couldn't really blame her for being so intransigent. There comes a point when you can't stand the thought of running away any more. I suspected in a comparable situation I might have acted much the same way myself.

'All right,' I said to her. 'Here's the deal. If we start going randomly off on our own then we're all screwed. Anything we do about this, the three of us, we tell each other in advance, and we do it together. You stay involved right to the end. But, in the meantime, you move out of the apartment a while, just as a precaution. Deal?'

Saskia looked at me for a long moment.

'All right,' she said. 'Thank you, Paul. Yes. I agree.'

```
From:     balthazarwood@yahoo.com
To:       raskolnikov@hushmail.com
Subject:  Re: what up?
Date:     16 Aug 2003 18:11 GMT
```

There's things I need to tell you. There's things you need to tell me. Pick a time and place. Be paranoid. A public place.

```
From:     raskolnikov@hushmail.com
To:       balthazarwood@yahoo.com
Subject:  Re: what up?
Date:     16 Aug 2003 18:33 GMT
```

i don't need you to tell me to be paranoid, paul. i really fucking don't.

last night zoltan calls and says he needs to meet me. cuz the fbi is after me and you told them all about me and shit. glad i checked my messages first. never mind the fbi. he's the fucking scary one. what the fuck is happening?

you should go for a romantic sunset walk
on the beach tonight. start at judah and
go south. and you fucking well better be
alone.

The beach that demarcates San Francisco's Pacific coast is one of the city's favourite playgrounds, but near sunset it is almost deserted. I passed only a few dozen people during my twenty-minute walk. A few joggers, some Asian and Mexican fishermen patiently waiting near poles that jutted out of hastily erected pillars of sand, a pair of hardcore surfers in wet suits emerging from the waves, couples walking dogs, a few solitary men and women sitting in the sand and staring wistfully at the sun as it set behind the mighty Pacific. I wondered what they were thinking about. Maybe they were meditating. This was, after all, northern California, and the beach was probably a good place for meditation. Roaring ocean, soft sand, whistling salt wind, whirling flocks of seabirds stained red by the sunset, it was like a New Age postcard. Maybe I should take up meditation myself. I could use some inner peace.

'Wazzup?' Arwin demanded. I jumped. He had snuck up behind me.

'Hey,' I said. 'How you doing?'

'You tell me,' he said.

'You're doing pretty shitty.'

'Yeah,' he said. 'I was afraid of that. But Zoltan lied about the FBI, right?'

'No. It's true. I went to them.'

Arwin stopped dead in his tracks. 'You what?'

'I talked to the FBI. And I told them all about you.'

343

'*What?* What did you do that for?'

'Because Zoltan's a fucking war criminal,' I said.

He looked bewildered. 'So?'

'So? You knew?'

'What, that he did fucked-up shit? I didn't *know* know, but, man, you look at him and you're not too surprised, right? What did you expect? You thought he was a Boy Scout? You find out he isn't and you're all surprised and you go to the cops? And you tell them about *me?* What the fucking fuck?' He pushed me, two-handed, hard enough that I had to take a step back to maintain my balance. 'You ratted me out? I don't believe this! Why are we even talking? You find out Zoltan's got a history and you go crazy? You fucking *fuck!* They're going to find me. They've got my fingerprints already, you know, I got a record here. You ratted me out just cause you found out Zoltan did some bad shit during the war? It was a fucking war! Newsflash: bad shit happens during wars!'

'Bad shit?' I said. 'Try putting thousands of people in concentration camps and then torturing men and gang-raping women until they bled to death. Try helping murder seven thousand unarmed men. I'm not exaggerating. You can look it up.'

Arwin didn't say anything.

'Oh, I'm sorry, why would you want to, right?' I injected as much sarcasm and contempt into my voice as I could. 'Why should you care? Industrial rape and murder and people tortured to death in concentration camps or being lined up and shot in the back of the head by the thousand, that's just bad shit happening to someone else, why should you give a flying fuck, right?'

'Concentration camps,' Arwin repeated. 'Really?'

'Yeah.'

He looked at me for a moment. Then he started walking again. I stayed next to him.

'I read about those,' he said, his voice softer. 'I saw pictures.'

'Yeah? Don't let them get to you. They were just bad shit. It happens during wars.'

'You know I'm Jewish, right?'

I blinked. 'Actually,' I said, 'I'd forgotten.'

'So concentration camps, they feel kind of fucking personal, even when they're not.'

'Yeah.'

'Zoltan ran one of those, huh? Our man Zoltan ran a concentration camp?'

He hadn't exactly run them, from what Talena had said, but I sensed it was a bad time to split hairs. 'Yep.'

'No shit. Huh. Well, fine, okay then, whatever, go get him, I'll fucking cheer. But why did you have to tell them about *me*? And never mind the cops, how the fuck does Zoltan or anyone else know about that back door?'

'Because I told the FBI about it,' I said.

He twitched with surprise. 'You found it?'

'Yeah.'

'Shit. Shit. I didn't think your C was good enough. But, wait a minute, so you told the FBI, how did Zoltan find out?'

'Because Zoltan's got a friend in the FBI,' I said. 'You want to know how I found that out? I found out last night when he and Zorana came to my house and beat the living shit out of me and my girlfriend.'

345

'Huh,' Arwin said. 'I thought you were walking funny.'

'Yeah.'

'Shit. Mother*fucker*. This is so fucked up.'

'Yeah,' I agreed. 'Why did you build that back door into Mycroft?'

'I *knew* that was gonna get me into trouble. I knew it and I did it anyway.' He sighed. 'I figured maybe there'd be some money if I wanted to live dangerously. Sell it to someone else or something. And, you know, it was kind of an Easter egg.'

Easter egg: a flashy piece of code hidden in a program as a kind of signature. I had written a few myself.

'Doesn't matter,' he said. 'Shit. This would be funny if it wasn't so sad. You sicced both Zoltan and the FBI on me because I wrote a back door that doesn't even fucking work. There's a bug on the live site. I don't know what it is but that back door is fucked.'

'Guess again,' I said.

'Huh? I'm not guessing. I've tried. I've . . . '

He stopped talking. A metaphorical light bulb lit up over his head.

'Aw, no,' he said. 'You're shitting me.'

'Nope.'

'What did you do to it?'

'Basic substitution cipher,' I said.

'No shit. Well, fuck me gently with a chainsaw. Either I'm dumber than I thought or you're a whole lot smarter.'

'Thanks. Might be both. Now listen carefully. If you give me the key, I think I can get the FBI to forget all about you. Maybe even give you some protection.'

He looked amazed. 'You've got to be kidding me.'

'I'm serious. Give me the key and I'll tell them to leave you alone.'

'No fucking *way!* What are you, stupid all of a sudden? That key is the only thing I got. Zoltan's a big-shot war criminal, huh? Man, all of a sudden that's great news. That's fucking great. You go back to them and tell them I'll trade the key for immunity. And citizenship. And a clean record. And ten thousand bucks.'

I winced. I should have seen that coming. It had never occurred to me that Arwin's back door was now supremely valuable to him, his only bargaining chip, and he wasn't likely to give it away for free. 'I'm . . . Arwin, I'm not negotiating for the FBI. They don't even know I'm here talking to you.'

'So go and tell them. What did you expect, that you'd rat me out and I'd be so grateful I'd turn around and give you the only thing I've got? I should kick the shit out of you right now is what I should do.'

'I'm bigger than you are,' I pointed out.

'Yeah? How about Zoltan? Maybe I should say fuck the FBI and go tell him that the keep-your-mouth-shut memo he sent you last night doesn't seem to have stuck.'

I snorted. 'Good luck living long enough to finish the first sentence.'

He paused. 'Yeah. True.'

'I'll talk to the FBI. You don't talk to anyone.'

'Fine,' he said.

We looked at one another.

'You still want that job?' I asked.

'Fuck you.' He sounded more sour than furious. 'I'd rather work in a kitchen with Jeffrey fucking Dahmer than work with you again, you ratfuck piece of shit.'

'Always nice to see you too,' I said. 'I'll be in touch.'

Talena was out at her rescheduled poetry reading, trying to live a normal life as Agent Turner had ordered. I decided to go to the Metreon and watch Johnny Depp play a zombie pirate. Hollywood escapism was just what the doctor ordered. I had rarely wanted to escape reality with such passion. I felt like I had been sucked into a vortex of chaos. Zoltan was a psycho bloodsoaked war criminal, Sinisa was an international smuggler of psycho bloodsoaked war criminals, Zoltan and Zorana had beaten and humiliated Talena and me and threatened to murder us, the FBI didn't know how long it would take to catch them because one of their agents was a mole, and now Arwin, the only man who had the key that could open Sinisa's vault of secret messages, the vault that I had helped build, wanted to negotiate a package deal with the FBI before he turned it over.

In a weird way I blamed Dragan. If Saskia's husband hadn't been such a sick thug, we would never have got involved in this. It was funny that just a few months ago it was Dragan who was the bogeyman we feared, when Saskia and I were living in Albania, when Sinisa and Arwin and Zoltan and Zorana were colourful friends and acquaintances. Now when I thought of Dragan, rendered small by time and distance, compared to Zoltan and Zorana he seemed about as scary as Johnny Depp.

At least Steve and Lawrence had responded to my call for desperate-times reinforcements, and were due to arrive on Friday. I knew I would feel a lot better with them around. But I also knew they couldn't stay more than a couple of weeks.

When the credits rolled I reluctantly got to my feet, energized by the sight of a good old-fashioned summer Hollywood blockbuster, but dejected at being flung back into the real world and all its treacherous chaos.

My cellphone rang as I walked on to Mission Street. I dug it out of my pocket, unwillingly envisioning terrible things, Agent Turner calling me to tell me in a grim voice that Talena's mutilated corpse had been found. I looked at the caller ID and was semi-relieved to see it was Arwin.

'Yeah,' I answered.

'Hey. I broke your cipher.'

'Not hard. So you looked at Mycroft?'

'Yeah. And I'm not giving you the key until I can cut some kind of deal, but you should come shoulder-surf some of this shit.'

'All right. Now?'

'I gotta eat. In, like, an hour.'

He gave me an address: the Deluxe Hotel on Leavenworth near O'Farrell. With a location like that I was pretty sure it didn't live up to its name. That was right in the decaying heart of the Tenderloin ghetto.

'See you in an hour,' I said.

'And we'll both be alone, right?'

'Right,' I agreed.

***

I called Talena and updated her on the situation. It was a relief to hear her voice. I knew that every time we parted, for the foreseeable future, a terrible fear would begin to cloud my mind, fear that we might never meet again, that Zoltan and Zorana might have found out we had disobeyed

349

them, might have found Talena and taken her away and hurt her and killed her.

After talking to Talena, I killed forty minutes reading magazines at the Borders bookstore off Union Square, then walked down Market Street, which was clogged with the usual crowd of downtown San Francisco's homeless, filthy and bearded with running sores on their arms and faces, parked next to shapeless heaps that were all their worldly possessions, grimy lumps of clothes and sleeping bags, maybe a few books or a shopping bag full of recyclable cans. Some of them were addicts, some of them were deranged, some of them were just way down on their luck. They reminded me very much of the refugees I had seen on Sinisa's fishing boat in Albania.

From Market I turned up Leavenworth Street into the Tenderloin, the rotting core of downtown San Francisco, a ghetto populated by hookers and junkies, last-chancers and no-hopers, the homeless and those lucky enough to live in the squalid junkyard single-room-occupancy hotels that occupied virtually every corner. I passed broken windows and empty storefronts, porn stores, cheque-cashing stalls whose tellers sat nervously behind thick walls of bulletproof glass.

The Deluxe Hotel was ironically named. At first glance it looked physically lopsided, but it wasn't really, just viciously ugly, poorly maintained, coated with grime and smeared with half-erased graffiti. Two of the second-floor windows were broken, apparently from the inside. I was pretty sure that California's next half-decent earthquake would reduce the whole building to rubble. Two wild-haired homeless men were passed out on the sidewalk in front of the iron cage that guarded the entrance. The whole area stank of urine.

I gingerly stepped around the homeless men and pushed the stained white button next to the iron cage. After a moment the intercom grille above the button barked, 'What?' in a distorted, inhuman, barely understandable voice.

'I'm visiting Arwin. Room 309,' I said.

'I ain't got no note about no other visitor.'

'Call him up and ask,' I suggested.

Laughter filtered through that intercom sounded downright scary. 'Call him up? You think this the Fairmont? We ain't got no telephones.'

'Well, I don't know. He asked me to come here.'

'Well,' the voice said dubiously, 'you know his name. And you look all right.'

I supposed a camera was watching me from somewhere. The door buzzed. I went through the cage of the outer door, and the ancient interior door, to the desk, behind which sat a fat bald black man with a thick beard, a pierced septum, and at least twenty earrings, wearing a leather vest.

The green paint on the stairs was faded, the air was thick with a whole collection of noxious smells, and I carefully avoided a syringe that had been abandoned on the first landing. The hallway, probably last cleaned in the 1930s, was an instant asthma attack. The door to room 309 was slightly ajar. I knocked and it yawned open. The room within was empty. After a moment I walked in. Maybe Arwin was still out at Burger King or something.

The room was quite small. Everything was a uniform faded beige. The ceiling was low, uneven and water-stained. The walls were dusty and peeling. The bed was beneath the only window and was visibly lumpy. On one side there was a bedside table, its ashtray half full, and on the other side two rickety chairs. A tiny TV was in the corner of the room, high up on a stand that screwed into the wall. The bathroom door was closed. I was surprised that the hotel had individual bathrooms but no phones. I supposed Arwin connected to the Net via some kind of wireless connection. But no computer was visible.

I wondered how long Arwin had been living here. I felt vaguely guilty that he was living in a place like this. Despite our recent hostility, he was a friend. I should try to set him up in something better. Maybe he had just moved here today, in response to yesterday's phone warning. I hoped so.

'Arwin?' I asked, loudly, but there was no response. 'You home?'

I approached the bathroom door, intending to knock, but then the smell hit me. The rich iron smell of fresh blood. I knew right away what had happened.

My hand, operating on autopilot inertia, reached out and pulled open the bathroom door. I watched it creak open like I was a passenger in my own skull.

Arwin was arranged on his knees, arms cuffed behind his back, bent forward with his head thrust into the toilet. He had been gagged by some bloodsoaked cloth. The soles of his shoes were still covered with wet beach sand. There was a great deal of blood smeared and spattered everywhere, all over Arwin and the toilet and the floor and on the lip of the ancient clawfooted tub. It had just begun to dry.

I didn't quite compute what had happened to his head at first. It looked shrunken and misshapen, and at the same time he seemed to be wearing some kind of pale baseball cap. I looked at the bloody rag dangling from the shower-curtain rail for a moment and then understanding hit, my knees buckled, and I sat down hard on the floor.

The dark rag tied to the shower rail, with the big bloody clump hanging from it, was Arwin's long hair. He wasn't wearing a cap. The pale bloodstreaked hemisphere I saw half dunked in the toilet was his bare skull. Arwin had been scalped, and his scalp hung over the tub.

Five hours ago we had walked along the beach and talked. Ninety minutes ago I had spoken to him on the phone. Now he was dead. Zoltan and Zorana had somehow found him and come and killed him. Executed him, nineteenth-century style.

I pulled my cellphone from my pocket with shaking hands and pushed 911. But I didn't initiate the call. If it got out that I was the one who had reported Arwin's death, Zoltan and Zorana might unsuspend the death sentence that hung over us. Better to make it an anonymous tip from a pay phone, at least for now, lie low until Agent Turner found the mole.

If she found the mole. She would have to do it without Arwin's back door. It would never open again. I was sure Zoltan and Zorana had taken Arwin's computer, but that didn't matter. Arwin would not have been so stupid as to write down his private key. It had died with him.

I called the police from a pay phone across the street. I was surprised by my strong and steady voice. I thought of wiping the phone buttons clean, but my prints were probably already on the bathroom door and the hotel doors, and they weren't on file anywhere, and anyway the cops would be able to work out from time of death that I couldn't have been the killer. And being a suspect in Arwin's murder was one of the least of my concerns.

The initial shock of seeing the body had impelled a rush of cool, detached capability, the ability to calmly do what needed to be done. That ended after calling the police. I walked back down Leavenworth, dragging my feet, stumbling twice on kerbs. I felt shaky and nauseous. The thick foetid air of the Tenderloin did nothing to help me forget the stench of blood. After a couple of blocks I stopped and leaned against a brick wall, breathing heavily. The gritty texture of brick against my palms steadied me a little. I tried closing my eyes, but the image of Arwin's kneeling and mutilated corpse danced on the back of my eyelids, as if etched into my retinas. I already knew that sleep that night would be little more than a series of blood-drenched nightmares.

I wanted to walk and keep walking, right out of San Francisco, out of this awful tangle that had become my life. I crazily envisioned calling Talena on my cellphone and having her join me, and the two of us walking south down the peninsula, past the airport, through Silicon Valley, walking for days until we reached Santa Cruz or Big Sur or somewhere all this madness could not follow us. If such a place existed. I had my doubts.

21 Dead Man's Switch

Arwin's death merited a two-paragraph item deep inside the Bay Area section of the *Sunday Chronicle,* ending with:

The victim was identified as Arwin Shostakoff, an illegal immigrant with a lengthy criminal record. INS records indicate that Shostakoff was deported from America in late 2001. Police refused to speculate on how he returned to the country or whether the crime was gang-related.

I crumpled the newspaper into a ball and did my best Greg Maddux impersonation. 'They make him sound like some kind of low-life gangbanger who got what he deserved,' I said, irrationally angry at the *Chronicle* for not having given Arwin a lengthy and balanced obituary. 'He was a good guy, he was really smart, he worked hard, I don't think he was ever violent unless you count bar fights. He was fucking funny. Was.'

'I'm sorry,' Talena said quietly. 'I'm so sorry.'

'Fuck. Never—shit!'

'What?'

'I just realized. Arwin might have talked. Before they killed him. He might have told them that I talked to him on the beach. About negotiating with the FBI.'

We stared at each other for a second, wide-eyed with panic, before Talena shook her head and smiled ruefully.

'Now it crosses our minds,' she said. 'Well, I guess he didn't. Or we'd be having this conversation in the afterlife.'

'Good point.' I shook my head. 'I can't believe he's actually dead. Not in my gut. Even if I could believe he was actually dead, I couldn't believe he was actually murdered. And even if I could believe that, there's no way I could believe all the rest of this shit.'

Talena got up, walked behind me, and massaged my shoulder muscles, which were about as loose as concrete. She leaned over and kissed me on the cheek.

'Was it true, what Saskia said?' I asked. 'About you making a point of walking slowly across Sniper's Alley?'

Talena nodded. 'For a while,' she said. 'Maybe two months, after Davor died. You met his little brother in Sarajevo, you probably don't remember. Davor died trying to get a little girl's doll back. I wasn't there. His girlfriend—I don't even remember her name any more, isn't that awful? His girlfriend came to the apartment where I was staying, because I was her nearest friend to the hospital; she was just covered with his blood. She couldn't talk. And the next day she went out and walked up and down Zmaja od Bosne until one of them shot her. Suicide by sniper. It was a head shot, at least she didn't suffer. Anyway, after Davor, I didn't want to die, I don't think, but who lived and who died seemed so random, and I hated them so much, I didn't want to scurry around like a mouse, running from them all the time. So I started doing the slow defiant walk thing. I wasn't the only one. Lots of people did it.'

'Why did you stop?'

'Eventually they shot at me.' She smiled bleakly. 'After that my self-preservation instinct took over and I ran like hell every time.'

'Hurrah for your self-preservation instinct.'

She kissed me again.

'All right,' I said. 'What do you want to do today?'

'I don't know. I didn't have any plans.' She sighed. 'Oh, the irony. Normally it'd be great to have a whole Sunday afternoon with nothing to do but lie around together.'

'Yeah. But, um, Friday's no-sex stance, that still stands for a while for me.' I was healing, but still sore and sensitive, and I had an amazing dark fist-sized bruise where

Zoltan had hit me. So did Talena, but mine, as I had pointed out proudly to her in the shower, was bigger. Laughter still hurt; sex would probably be agonizing.

'Me too. I mean'—she waved her hands dismissively—'I don't want you worrying about me, honestly; just because with me it's mostly psychological doesn't mean it's more serious than you getting your balls kicked in, but the whole "psycho madman ripping your clothes off and threatening to rape you and running his knife all over you before cutting your chest open" thing, I think it might take another couple weeks before I'm real sexually comfortable again.'

'Psycho madman?' I asked. 'You think he's crazy?'

She thought about it for a moment. 'I guess not. Evil isn't crazy. Different things.'

'Yeah.' I glanced at the rest of the paper and decided I wasn't interested. 'You know what? Let's go get a drink.'

'A—Paul, it's not even noon yet.'

'Well, whenever Noc Noc opens. Arwin liked that place. I owe him . . . I don't know. A wake. Fuck being safe and responsible. Let's go get Saskia and get a drink.'

I expected Talena to object further, but, 'Yeah,' she said. 'Okay. Let's blow off some steam. In case they come kill us tonight, we might as well pickle ourselves first.'

Monday through Thursday of that week passed uneventfully. The constant unease, the unending stress, the not knowing what Agent Turner was doing or what Zoltan and Zorana planned, was a physical weight like wearing a lead coat all day long. Both Talena and I threw ourselves into work. I worked forty-eight hours those four days, even though I was only allowed to bill Autarch twenty hours for the whole week. Each night we held each other tightly until we fell asleep in one another's arms. Even so our sleep was fitful and restless. Talena twitched and murmured desperate words of Croatian, and I often woke from nightmares in which I was back in Albania, working next to Arwin, and he seemed alive and fine, except he had been scalped and endless rivers of blood flowed down his face.

And then, Thursday night, as we watched TV on the couch, Arwin emailed me.

'What the hell?' I said, astonished, staring bug-eyed at my laptop.

'What?' Talena asked, worried.

'It's Arwin. I just got email from Arwin!'

'You what? From *Arwin?*'

'Pretty good trick seeing as how he's been very dead for the last five days. Get this! The subject line is Dead Man Talking!' I clicked excitedly. Had he somehow faked his own death? Had that been someone else's body? Was Arwin alive?

```
From:     raskolnikov@hushmail.com
To:       balthazarwood@yahoo.com
Subject:  dead man talking
Date:     21 Aug 2003 05:00 GMT


so if you're reading this, either i'm dead
or i fucked up my dead man's switch, and
if it's a fuckup then i'll probably be dead
soon anyway, so goodbye.

this is supposed to be triggered by an obit-
uary with my name and birthdate appearing
```

in my hometown paper. i got a cron job running twice a week checking its web page and
if it gets a hit it sends two emails. pretty
sneaky, huh?

the first email goes to the nypd and talks
about some mafia guys i know in brighton
beach. watch the news closely. you'll probably hear about it.

the second email goes to you. you remember
our little walk on the beach? hell, i don't
know, could be sixty years ago. sure hope
so. anyway we went for a walk on the beach
and i came back and looked up our mutual
friend Zoltan. the shit he did is so fucked
up. in case it wasn't so long ago, and i
stepped in front of a bus or a flamethrower
or something, do me a favour and get the
fucker.

it's a dostoyevsky quote. and ain't it the
truth?

'i tell you that to think too much is a disease, a real actual disease.'

take care of yo'self, you ratfuck sonofabitch.

-arwin

'Goddamn,' I said, bitterly disappointed, and pleased, and impressed.

'Is he alive?' Talena scrambled across to look over my shoulder.

'No,' I said. 'No. But he gave us the key.'

'The key to his back door? How? Oh,' she said, reading.

'The very same,' I said. Without stopping to think I called up a new browser window and pointed it to Mycroft. 'Let's you and me open it up and break on through.'

It wasn't hard. After all I had built the website myself. I directed Internet Explorer to Mycroft's IP number, the unique Internet address I knew by heart, and the login web page I had built myself filled the screen. A couple of logins I had installed for test purposes were probably still there, but there was no point in logging in. I just added '/upload/' after the IP number in Explorer's address bar, and seconds later, a list of every stegosaurized picture that anyone had uploaded to the system filled the screen. I hadn't bothered securing this list. The whole point of public-key cryptography is that you don't care if your encrypted messages are available to the whole world, because only the recipient can read them.

But in this case, the secret message contained in each picture had been encrypted three times: once for the intended recipient; once for Sinisa; and once for anyone who knew the pass phrase Arwin had just sent me from beyond the grave.

There were a lot of messages. Collectively they told a fascinating story. Talena had been right, they were smuggling drugs. But there was so much more to it than that.

Six months ago, Sinisa Obradovic had been just what he seemed, an effective but small-time smuggler who moved people into and out of the Balkans. But that wasn't enough for him. Sinisa had ambition. Sinisa had a dream. And Sinisa had a golden opportunity hammering away on his mansion's wrought-iron gates.

The zombies hadn't wanted to come to Albania. They had expected to live out their years in their homes in Bosnia and Serbia. When the war finally ended, in 1995, all three sides fiercely protected those accused—unjustly, all claimed—of war crimes. NATO, particularly the French, made a few arrests, but generally turned a deliberate blind eye to war criminals, for fear their arrest might spark a renewed guerrilla civil war. I well remembered Talena's frequent laments that the locations of Ratko Mladic and Radovan Karadzic were open secrets, but NATO refused to pursue Bosnia's most theoretically wanted war criminals.

It wasn't the half-hearted hunt of NATO and the UN that drove the zombies into Sinisa's arms. It wasn't the efforts of those few of their victims who survived. It was the increasing pressure of their own countrymen. Several messages I read on Mycroft, messages sent from one zombie to another and translated by Talena, condemned the 'betrayal' by the new Westernized generation of Serbs, sick of war, appalled by what had been done in their name. The first zombie to escape to Albania was a distant relative of Sinisa. Others trickled in by twos and threes. And then, on 12 March, one month before Talena and I arrived in Bosnia, Serbia's Prime Minister was assassinated, and the resulting crackdown on organized crime prompted a new spate of construction work down the street from Sinisa's Albanian mansion, as a dozen zombies fled from what they bitterly called a 'witch hunt.' A few of them hadn't made it out of Serbia; that was why Saskia and I had received a house of our own.

No wonder Sinisa had been in such a hurry to finish Mycroft and get the zombies out of the country. Albania was awfully close to Serbia, and if word got out that Sinisa was hiding them in Vlore, the diplomatic pressure on the Albanian government would have been intense. Belize, sleepy backwater, faraway Belize, where nobody knew a Serb from a Croat from a Muslim, was a much safer base of operations.

At first Sinisa's zombie zoo was a simple exchange of services. The zombies paid with blood money for security and anonymity. But Sinisa slowly began to realize that the increasingly bored and listless zombies could be more than just dependents. That was his real genius. Anyone else would have looked at this vilest group of criminals Europe had seen since the Nuremberg trials, considered their horrific histories and outstanding arrest warrants, and seen a massive liability. Sinisa saw one of the most extraordinary economic assets on the planet. He saw a group of people capable of any kind of crime or violence, fiercely loyal to one another, sitting on a pile of ill-gotten money, and desperate to avoid capture.

Sinisa struck a deal with them. He would get them out of the Balkans and into relative safety. They would scatter in twos and threes, each little group getting their own little Third World sub-empire, and oversee his smuggling operations for him. They were perfect for the job. A smart, competent, ruthless, tight-knit group who would never dare betray Sinisa for fear of the warrants hanging over their collective heads.

Sinisa's dream was, just as he had said, to become the Amazon and eBay of human trafficking, to build a people-smuggling empire on which the sun would never set. He had connections. He had the zombies. And soon enough he had Mycroft, perfect secure communications, miles better than passing slips of paper with cellphone numbers on them back and forth in shady bars in Tijuana or Guangzhou or Istanbul.

It was fascinating, reading the messages in sequence, watching Sinisa's Latin American business grow, like time-lapse photography of a blooming flower. Belize was already a drug-smuggling nexus, but there was hardly any human traffic; you had to go out of your way to get there. Sinisa reached into the constant stream of would-be immigrants that flowed from Colombia and El Salvador and Guatemala and the rest of Central America into Mexico and to the USA, and began to divert some of that into Belize. He was cheaper than his rivals, and he quickly developed a reputation for reliability. Sinisa became a big customer of a cabal of Mexican coyotes who led people through the Arizonan desert, and then he was their biggest customer, and I could tell, from the tone and content and number of messages, that by degrees he was becoming their employer.

Further tendrils of empire were already growing around the globe. One of the reasons Sinisa had chosen Belize was its surprisingly good connections to the Orient; many Taiwanese and wealthy Chinese had purchased Belizean passports. The two visitors from Taiwan whose presence I had wondered about, Mr Chang and Mr Lee? Major snake-heads, smugglers who shipped literal boatloads of Chinese from Fujian province into America every month. Mr Chang and Mr Lee were very interested in the new route and new communications network that Sinisa had opened up. A pilot joint venture was due to begin next month.

There were messages from Africans in Angola and the Congo and Liberia and the Sudan, discussing how they might move people across the Sahara and into Europe. There was talk of sending Indonesians into Australia. There were discussions of how many Moldovan women the American sex trade could handle. And his Balkans business continued to thrive, taking people from Central Asia, India, the Middle East, and bringing them to Western Europe.

Sinisa, like the CEO he was, stayed laser-focused on his one business, people smuggling. Time and again people suggested he used his network to transport drugs, or weapons, or blood diamonds, and time and again he shot them down. Those businesses were too dangerous, too violent, too politically volatile. He did not want to find himself in the crosshairs of America's long-standing War On Drugs or more recent War On Terrorism. That was too risky. But people smuggling was sufficiently morally ambiguous that it remained a much lower enforcement priority for Western governments. Its slightly lower profits were worth the considerably lower risk.

Like any other start-up business he had worries aplenty, a new fire to fight every day. The Belizean government needed careful care and bribery. Existing people-smuggling rings, although scattered and disorganized, were angry at their loss of business. Sinisa played them off against each other, bringing some under his organization's loose umbrella, intimidating others, and, judging from a couple of more cryptic than usual messages, murdering a few Guatemalan hotheads who weren't willing to listen to reason. His rivals, small and fragmented and poorly organized, were minor obstacles. His biggest problem, like any other start-up, was cash flow.

You can't build a business without capital, but neither banks nor venture capitalists offer money to smuggling syndicates. A problem. But there was a third head of the Cerberus that led Sinisa down the road to empire. He had the zombies; he had Mycroft; and he had a whole lot of heroin.

Sinisa's original Balkans business had stretched all the way to Afghanistan, still the source of half the world's heroin despite the best attempts of the American-backed government, and somehow he had gotten his paws on a mountain of pure Afghani heroin with a street value approaching forty million dollars. Sinisa's policy was to stay far away from drugs, they were too dangerous, but just this once, this was different. This was start-up capital for a billion-dollar enterprise. 'Billion,' with a 'b,' as in one thousand million; that staggering sum was his long-term goal. Sinisa wanted to be the CEO of an organization with gross revenues of one billion dollars a year.

I wondered if CEO was really the right term. Sinisa had the CEO mindset, he thought of himself as a CEO, but chief executive officers have boards and shareholders, and they operate inside the law, carefully regulated. Sinisa worked in the last shadowy corner of this world where the feudal system reigns, knights and dukes and kings and emperors of crime. Smuggling refugees across the Balkans had made him a duke, but that wasn't enough. On the other hand he didn't want to be an emperor; he knew that was too much, would make him a target, like Pablo Escobar.

The analogy got better the more I thought about it. The zombies were his Knights of the Round Table. Zoltan and Zorana were his co-Lancelots. Arwin and I had been the wizards. And Sinisa, of course, was the king.

You should have meddled not in the affairs of wizards, King Sinisa, I advised him mentally. *For as you can see, we can haunt your ass even after we are dead.*

There were only a few messages that referred specifically to me.

```
From:    M To: S
Subject: READ ME IMMEDIATELY
```

```
Critically important. The attached report
was filed on the FBI infobase today. Balt-
hazar Wood has reported that you are smug-
gling war criminals into the USA and that
ZK is at large in America. This is a massive
security breach and we need to deal with it
immediately.
```

```
From:    S To: ZZ
```

```
I have sad and disappointing news. Our ex-
friend Paul Wood has found out who you are,
and has talked to the FBI.
```

```
Not as bad as it sounds. The FBI cannot
start pursuing you yet, but if he tells them
that he saw you personally, they will begin
```

an investigation. Of course if they do we will know about it immediately.

But that will not happen. Because you will go to Paul—who lives at 1256 Rhode Island Street, in San Francisco—and you will make it very clear to him that he will never talk to anyone about this again. You will not cause any permanent damage to him or anyone else.

The timing is terrible, but remember, we only need his mouth shut for the next few weeks.

From: S To: M

Thank you for the warning. Regardless of what happens you are not to risk discovery in any way. You are more valuable than ZZ and the money combined.

Obviously we will need to find new programmers for Mycroft 2.0. A shame. Finding trustworthy people is difficult and may delay the project.

I cannot tell you how much I look forward to seeing you again.

From: ZZ To: S

Paul will never speak of us.

We have made arrangements for the sale and
the flight. The agreed price is 13 million
dollars. The exchange will take place at an
event called Burning Man. The pilot will
charge 250,000 dollars. M reports the pilot is wanted by the FBI and desperate to
get into Mexico. Tijuana arrival is scheduled for approximately 0300 on Sunday 31
August.

'So S is Sinisa,' Talena said, near midnight, when we
had finally exhausted the mysteries of Mycroft. 'And ZZ is
Zoltan and Zorana.'

'It's probably Zorana who writes them,' I said. 'Her
English was always better.'

'And M is the mole.'

I nodded. Sinisa's source in the FBI, the fourth and most
rabid head of Cerberus, the crown jewel of his kingdom.

'I guess ZZ are just visiting after all,' I said.

The last message implied that Zoltan and Zorana had
not come to America to live, but only because Sinisa's criminal start-up needed funds. They had brought a staggering
amount of pure Afghani heroin into America, they had
found a buyer, and they were going to sell it, fly the money
to Mexico, and then courier it back to Sinisa in Belize.

I had heard of Burning Man. Some kind of counter-culture
arts festival in the Nevada Desert held every year, in the week

before Labor Day. Lots of drugs and naked people, a huge crowd of suspicious characters and distracting sights, with basically zero police presence, in the middle of the empty desert. Anything could happen at Burning Man, from the stories I'd heard, and in the chaos and confusion and drug-maddened haze, nobody would pay attention. The perfect place to trade a lot of drugs for a lot of money and then fly that money south to Mexico.

'They'll be leaving the country in ten days,' Talena said. 'And maybe not coming back.'

'None of this really helps, does it?' I asked. I wanted to hit something, spend an hour beating up on punching bags, but I knew that even if I did, I would find this hard reality no less infuriating. 'We know exactly what they're doing and we can't do a thing about it. We have to sit back and do nothing, because Agent Turner has to be all slow and quiet to find whoever the fuck M is, and I don't think all this shit we just read is really going to help her that much. If she tries to do anything to stop them, they'll find out. She's not going to find M in the next ten days. They're going to get *thirteen million dollars* for Sinisa and his zombie buddies, and then they're going to get away, and we can't do fuck-all.'

I woke unusually early the next morning, just past dawn. I tried to fall back asleep but couldn't. Eventually I surrendered to wakefulness and padded to the shower. When I came out, a damp towel wrapped around my waist, Talena was up.

'I'm tired,' she said, 'but I can't sleep.'

'Me too. Doesn't it suck.'

I dressed and prepared coffee and bagels as she showered. I wanted to read the paper, but we hadn't arranged for delivery yet, it was a six-block walk to the nearest newspaper box, and I wasn't ready to face the world outside.

Talena pulled on underwear and a Ramones T-shirt and sat at the kitchen table with me. The same kitchen table she had bled on, when Zoltan and Zorana had attacked us.

'Tell me something,' she said. 'Does this place feel like home to you?'

'It might have some day if it wasn't for them,' I said.

'Yeah. For me too.'

We looked at each other.

'Does anyplace feel like home?' she asked.

I said, 'I don't know. Not really.'

'Huh.' She sipped her coffee. After a moment she said, 'That's not a real reassuring answer.'

'Not reassuring how?' I asked cautiously.

'For, like, the future. You know. Our future.'

I decided it was wisest to wait for her to explain.

'I didn't sleep much,' Talena said. 'Tossing and turning and thinking. If we don't do anything, then what do we do? You know? Get married and have kids?' I twitched. 'Relax, Paul, I'm speculating, not proposing. You don't feel like you belong anywhere. I don't feel like I belong anywhere. So what the hell do we do? Try and settle down and have a normal life and forget that we didn't do anything?'

'I don't understand,' I said. 'What do you mean, didn't do anything? We've done lots—'

'I mean, about them.'

'About them? I . . . I thought we agreed we *can't* do anything.'

'No. Agent Turner can't do anything. We could do something. We could go to Burning Man ourselves, try to find them, try to fuck up their plan.'

I looked at her for a long time.

'You're serious,' I said.

'Like a bullet. Like a heart attack. Yeah, I'm serious. Paul, these people, not just Zoltan and Zorana, them too, but the people the money will go to—besides what they did to us, these are the people who destroyed, slaughtered . . . ravaged . . . my city, my country, my family, my friends, my home. Honestly, this may sound crazy, but honestly, I was thinking about it, and if we died and they all died, I swear to God, I would call that a fair trade.'

'Talena,' I said. 'Please. Do not get all martyrish. I'm very sorry, but I am not going to let you die on me.'

'I'm not about to strap on a suicide vest and go bomb them,' she said. 'But . . . I don't know. Do you want to sit here and be safe? If you call this safe, knowing they might change their minds some day and decide to off all us witnesses? I remember you said you wanted them dead. You said you would kill them yourself.'

'I would,' I said.

That hadn't been a thin emotional flash. I was still willing, still eager. I wouldn't hesitate for a second. They had tortured, raped and murdered scores of people, had come into my home, beaten me to a pulp, tormented and cut and scarred the woman I loved. Would killing them be justice? Who cared? I wasn't interested in philosophical discussions of the death penalty, of whether either or both of them could hypothetically some day be rehabilitated into the next incarnation of Mahatma Gandhi. We were way past justice. I wanted revenge so badly that my hands shook and I groaned audibly whenever I thought of Zoltan smiling and caressing Talena's naked body with the point of his knife.

We knew where they were going. Burning Man. Talena was right. They were going there because it was the perfect place for a drug deal, the perfect place for a getaway, a place where anything could happen and no one would notice. And that also made it the perfect place for an ambush. But was I willing to risk my life, and more importantly Talena's life, for my revenge? Even if, maybe especially if, Talena wanted it even worse than I did?

'This is crazy,' I said. 'You want to go, just you and me, to somehow stop two incredibly dangerous mass murderers from doing a multimillion-dollar drug deal. To kill them, if we can. Am I hearing you correctly?'

'Maybe your friends would help. Steve and Lawrence.'

'They probably would. That's not the point. Yes, I want them dead. Yes, I would kill them myself. No, I don't want to sit back and let them get away. But there has to be some other way of doing it than us going in like vigilantes. I mean, who are we? We . . . This isn't our job. I don't know whose it is, but this isn't our job. We've done enough.'

'If not us, then who? They'll be gone in ten days. We have to do something, Paul. *Somebody* has to do something. And there's nobody but us.'

She was right. The FBI were hamstrung by Sinisa's mole. Even if we could notify the police, even if they believed us, the odds of them stopping anything at Burning Man, without the mole finding out, were on the wrong side of slim and none.

The hard truth was that nobody would do anything unless we did something.

'I'll go,' I said. 'Steve and Lawrence and me. Not you.' I searched for a reason. 'We'll need someone to coordinate things from outside, who we can call if we need—'

'No. Paul, I am not your little princess on a pedestal who you go home to and build walls around. I'm your partner in crime. What we do, we do together.'

We looked at each other for a few seconds.

'All right,' I said, fearing as the words left my mouth that I would regret them for the rest of my life, that something terrible would happen to Talena out there in the desert.

'All right?'

'All right.'

We looked at one another. Talena smiled.

'You know, I always wanted to go to Burning Man,' she said. 'It might even be fun.'

'I sure hope so,' I said. 'God knows we need a vacation.'

5 Black Rock City

22 Monday: Lay of the Land

We reached Pyramid Lake at sunset, as the dying sun illuminated the landscape with dark and shimmering shades of red, instilling with unearthly beauty the mirror-still water, the single central island that gave the lake its name, the pale flat striated desert that surrounded us. The single ribbon of black road looked like a wound, as if the earth's blood had thickened and dried into asphalt. The distant ridge to our east glittered like it was full of rubies. Its twin to the west was shrouded in shadow. Ominous, slow-thumping industrial music boomed from the car stereo.

'Bit like home, this,' Steve said. 'Except there'd be more dead roos on the road.'

'It is like Australia,' Lawrence agreed. 'Nice aesthetics, but a little light on survivability. In a state populated by lawless gambling addicts. The similarities are striking.'

'There's heaps more gambling here than home. We don't have pokies in petrol stations. I don't reckon Australians would stand for that.'

'No, you'd insist on sitting, wouldn't you? Lazy bastards.'

I grinned. It was good to have my friends with me. Steve, the mountainous blond Australian, mechanic extraordinaire, tough-as-titanium ex-con and one of the nicest guys in the world, who talked slowly and with small words but was smarter than he seemed. Lawrence, the wiry hard-drinking New Zealander, sharp as a scalpel, not quite the cynical misanthrope he acted. Friends, blood brothers, members of my tribe. Saskia sat to their left, behind me.

'I hope we haven't forgotten anything critical,' Talena said.

'You've got the tickets?' I asked.

She nodded.

'How about the good sense God gave you?' Lawrence asked. 'You seem to have mislaid that some time before we showed up.'

'What do you want us to do?' Talena asked. 'We know what we're doing is stupid and dangerous. But tell us what else we can possibly do. Sit around and do nothing and let them get away with everything? Go to the police and have their friend in the FBI find out all about it and warn them? Do you have a third choice, Lawrence? Because those two don't fly.'

An uncomfortable silence fell.

'I'm sorry,' Talena said. 'Lawrence, I'm sorry. You're doing us a huge favour just being here. I know that. I'm being rude because I'm stressed. I apologize.'

'No worries,' Lawrence said. 'Between the Brady Bill and imminent mortal danger, you've got a right to vent. I do hear you. I just can't help thinking that there must be someone else who can deal with this Zoltan.'

'I wish there was,' I said. 'Believe me. But there isn't.'

'Brady Bill?' Saskia asked, puzzled.

'The reason we don't have guns,' Talena explained. 'Federal law. Ten-day waiting period between asking for one and getting one.' She sighed. 'It's a good law. Tells you something about how fucked up our life has become that I'm complaining about the Brady Bill.'

'I thought cheap and widely available machines of death were an inalienable constitutional right in America,' Lawrence said. 'Can't you buy one on the black market?'

I shrugged. 'Maybe in Tangiers or Jo'burg or Bangkok. But here, I'm a white-bread computer programmer and she's an editor. I don't think we know anyone who even has a criminal record, much less anyone who can connect us to an illegal gun.' I paused for a second and thought of Arwin. 'At least nobody who's still alive.'

'I wish old Hallam was here,' Steve said.

'Me too,' Lawrence said.

I nodded my agreement. Back when Steve and Lawrence and I had met, back when we had trucked across half of Africa, Hallam had been our driver and leader. When we had faced down a killer in Morocco, it was Hallam who had won the battle. But his adventuring days were over; he and his wife Nicole now had two infant children.

I pulled into the left lane and passed a bus overloaded with boxes and bags duct-taped on to the roof. The back was adorned with huge Om and Peace and Burning Man sigils, and the entire left side of the bus was a huge mural of a galactic firedancer using the stars as his fuel. The sun had almost set, and the headlights of the dense chain of BM-bound vehicles stitched an endless line through the night. I knew from their website that they were expecting more than thirty thousand attendees.

We drove deep into the desert for another hour, through Indian reservations, past tiny towns whose very existence was mysterious, until we reached Empire, the second last town before Burning Man. By this time it was fully dark. Empire had a population of about a hundred and vanished behind us in a flash. We went up and over a hill. As we crested the top, I caught my breath.

'Crikey,' Steve said.

Gerlach, the last town, was only a handful of small buildings. But beyond, amidst the velvet darkness of the desert, we saw ten thousand twinkling electric lights, arranged in a horseshoe shape a good quarter of a mile thick with an interior diameter of a mile. In the centre of the horseshoe, clearly visible although we were at least ten miles away, loomed the stylized figure of a man, his neon bones glowing bright blue, rising at least a hundred feet above the desert. Our first view of Black Rock City, and of the Man.

Two days earlier I had paid one thousand dollars cash to a heavily tattooed woman in a hipper-and-freakier-than-thou body modification shop in the Lower Haight, and in exchange received five Burning Man tickets. The survival guides that came with the tickets made it clear that Burning Man, held in Nevada's barren Black Rock Desert, was very much a Bring Your Own event. Participants were required to bring, at the very least, their own food, water, shelter, bedding, clothing, garbage disposal, sunscreen and 'an open mind and a positive attitude.'

The next day we picked up Steve and Lawrence at the airport, drove six hours through heavy traffic to Reno, and went on a massive shopping binge at the local twenty-four-hour Wal-Mart. By the time we finished, both my MasterCard and our rented Chevy Malibu wheezed and groaned beneath their new loads. We bought tents, sleeping bags, camp cookware, food, hats, sunglasses, toiletries, camping tools and whatever other sundries looked potentially useful for a seven-day stay in the desert, a counter-culture arts festival, and/or a pitched battle with international war criminals and multimillionaire drug dealers.

Past Gerlach we followed the slow-trickling line of vehicles off paved road and on to the desert, along a trail marked with orange cones. A sign at the turnoff warned us that Burning Man's speed limit was five miles per hour. I could see why. While the Black Rock Desert, actually an endless monochrome sea of pale grey, was absolutely flat, a dream to drive on, the top layer was talcum-fine dust that rose and hung in head-high clouds all around our teeming convoy.

We eased our way through stop-and-go traffic towards the blue figure of the Man. About the only thing I already knew about Burning Man was that the week-long event culminated with the burning of that colossal figure. The road was lined with signs. The first said:

BURNING MAN IS A SELF-SERVICE CULT.
WASH YOUR OWN BRAIN.

It took another half-hour to get to the Gate, where our greeter, a pretty blonde Southern girl wearing an orange vest and a deer-antler headdress, took our tickets and gave us glossy maps of Black Rock City and thick booklets called *What Where When* that listed Burning Man's many semi-scheduled events.

'Where do we camp?' I asked.

'Depends. Are y'all part of a theme camp?'

After a pause Talena admitted, 'We don't even know what a theme camp is.'

She laughed. 'Virgins! I knew it. Just camp anyplace that's free and doesn't have a reserved sign. Otherwise, round here it's first come, first serve.'

She waved us on. I shifted our trusty Chevy Malibu into first gear and allowed it to drift forward. Our windows were open and we could taste the bone-dry air and the fine alkaline dust that permeated it. In the distance we heard rattling techno music. The electric-blue neon skeleton of the Man loomed ahead of us, his arms by his side, and in the city that surrounded him other lights whirled and flickered, too distant to be deciphered. I had not expected so much electricity. Later I learned that most of the larger camps brought massive truck-mounted generators.

Far ahead, a gout of flame leaped at least thirty feet into the sky. A second later its shuddering roar tore through the air. We reached the outer road of the city, the edge of a colossal ragged forest of tents and RVs. A street sign told us we were at the corner of Vision and 6:30. Our headlights splashed over four people walking past. Two men and two women, thirty-something. The women wore tribal-patterned body paint, thongs, boots, fairy wings, and nothing else. One of the men wore jeans and a black T-shirt. The other was naked but for a horned gorilla mask and various tattoos. At the intersection ahead of us a twenty-foot-high banana on wheels crossed from left to right. There were a dozen people riding on it.

'Toto,' Lawrence said, 'I don't think we're in Kansas any more.'

We drove aimlessly around Black Rock City for a while, getting the lay of the land. I quickly decided that the other reason for Burning Man's speed limit was because if you went faster than five miles an hour you encountered so much sensory stimulation that your brain might explode.

The outer district of the city was mostly tents and RVs, but as we moved in towards the inner edge of the horse-shoe-shaped city, towards the Man, we drifted past geodesic domes, circus tents, multi-storey wooden buildings, painted and draped in bright colours. It was hard to imagine that just a few days ago this had all been barren desert, and would be again in a week. We heard a half-dozen types of distant music, and an occasional flame-thrower roar. We passed a car with a glowing pink ten-foot-diameter dread-locked head mounted above it on steel rods.

Gaggles of people drifted past, dressed in flashy clubwear, body paint, elaborate costumes, nothing at all, or some combination of all four. I aimed for the inside edge of the city, which boasted the biggest and brightest structures, but when we were a block away a purple-haired man warned us, 'Dude, no driving on the Esplanade unless you're an art car!' and we retreated. Shortly afterwards, we stumbled across a colossal, brightly lit, many-pillared tent festooned with flags and banners, with its own ring road around it, midway between the Man and the gate.

'Center Camp Café,' Lawrence reported, looking at his map. They were the first words, other than soft expostula-tions of amazement, that any of us had spoken for some time.

I pulled over and looked at my own map. Black Rock City looked like a one-third-eaten doughnut centred around the Man. The city's inner edge was the Esplanade. Nine other streets, this year named Authority, Creed, Dogma, Evidence,

Faith, Gospel, Reality, Theory and Vision, marched concentrically outwards from the Esplanade. They in turn were carved into blocks by seventeen radial streets, like spokes from a wheel, with the Man as the hub. The spoke streets had clock coordinates, with Center Camp at 6:00 and the bitten edges of the doughnut at 2:00 and 10:00.

'I think I am dreaming,' Saskia said, as a woman walked past wearing an enormous hoop dress made entirely of plastic sporks, chatting to a man painted gold.

'No,' Lawrence said. 'This place is much weirder than any dream I've ever had.'

'We should find a campsite,' I said. 'It's getting late.'

'Yes,' Talena said. 'And it's an amazing place but let's remember we're here on business.'

I paused a moment to absorb that. For a while, in the face of Burning Man's overwhelming kaleidoscopic strangeness, I had lost track of why we were here.

'I can't believe we forgot a *hammer*,' Talena said, disgusted.

'This tent isn't going anywhere unless a hurricane hits,' I pointed out. 'Not with all that water in it.'

'But it's all collapsed and squishy.'

I looked at her. 'Did you say "squishy"? Did you buy a Jello tent when I wasn't looking?'

She started to laugh. 'Well, it *feels* squishy.'

'Somebody here call for a hammer?' Lawrence asked, hefting one as he approached, one hand concealed behind his back.

'Where did you get that?' I asked, amazed.

'Our neighbour in the trailer on the corner. Anders. Swedish bloke, very interesting, worked all around the world on the merchant marine. He pointed out that we forgot something absolutely critical. Something more important than water. Rivalling oxygen.'

'What is that?' Saskia asked.

I, who had known Lawrence a long time, saw the punch line coming and grinned.

'Beer,' he said, revealing a six-pack of Michelob. 'Fortunately our man Anders is the generous type. Drink, drink and be merry, for tomorrow we will wish to die.'

Our camp's four tents—three for sleeping, one for storage—were soon fully erected and we sat cross-legged on the desert, newly aware of important things we had forgotten to bring. Seats, for one, as the ground was hard and uncomfortable, a thin layer of dust over a base baked to nearly the consistency of brick. And we were the only camp in sight without any kind of shade structure to escape the blistering daylight sun.

'No worries,' Steve said. 'We'll rig something up. But right now I wouldn't mind going for a bit of a walkabout.'

'Me too,' I said. I was tired, it had been a long day and a long week, but I had rarely been so eager to explore a place. 'Anybody else?'

We were all tired, Steve and Lawrence were still jet-lagged, but all five of us set out on foot to explore. We walked down 5:00 towards the Man. A UFO on wheels passed us, lights blinking. When we finally reached the Esplanade, we all stopped and gaped, as the sheer scale of Black Rock City became apparent for the first time.

The Esplanade, from dusk until dawn the world's largest party zone, was lined by Burning Man's brightest and flashiest camps and compounds. We stood near a full-size pirate ship, a pillared Roman temple, a huge video projection screen, and a palatial Arabian tent. The moon was nearly new, but the Esplanade's three-mile arc was lit by neon signs, thousand-watt lights, bonfires, laser beams, video projections, illuminated art, firedancers, flashlights, flame-throwers, and the ten thousand glowsticks carried by the seething crowds. Huge rave camps blasted psychedelic trance for thousands of dancers. Firedancers and live bands and stilt walkers and glassblowers and video artists performed. Dozens of improvised bars helped quench dusty and thirsty throats.

The mile-wide disc of desert surrounded by the Esplanade, the area around the Man, was uninhabited but far from barren. Busy walkways marked the 3:00, 6:00 and 9:00 routes to the Man, lit by kerosene lamps hanging from paired rows of fifteen-foot wooden pillars. The rest of the space was criss-crossed by art cars large and small, carrying the teeming partying masses from one distraction to the next. There was a reticulated bus that had been transformed into a whale. There was an Egyptian chariot drawn by a motorcycle. There was a fire-breathing dragon the length of a tractor trailor. And dozens of others, too distant to be seen in detail.

'Where do you want to go?' I asked the others.

Talena shook her head, bemused. 'Everywhere,' she said.

'Let's go see the big fella,' Steve suggested. 'Save the rest for tomorrow.'

It took ten minutes to walk to the Man, seventy feet of two-by-four planks and neon tubes atop a wooden ziggurat four storeys tall. We climbed the ziggurat and edged through the crowd atop it until we stood directly beneath the Man's gigantic wooden bones, looking across the desert night at the vast glittering arc of Black Rock City. After a little while we descended into the ziggurat, where tiny clumps of dirt and grass hung suspended on ropes from the top rafters. In the desiccated desert air the grass's rich thick smell, the smell of life, was overpowering. I admired the solid carpentry and wondered how the constructors felt, spending weeks building this structure and then, after only a week, on Saturday night, watching it burn.

'Do you know where Hatter is camping?' Talena asked on the way back to camp.

We had one friend here, Chris Aanansen, aka the Mad Hatter. He had been here for nearly two weeks already because he was a member of the Department of Public Works, the mostly volunteer crew who built the city's infrastructure from scratch every year.

'A camp called Crackhaus.'

'Sounds charming. Did he say where?'

'He said they'd be registered at Center Camp. We can look it up.'

'Don't suppose your friend Zoltan will be registered too,' Lawrence said. 'International House of War Criminals and Heroin Dealers, maybe? It's got a ring to it. We should suggest it when we find him.'

'Finding him could be tricky,' Steve said. 'This is a bloody big place.'

'We came prepared with a plan,' I said. 'You know that poster tube we brought?' Lawrence and Steve nodded. 'Well, finding Zoltan sounds like too much trouble. Much easier to make him come to us.'

23 Tuesday: Honey Pot

Up close, the pixillated images of Zoltan blown up to two-by-three-foot poster size looked like abstract art, but from ten feet away or further his grim features were recognizable. Lawrence, Talena and I took two of our four copies to Center Camp Café, Burning Man's nerve centre, while Steve and Saskia set up the honey-pot camp. An odd combination: Saskia looked like a pygmy next to Steve.

It was only ten in the morning and the heat of the sun already felt like a physical weight. We had been driven from our tents an hour earlier thanks to their tendency to turn into ovens in direct sunlight. Again I wished for a shade structure. At least we had brought hats and sunscreen. I wondered how long it would take to die of exposure out here, if you were abandoned naked in the desert. A few days at most.

By night, Black Rock City was a phantasmagoric, glittering wonderland; by stark colour-draining sunlight, it looked like some kind of avant-garde apocalypse, Mad Max meets Mardi Gras, as if all of America's colourful mutant social subspecies had been driven into the desert by some disaster. Pierced and tattooed people with unnatural hair colours whizzed by on bicycles already thickly tarnished with pale dust. We passed a row of blue Porta-Potties. The heat and stench inside those plastic cubicles guaranteed that people with delicate sensibilities steered far clear of Burning Man. People were lined up, mostly in pyjamas or jeans, most of the men and some of the women topless, but even by day there were many retina-scarring outfits. A couple of men wore nothing at all. I wondered how much sunscreen they went through. Talena and Lawrence and I were hopelessly mundane in yoga pants and halter top, shorts and T-shirt, and sweat pants and no shirt, respectively.

Center Camp Café had room for maybe a thousand people. Long lines stretched up to the coffee bar. A couple of dozen near-naked men and women, several of them elaborately tattooed, did yoga on the performance mat. A woman played an accordion on one stage, and a man ranted on the other, each amplified just enough that they wouldn't interfere with one another. There were massage tables and feathered art installations and heaps of benches and couches and cushions and chairs, and the ground was covered by hundreds of overlapping carpets, and there was shade, for which I was very thankful.

'Look at this. We're surrounded by dozens of fit half-naked women,' Lawrence said. 'That's morally wrong. They should be fully naked.'

'Some of them are,' Talena said, nodding towards a tiny, pretty and natural blonde chatting with a man in leather hot pants.

'Ah. Well. I suppose that's a start.' I think Lawrence was a little shocked. I know I was. Topless women and naked men were common Burning Man sights, but full female nudity was unusual. He changed the subject quickly. 'Where do you think we can put up our Wanted Dead or Alive posters?'

'Maybe we should ask the coffee people,' I suggested.

'Ask someone in charge if it's okay,' Talena said, amused. 'How Canadian.'

'You think it's easier to ask forgiveness than permission?' I asked.

'I think it's anarchy and there's nobody to ask. One on the wall, here, and then one on the other side.' She led the way, posters in one hand, duct tape in the other.

My plan was a variant of what the hacking world called a 'honey pot': set up an invitingly open computer system that would-be intruders will flock to, not knowing their every move is tracked. For our honey pot we had annexed a second patch of real estate, across the street and down about fifty feet from our real camp. Steve had erected a tent there and affixed one of Zoltan's posters, a pad of paper and a pen. The two Zoltan posters in Center Camp Café were adorned with helpful Magic Marker captions:

HAVE YOU SEEN THIS MAN? COME TO GOSPEL AND 5:10! TELL US WHERE AND WHEN!

With any luck people would interpret it as a weird social-art piece and enlist themselves in our hunt, recording Zoltan sightings for us. But what we were really counting on was that Zoltan or Zorana themselves would see the poster and come investigate. One of us would keep a discreet eye on the honey-pot tent at all times. Between turning our hunt for Zoltan into performance art, staking out the honey pot in case they showed up in person, and the high-tech toys I had bought in San Francisco's International Spy Shop, I figured our chances were pretty good.

We purchased iced lattes—when in the desert, ice seems like the apotheosis of all human endeavour—and went back to our camp to deliver two to Steve and Saskia as a reward for their work. Zoltan's mug was securely taped to the honey-pot tent, and its odd blown-up-tiny-picture appearance serendipitously made it actually stand out a little in the sea of visual stimulation that was Burning Man. A pad of paper and a pen were lashed securely to the honey pot's tent pole.

Steve had even managed to rig a kind of shade structure for us between the tents and the car, made out of tent flies. It wasn't much compared to most of the camps we had passed—even the humdrum ones generally had a geodesic dome, covered in parachute fabric and decorated with couches, chairs, carpets, pillows and mountains of water—but it sure beat sitting in the blazing sun.

'Now we start sitting around watching?' Talena asked.

I nodded. 'I was figuring three-hour shifts.'

'I'll start,' Lawrence said. 'It's noon. I'll expect reinforcements at three.'

'Try not to get distracted by the naked ladies,' Talena cautioned.

'Never,' Lawrence swore unconvincingly. 'Where are your James Bond toys?'

'In our tent,' I said.

San Francisco, like London and New York, boasts a branch of the International Spy Shop. Its Folsom Street store sadly does not sell poisons, explosives, or Aston Martins outfitted with laser beams; it does not even sell guns; but it does sell tear gas and gas masks, plus powerful binoculars and shotgun microphones with which one can watch and listen from hundreds of feet away. Another authorized expenditure of Sinisa's blood money.

'Maybe I stay here,' Saskia said. She seemed a little overwhelmed and unsettled by Burning Man. I couldn't blame her.

'Let's go find my friend,' I said to Steve and Talena. 'He's all plugged in, he can tell us where we should go. The Mad Hatter.'

Years ago I had worked with Chris Aanansen, universally known as the Mad Hatter, or just Hatter. Back then it said 'guru' on his business card. Testament to the excesses of the dot-com boom, yes, but also accurate: Hatter was a brilliant programmer. Unfortunately he hated programming. So when boom went bust he turned his back on computers and morphed rather bizarrely into an adrenaline junkie. Now he made his living as a smoke-jumper, parachuting out of airplanes to fight forest fires, arguably the world's most intense job. Like Steve, Hallam and many other of my friends, Hatter would have made me feel incompetent, inadequate, unmanly and inconsequential if he hadn't been such a helluva nice guy.

He was also a hard partier. When we showed up at Camp Crackhaus it was littered with discarded beer and whisky bottles, empty nitrous oxide canisters and unconscious semi-human forms sleeping off the night's revelry. There was an art car parked out front, a straight-out-of-Mad-Max pick-up truck, painted to look like a post-apocalyptic relic, armed with a pair of turret-mounted propane-powered flame-throwers. Excessive pyromania was apparently a signature element of Burning Man from the name on down. The art car's engine seemed to have fallen victim to dust, mortal enemy to all moving parts; its bonnet was up and two men dressed in black looked into it and muttered grimly to one another.

Hatter, a tall, lean, cadaverous man with a lined face

that made him look older than his thirty years, sat slumped on a folding chair, sipping from a can of beer, smoking a cigarette. A large patch of the left side of his face appeared to have been scraped off with a cheese grater. One of the many spectacular hats he owned, hence his nickname, sat on the ground next to him, two feet tall and zebra-striped. A walkie-talkie rested atop the hat.

'Hatter! What happened?' I asked.

'Paul!' he exclaimed, pleased and surprised. He leaped up and hugged me. 'I didn't know you were coming! And Tally, right?' They had only met a couple of times.

'Talena,' she corrected him politely. She didn't like the diminutive.

'This is—where's Steve?' I asked.

Talena pointed to the broken-down art car. Steve's blond, smiling face appeared for a moment from behind the bonnet. 'Just having a bit of a go,' he called out, before diving back into the engine. There was nothing that made Steve happier than fixing a broken machine. The two black-clad men next to him looked on with bemused awe as he worked.

'What happened to your face?' Talena asked Hatter.

He waved dismissively. 'I fell off an art car. At the DPW party. Hurts like a sonofabitch, but we've got plenty of illegal analgesics around here. So what made you come? When did you arrive?'

'Last night. Kind of a last-minute decision,' I said, avoiding the whole story. Hatter was a good friend but not a tribal brother; I couldn't enlist him the way I had Steve and Lawrence.

'And how are you liking the playa?'

'The what?' Talena asked.

'Playa. Spanish for beach. This whole desert was a lake-bed a few million years ago. Burners call the desert the playa.'

'Burners,' I said cautiously.

'Right. Sorry. You're new around here. "Burners" means anyone at Burning Man.'

'Oh. Okay. Anything else we should know? Advice for newbies?'

'Sure,' Hatter said. 'Let's see. Hydrate. That's the most important thing. Keep water with you at all times, and keep drinking it. What else . . . It's a gift economy out here. The only things you buy are coffee and ice. Otherwise, just ask for stuff, and people will probably give it to you, if it's at all reasonable.'

'And then you give them something back?' Talena asked.

'Gift economy, not barter. Giving back is nice but not necessary. You'll even find random people walking around giving you things.' He shrugged. 'Crappy little trinkets, mostly, but the symbolism matters. I don't mean to get all hippie on you, but honestly, out here there really is a genuine general sense that sharing is good, and you take care of everyone, neighbours, strangers, anyone. It's pretty amazing.'

I nodded, though I wasn't all that amazed. I had trav-elled enough to know that this attitude was common to all desert cultures.

'Did you bring bicycles?' he asked.

We shook our heads.

'Too bad. Best way to get around. You're not supposed to use any non-art car after you've arrived. You can hop rides in art cars, but it's not like they follow any kind of route or schedule.' He grinned. 'That's what makes them fun.'

'What happens if we do use our car?' I asked. 'Do we get kicked out?'

'It's happened.'

'Who does the kicking? Who runs this place?'

'Runs is a dangerous word,' Hatter said cautiously. 'This is more an anarchic bazaar than a structured event. But there is a group that orchestrates it, organizes all the volunteers. If you manage to really piss a lot of people off, the Black Rock Rangers will throw you out. They make sure everybody plays nice. Volunteers. Like the rest of the infrastructure people. DPW, the lamplighters, the coffee people, the medical centre, the firefighters, the post office, the clean-up crew, almost everyone's a volunteer. Hey, what time is it?'

I glanced at my watch. 'About eleven.'

'Eleven? Shit. I should get going. I'm supposed to be jumping in half an hour.'

'Jumping?' Talena asked.

'Skydiving. World's greatest hangover cure. But, shit, I don't know. It's a long walk on a hot day. The DeathGuild boyz were going to give me a ride on Rogue, but it's busted.'

'Rogue? DeathGuild?' Talena asked.

'DeathGuild is the big goth camp on the Esplanade,' Hatter said, gesturing vaguely towards the Man, whose wooden form was visible from most of Black Rock City by day. 'They run Thunderdome. The big bungee-fighting place. Rogue is one of their art cars. But her engine crapped out last night and nobody here knows how to fix it.'

'Don't be so sure,' I said. 'Steve! How's it looking?'

'She'll be right in a minute, mate, no worries! Just need to grease the wurblesnatcher and cobblegrind the ozone belt!' Steve called back, or might as well have for all I understood him.

Hatter nodded as if Steve's response had made sense to him.

'Maybe we'll ride along with you to the airstrip, if that's okay,' I suggested.

'Sure, yeah. I mean, if the DeathGuilders say it's okay. It's their car,' he said, motioning to the two men wearing far too much black leather for this heat.

'Give her a go, mate!' Steve said to one of them.

He blinked, obviously not accustomed to being so addressed by gigantic blond Australians, but once he deciphered Steve's meaning he went to the driver's seat and turned the key. Rogue's engine roared into life. Wide smiles broke out on the faces of the two DeathGuilders before they remembered they were goths and recomposed their expressions into menacing gloom.

'You blokes mind if we borrow your ute for a bit of a recce?' Steve asked.

They looked at one another.

'Sure,' one of them said cautiously, almost as if he had understood.

'Outstanding. Paul! Talena! Hop in!'

'Come on,' I said to the Hatter, 'you've got yourself an airport limousine. Do those flame-throwers actually work?'

'Like a charm. I'll show you.'

The two goths drove. Steve, Talena, Hatter and I perched atop the back, occasionally startling those around us with

Rogue's twin turret-mounted flame-throwers, each of which belched flame about twenty feet.

'Bit of an amateur job, this,' Steve said reflectively as he examined the pipes, valves, tubes and Zippo lighters that comprised the flame-throwers. His hands were dark with grease.

'Please try not to blow yourself up,' I said. 'It would be hard to explain to Hallam.'

'I reckon that's just how Hallam figures I'll buy the farm,' Steve pointed out.

I chuckled. 'True. But still. Try not to make a down payment while you're here.'

Burning Man's airstrip was some distance south-east of the horsehoe that was Black Rock City. The city proper was only a fraction of Burning Man's geography, which in turn occupied only a tiny patch of the desert. The playa. The border between Burning Man and raw desert was demarcated by a three-foot-high orange 'trash fence.' Beyond that fence, the lone and level playa, one of the most visually barren landscapes on the planet, stretched far away. The jagged, arid hills that surrounded the desert looked close enough to touch, but I knew they were thirty miles distant. The wind was beginning to pick up and in the distance I saw a vortex of dust easily a hundred feet tall.

The desert was so flat, hard and endless that planes could actually land anywhere, but they were supposed to use the airstrip's fenced-off landing zone. Black Rock Airport even had a terminal, albeit one that consisted of a shack dressed with signs warning pilots they were basically on their own. A couple of dozen light airplanes were parked in neat rows between the airstrip and the terminal.

'Hey, Hatter,' I said, 'tell me, how far can these planes go?'

He looked at them with a jaundiced professional eye. 'It varies. Mostly a few hundred miles. A few of them can go further.'

'How much further? Like to Mexico?'

'Hmm.' He considered. 'Mexico's about seven hundred knots from here. That's a long way. The only ones that could make it are those two, there and there.' He pointed to two airplanes very similar in appearance, larger than most. 'Cessna 182s with long-range tanks. Why do you ask?'

'Just curious,' I lied. Zoltan and Zorana's getaway plane might not have arrived yet. It might be hidden somewhere in the empty miles of Black Rock City beyond the trash fence. But it might be one of the two that Hatter had just pointed out.

'That's my ride,' Hatter said excitedly, pointing to a half-dozen skydivers strapping on their harnesses next to a small plane. 'See you back in camp, Paul. Drop by Crackhaus any time!'

'Count on it,' I assured him.

We left Steve with the goths at DeathGuild's workshop. After he suggested doubling the range of Rogue's flame-throwers they all but adopted him. DeathGuild was a huge camp, the only one I had seen with a fence, where the big attraction was a thirty-foot-high geodesic battledome out front. Every night would-be combatants strapped them-selves into bungee cords and fought for bragging rights with padded clubs while hundreds cheered them on.

We had ninety minutes before Lawrence was due to be relieved, and we decided to go for a walk. Enjoying ourselves was surprisingly easy, despite the sword of Zoltan hanging over our heads, thanks to the sea of distractions that surrounded us. I began to understand, as we wandered, what Hatter had meant by a bazaar. There were hundreds of 'theme camps,' groups ranging in size anywhere from a few people up to maybe a hundred, and each camp did something to entertain, amuse, aid, delight, feed, bewilder, or annoy the passing crowds. Giving out coffee, or Kool-Aid, or pancakes, or massages, or sunscreen. Showing movies. Constructing a merry-go-round, roller-skating rink, bowling alley, or haunted house ride. Creating an Irish pub, hosting live music, and giving drinks to all. Littering their turf with weird sculptures and croaking menacingly at those who approach. Firedancers, flame guns, naked brunches, bondage tutorials, costume workshops, dance clubs, temporary tattoos, DJs, art cars—Black Rock City was such a giddily unreal place that I was able to spend as long as half an hour gaping at its many spectacles before suddenly remembering why we were here.

Those were bad moments. I shuddered despite the heat, and heavy slimy trepidation congealed in the pit of my stomach when I realized that we were chasing the two people who had left the dark bruises on my belly and Talena's, the angry red scab that still lay between her breasts: two people who were perfectly willing and able to kill us both. We had come here because Burning Man's anarchy was a world of its own, with no authority oversight. But that worked both ways. We would not be rescued if something went terribly wrong. We were on our own.

Eventually we ventured into the playa and past the Man, along the 12:00 walkway that led to Burning Man's second largest structure, a mosque-like edifice called the Temple of Honor. Above us, as we walked, an airplane disgorged its load of skydivers, one of them presumably the Hatter. In the distant west, clouds of dust were beginning to form and drift above the playa.

The Temple was gorgeous, fluted pillars supporting enormous bulbs and spires, breathtaking art and architecture made of humble papier-mâché and black and white wallpaper. Talena and I chatted and chuckled and held hands during the walk, but as we approached, we fell quiet. The dozens of other burners who stood beneath and around the Temple were hushed and serious. This was a solemn place.

Couples held each other tightly. People spoke in soft murmurs. Half a dozen people were quietly weeping. Others stood or knelt as they wrote on the Temple's walls. The wallpapered exterior was mazily patterned in black and white, and most of the strips and patches of white that could be reached from the ground had been covered with spidery handwriting. We approached and read some of what had been written.

Philip Hann 1971–2003 He was a good man and his wife and son and friends loved him and miss him very much

I loved you, Lisa. I will always love you. All I ever wanted to know was why.

Dad I'm trying to understand how you could have done it and what must have happened to you to make you do it but it's SO FUCKING HARD I'll try I promise I swear

After this temple burns I will stop cutting myself

david i'm so sorry it was the worst mistake of my life. it was the worst thing i ever did. i should have believed you. i should have trusted you. it was my fault you did it. it was my fault. god please believe me i'm so so sorry.

Naomi Anne Foster 1974–2002 Elena Sophia Anderson 1999–2002 I never believed in Heaven until I met you my daughter I will see you and mommy there I promise

There was more, much more, some of the entries so harrowingly personal that I couldn't finish them. There were books chained to the base of the Temple for longer messages. Some of them went on for pages. All of them were anguished, heart-rending, mournful. Requiems and regrets, story after story that told of awful loss and pain.

I began to understand. The Temple of Honor was not meant as art or architecture. It was a literal temple, a place to honour the dead, the lost, the mourned. On Sunday the entire temple would burn to the ground. Every message here, every word that had been written, would be consumed by flame and reduced to ash by the temple's funeral pyre. It was a powerful thought.

After several minutes I had to stop reading. The words were too raw, too electric, and the abrupt transition from the bacchanal that was the rest of Burning Man worked like an emotional sucker punch. The overflowing sorrow of the epitaphs and lamentations all around us, the soundtrack of quiet sobs and whispers, and the colossal austere beauty of the temple amid this dead arid land, were overwhelming. I felt like I had been immersed in terrible sadness, like it was a physical thing, a fog, and I couldn't help but think of all the people, all the futures I had ever lost. I took Talena's hand, my throat thick, my eyes damp.

'Do you have a pen?' she asked me quietly.

I nodded, not trusting myself to speak, shrugged off my day pack, and unearthed a pen. She took it and led me to a bare patch of wall. There she wrote: *Goodbye Mom. Goodbye Dad. Goodbye Zlatan. Goodbye Sarajevo. Goodbye Bosnia. Goodbye my home. I loved you all.* Then she wrote it again in Croatian.

'Here,' she said, handing me the pen, her voice cracking, her lips quavering. 'Write something. Please.'

I hesitated for a moment. Then I turned to the wall and wrote next to her entry, with a shaking hand, the words barely legible even to me: *Goodbye, Laura. In another world.*

I felt cold tears slide down my cheeks. I tried to ignore them while I put the pen back in the day pack but I couldn't make my limbs work properly. In the end I just dropped them both and put my arms around Talena and for some time we held each other tightly.

The dust storm hit us as we leaned on one another. It wasn't as bad as the Sahara's skin-grating sandstorms, but it was rough. The playa dust was alkaline and burned our tear-soaked eyes. We took our T-shirts off and wrapped them around our heads, baring the wounds Zoltan and Zorana had left on us, not that anyone could see them in the storm's whiteout. Between the thick whirling dust and the thin cotton we could barely see each other. We had to wait for the storm to lessen before we dared leave the temple.

'You're late,' Lawrence cheerfully accused when we arrived back at our camp, our eyes red with tears and playa dust, but feeling stronger, like we had left a physical burden behind at the temple. He sat on a folding seat he had somehow scrounged and sipped a Michelob. Saskia sat on the ground next to him, relaxed and smiling.

'Your friend Anders is impressively generous with his beer,' I said.

'I told him we'd go out tomorrow to get more water and resupply his beer fridge.'

'Any flies at the honey pot?'

'Two people wrote in the book,' Lawrence said. 'Normal people. Given the highly flexible definition of 'normal' one uses around here. Apparently he's been seen earlier today at the Man and walking along the Esplanade around three.'

'Sweet,' I said. 'I wasn't sure people would participate.'

'I suppose it's just weird enough for burners to approve,' Lawrence said.

'Burners. I see you're picking up the lingo,' Talena said, amused.

'Yes. And now, if you'll excuse me, I'm going to try picking up the women.' He looked over to Saskia and gave her an up-and-down leer. 'Want to go for a walk, my dear?'

'Lawrence!' she said, scandalized. 'It is rude to look at a woman like that.'

'She acts like she thinks I don't know that already,' Lawrence said to me.

'I will walk with you,' Saskia said. 'But you must behave.'

Lawrence winced with exaggerated pain at the last stricture, and then the two of them left. Talena looked at me and arched a single eyebrow, smiling faintly.

'You will not matchmake,' I said sternly.

She smiled. 'I don't know if I need to.'

Talena and I stayed in camp for the rest of the afternoon, screened behind our tents lest Zoltan and Zorana walk down Gospel Street and recognize us. We didn't talk much, but our silence was warm and comfortable. Two more people entered Zoltan sightings, both citing Center Camp Café as the location.

Steve and Saskia and Lawrence returned around sunset for our dinner of corned beef, rice, canned vegetables and canned peaches. Lawrence and Saskia brought disquieting news.

'The Center Camp posters have been torn down,' he reported.

We paused to absorb that.

'Probably not randam vandals,' I said.

'Probably not,' Talena agreed.

'So they've seen the posters. But we haven't seen them at the honey pot yet.'

'Might be they'll come visiting tonight,' Steve said.

I nodded. 'Maybe. Or maybe they saw us first, and now they're the ones planning an ambush.'

A silence fell.

'So much for my hopes for a good night's sleep,' Lawrence muttered. 'Cheers, mate.'

By night, Gospel Street and 5:00 was dark and quiet, except when large groups stopped at the nearby Porta-Potties. Occasional art cars drifted by, a bus with a tall ship's superstructure, a van lit by ten thousand LEDs, a pick-up truck and trailer covered in shag carpet, but they never stopped.

The five of us sat in the dark, watching the lantern in front of the honey-pot tent, and waited.

At midnight we decided that there was no sense in all of us staying up all night. Talena volunteered to watch until three in the morning, and I reluctantly agreed to wake up at three and stay on watch until six, when Saskia would take over. Steve and Lawrence, still jet-lagged, didn't argue.

24 Wednesday: Smack Dealer Camp

'Paul,' Talena whispered urgently, shaking me awake. 'Paul, someone's here.'

'Muh,' I croaked, wishing she would just go away and let me sleep. Then I remembered where we were. I sat straight up, burying my head in the tent fabric for a moment. 'At the honey pot?'

'Yes. Hurry.'

I wriggled out of the sleeping bag and the tent as quickly and quietly as possible, remembering just in time to grab the shotgun mike and binoculars. I glanced at my watch. Two in the morning. The desert air was cold and windless.

A gigantic tricycle, fifteen feet high, painted in gleaming lacquered primary colours, was parked in front of the honey pot. Dim lights emanated from the hubs of its three wheels, red and green and blue. A single brilliant headlight perched atop a pole that protruded up from its cab, like a giant glowing eye on a stalk. The tricycle was so elegantly designed it looked like it had come straight from the set of *Alice in Wonderland* as directed by Tim Burton. If I had seen it anywhere other than Burning Man I would have assumed someone had slipped hallucinogens into my food.

I saw flickers of motion, someone descending the ladder that hung from the tricycle's side, someone else in front of the tent. I couldn't tell how many. The lantern in front of the honey pot had gone out or been extinguished. I fumbled with the shotgun mike, which looked a lot like a police billy club, putting its headphones in my ears and trying to find the on switch. Eventually I succeeded and aimed it at the honey pot. Nothing happened. After a moment I realized I was holding it backwards and rotated it a hundred and eighty degrees.

The noise was deafening, like the sound of plastic being torn amplified to hardcore-clubber levels. I grabbed frantically at the volume control and turned it down. When the noise dropped to sane levels I realized it was the sound of someone going through a tent door.

'What is it?' Talena whispered. I removed a headphone and passed it to her. We stood next to one another, listening.

'There's nothing in there but a bunch of water,' a voice said. Neither Zoltan nor Zorana: an American voice, male.

'But it's him, right?' Another male American voice.

A light went on at the honey pot, aimed at the picture of Zoltan duct-taped to the tent's exterior. We saw three people silhouetted, two men and one woman, before it switched off.

'It's definitely him,' said the first voice.

'I don't like it,' an American woman said. 'Maybe we should call it off.'

'It's weird, but it's not cops,' the first voice said. 'I don't know what it is.'

'We should make him tell us,' the woman said.

'Make him?' the second voice asked, incredulous. 'I'm not going to try to make that motherfucker tell me anything. I'm going to smile at him and his crazy wife real nicely and pay them for their cargo and get the fuck out of there. And I'm sure as hell not going to tell them we're calling it off. Those two are fucking *crazy*.'

'We shouldn't have agreed to this,' the woman said.

'Too late,' the first man said. 'Kevin's right. I don't think we can back out now.'

Talena and I looked at each other and nodded our mutual understanding. It wasn't Zoltan or Zorana. These were the drug dealers, the ones who had come to Burning Man with thirteen million US dollars cash to buy Sinisa's high-grade Afghani heroin. They had obviously already met the Couple From Hell.

'Whatever,' the first voice said. 'There's nothing else here. Let's go.'

The light went back on and the three figures climbed back on to the tricycle.

'We should follow them,' Talena whispered.

'I know,' I said. 'Let's wake up the others.'

The headlight on the spire atop the tricycle's cab lit up and it started to move away, even though the third climber was still only halfway up the ladder.

'Shit,' Talena said. 'No time. Come on.'

Black Rock City's five mph speed limit made for a low-speed pursuit, but we still had to jog to keep up. The tricycle went inward, towards the Esplanade, and then to our dismay it continued across the playa towards the Man, picking up speed as it went, breaking the speed limit and getting up to the speed of a fast run. Both Talena and I were wearing socks and no shoes; there was no way we could keep up with it all the way across the playa.

'Shit,' I panted. 'Fuck!'

'Wait! Come here! Please!' Talena called out—not to me, but to an art car she noticed driving along Authority, the first street out from the Esplanade. 'Car' was really too grand a term. The vehicle that swerved and turned towards us was a motorized couch on wheels, piloted by a naked old man with a beard that descended to his navel. He sat in the middle of the couch, directing its motion with a joystick between his legs.

'Give you a ride, darling?' he asked Talena, leering.

'Yes!' Talena said.

We boarded the couch, Talena to his left, me to his right.

'I can't believe I'm about to say this,' Talena said, 'but follow that art car!' She pointed at the light of the tricycle, fading in the distance.

The old man looked at her for a moment, looked at me, shrugged, laughed, and pushed the joystick forward. The couch leaped forward, pushing us back into its lumpy seats.

'Holy shit, this thing is *fast,*' I said approvingly, part flattery, partly genuinely impressed.

'It's all about the power to mass ratio,' the old man said. 'What's that you got there?'

I saw no point in lying. 'Binoculars and a shotgun microphone.'

He raised his eyebrows. 'Spying on someone?'

'Yes,' Talena said.

'Well then. I'll keep a discreet distance.'

We followed the tricycle all the way to 10:00, one of the

ends of Black Rock City's horseshoe, where music from a half-dozen rave camps still pounded rhythmically and would until dawn, and along 10:00, all the way to Vision, near the city's uttermost edge, and to the only camp we had seen other than DeathGuild that had a fence. A six-foot-high chain-link fence with a gate, guarding a large trapezoidal area that contained a half-dozen geodesic domes and three Ryder trucks.

One of the trucks hummed with generator noise, and there was enough light to make out some details through my binoculars. There were only about a half-dozen figures moving about, but I guessed the camp as a whole had some forty residents. Each dome had not just its own electric light but a fridge, unthinkably decadent luxury for Burning Man. I thought I saw an espresso machine. And there were three other art cars parked in the complex: a giant spider, a Batmobile straight out of the movie, and a van dressed up as a great white shark. Like the tricycle, and like everything else in this camp, the production values were very high. Which made sense. After all, if we were right, this was a camp of multimillionaire drug dealers.

'You want to go knock on their door?' our driver asked.

'Not tonight, thank you,' Talena said politely. 'That'll be fine.'

The driver turned the couch around and returned to the Man.

'Have a good burn,' he said cheerfully when we disembarked.

'Have a good burn,' we echoed, and walked back to camp, feeling triumphant.

Major heroin dealers lived the high life. No question about it. The crew at Smack Dealer Camp, as we christened it, dressed in expensive clothes, did a lot of expensive drugs, and surrounded themselves with expensive toys and expensive women. They talked about chalets in Lake Tahoe and yachts docked in Honolulu and booking whole floors of Manhattan hotels. Mostly they were at Burning Man to party, although a few of them seemed to have come for the art, and one talked learnedly about studying Burning Man's distributed community as an example of what the future would bring.

You can learn a lot about a group of people if you spend a whole day spying on them. Of the dozen men and two dozen women, only five men and two women were actually involved in the business. The rest were buddies and hangers-on. High-school friends who had grown up in suburban Orange County with the core crew and now acted as gofers and kept the camp running smoothly so the real dealers didn't have to do any work, and lithe young women who were there for decorative value and/or to sleep with the men in exchange for living off their largesse, playing with their many toys, and partaking of their endless supply of drugs. Ecstasy, acid and nitrous oxide were the most popular substances. The dealers themselves used drugs only sparingly, and no one was allowed to touch the hard drugs that were their business.

The core crew and most of the men were in their early thirties, and all their money and flashy tattoos couldn't hide the fact that the men in the camp tended towards pudgy, greasy, slovenly, lazy and unattractive. The cloud of decorative women—Talena quickly took to calling them 'concubines'—were in their early twenties, some of them embracing their party-across-America lifestyle, others torn by moral qualms, sexual repulsion, or the desire for some kind of normalcy. It was an interesting crowd and under other circumstances I would have studied them with utter fascination. The intellectual member of the core crew wanted to retire, but the rest wanted to move from rich to ultra-rich, from first class to corporate jets, and that conflict simmered all day. They complained about money launderers who took forty per cent of their hard-earned money. A woman agonized to another about whether she should sleep with the man who invited her; she wanted to but worried he would then lose interest and expel her from this drug dealers' Eden she was enjoying so much. Another told her friend in strict confidence that she couldn't stand the lifestyle any more and she was going to return to stripping as soon as they got back from Burning Man. Two of the gofers resented the core crew because they couldn't get promoted into membership and were thinking of striking out on their own. Just a few of Smack Dealer Camp's dozen in-progress micro soap operas.

For a group of big-money drug dealers they were amazingly easy to spy on. Maybe they had let their guard down for Burning Man. Maybe they had just grown overconfident. They seemed to be good at their business. None of the core crew had ever been arrested, and while one of them talked about guns a lot, and we briefly saw one of the gofers carry two handguns from one Ryder truck to another, we overheard no anecdotes of violence.

We had moved our camp almost next door to theirs, killing two birds with one stone: we no longer risked discovery by staying close to the address Zoltan and Zorana knew from the posters they had torn down, and we were close enough to Smack Dealer Camp that we could sit in our tent with binoculars and shotgun mike and see and hear just about everything that went on. It was uncomfortable work—our tent was like an oven even with door and window flaps wide open and two rapidly melting bags of newly purchased ice cooling the air a little—but at the same time it was voyeuristically fun.

'Smack Dealer Camp,' I suggested to Talena at lunch, crackers with corned beef and soup, 'would be the greatest reality TV show ever.'

In the afternoon, when Steve and Lawrence and Saskia took over the eyes-and-ears work, Talena and I went roving across the disc of playa that surrounded the Man, and the vast wedge between the Man and the trash fence, looking at the art installations. Some of them were amazing. Some of them were just weird. A vividly painted forty-foot-tall fallen chandelier. A huge ball of fire on a chain that endlessly wound and unwound itself around an iron pillar. A three-storey house of wood made of fifty-two wooden panels, each one painted as a different playing card. A field of little bobblehead dogs rippling in the wind. A telephone with which one could talk to God, who had an unexpectedly nasal voice. A tall and disturbing jagged metal sculpture of some inhuman beast. A row of blown-up, six-by-four-foot pictures of two dozen people, along with a note from the artist explaining that she rejected family and country and religion; these pictures were of her closest friends, who she saw as her nation, her tribe, her gods. I looked at that one for a long time.

After the art we went to the trapeze. I expected a long line but there were only a few other burners and we both spent a giddy hour leaping and swinging about, high above the net, learning how to swing from our legs, to backflip into the net, to do a two-person catch-and-release. We cruised back to dinner high on endorphins, giggling and nudging one another like teenagers.

By the time we got back our camp had changed. Steve and Lawrence and Saskia sat on folding seats beneath a tall shade canopy, drinking bottles of Stella Artois, playing cards on the red surface of a brand-new cooler. As we approached, flabbergasted, Steve and Lawrence loudly started to complain that Saskia, who had a much larger pile of paperclips in front of her, was clearly cheating.

'What the hell?' Talena asked. 'Where did you get all this?'

'Empire. Turns out they stock up on all this gear so lazy forgetful people like us don't have to drive all the way back to Reno,' Lawrence said. 'Very thoughtful of them. Can you believe Anders wasn't happy I bought him Stella? He wanted Michelob instead? There's just no telling with some people. It's good that we moved. He's clearly not a trustworthy neighbour.'

'Speaking of neighbours,' I said, 'what happened to keeping an eye on our new ones?'

'No need, mate,' Steve said. 'They went and blabbed it all.'

'Blabbed what?'

'Tomorrow night,' Lawrence said. 'Four and thirty, ante meridian. Between the Temple of Gravity and the trash fence. That's where the deal goes down.' He grinned.

'You like that? "The deal goes down"? Very convincingly American of me, no?'

'Lawrence,' Talena said, 'you couldn't convince Helen Keller that you were American.'

'Flattery will get you everywhere,' he said, pleased.

'Tomorrow night,' I repeated. Somehow it seemed too soon. I had thought it would happen Saturday, the night of the Burn, when all the rest of Burning Man clustered around the Man and watched him erupt into a pillar of flame.

'A bit of action,' Steve said, cracking his knuckles. 'About bloody time. Tell you the truth, all this sitting around watching was getting a bit dull.'

25 Thursday: Coffee and Heroin

The downside to our new camp was that it took half an hour to walk to Center Camp for coffee. Steve and Saskia and Lawrence remained behind; Saskia had won almost a hundred dollars at cards and was eager to continue her streak, while Steve and Lawrence wanted to win it back, and, besides, both of them claimed, a quick bottle of beer was all the morning pick-me-up they needed.

The café was buzzing with activity and we had to stand in line for fifteen minutes before a gorgeous redhead wearing stripey orange and black tights and a cowboy hat covered with plastic cockroaches sold us our morning mochas. We turned, headed across the café to find a place to sit, walked maybe twenty steps, and very nearly collided with Zoltan and Zorana as they cut across one of the coffee line-ups.

I went cold before I even consciously recognized them. My stomach tightened painfully and my hands started to shake, spilling hot mocha on my fingers. Pavlovian fight-or-flight response. Talena gasped. They were no less surprised to see us. All four of us froze dead still for several seconds, staring at one another in shock. The burners in the nearby coffee line-up turned and curiously observed our tableau.

I told myself that we weren't in immediate danger. They wouldn't dare try anything here in the café. The important thing was to ensure that they didn't find out where we were camped, and to stay cool. I tried to tell my nervous system that neither fight nor flight was the right response. It didn't seem at all convinced.

Zorana recovered first. 'Balthazar,' she said, smiling as if with delight, her voice so smooth she was practically purring. 'Talena. What a pleasure it is to see you.'

Talena smiled thinly back. 'The pleasure is all yours.'

'You know what I see?' Zoltan growled. 'I see two dead people.'

'Wow, just like *The Sixth Sense*,' I said, managing to keep my voice amused and dismissive. As I expected he didn't get the reference and for a second his menace turned to bewilderment. Fine by me. If you can't beat 'em, out-weird 'em.

'We gave you a chance,' Zorana said to me. 'We should have known you would spurn it. You stupid, stupid man.'

'I will finish with you,' Zoltan said to Talena. 'I will finish you. I will make you—'

I said, 'Shut the fuck up, you bloated sack of shit.'

They were so surprised at being addressed in that way— I was probably the first person to do so in a long, long time—that they actually did shut up. Zoltan and Zorana, very accustomed to fear, were much less familiar with anger. And when Zoltan had threatened Talena it was like he had flicked a switch in my mind from fear to rage. I wanted to gouge his eyes out, tear his head off, plunge my fist into his chest and pull out his still-beating heart.

'I was going to give you a chance,' I said. 'I was going to say, go out and give yourself up to the FBI and we'll all call it a day. But fuck that. Fuck prison. Prison's too good for you.'

'Your mouth,' Zoltan said contemptuously. 'It flaps like the wings of a bird.'

Now he had weirded me out. I had never heard Zoltan wax poetic before.

'One day soon,' he continued, 'I will make it stop flapping and start to scream. Your mouth, Paul Wood, it will scream for very long. Your mouth, but first, hers. She will scream for very long, and I will make you watch.'

'Promises, promises,' Talena said airily.

I forced a casual smile and inwardly raged at the Brady Bill. If I had had a gun I would have shot him right then and there, in the middle of Center Camp Café, to hell with the spectators. I was tempted to fling my hot mocha in his eyes. But with his boxer's reflexes he might well dodge, and even if I succeeded there were surely Black Rock Rangers present, Burning Man's unofficial and unarmed law enforcement, who would expel me from Black Rock City. It wasn't quite worth it.

'Not promises,' Zorana said. 'Prophecy.'

'Are you about finished,' I asked, 'or would you like to vomit out more horseshit and call it conversation?'

'So proud,' Zoltan said. 'Such a man. Such a big man. Do you know, Paul Wood, do you know how many big men like you I have watched die?'

I wanted to say something to rattle him. Something like 'So how's tonight's drug deal going?' or 'Booked your flight to Tijuana yet?' I nearly did. It would have almost been worth it to reveal that we knew exactly why he was here, just to shake his implacably menacing composure for a moment.

'What did you do, bore them to death?' I asked instead. Not much of a comeback.

Zorana said something to Zoltan in a low voice, in Serbian. Later Talena told me it was 'We should go.'

'Goodbye, Paul,' Zoltan said, staring straight into my eyes. 'You should pray to every God, every night, that I never again see you.'

'Oh, no no no. We will meet again,' I said. 'Once. Very, very briefly.'

'On the contrary,' Zorana said to us both, 'when we meet again, it will feel like a long time. A terribly long time. For you it will feel like forever. And when it is over, I will know both of you so well. Better than you know each other. You can learn so much about a person. You have no idea how much.'

I began to wonder if Zorana was the really crazy one.

'Until we meet again,' she said.

They turned and walked away, inwards, towards the Man. We watched them until they were well past the Esplanade, into the playa. I was pleased to see them furtively glance over their shoulders several times. For all their threats and intimidation they were at least a little worried about us following them.

'Are you frightened?' Talena asked me quietly, as we walked back towards our camp.

'Yes. Are you?'

'Yes.'

We walked a little further.

'But I'm angry too,' I said. 'I'm more angry than scared. I'm furious.'

'Good,' Talena said. 'Me too. Me too very fucking much.'

The Temple of Gravity was in the empty playa beyond Black Rock City and the Man, a good twenty-minute walk from the nearest camps. This temple was half art, half dance club. Four enormous slabs of concrete hung on chains at a sixty-degree angle from two high intersecting arches of solid steel. A huge brass brazier in the middle still burned when we arrived at 4.15 in the morning, and more than a hundred people remained perched on the concrete slabs or swayed to the throbbing music. I assumed most of them were on drugs, coming down from E or acid or something else that gives you unnatural stamina.

At this hour the desert was very cold, the day's blistering heat a distant memory. We all wore jackets or sweaters, but I don't think we really needed them. The adrenaline alone would have kept us warm.

Despite Steve's desire for action our plan featured yet more waiting and watching. Watch the deal take place, and then follow Zoltan and Zorana back to their camp. When we found out where they lived, we would be able to make some informed decisions about what to do next. I wasn't looking forward to that part. I knew that the road we had begun to walk had only one logical conclusion. Sneak into their camp at night and murder them as they slept. I could barely even think of it. I didn't know if I could do that. Not for practical reasons, not because they might ambush us, or because the authorities might catch us and jail us forever. I just didn't think I could bring myself to kill someone like that, cold-blooded, premeditated, not even a monster like Zoltan, not even after what he had done to us. In hot blood, if he threatened Talena in front of me, sure. But crouched over his sleeping form? I didn't know if I would be able to do that. I didn't know if I wanted to be able to do that.

'They're on the move,' Lawrence said, his voice low.

The tricycle and spider-car moved slowly enough that we were easily able to follow at walking speed, probably because they didn't want to attract any adverse attention. We knew there were two people riding in the tricycle's cab and three more in the spider-car, a Volkswagen Beetle tricked out with eight welded steel limbs, a spider's head and mandibles, all made of gleaming albeit playa-dusted chrome. There were guns aboard the tricycle. We had watched and listened as they had loaded it. And the spider-car contained a crate carrying thirteen million US dollars. Judging from their grunts as they had hoisted it into the trunk, that much money weighed a whole hell of a lot.

We stayed far enough away that we could only just see the headlight perched above the tricycle. We followed that light into utter darkness for several minutes. A light breeze blew. The moon was new, and above us the sky was full of so many stars there barely seemed to be room for them all. The pale band of the Milky Way was clearly visible. Talena held our shotgun mike, Lawrence the binoculars. Behind us, we could see the glow of the Temple of Gravity, the Man and the Esplanade, but before us the darkness was broken only by the tricycle's headlight and, far away, a faint dim red light moving slowly left to right. Hatter had told me about the perimeter scouts, Black Rock Coyotes, armed with heat and motion sensors, patrolling the fence lest people enter without paying. It was ironic that up here 'coyote' meant someone who prevented a border crossing.

Talena and I held hands tightly as we walked. We each wore one of the shotgun mike's two headphones, which were the kind that clipped individually on to one's ear. It was so dark that I only knew the others were still with me from the soft crunching sounds of their boots on the playa. The wind grew stronger, a blessing and a curse. It obscured the air with playa dust and drowned out small sounds, which made it easier for us to go undiscovered, but harder to see and hear with the binoculars and shotgun mike.

Now that something was finally happening I was alert, adrenalized, more excited than scared. The situation felt unreal and dreamlike. Every physical sense seemed to have been artificially heightened. I imagined I could feel individual motes of playa dust as they brushed against my skin, could pick out individual lines on Talena's palm.

We closed to maybe three hundred feet from the tricycle. It was hard to judge distance. The headlight went out. A moment later, two flashlights winked on next to it. I listened intently, but the shotgun mike amplified the whistling wind into the howl of an oncoming gale; I could hear that words were being spoken, but not what they were.

'We have to get closer,' Talena said.

'Won't you come a little closer, said the spider to the fly,' I murmured to myself.

We began to approach.

'No,' Saskia said. 'We should go to the left.'

I stopped, surprised to hear Saskia volunteer a suggestion. 'Why?'

'So the wind blows from them to us. We will hear them much better that way. If we go too much closer, and they have other people watching, they will see us.'

'What other people?' Talena asked, low-voiced.

'Snipers. Sometimes we had meetings like this to exchange prisoners, in the war. Always both sides had many snipers watching.'

I had forgotten that Saskia had actually fought on the front lines, in Sarajevo. 'All right,' I said. We circled to the left.

'We'll need to run some tests,' a nervous voice said over the wind noises in my right ear, and I twitched with surprise at the voice's unexpected volume and clarity, as if the speaker stood as close to me as Talena. Saskia had been right. We were no nearer, but standing downwind of them, the sound was much clearer.

'Tests, yes, okay,' a voice said. Zoltan's voice. He sounded bored.

Lawrence passed me the binoculars. Four figures I recognized from Smack Dealer Camp stood in the light of two flashlights, presumably held by Zoltan and Zorana. Between them, on the playa, lay an open duffel bag full of bags of white powder. Just like the movies. One of the Smack Dealer Camp boys knelt beside the backpack, opened a small briefcase next to it, and began to perform a set of delicate manoeuvres, presumably making sure that what they were buying was in fact reasonably pure heroin. I handed the binoculars to Saskia, wondering how it could be that we lived in a world where this single duffel bag, full of the slightly processed seed-pods of a flower so common it was practically a weed, was worth so much.

Zorana said something in Serbian. Talena stiffened next to me.

'What?' I whispered.

'She said, "They have a clear view,"' Talena whispered back.

I didn't like the sound of that at all. It had to mean that Saskia was right, there were other people out here, allies of Zoltan and Zorana, watching the deal as it happened. Their insurance. Which was very bad news. First of all it meant that we had more than just Zoltan and Zorana to deal with. Second it meant that their friends, presumably armed, could be anywhere around us, and could spot us at any minute.

'It's good,' the crouching man reported.

'The money?' Zorana asked.

'It's in there,' one of the Smack Dealer Camp representatives, a woman, said. 'We can stay while you count it.'

'No need,' Zorana said.

'That's very trusting of you,' the other woman said, surprised.

'It is not you we trust,' Zoltan said. 'It is your fear.'

A brief silence followed.

'Well. Pleasure doing business with you,' the Smack Dealer Camp man lied. 'We look forward to a long and mutually prosperous relationship. The key's in the ignition. Enjoy.'

The crouching man zipped up and picked up the duffel

bag. It was obviously heavy. The four from Smack Dealer Camp made their way back to the tricycle, leaving the spider-car unoccupied. I nodded slowly, understanding. There was so much money, it was so heavy, that the deal had to include a transport vehicle.

Zoltan and Zorana approached the spider-car and were about to enter its open doors. Then Zorana stopped, abruptly, in mid-motion, and said something in harsh urgent Serbian.

'Shit,' Talena said. 'They've seen us.'

We all took a quick moment to absorb that.

'We better go,' Lawrence said.

I shook my head. 'We have to find out where their camp is.'

'All we have to do is find that spider car tomorrow. Come on.'

'No,' I said. 'They'll think of that. They'll hide it somehow. We have to find—'

I saw something flicker below my field of vision. I looked down to my chest and the dim red dot that had materialized there. I still hadn't quite worked out its implications when Saskia tackled me. Despite her size she hit me hard enough that I let go of Talena's hand and fell to the ground. The headphone tore free of my ear.

I stumbled to my feet. 'What was that?'

'Laser sight,' Saskia said.

Lawrence said, 'It is definitely time for us to go.'

The headlights of the spider-car lit up and it began to move in our general direction. In its windows, two flashlights winked on and began to scan back and forth across the playa.

The situation was bad and could quickly become disastrous. Zoltan and Zorana had completed their transaction and had the money and a vehicle. They were certainly armed, and they had allies somewhere out here in the darkness who had guns with laser sights. Once they knew it was us, they wouldn't hesitate to shoot. And they had inadvertently lured us out into an ideal kill site; late at night, an unoccupied patch of playa, nobody around. Lawrence was right, we had to run, now, and there was no way to follow them back to their camp. Even if we could circle around somehow, they were in a car, they moved too fast. We would lose them.

Unless. 'We split up,' I said. I grabbed the binoculars from Lawrence and took Talena's hand. 'Talena and Saskia come with me. Steve, Lawrence, run back to the Temple of Gravity. Make noise, draw them after you. Go. Now.'

Without even pausing for a beat they turned and ran.

'I have a plan,' I whispered to Talena and Saskia, as I led them perpendicular to Steve and Lawrence's direction, further into the darkness, walking instead of running.

Steve bellowed convincingly with pain, as if he had stubbed a toe. The spider-car swerved to pursue his voice. I smiled with relief. Zoltan and Zorana wouldn't recognize Steve and Lawrence, and I knew that both of them could do very convincing versions of Stupid Inebriated Tourist. They would be fine.

Talena and Saskia and I walked for another few seconds, then I stopped.

'Lie down,' I whispered, and lay down next to them. 'Use the mike. Find them.'

'Oh,' Talena whispered. 'I understand.'

We lay so close I could see her outline against the pale playa by starlight. She aimed the shotgun mike in the general direction where the laser sight must have been in order to draw a bead on my chest, then panned it back and forth. With her free hand she offered me one of the headphones but I declined. She might need both to make out any telltale noises. Thankfully the wind had died down a little. The spider-car rattled past, within a hundred feet, but Zoltan and Zorana were too intent on pursuing Steve and Lawrence to notice us.

'I hear something,' Talena whispered. 'They're talking. Must have radios or walkie-talkies. Two men, with different accents. They say they can't see anything out here. They just agreed to something.' Then, 'I can hear their footsteps.'

She slowly rotated the shotgun mike towards the Man, listening. I looked over to the spider-car and saw it moving fast, past the Temple of Gravity, towards Black Rock City. Steve and Lawrence had either eluded the Couple From Hell or convinced them of their harmlessness.

'Perfect,' I whispered. 'Now we follow them.'

It wasn't difficult. We were far out of their earshot, but thanks to the mike, they were well within ours. When they reached 2:30 and the Esplanade, we saw them by the light of the huge rave camps there. Both of them carried poster tubes slung over their shoulders, tubes which I supposed contained their guns. One of them was a skinny Latino man, presumably the pilot who would fly them to Mexico, wearing a long white fake-fur coat open over a thong swimsuit. The other was a tall, wiry blond man with a ponytail, shirtless, in track pants and sandals. Saskia and I recognized him immediately. Sinisa Obradovic. Both of us gasped.

425

'That's him,' I murmured to Talena. 'Sinisa. You remember?'

'I remember,' she said.

'Why is he here?' Saskia asked. She sounded frightened.

I shook my head. I wasn't happy to see him either. Dealing with Zoltan and Zorana was bad enough. Sinisa's presence was an unexpected blow. Our enemies were more numerous and more dangerous than anticipated.

We followed them to a big rented Winnebago at 2:30 and Faith. They entered the Winnebago and didn't come out again. We sat beneath somebody's shade structure fifty feet away and watched. I wondered why the king of the criminals himself had blessed Burning Man with his presence. I guessed this drug deal was so important to his organization that he didn't want to delegate.

We were exhausted, but fortunately it was too cold to fall asleep. A thin streak of dawn began to stain the eastern sky. I had started to wonder if Zoltan and Zorana were camping separately when the spider-car finally rolled up.

We watched Zoltan and Zorana roust Sinisa and the Mexican from bed, open the spider-car's trunk, and transfer a wooden crate into the Winnebago. It was so heavy it took all four of them to lift it. Sinisa drove the spider-car away, and the other three retreated into the Winnebago. The sun had begun to warm the desert air by the time Sinisa returned and, yawning, climbed into the Winnebago and shut the door. We waited another twenty minutes just to be sure, but there was no more movement, no more noise.

We knew where they lived.

26 Friday: Best Laid Plans

'It is still not easy,' Saskia said, at breakfast the next morning. 'We have surprise, but they have weapons. They are very dangerous. I was thinking, perhaps we could use your tear gas to drive them from their vehicle, then take them as they exit, but now I think they are too dangerous. I think we must attack their vehicle as they sleep. I think we must burn it.'

She sounded intent but calm, as if arguing some interesting philosophical point, rather than planning the deaths of four people. I stared bemusedly at her. The meek and terrified woman I had first met had transformed into a decisive general. I supposed Saskia had been like this in the years when she fought for Sarajevo and protected Talena, before seven years of Dragan's inescapable abuse reduced her to cringing timidity.

'So you're planning to murder them in their sleep,' Lawrence said.

Talena and I looked at each other uncomfortably and didn't say anything.

Steve shook his head. 'Whatever you figure on doing, mate, we're in your corner, you know that. But walking up to their camp tonight and setting up a propane bomb or something like . . . I'll put one together if you ask, and I'm sure they deserve it, but I don't mind saying it'll leave a bad taste.'

'Likewise,' Lawrence said. 'Maybe I've seen too many Westerns, but that just feels wrong.'

'Yeah,' I said. 'It's wrong. I know that. We know that. But what the fuck else do we do? You'd rather we woke them up and challenged them to a duel?'

'No, wait, let me guess,' Talena said. 'You'd rather we just let them go. Let them fly back to Mexico with thirteen million dollars for war criminals. After what they did to us, after what they did to my home, we just let them go.'

'Not exactly,' Lawrence said.

'Then what?'

'Let them live. Wait for the FBI to catch the mouse in their house. Come visit London for a few months while they clean up. You've still got that crystal ball that lets you read their secret messages. When they come back, you have a whole FBI welcoming committee waiting for them.'

'Let them go and catch them when they come back.' I shook my head. 'Sorry. No. If they get to Mexico I don't think they'll come back at all. Especially if their friend in the FBI gets busted. They'll stay out of the country for good. Besides, we can't come to London. We've got Saskia to worry about. She can't leave the country. And we can't afford to go on the run while the FBI cleans house.'

A gloomy silence followed. But it was brief. Steve and Lawrence looked at one another, and diabolical smiles began to spread across their faces.

'Well now,' Steve said. 'Lawrence and me had a little talk last night, hypothetical like, figured this might be where things were going. We came up with a bit of a plan. We reckon maybe there's one little thing we can do to get them a bit shirty at us, make sure they come back in a hurry, maybe not leave at all.'

'One little thing,' Lawrence agreed.

Talena looked wary. 'What one little thing?'

Steve and Lawrence grinned at one another, obviously savouring the moment, and then Steve said, 'We nick the money.'

My mouth fell open.

'Steal the money?' Saskia asked. 'Yes, but how?'

'It's funny you should ask,' Lawrence said. 'I happen to have a cunning plan.'

The money we intended to steal was very heavy, locked inside a Winnebago, and guarded by four criminals, all of them presumably paranoid, trigger-happy and heavily armed. The casual observer might think that we had first to gain access to the Winnebago, then somehow separate the money from its guardians, and finally lug the money to our getaway vehicle. But the casual observer did not have Lawrence's evilly brilliant mind.

Sinisa had parked the spider-car some distance away from the Winnebago in order to avoid discovery. He was presumably worried that the denizens of Smack Dealer Camp might attempt to recover the money now that they had his heroin, and figured that his new vehicle was too easy to find, maybe bugged with a location transmitter, and wasn't needed now that the money was safely in the Winnebago that would carry it to his getaway plane. Fortunately, even at Burning Man, the spider-car's high production values stood out, and it didn't take us long to find it parked between two stoner camps near 4:30 and Faith. Their denizens took the late afternoon appearance of Steve, Talena and me, and our excuse that we had lost the keys, in stride. A few of them clustered around as Steve broke into the car and began working under the steering wheel.

'That's a totally amazing art car, dude,' a blond, bearded, bong-wielding man said. 'It's just, like, beautiful.' His friends and neighbours nodded and offered us bong hits. We politely declined.

When Steve's automotive refurbishment was finished, he covered the traces of his forced access as best he could, relocked the door, and went to relieve Lawrence at the Winnebago stakeout. Talena and I didn't dare go on lookout for fear of being spotted, but the Couple From Hell still didn't know that Steve and Lawrence were associated with us. Saskia made dinner for the rest of us, freeze-dried beef stroganoff with granola bars for dessert, and we went over the finer points of our plan.

We waited until an hour past sunset, when it was fully dark.

None of the subjects of our surveillance had left the Winnebago since we had begun watching at three in the afternoon. Apparently they had decided that their share of the thirteen million dollars was worth missing all of Burning Man's frenetic final weekend. As thirty thousand people danced, drank, whooped, hollered, ingested massive quantities of illegal drugs, had sex, and/or sampled the many delights of the Esplanade in this last night before the Man burned, Sinisa, Zoltan, Zorana and the Mexican, christened the 'Fearsome Foursome' by Lawrence, played cards and drank beer; and Lawrence, Saskia, Talena and I watched them. Watched them and watched Steve as he lay beneath the Winnebago for a good twenty minutes, working with his skilled hands and a sharp knife.

'That was a good little engine under there,' he said sadly when he returned to our discreet shelter between two tents of a nearby camp abandoned for the evening. 'And that chemical loo was a tidy little piece of work. Ripping it all up, that wasn't right.' He seemed genuinely repentant, as if he had committed some sort of mechanical sin and was now doomed to engineering hell.

'Here we go,' Talena said sharply, watching through the binoculars. 'Zoltan's going for the toilet.'

'That didn't take long,' Lawrence said. 'Hope they're drinking a lot of beer in there. And they all ate some bad enchiladas last night.'

The cry of dismay was easily audible without the shotgun mike.

'Beautiful,' Lawrence said. 'Backed up like a charm. Well done, mate.'

He clapped Steve on the shoulder. Steve grunted sourly, unhappy at being praised for fouling up perfectly good machinery.

There was a brief and high-volume discussion inside the Winnebago, and then the door banged open and Zoltan and Sinisa went outside to inspect the chemical toilet. After they left the well-lit doorway all we could see was two flashlights disappear around the back of the Winnebago, then drop down to near playa level, aimed up at the newly wrecked Winnebago.

The lights hung utterly still for a moment. Then both flashlights flickered off. Sinisa shouted something in Serbian and a moment later Zorana turned off the Winnebago's interior lights. There was just enough ambient light, and we were just close enough, to see motion in front of the Winnebago as Zoltan and Sinisa returned to the front. There they stopped and Sinisa and Zorana had a brief and tense conversation in Serbian, which ended, according to Talena, with Sinisa ordering Zorana to be quiet and let him think.

After that there was a long silence.

I knew what Sinisa was thinking. Either this was random vandalism—not at all likely—or somebody was after them. Somebody who didn't act like the police. There would be two possibilities uppermost in his mind: either Smack Dealer Camp wanted to have their drugs and keep their money too; or Talena and I were here to wreak revenge.

I was sure what he wanted to do was venture out from the Winnebago and search the neighbourhood for his watchers. But he feared being lured away from the money. The treasure chest within the Winnebago was like an anchor, limiting him to only two choices; stay with the money, or carry the money away.

If it was Smack Dealer Camp, then the denizens of the Winnebago were outnumbered and outgunned and should try to get away while they could. If it was Talena and me, this was some kind of trick and they should stay where they were. Our plan relied on Sinisa not taking Talena and me seriously, and on him being a man of action who would rather do something active than passively wait. Especially if passively waiting meant spending the next twenty-four hours in a Winnebago that now reeked of shit.

'I will be back soon,' Sinisa said, in English, and broke into a run, heading towards 4:00 and Faith. Towards the spider-car. Perfect.

We waited. In the distance, huge columns of flame leaped up from the Esplanade, some new über-flame-thrower capable of launching curling gouts of fire some eighty feet into the sky, cueing roars of applause. The show had just ended when the spider-car appeared. We watched as Sinisa climbed out, barking orders in Serbian.

Soon Zoltan, Sinisa and the Mexican staggered beneath the burden of the crate full of money, grunting and groaning, while Zorana covered them from the doorway of the Winnebago with a rifle more than three feet long. I idly passed the time by trying to guess how much the money weighed. I knew a dollar bill weighed about one gram, so if it was all in hundreds, then that crate contained some three hundred pounds of money.

Finally, after twice dropping it, they got the money into the trunk. Zoltan and the Mexican got into the front of the spider-car, the Mexican in the driver's seat. Sinisa and Zorana got into the back, an awkward fit with their rifles slung over their shoulders.

'Perfect,' Lawrence said, with authorial pride. His plan had deceived our enemies to such an extent that they had actually carried the money out of the Winnebago and into our getaway vehicle for us, eliminating the weight-of-thirteen-million-dollars problem. Now all we had to do was take custody of the said vehicle.

A trivial problem. We waited until all four of them were in the car and the doors were shut. The engine roared to life, the headlights lit up, and Talena took one of the two walkie-talkies we had borrowed from the Hatter and pressed the red Push-to-Talk button.

The other borrowed walkie-talkie was duct-taped beneath the front seat of the spider-car, wired to a canister of the tear gas we had purchased at the International Spy Shop. Steve's work was as reliable as ever. Alarmed voices from inside the custom Beetle quickly morphed into a plaintive cacophony of hoarse, choking cries. A few seconds later, four figures climbed blindly and spastically out of the spider-car and staggered towards fresh air, clutching at their eyes as if they wanted to tear them out.

Lawrence had already strapped on the gas mask, purchased with the tear gas as part of a set, and he sprinted towards the Beetle like he was going for Olympic gold. In fact there was no need for speed. All four of the tear-gas victims still moaned and thrashed with pain, hands over their burning eyes, completely unaware that Lawrence was commandeering the vehicle they had just vacated. The Mexican had had the presence of mind to remove the key, but Steve had rewired the spider-car's ignition so that once the engine started it could not be stopped so easily. Lawrence reversed the arachnidized Beetle away from the Winnebago and on to Faith Street, then accelerated away, violating Burning Man's speed limit and going up to maybe fifteen miles an hour. After five days in Black Rock City, that seemed terrifyingly fast. By the time its four previous inhabitants were on their feet, the spider-car and its cargo of thirteen million dollars had vanished in a cloud of playa dust.

Up to that point the plan had worked perfectly. Talena and Saskia and Steve and I were triumphant. We thought we had won. All we had to do now was sidle off to the Esplanade, disappear into the crowds, go back to our camp, rendezvous with Lawrence, transfer the money into our Chevy Malibu, and get the hell out of Dodge.

If only we had known that they could see in the dark.

We had watched the excitement from a camp about a hundred feet away from the Winnebago, in the middle of the block. We had a fairly clear view, but there were several camps between us and the distance between was partially interrupted by vehicles, tents, shade structures, rebar-anchored guy lines, solar showers, the usual detritus of the back streets of Black Rock City. Steve and Talena and Saskia and I stood and began slowly and quietly to walk away, confident that we were safe. We were wrapped in a blanket of darkness, surrounded on all sides by visual distractions, indistinguishable from innocent passers-by.

But there were no other passers-by. And when we stood from behind the tents that had sheltered us, Zorana, blinking her eyes clear of tear gas, looked through the scope on her grotesquely huge rifle, a scope that exemplified the finest in American military techno-fetishism, featuring both night vision and heat vision, and saw the three of us walking away.

We had been lucky when we had witnessed the drugs for money exchange in the playa last night, lucky that the wind and whirling dust had obscured both starlight and heat, that they had been distracted by the scrambling figures of Steve and Lawrence, lucky that Talena and Saskia and I had not been seen as we lay prone and tracked them with our shotgun mike. Our luck had run out.

We didn't know any of this at the time. All we knew was that four flashlights were trained on us, and then the lights were jostling up and down and growing brighter as all four of them, Zoltan and Zorana and Sinisa and the Mexican, sprinted towards us. We hesitated for what might have been a fatal second before turning and trying to flee.

We probably didn't have a chance in a foot race anyway. We were all in reasonably good condition, but none of us was a natural sprinter, and our pursuers were fit and fast and furious. Our only hope was to make it into a crowd of people before they caught us. And that hope died about three seconds into the chase when Talena, running next to me, tripped on a rebar tent pole and slammed face-first into the ground.

Time slowed to a glacial crawl. I felt like I was moving in slow motion, like the Six Million Dollar Man, as Steve and Saskia and I screeched to a halt and turned to help her. Talena tried to get up, but the fall had stunned her and she couldn't find her footing. Behind her, maybe forty feet away, four darting flashlights were closing and converging on us.

I realized with a sickening vertiginous sensation like falling off a cliff that the four of us no longer had any chance of getting away.

Only one thing to do.

'Get them out of here,' I ordered Steve. Then I ran straight at the flashlights.

They wavered and halted, confused that their prey was charging straight at them, and they were just close enough together, and I opened my arms wide and leaped off my feet at the last minute, kicking my legs out to make the path of my impact as wide as possible, and knocked all of them down like bowling pins.

'Paul!' I heard Talena shriek. I wanted to turn and give her one last look, but I was too occupied with trying to pull down all four of my opponents, ensuring that they could not break free of me to chase her. I scrambled and wrestled for what felt like a long time with a tangle of arms and legs and torsos.

The last thing I heard was Talena cry, 'Let me go!' her voice gratifyingly further away. I imagined Steve throwing her over his Herculean shoulder and running for the

Esplanade, Saskia in tow, and in the moment before Zoltan slammed my forehead into the ground with all the considerable force he could muster, I offered Steve a thousand mental thanks. Then the world went away.

27 Saturday: The Burn

'He's waking up,' a rough male voice reported.

It was very hot. I was nauseous. My head hurt like somebody had drilled a hole in my forehead and dumped half a litre of sulphuric acid into my skull. My shoulders ached, because my arms were drawn uncomfortably behind me, and my hands were half numb, half agony. I hurt almost everywhere, and I knew without trying that breathing deeply would be a very bad idea. My mouth was full of something cotton. I tried to spit whatever it was out, but it seemed to be stuck in place.

I tried to remember why I hurt so much. I must have been in a car accident. Yes, and suffered a concussion, that was why I couldn't remember anything. But what had the doctors done to my arms? Why was I sitting instead of lying down? And why did the furnace-hot hospital room smell so pungently of shit?

I made my left eye flutter open. For some reason my right eye wouldn't. I saw Zoltan, Zorana, Sinisa and the Mexican in front of me, the full Fearsome Foursome, all of them barely dressed thanks to the heat, the men shirtless, Zorana in a blue bikini. The gates of memory opened and I cringed with understanding. I had been captured. I was in the Winnebago, stripped naked, perched on a folding chair next to the sabotaged toilet, my arms bound behind me. The worst-case scenario.

No: second-worst. Talena had gotten away.

Zorana approached, holding a curved blade, smiling cheerfully.

'Do you know what kind of knife this is?' she asked, in the same tone of voice she might use if she wanted to know the time. 'It is a very sharp knife used to skin animals. My mother taught me how to use it, a long time ago, before the Ustasha killed her.'

I looked at her dully. I was already in too much pain, my mind too muddled and quicksand-thick, to have room to feel any more fear. All I felt was vague surprise that I was still alive and still at Burning Man. I had assumed, when I charged them, that after catching me they would take me out to some empty patch of playa, kill me, and leave. Keeping me alive was risky. By now Talena and Steve and Lawrence had surely gone to the police.

'He does not listen,' Zoltan said. 'I think we scrambled his head.'

'You would have killed him if I had not stopped you,' Sinisa scolded him.

Zoltan muttered something angry in Serbian. I struggled to open my right eye but nothing happened. For a moment I was afraid the eye was gone, but then I realized what had happened: the whole right side of my face was covered with dried blood, gluing my eye shut. I was surprised the heat hadn't made the blood melt again. It had to be well over forty degrees in the Winnebago.

'This is so messed up,' the Mexican said, his accent more

American than mine. 'I just came here to help fly you out of here. This is *kidnapping*. It was almost *murder*. I don't know—'

I never found out what he didn't know, because that was when I ceased to be able to hold back my nausea, and just as I had when Zoltan and Zorana had invaded our home and tied me up in this same manner, I started to throw up. But this time was infinitely worse. For one thing, the beating they had given me had cracked at least two ribs, and with every convulsion a white-hot bolt of pain lanced through my chest, as if somebody had made me swallow a huge fish-hook with a line still attached and then repeatedly yanked on the line as hard as they could. For another, they had gagged me, and I immediately started to choke.

My gut was still trying to expel its contents, my lungs were desperately trying to draw in air, my throat seemed to have been filled with concrete, and as I thrashed every twitch caused my cracked ribs to erupt with further agony. This seemed to go on for hours. I would have fallen over if the tattooed Mexican had not rushed over and righted the chair. My vision started to fade, like the colour draining from an old TV after the plug is pulled. I was distantly aware that I was on the verge of passing out, and maybe dying, when Zorana pushed the Mexican aside, ripped the gag from my mouth, and performed a Heimlich manoeuvre. I coughed a fountain of vomit all over myself and started to breathe again, in great whooping gasps.

I moaned incoherently as my vision returned. I almost wished I had been allowed to sink into unconsciousness. I felt newly alert, almost energetic, acutely aware of the myriad agonies throbbing throughout my body.

Zorana turned to the Mexican and said, 'Clean him up.'

'What? Fuck you! I'm not cleaning up puke!'

Zoltan took a step towards the Mexican before Sinisa intervened.

'Never mind,' he said. 'We will leave him like this.'

I thought he was talking about leaving my corpse. I closed my working eye and tried to steel myself for death. Not today, I supposed, not in the sun, but tonight, as the Man burned, they would kill me and leave me in the playa.

'You should pray,' Zorana said to me. 'Pray your friends did not lie to us. Pray they are not so stupid that they attempt to deceive us.'

My left eye snapped open and I stared at him with new understanding. Ransom. Of course. They were holding me for ransom. That was why I was still alive.

'Personally,' Sinisa said, 'I hope they are neither liars nor stupid. You have betrayed us, Paul, and gravely inconvenienced us, but I do admire your courage. You are not the little man I thought. You do not deserve to die. And I do not kill those who do not deserve it.'

I should have kept my mouth shut. I could only cause trouble for myself and the effort required to speak made my head spin, but his hypocrisy made me irrationally furious. 'Like all those bodies in the forest in Albania?' I asked, my voice a hoarse croak. 'Did they deserve it?'

He raised his eyebrows. 'Interesting. How interesting. I did not know you had discovered those. But the answer is yes. Except for one man whose death was an unavoidable necessity. As yours may yet become. But if your friends return my property, I promise, Paul, you will all be spared. I am a man of honour.'

'Who hires war criminals to do his dirty work.'

He sighed. 'You disappoint me. As I told you once before, Zoltan, Zorana, the rest of my associates, they were created by the war, not the other way around. Afterwards, of course, they were considered monsters, irredeemable, fit only for prison or death. The usual terrified simplistic morality of the weak. I had hoped for better from you. Think about it, Paul. Far better that they work for me, helping bring the victims of war to freedom and safety, than languish in prison at great public expense, no?'

I didn't answer.

'I suppose you are in no condition for a philosophical discussion,' he said. He actually sounded disappointed.

They left me alone after that, left me to sit in my own filth and agony for the rest of the day, drifting in and out of consciousness. That day seemed to move so glacially that I remember wondering if the earth's revolution had slowed, or halted, or even reversed. It was an endless shapeless miasma of pain, fear, hate, exhaustion, rage and powerlessness. But finally, like a kidney stone, it passed.

'Get up,' Sinisa said to me. 'It is time to go.'

I had somehow managed to doze off. I opened my left eye—the right was still, amazingly, glued shut by my own dried blood—and looked around. The Fearsome Foursome were all dressed in black. Sinisa and the Mexican carried poster tubes and the Couple From Hell wore zipped-up gun-concealing windbreakers.

I managed to stand. It wasn't easy; my legs felt weak, filled with mercury rather than muscle. Motion caused my head to start pounding once more, as if pain was a physical thing that had condensed into a large amorphous glob right behind my eyes. My shoulders were on fire, I could no longer feel my hands, most of my muscles were cramped or bruised or both, and every breath reminded me of my cracked ribs.

Zorana smiled, amused, as she tightened a yellow rope around my neck. 'My little pet,' she said fondly, and kissed me on the back of my neck. 'Walk. Be quiet. You know I can make you quiet very quickly if I want.'

Anywhere else it would have been an unthinkably bizarre and surreal sight: four people leading a man, naked and drenched in blood and sweat and vomit, on a leash. At Burning Man we could easily have been written off as some particularly weird fetish camp. A moot point; nobody was witnessing anything. This was the night of the Burn, the pyromaniacal bacchanal that was Burning Man's climax, and all thirty thousand burners in attendance were crammed into a thick riotous crowd surrounding the Man. Around that hundred-foot neon and wood statue, a mile behind us, hundreds of drums thumped and rattled in tribal blood-maddening rhythms. The hum of the crowd was savage, primal, electric.

I suppose there must have been a few other stragglers, substance abusers sleeping off an overdose, thieves prowling through the sea of empty camps looking for anything valuable, adulterous lovers slipping off to a pre-arranged tent, but we didn't see any. The back streets of Black Rock City were dark and post-apocalyptically quiet. We walked along 3:00 to Vision Street, the very edge of Black Rock City's horseshoe, and into the empty playa, towards the distant silhouette, barely visible, of the spider-car we had so recently stolen from Sinisa.

We paused so Sinisa and the Mexican could withdraw their sniper rifles from the poster tubes that concealed them. Zoltan and Zorana drew guns from beneath their windbreakers as we walked. The spider-car's lights were off, and we saw no movement, no one around.

When we were about two hundred feet away, Zorana froze and said something to Zoltan and Sinisa. I followed their gaze, dully, just wishing that it was all over. A little distance from the spider-car, parked behind it and to its left, separated by maybe fifty feet, there was another vehicle, a pick-up truck. And resting between the spider-car and the pick-up I saw the dark shape of a familiar crate against the pale desert. The money.

The pick-up's engine roared and its headlights came on, high-beam, all but blinding us. Zoltan and Sinisa and the Mexican dropped prone, aiming guns at it. Zorana pulled hard on the leash and dragged me in front of her.

'Paul!' Talena cried, her voice desperate. 'Paul! Are you okay? Are you *okay*?'

I didn't trust myself to speak loudly enough to be heard so far, so I just nodded.

'All right,' a voice called out, Lawrence's voice. 'Let him go. Let him walk over here.'

Zorana looked over at Sinisa. Sinisa nodded.

'Just one thing,' Lawrence said. 'If anything happens before we're all safe and sound . . . show them, Steve.'

A torrent of flame leaped out of the back of the pick-up truck and through the air, angled upwards, passing over the wooden crate and some distance beyond, very nearly reaching the spider-car. Sinisa grunted with disconcerted surprise. I smiled for the first time all day. Rogue. They were in Rogue, DeathGuild's art car, armed with souped-up-by-Steve flame-throwers, and they had the money hostage.

'I realize modern financial instruments have grown increasingly abstract,' Lawrence said, 'but you'll still find it difficult to spend that money if it all goes up in smoke.'

Sinisa and Zoltan and Zorana muttered to one another. Finally Sinisa called out, 'And how can I be assured that that is in fact my money in there?'

'Come on up and see for yourself,' Lawrence said.

After a brief discussion it was Zoltan who advanced towards the crate.

'In the interests of a peaceful exchange,' Lawrence said, 'please remember we can turn you into kebab meat with one squeeze of the trigger.'

Zoltan knelt over the crate, inspected it by flashlight, and walked back to us. He said something to Sinisa, which I guess meant that the money was real, because he said something to Zorana, and she let me go and gave me a little push.

'Goodbye, Paul,' she said. 'I do so hope we meet again some day.'

It was a long walk on weak legs, but it was a walk to freedom, and that gave me all the strength I needed. When I finally reached Rogue, Steve and Talena grabbed me and lifted me bodily up and into the bed of the pick-up. I didn't have to move a muscle.

Talena turned on her Maglite and played it over me.

'Oh, my God,' she said, horrified. 'Oh, God. Oh, God. What did they do to you?'

'Looks worse than it is,' I croaked. 'I'll be okay. Maybe . . . do you have a towel or something?'

'Not to worry, mate,' Steve said as he cut my hands free. 'We'll clean you up. But first I reckon we better bail out.'

He rapped twice on the cab, which contained Lawrence and Saskia. Lawrence switched off the headlights, shifted into reverse, and stamped on the accelerator. I would have fallen over if Talena hadn't held me. Rogue swung around and sped away, trailing a plume of playa dust. I struggled to keep my balance. Steve took off his T-shirt, wet it with some water from a four-litre container, and gave it to Talena, who began to wipe the blood off my head. I motioned for water and when Steve gave me his bottle I drank deeply.

'We should have burned the money,' I said. 'Fuck. We shouldn't have left it with them.'

'*Au contraire,* mate,' Steve said. 'We wanted to give them a reason to fly away home.'

'What do you mean?'

'He means this isn't over,' Talena said grimly. 'We're not letting them go.'

Lawrence drove Rogue most of the way to Black Rock City's outskirts, then swerved around in a quick circle and stopped dead, facing the distant spider-car. Steve peered through the binoculars.

'They're taking a look-see before they put the money in,' he reported. 'Let's move.'

'And let's hope they're heading for the airstrip,' Lawrence said from the cab. He kicked Rogue into gear and we leaped away, headed for Black Rock Airport.

'Why?' I asked.

Lawrence explained. 'Both of the planes big enough to reach Mexico now have propane tanks discreetly duct-taped on to them. The idea is we get there before they do, turn on the tanks, hurry them along so they don't notice what's going on, and just as they take off we drive along beside them and light them up with a blast from one of these flame-throwers. Steve rigged the tanks so if the propane catches it'll be like a fuse and the tank will blow a few minutes later.'

'Oh,' I said. It didn't sound like a very good plan to me, but it wasn't like I had a better one handy, and my mind and body were both badly shaken. Still, there was something about it that bothered me, and not just the fact it relied on Rube Goldberg propane bombs. I tried to work out what it was. I was distracted by sensation slowly returning to my hands. An intensely painful, pins-and-needles-on-fire sensation that brought tears to my eyes. But there was something wrong, something very wrong.

'Shit,' I said. 'They can see us.'

'What?'

'They've got two rifles with fuck-off night-vision scopes. That's how they caught me. They can see us fine right—'

There was a loud bang as something metallic slammed hard into Rogue's side. Steve, Talena and I fell to the bed. I howled as my cracked ribs collided with a propane tank.

'Fucking hell,' Steve said.

Another loud bang followed, and Rogue's engine developed a loud, unhealthy whop-whop-whop noise. Then a popping noise, which I guess was a shot that missed. It didn't matter. The previous shot had been sufficient. Rogue's engine faltered, sputtered, slowed and stopped.

I got to my knees and looked around. Ahead and to our right, about a mile away, two lines of lights indicated the location of Black Rock City's airstrip. Steve knelt up next to me and looked through the binoculars at the spider-car, maybe half a mile away ahead and to our left.

'The money's in the boot,' Steve reported. 'They're climbing in now.'

The spider-car's headlights winked on and began to move. Away from Black Rock City, away from us, towards the airstrip and plane that would take them to Mexico.

'It is not too late,' Saskia said fiercely.

Lawrence said, 'Steve. Can you fix her?'

Steve vaulted to the playa, popped open Rogue's bonnet, and illuminated the engine with his flashlight. 'Maybe,' he said doubtfully. 'She doesn't look good. Hard to say without giving it a go.'

Saskia jumped down too. 'Lawrence. Talena. Come. We must light the propane before they take off.'

'No,' I said weakly. 'No. They'll see you coming.'

'They won't be looking for us,' Talena said. 'They think they've won.'

'They have won. Accept it. We're alive. That's all we get.'

'No,' Saskia said. 'I will not allow it. I will stop them myself if I must.'

'Stop her,' I said. 'Don't let her go.'

Talena thought about it a moment as I climbed painfully down from Rogue.

'No,' she said. 'I'm not letting them go that easy. Lawrence, you coming?'

'Well,' Lawrence drawled, getting out of the cab, 'I suppose after all this driving, stretching my legs would do me good.'

'Don't,' I said to Talena. 'Stop it. Don't be an idiot.'

She kissed me on the cheek. 'See you in a bit,' she said. Her voice was cheerful, mischievous. 'I love you. See you in just a little while. Steve, keep an eye on him, don't let him go anywhere, he's too badly hurt.'

I reached out to grab her but she was gone.

I watched her and Lawrence and Saskia sprint across the desert towards the airstrip. I was coldly certain that they were being watched. I almost hoped they would be shot at. If that didn't happen, it probably meant they were being lured in so Zoltan and Zorana could be sure of killing them.

There had to be something I could do. 'Steve,' I said. 'I'm going for a walk.'

He emerged from Rogue's bonnet and looked at me. 'Paul mate. Don't know if that's such a grand idea.'

'You going to stop me?'

He thought about it for a second. 'I reckon not. Might come with you though.'

'Don't,' I said. 'If you can fix this beast, that's our best chance. Good luck.'

I didn't stay to hear his response.

My idea was so simple it barely qualified as a plan. Talena and Saskia and Lawrence were following the spider-car towards the airstrip from the Black Rock City side. I would simply cross the airstrip and approach from the other side. There was plenty of time. Zoltan and Zorana and company still had to transfer the money into the airplane, prepare it for flight, taxi out to the airstrip, and so forth. With any luck Talena and Saskia and Lawrence would find some way to harass them without getting shot. No one would expect me to show up from the other side. I might be able to do something useful.

Then again, one of the reasons no one expected me to show up was that no one thought I was capable of doing anything at all. I was battered, bruised and nauseous, with two cracked ribs and a concussion. I felt barely able to stand upright, much less fight bad guys. But the woman I loved was out there, with a woman I thought of as my little sister, and a man who was one of my closest friends, battling a woman and two men I hated.

I reached deep down and found a glowing coal of rage, somehow undimmed by pain and fear and nausea. I tried to fan the coal, to breathe on it, make it catch flame, make it burn. Fuck my throbbing dizzy head. Fuck my weak and wobbly muscles. Fuck the two knives that stabbed me every time I took a breath. Fuck pain. Pain is only a warning. Pain doesn't matter. The only things that matter are love and revenge.

I walked. Then I walked faster. I grunted under my breath, but it was as much with anger as with pain, and then the anger began to predominate, to burn, and then, somehow, somewhere, I found the strength to run.

I leaned against the cool metal of a tiny airplane and tried to catch my breath. I was covered in sweat. My forehead was bleeding again. I was torn between the need to breathe deeply to recover my strength, and the need to breathe shallowly to avoid the explosive agony of my cracked ribs. I was cold and naked and thirsty and dizzy. But I had made it to the airstrip and I hadn't yet heard any shots. That meant Lawrence and Talena and Saskia weren't far away, probably hiding on the other side of this airplane parking lot.

Two lines of little electric lights extended into the playa, outlining the Black Rock City airstrip. They provided the only illumination except for the flickering light of a single flashlight, its location also the source of the only sounds, the muffled grunts of Zoltan and Sinisa and the Mexican as they struggled to transfer the three-hundred-pound crate to their getaway plane. I could barely see Zorana's outline atop the spider-car, rifle to her shoulder, sighting towards the Man, away from me. They obviously knew they had been followed. The other airplanes, barely silhouetted against the night by the airstrip lights, looked like ghostly alien mausoleums, like this was some kind of surrealist cemetery.

I took stock of my surroundings. The thirty or so aircraft here were parked in a grid seven planes wide and four deep, facing along the airstrip, with about ten feet between wingtips and enough space between propellers and tail fins for planes to taxi in and out of the grid. Sinisa's airplane was the third airplane from the left, in the second row. The one I leaned against was on the far right of the front row.

I tried to think of something cunning I could do to cause a distraction. Blow up one of these other airplanes? Start one up and drive it into their getaway plane? Or at least find some kind of weapon? I reached for the door handle of the one I leaned against and gingerly tried it. It was locked. And even if it hadn't been, I knew nothing about airplanes and I doubted anyone had left a loaded .44 Magnum out for emergency use.

At least I had the element of surprise. I started moving towards the getaway plane. My bare feet were silent against the hard playa surface. I scuttled from plane to plane, staying underneath wings and behind cockpits, trying to stay unseen. Nobody shouted a warning, and soon I was lurking behind the getaway plane's neighbour, watching the situation. The spider-car was parked on the other side of the big Cessna 182. Zoltan and Sinisa and the Mexican were trying to wedge the money through the Cessna's cockpit door, but it was a poor fit, and very heavy, and they only had a single flashlight, resting somewhere in the cockpit, to guide them.

'Push,' Zoltan grated. 'Fucking push.'

'It won't fit. We have to turn it around,' the Mexican said.

'It will fit,' Sinisa said. 'Push. Harder. *Harder!*'

It occurred to me that if Zorana was looking the other way, I could walk right up to their airplane without being seen. The others were focused on the illuminated cockpit, not the dark exterior, too busy with the money to pay any attention to me. But Zorana might have seen me approach, might have the gun trained on me, waiting for me to step out into the open. I made myself take two quick steps towards the getaway plane before allowing myself to worry too much about that possibility, paused for a second, observed that I had not been shot, and walked up to the getaway plane, behind the wing where the fuselage tapered down to the tail. I was maybe fifteen feet away from the three men fighting with the crate full of money on the other side of the aircraft.

I squinted at the Cessna, trying to work out where the hell that propane tank had been affixed. At first I had thought that that was the weakest part of their plan: the tank was bound to be seen. But here I was actively looking and still unable to find it.

A shot blasted out and my whole body twanged and shuddered like a bowstring. I gasped and dropped to my knees. But it hadn't come anywhere near me.

'Get this fucking money in *now*,' Zoltan said.

From my new vantage point on my knees, I saw a stand-issue propane tank between the Cessna's rear wheels, attached to the fuselage by several miles of duct tape. The tank's nozzle faced towards the nose of the airplane and I had to crouch and reach as far as I could to turn it open. There was a loud *thunk* as the crate full of money finally got through the door and fell into the airplane. My fingers found the little wheel. I twisted it and was rewarded by a gaseous hiss. Now all I had to do was light it. Trying to clear my dizzy head and work out how I could acquire fire, I sat back on my haunches, cracked the back of my head against the Cessna's fuselage, and yowled.

Zoltan, Sinisa and the Mexican froze with surprise. I leaped to my feet and started to run. Two shots boomed through the night as I ducked behind the neighbouring airplane, and in the dim light I saw a jagged hole the size of my hand materalize in its fuselage. I didn't know what kind of ammunition Zorana had in that rifle but I guessed it would kill Kevlar-vested elephants with a single shot. Something, gasoline from the smell, began to leak out of the airplane. I decided this was not a safe place and kept running. Then I heard footsteps behind me. I glanced back. One of them was pursuing me. The Mexican, carrying one of the rifles.

I sprinted to the next airplane over and hid. He followed, walking leisurely. I could just barely make out the outline of his body. He walked with his rifle up against his shoulder so he could see through its night-vision scope. He knew which airplane I had hidden behind. He was coming straight for me.

I took two quick steps to my left, then abruptly reversed direction and sprinted to my right. The feint worked, he fired but missed, and I took cover behind the next plane. He kept walking, unhurried, unconcerned. It didn't matter how many times I could pull a trick like that. This game of cat-and-mouse would inevitably fall out in his favour. I was naked and unarmed and there was only one more airplane between me and the open playa. Desperate, I decided to wait beneath the wing strut of this airplane, make him come so close I might possibly be able to leap out and wrestle with him. He would probably get a shot before I reached him. Even if I didn't, he was stronger than me; in my current condition I would lose a wrestling match with Tori Amos, never mind a Mexican gangbanger with a gun. But I had no other chance at all.

The Mexican approached. I crouched and tensed and told myself to be ready for one final, desperate burst of strength. I wasn't sure I would even be able to stand up, much less launch myself at him like a tiger. He came closer still. I saw him silhouetted against the airstrip lights, right at the nose of the airplane I hid behind. I saw him turning to face me. He was still a good ten feet away.

'G'day mate,' a loud Australian voice said. 'Need a light?'

The Mexican jerked with surprise and spun around. Too late. The jet of flame hit him dead centre and he screamed. Steve kept the flame-thrower trained on the Mexican as he dropped his gun and flailed around madly, his clothes and hair on fire, and finally fell writhing and screaming to the ground. I smelled roast meat and for an instant I flashed back to the pig that Dragan and the Mostar Tigers had barbecued on a spit, centuries ago and parsecs away. I saw Steve by the firelight. He had not repaired Rogue; instead he had strapped a flame-thrower on to his back and come here on foot, just in time.

Another shot echoed through the night, and I heard the ear-splitting *krang!* of metal on metal. For a moment Steve looked like he had grown a halo of flame. Then he was shrugging off the flame-thrower and running. His back was on fire. He had gotten about ten steps away when the propane tank burst into a cloud of flame and Steve tumbled heavily to the ground. Shrapnel rattled loudly off airplanes. I rushed to help Steve, who had managed to roll on to his back and extinguish the fire, hoping that all this sudden heat had clouded Zorana's night-vision scope.

'You okay?' I asked, stupidly.

'Tell you the truth, mate,' he croaked, 'I've had better days.'

He managed to say it with a smile. I figured even Steve would stop smiling if something vital had been hit, and I sighed with relief. Behind me, an engine started, and a propeller began to rotate.

'I'll be right as rain,' Steve said. 'Go get the bastards.'

A fine idea. If only I knew how. The gun, the gun the Mexican had dropped. I turned to recover it, but somehow, amazingly, the Mexican was not only still alive, he had grabbed the gun and managed to stagger back towards the airplane noises. Patches of his clothing were still on fire, and he moved like a badly wounded animal, navigating as if he were blind, guiding himself only by sound. I tried to chase him but I had no strength with which to sprint and by the time he got to the getaway plane I had made it only as far as its neighbour, the airplane that had leaked a large puddle of gasoline from the gunshot hole the size of my hand.

There had been no gunfire since the shot that destroyed Steve's flame-thrower because Zorana had been busy climbing down from the spider-car and coming around to this side of the airplane. It was still dark but I could see her long hair blowing in the propeller wash. I half expected her to shoot the burned Mexican rather than burden themselves with him, but she stood still, holding the rifle to her shoulder, as Zoltan half guided, half pulled the burned man into the Cessna. Sinisa had donned a headset and was flicking switches and pulling levers, obviously making ready to depart. I remembered he had told me, long ago, that he was a licensed pilot.

I saw a light on the other side of the airplane. Fire. Saskia, standing alone, holding something aflame. She held some kind of torch in her hand, a stick soaked with oil by the way it had erupted in bright flame. I could see she was about to run for the airplane, try to turn on the propane tank—they didn't know I had already done that—and light the fuse that could destroy the getaway Cessna.

Zorana saw or heard something, and she turned around and knelt. She was going to shoot Saskia from underneath the fuselage, and Saskia couldn't see her.

'*No!*' I howled, ignoring the pain from my cracked ribs, bellowing as loudly as I could to be heard over the propeller. '*Don't!*'

My shout might have distracted Zorana. The strong propeller wash might have had something to do with it. But it helped, too, that in the distance, in the heart of Black Rock City, a blinding fusillade of fireworks, the overture to the

Burn, rocketed into the air and momentarily painted the night sky white. Zorana fired and missed. Lawrence leaped out of the darkness, grabbed Saskia, and pulled her behind the neighbouring airplane on the other side. She still held the lit torch in her hand.

'Throw it!' I bellowed. 'The tank is on!'

Zoltan shouted something Serbian at Zorana. She shouted back and started firing almost at random towards Lawrence and Saskia. Then she turned and fired four shots in my general direction. I dropped and huddled behind the airplane, my eyes tightly shut, as bullets tore past me and plunged into the playa. One of them struck some kind of spark and the pool of gasoline not ten feet away from me caught fire and began to burn.

The shooting stopped. The burning gasoline was so hot I felt my skin beginning to scald. I rolled away from it, half certain that Zorana would get a clear view and shoot me, and forced my eyes to open. Zorana was not looming over me with the gun. She was inside the cockpit and the door was closing. The Cessna taxied forward, turned to the right, and began to advance down the lane between the first two rows of airplanes.

Saskia rushed forward out of nowhere, the burning torch in her hand, and threw it at the Cessna. I held my breath, hoping—but it was just a stick of plywood half soaked with oil; the propeller wash caught it and flung it back before it could reach the propane tank duct-taped between the plane's rear wheels. We needed to throw something dense—like a flaming baseball, my mind gibbered—and we needed to throw it with impossible accuracy, into the propeller's gale-force artificial wind, to have any chance of igniting the propane. Even if I had a flaming baseball, it would be an impossible throw. They were going to get away. My whole body sagged with defeat for a moment.

Then inspiration struck. I knelt, newly adrenalized, and looked at the ground. The bullets that had missed me had plunged into the hard-baked playa surface, cracking it like a broken windshield. I reached for the nearest bullet hole and pried up a chunk of playa, a rough jagged diamond shape maybe four inches across and two inches thick. I steeled myself, told my hand not to let go, no matter what happened, until I said otherwise. I raced to the edge of the burning pool of gasoline, dipped my hand and the playa chunk in, and kept running, keeping pace with the Cessna.

Getting that close to the burning pool of gasoline had scorched the outside of my leg, but although my right hand was now on fire, amazingly it hadn't started to hurt yet, or I was in too much shock to feel it. I stopped, called twelve years of youthful baseball practice to mind, stepped into the throw, and hurled the gasoline-soaked, flaming chunk of playa at the Cessna as it turned towards the airstrip.

I immediately fell full-length on my hand to extinguish the flames. The impact on my cracked ribs made me howl with agony. But I kept my eyes open. I kept watching that jagged diamond of burning hard-baked desert soil as it whirled and cartwheeled through the air. I had aimed for the back of the propeller, but it didn't quite get that far, the propeller wash was too strong; it broke the burning chunk of earth into a hundred tiny clods and sent them spinning backwards. It looked like it disintegrated into a hundred fireflies, or a hundred matches, blown straight back from the propeller, straight towards the hissing tank of propane between the Cessna's wheels.

As the airplane climbed into the air, I saw a tiny blue tongue of flame beneath it.

In the distance, the Burn began. Flames crawled up the Man's bright blue skeleton, up the arms that today had been raised above his head, and in less than thirty seconds the Man was transformed into a gargantuan pillar of flame, amazingly bright, a second sun that cast shadows across the desert. Long shadows fell from Talena and Lawrence and Saskia and I as we stood together, from Steve as he shambled clumsily towards us, from the field of airplanes all around us. The Cessna gleamed in the Man's firelight as it gained altitude and banked south.

The Man burned. Whirling pillars of flame spun away from him and careened into the desert for a little way before dissipating into smoke. Steve joined us, breathing heavily, and all five of us stood in a row, watching their airplane dwindle into the distance. It had left the playa behind, it flew above the jagged crags and promontories of the desert hills to the south. We stood and watched, squinting, and as the burning Man fell backwards on to the desert, as a gigantic bloodthirsty howl of approval rose from thirty thousand throats and echoed across the playa, the Cessna suddenly, silently, gracefully, as if it were some kind of delicate flower, unfolded into vanishing, plummeting petals of flame. Blink and you would have missed it.

In unison, we gasped.

It was Lawrence who broke the silence, a full minute later, when the Man had dwindled to a bonfire, gigantic but only barely visible from where we stood.

'Christ,' he said. 'I don't know about you lot, but I could use a beer.'

Talena and Lawrence pushed Rogue across the playa. Saskia steered. Once they got some momentum going, we coasted across the playa with surprising speed. Steve and I were in the back. Steve lay on his stomach; his back was burned, and a large shard of the propane tank had bounced off his ribcage and carried a chunk of flesh away. I sat with my head slumped on my knees. I had added total exhaustion and a hand covered with burns—the pain had dwindled from 'unbelievable' to 'awful,' but I still breathed through gritted teeth—to my day's catalogue of misery.

We had left the spider-car at the airport, a kind of exchange payment for the airplane Zorana had shot to pieces. We wanted to get away from the scene so nobody could connect us to what had happened. It didn't take long—less than twenty minutes passed between leaving the airport and arriving at Camp Crackhaus—but in that time I felt like we passed through some kind of border, out of a mad world of gunshots and depravity and hate, back into the equally mad but much more civilized world of Burning Man. It was a transition I was very glad to make.

There was nobody at Crackhaus. We staggered in, found the cooler in the back corner of their shade structure, and opened it up, unconcerned by social niceties or the thought of being discovered stealing someone else's beer.

'Pabst Blue Ribbon,' Lawrence said, wrinkling his nose. 'In a can. Ah well, any port in a storm. At least it's cold.'

He distributed four cans, popping mine open for me so I didn't have to use my burned hand, and we sat and clicked them together. I was trying to think of an appropriate toast when Hatter walked in, dressed in a robe and a pointed wizard's hat covered with multicoloured glow-stick stars.

'What the—Paul? What are you doing here? What happened to Rogue?' he asked. He looked at me closer. 'My God. What the hell happened to you?'

'I fell off an art car,' I lied.

He looked entirely unconvinced.

'Hatter,' I said, 'you're my friend, right?'

'Yes,' he said warily.

'Then, as my friend, I need you to do me a very big favour.'

'All right. Sure. What?'

'Don't ask what happened to us tonight.'

He peered at me like he was trying to see right through my skull. Then, slowly, he nodded. 'Fair enough.'

'Also,' Lawrence added, 'while you're at it, you should probably pretend you didn't find us drinking your beer.'

Hatter laughed. 'You're welcome to the PBR. But Death-Guild is going to want to know what happened to Rogue.'

'I'll set the poor girl straight,' Steve assured him. 'No worries.'

'One day I want to hear the story,' Hatter said.

'One day I'll tell you,' I promised.

'Something smells like a burn,' he said. He examined me with a professional eye—like all smokejumpers, he was a trained paramedic—and winced. 'Jesus Christ. Your hand. Christ. Paul, you should get your ass to the medical centre right away.'

'We're taking him right there,' Lawrence said defensively. 'I mean, as soon as his beer is empty.'

'As soon as his beer is empty,' Hatter said sceptically. Then he shrugged and sat on a spare chair. 'Well. As long as you're dead set on drinking. There any more in there?'

We made it to Burning Man's impressively clean, professional and orderly medical centre, staffed by doctors and paramedics who also happened to be burners, about half an hour later. The medical staff listened to our outrageous lies about a home-made flame-thrower that had exploded in our hands, then cleaned and patched and bandaged my many wounds, and Steve's burned and shrapnelled back. He too had cracked ribs, but nothing more serious. When we were finally released, my head and hand and chest still hurt like a sonofabitch, but I hardly felt the pain through my brain-dimming exhaustion. I have only vague memories of collapsing into our tent and passing out.

28 Sunday: The Temple of Honor

On Sunday morning, Black Rock City began its long, slow process of disintegration. Tents were struck, domes deconstructed, cars and trucks loaded full of cargo, burnables dumped into the Community Burn Pits that raged all day. Exodus began, cars and trucks converging on the Gate from all points of the city, leaving blank patches of desert behind where their camp had once stood, forming a long snakelike line that trickled from the Gate to paved Nevada highway that led towards Reno and the real world.

Hatter had advised us to stay over Sunday night, so we could watch the Temple burn and avoid the worst of the exodus traffic. We would have stayed even without his advice. None of us was in the mood to pack and travel. I had a headache, countless cuts and bruises, cracked ribs, muscles so stiff they felt brittle, and a hand wrapped in gauze that hurt like it was still on fire. Steve's back was burned and cut in several places where shrapnel had bounced off his ribcage, but he turned down Hatter's offer of medication. I did not, and the pills from his medicine chest took some of the edge off my pain.

I didn't really mind the pain. It was uncomfortable and annoying, but I knew I would heal, and the pain would vanish. Any or all of the five of us could very easily have died the previous night. Walking stiffly and painfully feels like an enormously generous gift when you know that yesterday you came very close to never walking again.

'Hey, guess what?' Talena asked me, as we strolled along the Esplanade, watching the disassembly of the big theme camps.

'What?'

'I think we get our life back.'

'Oh,' I said. 'Good.'

'But I think we should move. Just in case. They still have our address. Saskia's too.'

'Saskia should move into a big house with room-mates,' I said. 'She'll make more friends that way.'

Talena nodded.

'Where do you want to move to?' she asked.

I shrugged. 'Maybe the Sunset?'

'Don't make assumptions.'

I looked at her cautiously. 'What kind of assumptions?'

'Like staying in San Francisco.'

I stopped walking. She followed suit.

'What exactly are you asking?' My voice was quiet.

'I'm asking you what you want,' Talena said. 'That's all. I know I sound like the kind of stereotypical clingy neurotic woman I make fun of a lot. Well, maybe today that's exactly what I am. I want to know. Where is your home, and do I live there? I don't think it's in San Francisco. Maybe I'm wrong. But that's the question you need to answer.'

'Today?'

'Whenever you know,' she said.

'What if I don't know what I want?'

'Then I kick your ass from here to Timbuktu.'

We laughed louder than the half-joke deserved.

'Okay,' she said. 'The ball is now in your court, right? And you will answer my questions in a future which is measured in days, right?'

'I will.'

'Thank God. I declare the relationship processing part of this conversation over. You may sigh with relief.' She reached her arms above her head and stretched, catlike. 'Shit, I'm still tense. Let's go to the Hatter's place and see if he's got any more beer. I could go for getting seriously drunk, how about you?'

'That sounds like a plan and a half,' I said.

When the Temple of Honor burned, there was no drumming, no dancing, no primitive howls in praise of destruction. Those of us who had stayed sat in solemn, peaceful rings around the Temple, thousands of us but far fewer than the throng who had stood and shrieked as the Man burned. We spoke in whispers, reverentially. Talena and I held hands. We didn't know where Steve and Lawrence and Saskia were. I think they made a point out of leaving Talena and I alone that day and night.

I heard quiet sobs from all around us as the flames licked at the base of the Temple, but otherwise we watched in utter silence as they mounted its bulbous spires and, like the Man had, briefly turned night into day. When the structure finally sagged and crashed and fell to the ground, a great quaking sigh ran through the crowd. We sat and watched it burn for a long time, before we stood and silently made our way back across the empty playa to the camps we would call home for only one more night.

'Wait,' I said, halfway back, as we reached the thick field of ashes that had once been the Man. 'Come here.' Our first words since we had sat to watch the Temple burn.

I led her into the centre of the still warm ashes, to the exact spot above which the Man had once stood. It seemed somehow appropriate. I took both her hands in mine and stood facing her.

'I've decided,' I said.

After a moment she understood. 'Oh,' she said.

I hesitated, trying to find the right words. Talena started to shiver.

'Tell me,' she said, her voice trembling. 'Please. Don't try to be fancy. Just tell me.'

'I'm already home,' I said. 'I'm home right now.'

'Right—you mean here? You mean the desert? Paul—Paul, no, that's crazy . . . '

'No. I don't mean the desert.'

'What do you mean?'

'I mean you,' I said. 'Wherever you are. That's my home.'

'Mr Wood, Miss Radovitch, good evening,' Agent Turner said, standing in her doorway. 'Please come in. You're just back from Burning Man?'

'Wow, you guys sure get some amazing Sherlock Holmes-type training,' I said. Both of us were still covered in playa dust.

'Technically we're not actually back yet,' Talena said. 'Just on the way.'

'Please,' Agent Turner said. 'Sit down. Tell me everything.'

Of course we didn't tell her everything.

'So you went to Burning Man just to be sure they were leaving the country,' Agent Turner said sceptically. 'Of course. What happened to your head?'

'I fell off an art car,' I said.

'How clumsy of you.'

'Let's not dwell on my physical inabilities,' I said. 'We just gave you the back door to a system used extensively by your turncoat agent. Are we boring you?'

'No,' Agent Turner said. 'Quite the opposite. An unsuspected window on their operations should help me track down Sinisa's FBI informant quite quickly. Thank you. Well done.'

'And what about the zombies?' Talena asked.

'I will file a report on our discoveries with other relevant governmental agencies. Hopefully this will filter up to our elected officials and they will muster enough political will to pressure the government of Belize to act with regard to the war criminals it now shelters.'

'File a report,' Talena said. 'That's all you're going to do.'

'Miss Radovich, I am sorry, I wish I could do more, but they remain far outside of FBI jurisdiction, and the only—'

I said, 'There's one thing you'll want to add to your report. In bold print. All capitals. We're giving you a deadline.'

'I beg your pardon?'

'A deadline. To catch the mole and to start the wheels of justice rolling towards our friends in Belize. One month.'

She looked at me distastefully. 'And what precisely do you intend to do if I fail to meet your deadline, *Mr* Wood?'

'Share the wealth,' I said. 'Give a few other people the key. The *New York Times,* the *Washington Post,* the *Guardian, Le Monde,* I don't know, whoever might find it interesting. Maybe CNN; it's probably too dry for them though. But I think at least a few reporters will find Mycroft very interesting. I think a few articles about a crew of war criminals hiding just around the corner from America, and the FBI agent who colluded with them, might amp that political will you're talking about, speed up those wheels of justice a little bit, don't you? I've noticed those wheels seem to move a whole lot faster when a few million eyes are watching them.' I paused. 'I don't really mean to threaten you. I'm just saying that if you catch your mole and deal with the zombies within the next month, you'll read fewer interesting articles about corruption within the FBI.'

'I see,' Agent Turner said. 'And you're not a little worried that these reporters will start asking some questions about you? Because, after all, what reporters do, at least in their Platonic ideal, is unearth the truth. And I don't believe for a second the two of you have told me anything near the complete truth of what happened at Burning Man.'

Talena and I said nothing.

'Do you recall when we first met?' Agent Turner asked.

'And the fate of the man we discussed then?'

'Yes, ma'am.'

'Are you going to try to go after them yourself? Am I going to receive word some time next month that Sinisa or Zoltan or Zorana have been found dead in a canyon in Mexico?'

I said, 'I can absolutely guarantee you that that will not happen.'

'Really. Is that because they are already dead?'

'All I can tell you is the last time I saw them, they were on a plane headed for Mexico.'

She frowned. 'You are a very bright man, Mr Wood. You and your girlfriend both. Very bright and brave and capable. So why is it that I don't trust you one iota?'

I squeezed Talena's hand, smiled innocently, and said, 'I really can't imagine.'

Epilogue

The Associated Press, 29 September 2003

THE HAGUE: The International Criminal Tribunal for the former Yugoslavia has confirmed last week's report from the government of Belize that it has killed or arrested nineteen alleged Bosnian war criminals found in a compound deep in the Belizean jungle.

'We can confirm that our inspectors have decisively identified at least seven of the individuals held by Belize as individuals indicted for war crimes, and that extradition proceedings have begun,' Femke Johanssen, a spokeswoman for the ICTY, said yesterday. She was unable to explain how the alleged war criminals travelled from Bosnia to Belize.

Eleven Europeans have been arrested on charges of drug smuggling. Eight others were reportedly killed while resisting arrest. The survivors will be held in Belize's notoriously over-crowded prison system, pending their extradition to the tribunal in The Hague. Their identities have not yet been released.

In Washington, John Romanov of the State Department said, 'The government of Belize, utilizing American intelligence, has identified and arrested a group of Bosnian war criminals hiding within its borders. This is a major victory for the international justice system, and we hope it serves as a reminder to war criminals around the world that their atrocities will not be forgotten, and their crimes will not go unpunished.' Mr Romanov refused to comment on speculation that the Belizean action was connected with last week's arrest of FBI agent Mary McLaren in San Francisco on conspiracy and drug-trafficking charges.

From the mines of Karnataka, India,
to the streets of Paris and the lights of Las Vegas,
Danielle Leaf is pursued by a terrible secret. . . .

Don't miss *Invisible Armies*, the compulsive,
fast-paced new novel from Jon Evans.

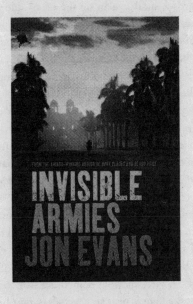

Turn the page for an excerpt

0-00-200769-X

www.harpercollins.ca • www.jonevans.ca

1

The bridge is out. No: it has never been in. Danielle nudges the gearshift into neutral, splays her legs out on either side to support the motorcycle, and stares disbelievingly. The road before her continues smoothly for some sixty feet, then unravels into a leprous mass of concrete, from which a tangle of rusted girders reaches across the Tungabhadra River towards a similar span on the other side. It fails to arrive by forty feet.

Whoever did not finish this bridge's midsection neglected to inform the National Geographical Survey of India, whose map of the state of Karnataka, currently tucked into Danielle's day pack, claims that the bridge successfully traverses the dark river below. The next nearest crossing is fifteen miles away, along gouged Indian roads that would eat up at least an hour, and it is already afternoon, and Danielle isn't sure that she can reach her destination at all from the other bridge. For a moment she feels defeated.

Which is fine. This is a chore, not a mission. A favour to a friend, and one she already wishes she had not accepted. A valid excuse to back out would be a relief, and how much more valid can you get than this impassable ruin of an incomplete bridge?

But wait. She sees motion. Something stirs in the water by the opposite shore, next to the pillars that hold up its third of a bridge, and then what looks like a large floating wicker basket shaped like an inverted dome, maybe ten feet in diameter, emerges from the shadowed water. It carries two men. One uses a leaf-shaped paddle to propel the basket-dome—*coracle*, a distant corner of her mind informs her—towards the south side of the river. The other man waves and points somewhere behind her. His smile flashes white against his dark skin. Danielle looks over her shoulder and sees a little dirt trail, about a hundred feet back, that separates from the road and falls steeply to a muddy landing on the riverbank.

They cannot seriously be thinking of ferrying her motorcycle across. It's a small bike, but still a heavy machine, and their overgrown basket looks like it has all the structural integrity of a banana leaf. But here is *another* coracle, coming behind the first, and this one moves slowly, because it is loaded with a half-dozen Indian villagers, several heavy sacks of grain, and a man sitting on a motorcycle much like hers. This coracle bobs low in the water but amazingly does not sink.

Danielle reluctantly decides she cannot abandon her errand just because the river must be crossed by fragile-seeming ferry instead of bridge. She wheels the bike around and steers down the dirt path to the riverbank, controlling brake and throttle gingerly; it has been years since she spent much time on a bike, she has no helmet, and low-speed motorcycle manoeuvres are always potentially treacherous. When she gets to the landing, a flat patch covered by shallow mud, she turns off the engine and looks towards the approaching coracle ferry. The paddling has stopped. Both men gape at her with wonder and bewilderment.

For a moment Danielle doesn't understand. Then she realizes. They thought she was a man, thanks to her close-cropped hair, and the truth has struck them dumb. She is probably the first woman riding a motorcycle by herself that these men have ever seen, and an exotic white woman at that. And this is the sticks. Yesterday's journey, Goa to

Hospet to Hampi, was a route that sees plenty of white women travelling solo, but although Hampi with its many Western backpackers is only ten miles away, this broken bridge is definitely off the beaten track. This is real rural India. A whole different world. She doesn't feel threatened by their stares, not with the sun beaming down, several women visible in the other coracle and a handful more now watching her from the opposite shore, but she does feel distinctly uncomfortable.

For a moment she wonders if this is what being a movie star is like; everybody wordlessly watching you, knowing that you belong to an infinitely glamorous and more exciting world than theirs. She wishes she had brought a male companion. Not that that wouldn't have created its own set of problems. But suddenly those problems seem better than feeling like a target. A target only of attention, right now, but such attention makes her nervous.

The empty coracle, a woven basket of thumb-thick branches lined on the outside with plastic wrap, reaches the shore. The non-paddling man steps out and motions her to get off the bike. She doesn't want to. She suddenly wants to turn around, ride straight back to Hampi, e-mail Keiran and tell him he can find someone else to run his international errands for him. But Danielle has spent the last few years of her life systematically forcing herself to do exactly those things that make her uncomfortable or frightened. She knows she is mostly the better for it. She wonders, though, as she stands back and allows the man to straddle her motorcycle and expertly roll it onto the coracle, whether one day this constant struggle for self-improvement will propel her into disaster.

The vessel's interior is wet, but the motorcycle's weight distorts the flexible hull enough that all the interior water pools beneath the bike's tires, and Danielle stays mostly dry. She sits crosslegged on the surprisingly comfortable wood, avoiding the ferrymen's unflagging stares, and watches the unearthly landscape around her.

The wide, fast Tungabhadra River, lined by tall coconut trees, carves a path through jumbled ridges of colossal reddish boulders that somehow look both crystalline and water-warped. Roads and villages are built in the shadow of these boulders, which look like handfuls of fifty-foot pebbles dropped by the gods, balancing and leaning on one another in seemingly unnatural ways, as if child-giants had used them as playthings, piled stacks and mounds of them, then abandoned them here when they grew bored. It's hard for Danielle to shake the notion that this place was meant for creatures on a far greater scale than mere human beings.

And then there are the ruins. Most human constructions here are ancient, the bones of the Vijayanagar empire that ten centuries ago ruled all of south India. Half-collapsed stonework; still-intact ziggurats densely carved with Hindu gods and idols, some of their features worn away by the centuries, but still enormously imposing; high ornate walls standing forlornly in tilled fields; half-mile-long pillared colonnades. Once these were royal residences, temples, elephant stables, public plazas. To the west, Danielle can make out the crumbling remains of a massive stone bridge that once spanned the palm-tree-lined river. This thousand-year relic doesn't seem much more ruined than the rusted iron and cratered concrete above her.

A few squat concrete boxes have grown around the northern end of the modern bridge, and clusters of thatched huts are visible in the distance, between the hills and ridges. Dots that are men and women can be seen cultivating small oblong properties, brown fields of grain and deep-green banana plantations. A large whitewashed temple to some Hindu god is visible at the top of the highest hill. But the modern buildings, roads and plantations look wildly out of place.

As they approach the northern bank Danielle winces, realizing that she forgot to agree to a price before embarking. She expects a demand for some outrageous amount of money, and she is not in a good position to argue; a woman on her own, on the wrong side of the river that only these men can help her cross. But the man asks her for only twenty rupees, less than fifty U.S. cents. His accent is so thick, and the price so surprising, that he has to repeat it three times before she is certain she understood. She wonders why, unlike just about everyone else in India, these men do not see the central goal of their interaction with a foreigner to be the acquisition of as much wealth as possible by any non-violent means available. Maybe so few tourists come here that these men have not learned how to be usurious.

Or maybe they are frightened of foreigners. If Keiran is right, they have good reason to be frightened.

She wonders what time the ferry stops. Surely she can get back before nightfall. Even if not, surely she can pay someone to paddle her back across. And even if that fails, surely some family will put her up for the night. She has money, after all, and a white woman's glamour. Even in the worst case, it will be an adventure. Danielle kicks her engine into life, shifts into gear, and starts north.